Daughter of a Thousand Pieces of Gold

by

Peg Helminski

Published by   **MNH Publications**
1251 NW Maynard Road, Suite 177
Cary, NC 27513

Layout, design and composition by Peg Helminski

Cover photo by Sears Portrait Studio, all rights have been purchased by the author.

Author photo by Qiu Qiang

Calligraphy by He Li-Ke

This book has been published in a variety of electronic and print formats. Some content that appears in one format may not be available in others.

Cataloging-in-Publication Data is on file with the Library of Congress

Helminski, Margaret Neral (Peg), 1955 -

Daughter of a Thousand Pieces of Gold, a novel

© 2012 Peg Helminski

ISBN-13: 978-0615661872 (Peg Helminski)

ISBN-10: 0615661874

peg@mnhpublications.com
www.facebook.com/PegHelminskiAuthor

publisher@mnhpublications.com
www.mnhpublications.com

Dedicated

To my delightful daughter, Elizabeth Qiu Qiang,
my precious son, Benjamin Gao Rong,
and all children whose lives have been touched
by the social welfare system of China.

and

To my wonderful eldest son, Nate
who desperately wanted a brother
and then warmly welcomed a sister
into our family.
He has become their beloved
blond, *da ge-ge*!

Table of Contents

Section Three: Family Life in America

Special thanks to:
The many children who shared their memories of China
and their adoption stories with me

and

to Jayne Tao Mei Forslind and Wu Rong
who read this manuscript in the early stages
checking facts and adding thoughtful comments,

and

to the members of my SCBWI critique groups
who read with an eye for detail
and helped me see
what strangers to China
and to adoption
might need to know.

and

to an enthusiastic team of proofreaders:
Barbara, Christy, Donna Rae, John, Kate and Kerri!

**I could not have written such a book
without your help.**

Please note:

Every effort has been made to reflect the truth of life in China in the late 1990's and around the turn of the 21st century in the social welfare institutes of that time which were home to thousands and thousands of China's children since the institution of the one child policy. China is a rapidly changing country and many things depicted in this book may no longer be the same by the time it is published.

The names of all the Chinese children in this story are names of real people; most of whom are or once were children living in China. Many of the events portrayed really happened. Still, this book is a work of fiction and, in no way portrays the actual events of any one child's life.

A special note about the calligraphy:

Each chapter begins with a number written in the elegant and graceful, form of calligraphy that Mei Lin's grandfather used. These were drawn by the very talented calligrapher, He Li-Ke. I am most grateful for his support and contribution to this book.

Introduction

In America, we place our family names last and our given names first. In China the family name comes first followed by the given name or title. It is most common to call a person by her whole name. Our heroine is *Zhong Mei Lin*, although friends and family sometimes call her *Mei Lin* for short.

In almost every language, "Mama" means the same thing. In Chinese, "Baba" means Daddy.

But, what one calls a person can be much more complicated. In China, one always knows where a person stands in a relationship by the terms of address used. In the countryside, between two men who are social equals, the term Lao, following the family name is common. Children, however, would call (or refer to) the same person as his family name followed by *Shu-shu* which is an informal title meaning something like, "uncle" although it does not necessarily mean the brother of one's father or mother, just a man who is at least a generation older than the one speaking. Therefore, the person whose name is Zhong Liang would be addressed as *Zhong Lao* by another man in his village and as *Zhong Shu-shu* by a child.

In this story, one family friend, "Uncle Charlie," whose real name is Cai Chao and who studied in the United States for several years, now prefers to be called by his "American name," including the English title, "Uncle."

An important or wealthy man would be addressed as, *Xian-sheng* which is something like the title, "Mr." But, *Qin Xian-sheng*, the restaurant manager, respected by others, is still *Qin Shu-shu* to Mei Lin because he is a family friend and treated like an uncle.

A teacher would be addressed as his or her family name followed by the title, *teacher* or *Laoshe* as in *Ma Laoshe* in this story. Likewise, a doctor would be addressed by his or her family name plus the title for *doctor, Yi-sheng,* as in *Gan Yi-sheng.*

In China a married woman retains the family name with which she was born. Her children take her husband's family name. A married woman would be called by her family name followed by her first name but also by her husband's family name and the title, *Tai-tai* in formal or business situations. So, Mei Lin's mother, Song An-Li is also Zhong Tai-tai meaning "Mrs." Zhong.

In the countryside, a married woman could also be referred to as her given name plus the title, Shen-shen which indicates that she is married or simply as *A-yi,* meaning *Auntie.*

Children, however, throughout China would refer to almost all grown women as *A-yi* following the family name of the woman they are talking to. A character in this book, *Qiu Qiang A-yi* is embarrassed by her lack of a *real* Chinese surname. Despite China's large population, there are only a handful of easily recognizable, authentic, Chinese family names. *Tai* is not one of them. This young Auntie also thinks of herself as an elder sister to all the children in the social welfare institute. So, she encourages this more informal use of her given name rather than the formal use of her assigned Orphanage surname, *Tai.*

Finally, in China there is a difference between the maternal (mother's) and paternal (father's) families. The term, *Ye-ye* refers to the grandfather of the paternal family: the father's father and *Nai-nai* is the word for a father's mother. A mother's father would be *Wai-gong* and a mother's mother would be *Wai-po.* Zhong Mei Lin has no known surviving relatives on her mother's side of the family.

In order of their introduction in the story

Zhong Mei-Lin Heroine, age 11 at story opening. Her name means, "Beauty" or as two different words used to express beauty are combined in the formation of her name, "Very Beautiful."

Zhong Liang Baba (father) of Mei Lin

Liu Long Tang He is the corrupt, local Communist cadre chief feared by all and opposed by none because he is a former general with high ranking cronies in the Beijing politburo. He is referred to as "Liu Shu-shu" by Mei Lin.

Song An-Li Mama of Mei Lin

Qiang Lao Elderly fisherman who taught Mei Lin to make traditional, old style split bamboo fish traps.

Liu Wei Lazy, spoiled son of Liu Long Tang

Ma Laoshe Mei Lin's teacher (Teacher Ma)

Zhong Chou Ye-ye (paternal Grandfather) of Mei Lin. Former professor of world literature and world-acclaimed author now "re-educated" as a farmer.

Qin Xian-sheng Mr. Qin, manager of the Golden Tiger Restaurant (Qin Shu-shu to Mei Lin)

Yin Tai-tai Shop owner who buys baby shoes that American tourists like. (Mrs. Yin)

Wan Lao and He Lao Two other farmers in the Longkou farming collective (Uncle Wan and Uncle He)

Nai-nai Mei Lin's paternal grandmother

Kitchen boy

Peter Schmitz American man who adopts a Chinese baby

Rebecca Schmitz American woman who adopts a Chinese baby

Anna Ai Lin Schmitz Their newly adopted daughter

Carol Another American, adoptive mother

Gan Yi-sheng Hotel doctor (Doctor Gan)

County Police officer

Di-di Mei Lin's little brother who will not be named until his first birthday.

Uncle Charlie, Cai Chao Good friend of Mama and Baba-and an engineer who is proud to have been chosen to study in the USA. He now prefers to be called by his "American name" including honorific of Uncle rather than Shu-shu.

Tang Gao Rong Civil Affairs Officer

Yan A-yi Baker of moon cakes (Auntie Yan)

Two police officers, one fat, one skinny.

Pan Ling Chicken thief

Pan Ching Pan Ling's son

Hong Rong Water-buffalo. Her name means, "Red Glory."

Yao Ting Mama's best friend, married to Uncle Charlie (Yao A-yi to Mei Lin)

Cai Wan Jen Uncle Charlie's and Yao A-yi's daughter

Jiang Shu-shu Village coroner (Uncle Jiang)

Xu A-yi Liu Lao's wife (Auntie Xu)

Xiao-xiao A friend from school. Her name means, "Very Little."

Old man in the market

Han Yueh Mei Provincial court official. Her name means "moon beautiful"

Officer Wang Police officer who brings Mei Lin to the social Welfare Center and who also is also in love with one of the A-yi's.

Tai Qiu Qiang Nursery auntie at the Baoshan City Social Welfare Institute. Her name means, "Autumn Strong" and she prefers to be called Qiu Qiang A-yi. She also hates the unrecognizable family name that marks her as not belonging to a family.

Ling A-yi SWI director (Auntie Ling)

Tong-Mi / Mi-Mi 4-year-old in Mei Lin's dormitory

Hua Surly eldest girl in Mei Lin's dormitory. Her name means, "Flower."

Wu Dan A girl close to Mei-Lin's age in her dormitory who becomes her best friend. Her name means, "Fifth Alone."

Da ge-ge Means "eldest brother." He is the eldest boy in the orphanage. His real name is **Hui Na-Te.** His name means, "Bring Excellence."

Kang Yi-sheng Orphanage doctor (Doctor Tong)

Tang A-yi Cook. (Auntie Tang)

Feng A-yi Laundress. (Auntie Feng

Guo-Jing A-yi The fat nursery auntie. Auntie Guo Jing.

Guan Fang Mei Baby with a deformed leg

Duo-duo Another baby in the nursery

Feng Cong Noisy boy who often gets in trouble

Fu Yuan Four year old in Mei Lin's room

Ji Qiao, Xiao Ping Younger girls.

Ni-Na and Gao Zhu Second graders from a third dormitory room

Mingsha Second grader.

Dong A-yi Another nursery auntie who switches night duty with Auntie Qiu Qiang

Yang Lan Crib mate with Duo-duo and Jin Ying but also another baby previously loved by Wu Dan who was adopted.

Elizabeth Talbot Adoptive mother

Michael Talbot Adoptive father

Su Xi Another of the "little kids"

Zao-zao Youngest girl in Mei Lin's room after Mi-mi is adopted.

Cindy Fernwelter American at the airport, a friend of the Talbot's

Jake Talbot Younger brother age 7

Evan Talbot Elder brother age 16

Taffy Cocker spaniel

Tyrone Percie Bennett/Bebo Mei Lin's first American school friend

Ellen Dawson Korean adoptee Mei Lin meets in her new American school

Marissa American cheerleader

Lin Pi-Jen Cashier at the Asian grocery store\

Grandma Talbot, Uncle Larry, Uncle Bob, Uncle Pete, Aunt Susan, Aunt Tina Extended family whom Molly Mei Lin meets at Grandma's house.

Jonathan Powers Boy on the ice

Rich, Tom and Tara Firefighter/rescue workers

Jessica Laughlin News reporter

Melinda and Todd Powers Jonathan's parents

Ms. Bordum and **Mr. Ditweiler** American high school teachers

Liu Lao's Old Tricks

***Real knowledge is to know
the extent of one's ignorance.***

"Ah, Zhong Lao. It is a fine day, is it not?" Liu Shu-shu walked up behind Baba and inspected the contents of the two-wheeled handcart.

"That, it is, Liu Lao; a fine day, indeed!" my father answered in the formal way and without looking up. He continued to load round, green watermelons onto the cart and tie them in with a net. It seemed as if there was hardly enough room for another melon. "Did you eat yet?" continued Liu Shu-shu in the traditional Chinese way of greeting. Liu Shu-shu was not my father's brother, but all Chinese children respectfully address elders as *Shu-shu: Uncle* and *A-yi: Auntie* whether or not they are related or even deserving of respect. His full name was Liu Long Tang and he was the Communist Party cadre chief for our village, so my Baba was always very polite when he addressed him, respecting the power of his position, if not the person of Liu Long Tang. Their exaggerated politeness underscored the fact that there was clearly no affection lost between them.

"Yes, yes, my wife prepared a fine breakfast already. Thank you."

"Ah, your wife. She is well? My wife and I were just speaking of her last night. We have not seen Song An-Li in quite some time. She has not left you for some Hong Kong merchant, has she?" Liu Shu-shu teased.

I peeked at the men on the road in front of our home through the crack between the moon gate and our courtyard wall. I could see the veins in my father's neck standing out. Baba was very insulted, but there was much at stake, so he joked back pleasantly with Liu Shu-shu. "No, no, no. She is quite well. She has been *very* busy. As you often say, Liu Lao, it is best to keep women working.

"See here," Baba opened a large sack on the ground for Liu Shu-shu to inspect. "In addition to working in the fields and caring for my home and daughter, according to the new economic reforms, my wife has made these embroidered silk baby shoes to sell in the big city tourist shops of Baoshan City. They will bring a high price."

"Ah," said Liu Shu-shu, "Song An-Li has not lost her fine skill with a needle. At least her right hand was not affected by the accident and she is not totally useless. It would be a double pity for you to be burdened with a useless wife and only a daughter to help with your farming responsibilities."

Baba did not respond. I knew there was a much bigger reason why Liu Shu-shu had not seen Mama these past three months but Baba was wise not to mention it, at least not until after the baby was born and the birth fine paid. Otherwise, Baba and Mama might both be fined, our home confiscated--or other things too terrible to mention, all because they had chosen to have a second child without a birth permit, despite the one child law.

Liu Shu-shu paused a moment, bent to look more closely at the contents of the hand cart, shook the basket full of water and wriggling fish and said, "If you take this basket off the end of the cart, you will be able to fit all the melons on safely as well as reduce the weight on this rickety old cart to a much more manageable load."

"Yes, of course, you are right," said Baba and he paused as if to consider the wisdom of this advice. "Ah, but if I do this, I will not be able to sell Mei Lin's fish to the fine tourist restaurant in Baoshan City."

"Eh? Your worthless-mouth-to-feed has been playing games in the river again?"

"Mei Lin is a *qian jin xiao jie*," said my father perhaps a little too proudly. I blushed from behind the corner of our courtyard wall. Baba had called me a "daughter of a thousand pieces of gold!" No one could see me, but such praise, the highest there is for a girl in China, was enough to cause me to lower my head and cover my face so that no one, not even I, could catch the smile of pleasure curving the corners of my mouth. It meant that Baba considered me as valuable as any son.

"Ai-ya! A daughter is nothing but an extra mouth to feed. You should have saved your birth permit for a son as my wife and I have done. You will live to regret your choice to keep this worthless girl. What will you do in your old age, Zhong? Who will care for you when she has gone to care for her husband's family?"

It is true that according to tradition, a woman is not her own person, but belongs to her husband's family in much the same way the family might own a water buffalo or a chicken. But things are changing swiftly in China. The bones of young girls' feet are no longer broken and bound, folded over so that they learn to walk, elegantly but painfully, in tiny, decorative shoes. Perhaps by the time I am fully grown, a woman will not only be able to walk wherever she wills and as easily as a man, but will be able to speak her own mind freely and determine her own destiny as well.

"Who knows what will happen that far in the future?" answered Baba as he echoed my thoughts. He stood up and paused from his work to daringly look Liu Shu-shu squarely in the face. "China is changing rapidly. Things may be very different by the time Mei Lin is grown. Already the government officials tell us that a girl is the same as a boy. Each can be a great happiness to parents. Glorious posters and billboards proclaim this message throughout the cities. All children are special to their parents."

"So they say. But, 5,000 years of Chinese tradition resists the wisdom of The People's government. We will see. It may be many generations before our far-seeing leaders' hopes are realized in the lives of ordinary Chinese citizens such as yourself, Zhong."

Baba should have stopped. Almost anyone else would have. "This may be true for all of China, but Mei Lin has proven herself to be both intelligent and resourceful. Already, at eleven years of age, she is in the top of her grade in school. She is a strong swimmer and can skillfully build as fine a bamboo fish trap as your son." Baba did not brag as strongly as he could have and say that I could build a far *better* fish trap than the useless son of Liu Shu-shu, although it was common knowledge in our village that I could weave a more beautiful and efficient fish trap than nearly anyone—except perhaps for Qiang Lao who taught me this ancient skill.

"You *waste* an education on a girl. You would do better to keep her in the fields until she marries. Get the most money out of her as you can. It is a good thing a father's time with a daughter is short! They cost more to feed than they can return to us in work."

Baba would not back down to Liu Shu-shu. "While she is at school or working in the rice paddies, her traps catch many fish. She tends these traps faithfully. She has caught more than enough for our family. I will take the extra fish she has caught to market and sell them. Someday, following the new economic reforms laid out by The

People's government, Mei Lin will be a wealthy business woman and her husband will count himself lucky to have married such a wise and competent woman."

"Ai-ya!" Liu Shu-shu exclaimed and spit. "If I believed in the old religions, which I certainly do *not*, I would say that the girl has put a spell on you and muddled your brain. That is what happens with the beautiful ones. They make idiots of even great men, so much more to the simple men such as you, Zhong. See if my words do not come true. You will live to regret the day you decided to keep that girl child and not drown her in the rice paddies as I did with the useless one my wife produced. When you are old and alone, do not come to me for help. I was wise enough to see that no girl child was registered as born alive in my household. My son will provide for me in fine style but I will not over-work him in order to care for a stupid, short-sighted man such as you. You think you are so wise, but you are foolish!"

Baba turned back to his work, and loaded another melon under the net. It was well known that Liu Shu-shu was nearly deaf in his right ear from hearing too many guns shot when he was a soldier during the Cultural Revolution. It was, therefore, no surprise that Liu Shu-shu couldn't hear exactly what Baba said when he turned away and continued talking softly under his breath. But, from my hiding place, I could hear, "Fine style, huh? His son is the laziest, worthless boy I ever laid eyes on. Mei Lin is worth more than ten of his kind!"

I almost gave away my hiding place by giggling. I bit my teeth into my lower lip and held my nose closed to keep any sound from escaping me. It was true. Liu Wei was already thirteen years old but still in my class at school where most of us would turn twelve next Chinese New Year. He never turned in assignments on time, his calligraphy was sloppy and he was always making our teacher, Ma Lao-shi angry with his unruly behavior. Whenever Ma Lao-shi made him stand in the corner, he would run home and complain to his Mama. She, in turn would tell his Baba. Liu Shu-shu would use his position as the most influential party member in the village and the former army officer (He once served directly under former Communist Party Chairman, Mao!) to publicly humiliate the teacher.

"What did you say, Zhong?" asked Liu Shu-shu.

"I was just wondering," said Baba, as he stood to wipe the sweat from his brow, "If you came here to discuss my daughter's skills or if some other business brought you to my gate?"

"Ah," said Liu Shu-shu with a fake laugh, "Yes, I did come to inform you that there will be a very important meeting regarding the farmers' quotas tomorrow morning."

"*Tomorrow* morning?"

"Ummm."

"Liu Lao, you know that tomorrow is market day. Any farmer with surplus to sell will be leaving tonight for Baoshan City. Few of us will be back before daylight the day after tomorrow."

"Ah, pity. There will be some important decisions made regarding an increase in the farmers' quotas due to the village central collective. But, perhaps ignorant farmers do not understand enough about their own business to worry about representation."

Liu Shu-shu particularly loved to stress the "ignorant" part of the phrase to my father. My grandfather had been an eminent professor at the National University in Beijing before the Cultural Revolution. Like many learned men in high positions, he was dragged out of his study one night and sent to the countryside to be "re-educated through labor" in Communist Party thought.

Even with tiny, bound feet that were painful to walk on, my very determined grandmother searched for him; following rumor after rumor, and found him after three years in this small farming village of Longkou where we still live. My Baba, who was a toddler at the time, has therefore been a farmer's son most of his life.

Although Liu Shu-shu often boasts of my grandfather as one of his reeducation success stories, in the evenings, Ye-ye is still a great professor. He taught Baba, and now me, to make beautiful Chinese letters in a flowing calligraphy style known as grass writing that he says I must never use in school. It is very elegant and complex calligraphy, not the simplified characters of the Communist Party that we are taught in school. Ye-ye taught me to speak and write not only the local dialect of our village, but Mandarin Chinese which is the official language of the government as well as French and English (which, during the struggle period known as the Cultural Revolution and until quite recently, were forbidden). When he talks of great poets, I see his eyes moisten as he quotes the words of the ancient ones whom he calls, "Lao-zi" and of foreigners such as William Shakespeare and Mark Twain by heart. So, my Baba is not really an ignorant farmer, but Liu Shu-shu will not ever admit this. To do so would be to admit his failure to reeducate three whole generations of the Zhong family.

Baba answered, "Thank you for your concern, Liu Lao. I will see what we can do."

Liu Shu-shu turned away toward the road and smiled in a way that reminded me of a poisonous snake sliding through bamboo grass. Baba continued loading melons. When Liu Shu-shu was out of hearing, I opened the moon gate and skipped out of the courtyard, onto the hard packed earth street where Baba still worked. My two long queues thumped against my back.

"Ah, Mei Lin, just in time. Come here and help me tie these melons in securely. I am about to entrust you with a great responsibility. To succeed, you must be twice as clever as any boy." He smiled at me teasingly and then continued, "Ten times as clever as Liu Wei."

"This will not be a problem!" I said and he laughed out loud before continuing seriously.

"I must go to an important meeting tomorrow. The farmers must have a voice. These melons must also get to market. They have been picked and will rot in this heat if we do not sell them for another week. Your Ye-ye is still strong so he can pull the handcart. You will go with him. You must walk the whole way. He is no longer as strong or as fast as I am, so you should probably start as soon as possible and walk most of the night. Help him push the cart when there are hills. Rest when you get to the place where the two rivers meet and the umbrella trees grow. Sleep there until the horizon between the two mountains turns gray. From there it is only a short walk to the market and you can enter the city by growing daylight, arriving before most of the farmers."

"Be sure to get the best price. Pretend that I am with you, only on other business elsewhere in the marketplace. Tell the dealers that I will be angry if you do not get a fair price and will report them to the police for thievery." Baba walked around the other side of the cart and tightened the net.

"In the market, the merchants may try to cheat your grandfather. He looks like a simple, old farmer. You are a daughter of modern China and expected to be nearly as educated as any city boy or girl. Remember though, to be humble and act simple, but bold enough to get the job done. Do not show off your extra learning."

"I won't, Baba."

"When you have sold all the melons," Baba paused to look at me, "Take your Mama's sewing to the small shop on the south side of People's Park. Tell Yin Tai-tai they were made by your mother. She knows your mother's work well and will give you a good price. Then, continue down the road another half li and take your fish to the back door of the *Golden Tiger Hotel and Restaurant for Foreigners*. See my good friend, Qin Shu-shu. Do you remember where it is? We sold some vegetables to him the last time we were in the city. Stress that these fine fish of yours were caught here in Longkou—upstream from the pollution of the big factories. He will

24

pay a good price. Foreigners demand quality food. The restaurant can sell them for a higher price if they advertise them as free from chemicals and mercury."

My fish! Baba had called them my fish.

As if reading my face, he continued, "Yes, they are *your* fish. You made and tended the traps. You caught them. You should share in the reward they will provide for our family. If you are not too tired, stop in the market and buy yourself a new quilted jacket and trousers for winter. You must be careful to return to me all of the money from the sale of the melons. This should nearly bring the sum we have saved to the full price of the birth penalty, but if there is enough money from the sale of the fish, also buy yourself a pair of warm shoes. I am counting on you Mei Lin. Now get ready for your journey. Pack some food for yourself and for your Ye-ye. Mama will help you. I will explain the situation to them and then I must visit Wang Lao and He Lao to see if they can also make arrangements to attend the meeting. I suspect Liu Long Tang is up to his old tricks and we must not let him succeed."

"Thank you Baba!" I said.

I could not believe my good fortune I would go to market. I was quite sure there was no place more exciting on Earth! Not only that, but I would have money of my own to spend! It was a good thing we were to start out immediately. I knew I wouldn't sleep tonight anyway. I was far too excited for sleep.

"I will not disappoint you. I will make you proud."

"I am already proud, little daughter." His eyes twinkled as he gave me a quick pat on the back of my shoulders. Though my Baba's hands are calloused and hard from the hard work of farming, I could feel the gentleness of his love and the assurance of trust in his touch.

Dreams and Realities

A single conversation with a wise man
Is better than ten years of study.

By the time Ye-ye and I began our journey, the sun had already been swallowed up beneath the western shore of the Nandu River. At first, there were lots of noises: the rushing of the water, the sounds of people talking as they made their way home from the fields, other people passing us along the road with push carts and pedicabs, bicycles, ox carts pulled by slow but strong water-buffalo, and every now and then, a truck or a shiny, black automobile with tinted glass and curtains on the windows. Two round tufted silk pillows always rested on the shelf behind the rear seat. I wondered what kind of person would be able to rest their head upon such a delicate pillow.

"Ye-ye," I asked after yet one more of these cars passed us, "What kind of person could own such a beautiful machine?"

"Humm." He paused as if considering my question a long while—too long, I thought.

"Ye-ye? Could I ever have a chance to ride in such a beautiful machine and rest my head on such a beautiful pillow?"

"Mei Lin! Look at yourself! You have sweat dripping off your forehead and dust caked to your clothes. You would ruin such a beautiful thing if you even touched it! You are the daughter of a poor farmer. You would do well to remember this. These cars are for rich businessmen from Hong Kong or for government officials. These are not things for the ordinary people of China to think about!"

"Yes, Ye-ye." His tone was scolding and I should have been shamed. Still there was something else in his voice and in the indulgent smile that curved the corners of his lips that allowed me to continue thinking as we walked.

After we had traveled another couple of li, I asked, "Ye-ye, what must I do to become a wealthy business woman from Hong Kong or a government official?"

"This is not something you—or even your Baba or I--can determine," he said gently, perhaps a little sadly. "You should not even speak of these thoughts to *anyone*. Work hard at whatever task you are assigned by The People's government. If others notice your good work, remain humble. If they decide to honor you or promote you, at first decline. If they insist, humbly accept the position but insist that you are doing so only because they believe it is for the good of the masses, for the welfare of all China. Mei Lin you have many abilities but it is sometimes wise not to let all of these abilities be seen by others. It can be very dangerous if others are threatened by your abilities. You must first test the waters of life to determine if you can swim in them."

Something in the way he spoke made me realize that he was saying something very important. Although I didn't understand what his words had to do with riding in a car, I determined to remember them always.

We walked on in silence for many more li--so many I lost count. Now, only the creaking of a loose board in the floor of the cart, the sloshing of water in the basket of fish and the evening song of crickets accompanied us.

"Was it this long to the city the last time we went to market?"

"Yes, but I had your father to help with pulling the load, so you were able to ride. You slept through the night. It seems a lot longer when you're walking, doesn't it?"

I covered my mouth and tried to hide the yawn, but it didn't escape Ye-ye's notice. "We are almost at the resting place," he said, "There will be one more big hill to climb, and then you can rest under the umbrella tree until the first hint of morning light."

I was very tired, so I wondered how it would be to rest my head on a silk pillow as grandfather drove a fine black car into Baoshan City.

"Ye-ye, Is it true that you used to be a famous professor at a very important university in Beijing?

"Yes, but that was a lifetime ago and I was a different person. Let us speak of present things."

"Why? I thought that being a professor would be a good thing, not a bad thing. You are very smart. You have taught me many useful things."

"Perhaps this is true, but being smart is not the most important thing in life."

"But, Ye-ye, being useful is very important, isn't it? You have helped our village many times. . . "

"Hush child. There is too much noise in the world already."

I was quiet for a few minutes but I couldn't hold the questions in. "But Ye-ye, I don't understand. You tell me I should prepare to go to university as you did. You became a famous professor and now you are a farmer. I just want to understand."

"China changes rapidly, child. Even in one lifetime, I have seen several different periods of history and many changes. Things are different now than they were even a few years ago." He was quiet for a moment and then continued, "I suppose, if you are old enough to ask the questions, you are old enough to be given a reasonable answer." He paused to think over what he had just said. "So, yes, I will tell you. Many years ago, when your father was a still a toddler, there came a time in our history that people refer to as the Cultural Revolution."

"Yes, I know all about this time in history," I replied enthusiastically. "We studied it in school. Before 1949, many people in China were starving. Evil landowners were making the people work very hard and not paying them enough to be able to feed and clothe their own families. Many people dressed in rags and ate barely enough to stay alive. Every day, children died in the streets and were swept away like garbage because their families could not afford a proper burial for them."

I thought I heard my Ye-ye sigh, but it could have been the wind. He didn't say anything, so I continued.

"Then, the great leader, Mao Zedong led the ordinary masses of Chinese people in a revolution. He led them to claim their rightful place. The tables were turned. The rich were made poor and the poor took over their fancy homes and made them into apartments so that there would be enough housing for everyone. Mao said that there was dignity in all work so jobs were reassigned and the wealth associated with some jobs was redistributed. Those who were doctors and professors became farmers and coal miners. Farmers and street sweepers staffed the hospitals and the splendid revolution continued."

"Yes," said Ye-ye a little impatiently. "This is all true. Many educated people were sent to the countryside to work in the fields. This was called 'reeducation.' It was believed that by such experience, our minds could be changed so that we could see how out-of-balance life had been under the old system. I think there was

29

great wisdom in this. However, I think the problem was bigger than even our great and honorable chairman Mao perceived and his solution was perhaps. . . " He paused again to consider his next words, "Perhaps, too simple."

"Why, Ye-ye? Teacher Ma says these changes brought more equality and opportunity to the great masses of Chinese people!"

"Yes, but in the process, many innocent people died at the hands of incompetent 'doctors' who were suited for nothing more than street sweeping while brilliant minds that should have been earning university degrees were driven to insanity by the tediousness of planting rice. This is a great price to pay for social change. While the rest of the world moved into the technological era, China remained a farming society. Now China is rushing to catch up, but for many of these brilliant young men and women it is too late. They are too old now to begin again as university students. Your father is one of those who should have been allowed to go to university. He would have made a fine diplomat. Even now, he prepares to work out an agreement with Liu Long Tang that will benefit both the farmers and The People's government."

Suddenly, I realized what Ye-ye had *not* said. "Ye-ye, was our family once rich?"

"Mei Lin, I do not want to burden you with too much information, it is a new day for China. Much that is past is not important for us today. It is only important that we do the best we are able with the task we have been appointed. I have told you too much already."

We were at the final big hill now. I moved behind the cart and leaned my shoulder into the back end of the cart and pushed while Ye-ye pulled hard at the ropes over his shoulders. Suddenly, I felt the cart jolt and water sloshed out of the basket and down my shirt.

"Ai!" Ye-ye shouted and he fell on his knee with a groan. All the melons wobbled. A small wave of water splashed out of the fish basket. I realized in that instant that it was only I who held the full weight of the loaded cart from rolling back down the hill.

"Ye-ye!" I shouted. "Ye-ye, What happened? Do you want me to come help you?"

"No, Mei Lin you are helping me as you are. Stay there. I have fallen and I need you to bear the weight of the cart so I can get up. Give me one minute. I think my foot slipped in a pile of water buffalo dung. It is too dark to see, but that smell is a pretty strong clue!"

I could hear him struggle to get up and then I felt him begin to pull the weight off of me. I pushed against the cart and we began again to make our way up the hill.

When we reached the top of the hill, I came to the front of the cart and took one of the ropes and one of the long arms of the hand cart. We each walked to one side of the front of the cart, each pulling on one arm of the cart, and tugging back on the ropes slung over our shoulders, we kept the cart from rolling away down the hill.

"Ye-ye," I asked, "was the Zhong family wealthy?"

"Mei Lin," he laughed, "You are as persistent as your grandmother! You should learn when to give up. Some things are not worth knowing. Still, you continue asking, so I will tell you. Yes," he sighed deeply as if it pained him to remember these things. "Our family was both esteemed and respected. People came from great distances to learn from me. My books were widely read. Even foreigners came to discuss great writings of all cultures with me. Sometimes they sent for me. I traveled by train to all the great cities of China and by airplane to America and Italy and England. I was paid very well. I wore fine silk suits and was accustomed to many servants. I owned many fine things. My father, too, had been well respected and, in fact, owned several businesses." He bowed his head and his voice trailed off, "I never knew what a need was until I was sent to the countryside during the Cultural Revolution to be reeducated. Though I have learned many things as a farmer, still, I think there is no guilt in having plenty. However, there is a responsibility to treat those who work with us and for us as well as we would wish to be treated if our places in society were suddenly reversed. And, I think this knowledge, if it lasts in the heart of China's people is, perhaps, one good that has come from all the pain and suffering of the Cultural Revolution."

"But Ye-ye, why are we not rich now?"

"We *are* rich, child. What greater treasure is there than a happy family?"

"But Ye-ye, you know what I mean . . .

"Now, Mei Lin, we must speak of these things no more! The past is gone. We cannot reclaim it. It is best to move on. We approach the resting place and others may already be gathered there. Enough now."

I was relieved to see the resting place in the distance. It was dominated by a very large umbrella tree with several others scattered around it. I was so tired that I really didn't have the strength to ask one more question anyway. I was almost asleep on my feet before Ye-ye laid out the blanket on the ground for me. "Sleep now," he said. "You will need all of your strength in the morning."

Morning Light Fills Ye-ye's Heart

Although my neighbors are all barbarians,
And you, you are a thousand li from here,
There are always two cups on my table.

"Mei Lin, get up." I could feel someone tapping on the bottom of my shoe. "The sun has already poked its head above the edge of the horizon. We must hurry." The sky was, indeed growing lighter, but the sun had just begun to crown the edge of the earth with gold. I rolled over and felt the damp chill of dew on my hair and face. Suddenly I remembered where I was.

"Is it morning already?"

"Almost. There is much to be done. We must hurry."

I scampered to my feet and snapped the dust and dew from my blanket, folded it and placed it back in the cart. Then I smoothed my hair with my hands and yanked my pants and jacket straight.

"Mei Lin, put on your hat. It will keep the sun off your head."

33

"Oh Ye-ye, I don't want to. These bamboo hats are so old fashioned. I don't want to look like a peasant in the city. People will think I am stupid all because of that hat!"

"People will know that you are a farmer and certainly not a scholar if the sun makes your face brown or covers it in freckles!"

"I don't care about freckles!"

"Granddaughter, one day, your stubbornness will become either your strength or your undoing! Make your own choice, but when you become weary from the heat, remember that I warned you. Sometimes there is wisdom in the old ways."

We began walking again heading downhill into the city. Ye-ye and I each took one long handle of the heavy cart and leaned back to keep the weight of the cart from pushing us down the hill too fast. Soon, I could feel a burning pain in my thigh muscles. When we reached the bottom of the hill, and the city limits, Ye-ye paused to wipe sweat from his brow with a handkerchief even though the air was still a bit chilly. It was then that I noticed the pained expression on his face.

"Ye-ye, what is wrong?"

"Little granddaughter, I hurt my knee when I fell last night much worse than I thought I had. It grew stiff and swollen in the night. I can barely walk now. I am sorry, I will slow us down."

"It is flat here with no more big hills. Perhaps I can pull the cart myself," I offered.

Ye-ye stopped to consider the possibility and finally laughed, "In the old days a girl could not do such a thing. It would have been impossible!" He continued as if remembering aloud. "When she was just learning to walk, your Nai-nai's feet were broken and bound. She could not walk even one step without great pain. Young girls could not run and play or prove their worth by working like boys. Just as they had no opportunity to show how smart they were because they could not go to school, they also had no opportunity to grow strong." He shook his head.

"You have grown up in the new China. You have not been raised in such a traditional way. You go to school and run and swim and ride a bicycle. You walk the river banks and haul in fish traps. You are small but, your legs and back are strong. Perhaps you are, indeed, as strong as any boy! And, even I don't see that we have much choice. If we are to get these things to market in time, you must at least try. He stood aside and smiled as he said, "In this instance, we should dispense with old ways and try the new ones. We will find out if you are, indeed, a *daughter of a thousand pieces of gold* as your father claims."

I stepped between the arms of the handcart. The worn wood was smooth to touch, but far too big for my small hands to wrap around firmly. Ye-ye tied both of the ropes from the base of the cart up and crossed them over my shoulders and across my chest. I pulled against the weight of the cart as the rope dug into shoulder. Perhaps just a few centimeters at first, but the cart slowly began to move. I leaned against the ropes and the cart rolled freely.

"Ah, you have done it!" shouted Ye-ye. While the cart was still moving, he grabbed onto the side rails and pulled himself up, hopping with his good foot onto a foot board beside the wheel.

Once I got moving, it was easier. The weight of the cart nearly pushed itself along.

Just as I had worked up a smooth momentum, a truck loaded with pigs swerved in front of me and I had to hold the cart back. I felt the full weight of the loaded cart in every vertebra of my back and across my shoulders! Starting up again was as much an effort as it had been the first time. Soon, a rivulet of sweat ran down my back from all the exertion.

By the time the sun was completely over the horizon, the morning rush had begun in Baoshan City. A steady stream of black bicycles ten across flowed past my left shoulder. "Briiing! Briiing!"

The bells jingled at me each time someone passed. Noisy motor scooters sputtered among them. Delivery trucks and farmers with handcarts wove in and out and around each other like partners in a delicate dance of time and space. A vast wave of people was moving, each only a few centimeters from the next, like a murmuration of blackbirds or the undulation of a giant human sea.

So much had changed since the last time I had been to the city. It was confusing. Old landmarks were gone. Where once there had been a dirt road, now an eight lane superhighway flowed.

A man drove past us on a motor scooter. A young woman, wearing a beautiful pink dress, nylon stockings and high heeled shoes sat sideways, balanced on the back fender holding out two large Kerosene tins so as not to let them touch her dress. Babies perched in bamboo seats on the handlebars of their mothers' bicycles and giggled as the breeze tickled their faces.

Cars and trucks, motor scooters and handcarts, ox carts and pedestrians carrying huge loads in baskets hanging from their yoked shoulders all converged at one intersection. To the right, a statue of goats climbed a steep rocky cliff. To the left, an American restaurant, with large golden arches dominated the corner. Overhead, pedestrians, wearing western style business clothes walked on the crisscross of bridges from one side of the busy streets to the other. Most of them were talking, not to each other, but into tiny machines that they snapped shut and slipped into pockets, when they were done. It was all so exciting compared to our simple quiet life in the countryside. I could hardly take it all in, but I wanted to absorb every detail, like a sponge absorbs water.

The thing that caught my attention and lingered most on my mind was the billboard straight ahead of me. Larger than life, a smiling woman in a green army uniform held one arm around a boy and another around a girl. The children smiled up at her admiringly. The slogan, in large, red, simple calligraphy proclaimed, "This is a new China. A girl is as good as a boy Have only one child. The future of China depends on you."

"Beep! Beep!" Another motor scooter passed us with three crates full of live golden-colored chickens stacked above the back fender. "Ji, ji, ji, ji!" they chattered in excitement. White chicken droppings splattered all over the road --and the scooter --and the back of the man on the motor scooter.

We passed a small park where columns of people practiced Tai Chi, a very slow moving form of exercise. They moved as one unit, each perfectly in time with the others from the "spread arms like fan" position to the "step around and chop" position. In one corner six very old men practiced an ancient form of this marital art with ceremonial swords.

Of course, my family practiced Tai Chi almost every morning in our courtyard. But there are only four of us. Here, there were hundreds of people, all in perfectly straight lines and all moving slowly, in graceful unison.

The speed of the traffic picked up. The noise grew louder. The sun was completely up now, peeking over the tops of the buildings. We passed a construction site where buildings that had stood for hundreds of years had been torn down to make way for a new, western-style high-rise apartment building. A skeleton of bamboo scaffolding surrounded the entire tower. The building was made of tinted blue glass and steel. Workmen, each carrying a yoke of two baskets filled with roofing materials climbed bare-foot up the scaffolding. Their toes wrapped around the smooth bamboo as they climbed. These workers had come from the countryside to find better paying jobs. They, too, wore bamboo hats but theirs, rounded like helmets with a shorter brim, lacked the broad brim and cone shape that marked mine as a farmer's hat.

Six workmen together, wearing simple, plastic flip-flops, pulled hand over hand, passing a rope behind them where the last worker, a boy who appeared to be younger than I, wound it into a neat coil. This thick rope was attached to a block and tackle: a network of pulleys, and they were hoisting a huge sheet of blue glass up to the top floor of the building. Their sleeves and pant legs were rolled up and sweat beaded on their arms and legs. Their well-defined muscles glowed in the golden light of this September morning.

Ah! Without realizing how we had gotten there, I was standing in front of the *Golden Tiger Hotel and Restaurant*. I pulled the cart into the service yard and rang the bell. The kitchen boy, wearing black trousers and a white shirt opened the door. His white apron was splattered with the blood of whatever animals he had butchered that morning.

"Ni hao," I said, "May I see Qin Shu-shu? My father, Zhong Liang told me to ask for him specifically."

"Qin Xian-sheng" he corrected my familiarity, "is a very busy man."

"I am Zhong Mei Lin. He is an old friend of my father's and will be most disappointed to learn that I have been here and he did not see me."

"Ai-ya!" The boy said nothing more, but his face told it all. He did not believe that I could possibly know such an important man as his boss, Qin Xian-sheng. How could I blame him? My clothes were dusty from the road and wrinkled from sleeping in them all night. My hair was probably sticking up and dirty. The now dried water mark on the front of my shirt still reeked of fish. My face was beaded with sweat and surely red from the exertion of pulling the cart for so long.

I returned to the parking area and sat on the tongue of the handcart while I rested a moment trying to think what to do if the boy did not summon Qin Shu-shu.

"Mei Lin!" Ye-ye's voice called me out of my thoughts. I had forgotten him! "Help me down. My good leg has grown stiff and I dare not step down on the bad one." I reached up to him and he dropped into my arms as he hopped down. I staggered backward and propped him against the edge of the cart.

"Snap!" I whirled around to see a very ugly foreigner with a camera aimed at Ye-ye and me. Though I had seen some pictures in school, I had never seen a real, live foreigner before. This one was as tall and as broad shouldered as a giant with a face as white as steamed rice. His straw-brown hair, as long as a girl's, was held at the back of his neck with a red band. He had brown fur on his chin and upper lip and a nose that stuck out from his face as far as a bird's beak! I suddenly knew why we called white foreigners, "Da bi-zi," --big noses! Most Chinese people have little noses that lie close to their faces. This American's nose stuck out in a point on the front of his face in a way that resembled the demons of ancient myths.

The most amazing thing however, was that he had a baby hanging in a blue cloth seat, strapped to his chest. The baby faced out and was laughing at me. She wore the most delicate, soft, pink clothes I had ever seen and in her shiny black hair sat a tiny bow made of white lace and pink silk strands.

"Sorry, I didn't mean to scare you. I should have asked. You just looked so beautiful in the morning sun, helping your father there . . ."

"Hello, I mean, ni hao," said the woman who popped out behind him smiling at me.

"Hello," said Ye-ye in English. "Are you Americans?"

"Yes! You speak English very well."

"Thank you, you are kind. I don't often get a chance to practice any more. I am Zhong Chou and this is my rude granddaughter, Zhong Mei Lin." Ye-ye switched to Chinese and said to me. "Stop staring! Close your mouth. You will catch flies!"

"But Ye-ye, the baby looks Chinese!"

"Dui. That's correct," said the man in perfect Mandarin dialect.

"Oh, and you speak Chinese!" said Ye-ye.

"A little," continued the American still speaking in Chinese. "I am Peter Schmitz. This is my wife; Rebecca Schmitz and this is our precious daughter, Anna Ai Lin Schmitz. We just adopted her six days ago in Anhui Province, but already it feels as if she has always been ours." The baby giggled and reached out a tiny hand to me.

I thought about Mama and the baby that would soon be arriving. I had always hoped it would be a boy as tradition seemed to demand, yet looking at this happy baby girl, I suddenly knew that the lady on the billboard was right. It truly didn't matter.

I remembered the bag of baby shoes. "Ye-ye, maybe they would like to buy some baby shoes!"

"Ah, my granddaughter is an entrepreneur! Bypass the merchant, eh? Well there is no time like the present to become a wealthy business-woman even if we are not in Hong Kong!"

I took down the sack and removed a pair of the baby shoes. This pair was green, the color of wealth, with tiny red and black dragons embroidered on the toes. Anyone with a foot small enough to fit into these shoes would have been born this year, the year of the dragon

"Oh Pete, they're beautiful!" said Rebecca Schmitz. "How much do they want for them?"

"Would eighty Yuan be enough?" asked Peter Schmitz in Chinese.

"For a pair?" I asked hardly able to believe my ears. I had thought eighty Yuan would be a good price for *all* of them.

"I am sorry, I didn't mean to insult you. I can tell the craftsmanship is superb. One hundred Yuan for the pair, then?"

"Sold!" I laughed.

Just then, some more foreigners walked up the sidewalk from the hotel toward the shops. Each of them was carrying a Chinese baby. "Carol, look what I just bought from this girl? Aren't they just darling?"

"Those are the cutest baby shoes I've ever seen! Does she have any more?"

I spread my blanket on the ground and dumped the contents of the sack onto it. The Da bi-ze bought every pair I had. They each paid 100 Yuan. I gave the money to Ye-ye who leaned against the cart smiling the whole time. I had never seen so much money at one time in my entire life! In less than twenty minutes I had made a small fortune—more than my father would earn in an entire year!

"Professor Zhong Chou! Is that you?" I spun around to see a well-dressed man in a black business suit, crisply starched white shirt and a red and black silk tie walking swiftly toward us. "The kitchen boy said Mei Lin was here but did not mention my honorable professor." The man first bowed, and then threw his arms around Ye-ye. "To what do I owe the great honor of such a visit?"

"You can thank Mei Lin. She has embraced the new economic reforms. I am only along for the ride to keep her company."

"Ah Mei Lin. You have grown so tall! Although in the old days, superstition would have prevented me from saying this, in the new China I can tell you that you truly favor your beautiful mother, Song An-Li."

I bowed my head and hid my face behind my hands. To be called beautiful in public was not something I was used to.

"Ah, you are a country girl. I embarrass you! I am sorry. Time advances faster in the cities. Today's city girls act almost Western. How is your mother? Has she recovered any of the use of her left arm or leg since the accident at her factory?"

"Yes, she is quite well, although we are told that she will never heal completely, and that one side will always remain a little weak. She can walk and hold things although her grasp is not sure. She is still not able to return to her factory job, but she can do simple house work and cook and sew."

"Ah, I am so glad to hear it. Perhaps each day she will continue to improve a little more. And your father, my dear friend? He is alright?"

"Yes, he is fine." I answered quickly. "He had an important meeting to attend for the farm collective quotas, so could not come to market with us today."

"What business is it that brings you to my door this fine day?"

"Baba thought you might be interested in buying the fish I have caught."

"Are they fresh?"

"Yes, they are alive. I trapped them and kept them until I could bring them to market. They are from the river near our village, upstream from the factories and pollution. They are healthy fish."

Qin Shu-shu walked around to the back of the cart, pulled up the sleeve of his jacket, unbuttoned his shirt cuff and pulled up that sleeve as well. Then he thrust his hand into the basket of fish and wriggled his fingers. Fish fluttered and splashed about. He grabbed one and held it up by the gill flap. "What a beautiful fish! It is nice and fat with good color and healthy scales." He did the same with two more fish. "A fine catch!" he proclaimed. "Of course, we will buy them all. The Americans will be eating fish tonight!" He looked at Ye-ye. "You will want cash, of course."

"They are Mei Lin's fish," said Ye-ye. "She is a country girl, but she lives in the new China where even a woman can manage a

business. She made and tended the traps that caught them. I
suppose you should ask the business woman."

They both laughed, "Ah it is a new day in China!" Qin Shu-
shu said, "Come to the kitchen with me Mei Lin and I will get your
money. I will have the kitchen boy come out and take the fish off the
cart for you. Are you thirsty?" he asked as we stepped inside the
kitchen door. "Would you like a Ke Kou Ke Le™"

At that very moment, I realized that I was very thirsty. Qin
Shu-shu reached inside a cooler and handed me an icy cold
Coke™. It had been many years since I had had one. In fact, it had
been many years since I had had any chilled drink. We almost
always drank tea: wolf-berry tea, jasmine tea, black tea, green tea. I
was not prepared for the unusual sensation. The cold burned my
throat and the bubbles tickled my nose and made me sneeze. I
choked.

"Not so fast!" he laughed. "You'll get a headache!" We went
into an office behind the kitchen where he opened a safe, counted
out some red, green and blue paper money and handed it to me. I
stuffed it in my pocket without counting it. "You know, it just occurred
to me that you also have some nice looking watermelons on that
cart. How long ago were they picked?"

"Just yesterday."

"Are they for sale as well? This current batch of Americans is
very fond of melon in the morning."

"Yes. I was headed to market to sell them."

"Don't bother. I'll buy them as well."

He turned back to the safe, removed another stack of money
and handed it to me. He called the kitchen boy I had seen earlier
and a second boy and told them to unload the whole cart. Then he
called a woman and asked her to pour three cups of oolong tea and
prepare a variety tray of steamed buns and two bowls of congee

and all the fixings: dried salted cucumber, pickled fish and some sweet things as well.

When it was prepared, he dismissed the woman and carried the tray out to the service courtyard. There, he set it on the small table overlooking the river. "Mei Lin, tell your Ye-ye to come sit with his old student. I wish to speak of philosophy and world literature and learn news of my good friend, Zhong Liang."

Ye-ye leaned heavily on my shoulder as we walked across the pavement toward the table.

"Laoshe, something is wrong with your leg!" said Qin Shu-shu. "You are in pain. Let me help you." He helped Ye-ye sit down and felt his leg through his trousers.

"Your knee is quite swollen. After we have tea, we will have the hotel doctor take a look at it."

"No, I feel fine," protested Ye-ye.

"Nonsense," said Qin Shu-shu. "I insist you see our doctor. It is the least I can do to return the favor of my most excellent education to you. Where would I be had you not forced me to learn so much when I was a stubborn youth? Now you try to be stubborn with me, but you see it will not work. I have learned many lessons from your example. After we have enjoyed our tea, I will call the house doctor, Gan Yi-sheng and he will give you good medicine to ease the pain."

After they had talked for quite some time, I began to grow bored speaking of Russian writers such as Chekhov and British poetry of masters such as Byron, and Keats. I am afraid I began to look a little restless I didn't mean to be rude, but I was eager to get to market. I knew I had enough money to buy some nice clothes for winter as well as present a good amount of money to Baba to add to the baby's birth penalty. If we were to sit here and visit and then to see a doctor, the whole day might be spent before I had time to get there. The morning was almost half over already. I began looking

out across the river, then back at the road, swinging my feet under
the table.

After they had spoken for nearly an hour, I picked up a
steamed bean paste bun and wandered down to the stone wall
above the river. The stone was hot now, having baked in the sun for
several hours. I climbed up and sat on it, watching the boats go by
on the mighty Pearl River--so much broader than our little Nandu
River that feeds into these waters. I thought about the fat baby
growing in Mama's belly and wondered if it was a girl or a boy. If it
turned out to be a girl, I would buy a beautiful silk and lace thing to
put in her hair like the Americans put on the babies I had seen that
morning.

Qin Shu-shu walked up behind me and startled me from my
daydreams when he said, "Mei Lin, I must get back to my work now,
although I would much rather visit with your Ye-ye all day. Gan Yi-
sheng will take good care of him. Your cart is empty now and ready
to go. The kitchen boys have left it over by that tree," he motioned to
a tree at the end of a long queue of bicycles.

"Xie, xie, Thank you Qin Shu-shu. We are most grateful for
your help." I said as I bowed to him.

"Bu ke qi--Don't mention it," said Qin Shu-shu as he returned
my bow. "It was my pleasure and my good fortune that you
happened to bring such beautiful fish and melons to me just when I
needed them most. Thank you for bringing your Ye-ye to visit with
me. Be sure to send my warm regards to your parents. I miss them
both very much." He paused a moment and looked at the ground as
if considering what he would say next.

"I have always thought of your father much as a younger
brother, you know. He was born when I was a student of your
grandfather's. A few of us more advanced students would gather for
discussions in your grandfather's study each evening. When he
began to walk, your father would toddle in and climb into your Ye-
ye's lap before his bedtime. Sometimes, while your grandfather

continued an important lesson, little Liang sat on my lap or played with my calligraphy brushes. He was just not yet three years old when your grandfather was taken away. In those days, I shared his grief.

"We both lost our future. He lost a father and I lost a man who was like a father to me in that one awful night.

"I helped your grandmother in every way that I could. Our shared grief grew an even stronger bond between your Baba and me that has lasted until today.

"So many things have changed since then. I was not able to finish my university degree or become a professor of world literature like your Ye-ye as I had hoped, but I am grateful the bond between your family and me remains." He bowed deeply to me and I returned his bow, feeling the weight of his words in my heart.

Qin Shu-shu returned to the kitchen and I walked over to Ye-ye. The doctor had applied a thick black paste of a very smelly Chinese medicine to his knee and covered it with a bandage. He had also given him a small plastic bottle, which he said was a popular American medicine. Ye-ye should swallow two pills now with a cup of tea and then again every four hours. For several days, he should take two more pills every four hours until the pain stopped and the swelling had gone down. I looked at the label. It said, *Extra Strength Tylenol*. The doctor also said that Ye-ye should avoid walking or standing on the sore leg as much as possible for several days.

Ye-ye smiled, took two of the pills, swallowed them with the last of his tea, placed the pill bottle in his jacket pocket and thanked the doctor. He asked how much money he owed the doctor and Gan Yi-sheng bowed deeply and said, "Most honorable professor, when I was a very young man, I read many of your great books before they were banned as a foreign influence by the leaders of the Cultural Revolution. It has been my very great privilege to help you in this small way."

Ye-ye and I both returned the bow and said, "Xie, xie."

Gan Yi-sheng helped Ye-ye walk back to our cart and settled him into the back with the blanket as a cushion before returning to the hotel. I noticed as I began to turn away, that Ye-ye's eyes were watery.

"Ye-ye, Is there something in your eye?"

"Yes child. The light of purpose floods my eyes, and just now, for a moment, overflows. After all these many years, my life's work is still remembered."

Qingpin Market

Judge not the horse by its saddle.

The sun was already quite high in the sky. "If we are to get to market, we must hurry," said Ye-ye. I picked up the arms of the cart and pulled against them. Compared to the weight I had pulled into this courtyard, the cart was so light, I felt like I could fly to the market. It was only Ye-ye, no melons, no water and no fish! I felt like running, but that was not possible. So many people and bicycles filled the streets. Here, there were also many foreigners, walking in the wrong places, creating obstacles that must be steered around. The foreigners seemed to have no sense of their part in the rhythm of the street. Didn't they understand that if anyone is to get anywhere, we must all move together? They, in fact, seemed totally unaware of their part in the flow of traffic—expecting everyone to steer around them much as a river winds its way around a water buffalo! I would forgive them however, as I suppose most of the people around me also did. The "Da bi-zi" had made me rich and given me a lightness of step. For this, I could excuse them almost anything.

We crossed over the canal and, because we had the cart, could not take the overpass footbridge across the divided freeway. We had to travel back to the place where the road curved into a wide circle, the place where the two, larger than life billboard children looked admiringly up at the woman soldier, where the American restaurant of large gold arches took up as much space as a rice paddy. There I could cross the freeway, turn the cart around and head up one of the small alleyways into the Qingpin Market.

Qingpin Market is a noisy place where farmers and vendors gather to sell what they have. They group together in sections according to whatever it is they have brought to sell. In the first section, there are all sorts of goods for sale, some old coins and various household items, a pearl merchant sits next to a man who has all kinds of locks and keys. They vie with each other for customer attention, each singing out his wares in a sort of song: "Pearls here! Quality pearls! Natural seawater pearls! Freshwater pearls! Cultured pearls! Here is my business card! Best prices in the market!"

While a meter away, another sings, "Pendants and broaches, original designs!"

"Antiques. Rare and valuable antiques!" sang a man operating from a push cart in front of the noodle shop. "If you can't buy today, come back tomorrow! Take my card! Tell your friends."

In another section one can buy any manner of Chinese medicine, from dried sea horses for gout and live scorpions used to treat liver cancer to herbs and powdered roots of exotic trees. One merchant sells only tea, but any kind of tea for any medicinal purpose. There were teas for headaches and teas for nausea, teas to prevent pregnancy and teas to ensure pregnancy. Here the melody of their song is the same, but the words are different.

"Cure your aches!"

"Ensure the birth of a healthy son!" shouted a toothless old woman when she saw us approach. As soon as she realized that I

49

was too young to have a baby and grandfather too old, she briskly pocketed her business card and returned to talking into a small plastic light she held in her hand and held up to the side of her face. "I wouldn't say that business is bad, but it certainly isn't what it could be. What if we expanded—say opened a web page and sold our teas internationally?"

We headed down one alley dedicated to pets of every kind. Here one can buy delicate bamboo birdcages complete with exquisite blue floral ceramic food dishes. One vender was pushing his customer toward a higher price:

"Eighty yuan? You embarrass me! No, this is a fine birdcage, completely lacquered. I couldn't sell it that cheaply! The feed dishes are of fine porcelain!"

One vendor had a huge bamboo basket filled with tiny plastic bags. Each bag had an individual Siamese fighting fish in a small amount of air and water. Next to him, a woman had sweet white Persian kittens for sale. Each had a red ribbon around its neck with a tiny comb attached to the end so you can comb its hair each day.

I was angry with myself. This was the wrong road to take, for it emptied into the big courtyard of the jade market. When I am old enough to marry, a young man will present me with a jade ring, and perhaps if he is wealthy, a jade bracelet as well.

Until then, I expect only to wear the jade Buddha, which hangs from my neck by a red silk cord. Most country girls have no jewelry or ornamentation and most people do not know I have this. I keep it under my shirt. For many years, all religion was considered a danger to the government. Now, there is more tolerance. I am not sure what I believe concerning religion. I wear the Buddha only because it belonged to my Nai-nai who died when I was very young. She cared for me when I was a baby while Mama was working in a factory. It is all I have to remind me of her. Whenever I miss my Nai-nai, I wrap my hand around it and feel the smooth surface with my fingers. The cart bounced behind me with a violent jolt.

"Mei Lin! Pay attention! What are you doing? Daydreaming?"

"Sorry, Ye-ye. All this jade reminded me of my jade Buddha and I was remembering Nai-nai."

"Ah, my old bones will forgive you, then. Your grandmother is certainly worthy of remembrance. However, do you think you could reminisce on a smoother section of the road?"

"Yes, Ye-ye. I am afraid I am quite lost. I cannot remember which road leads to the clothing section."

"Nor can I. So much has changed since we were here last."

Just then, a woman approached us. She was walking toward us pushing a bicycle along. From the handlebars hung ten golden-colored chickens. They were all alive, fluttering and flapping their wings and protesting loudly that their feet were above their heads, tied to the handlebars.

"Qing wen," I said, "May I ask please, where would I find the clothing merchants?"

"Ah," she said, and looked around as if getting her bearings again. "Take that alley," she pointed over my left shoulder. Go past the row of butchers and fishmongers. Turn left when you get to the man with the baskets of snakes and turtles. Don't turn right or you will find yourself surrounded by electronics: televisions and CD's, cell phones and microwaves. The alley you want is small and very narrow, but will take you directly to the best section for practical clothing."

"Xie-xie!" I said and nodded my head toward her.

"Ai-ya!" she screamed and held up her hand. A small trickle of blood dripped where one of the chickens had pecked her. I turned the cart around as she stood in the street, bracing the bicycle against her leg and scolding the chickens.

"Please," said Ye-ye, "Take this. You have been very helpful." He held up a clean and freshly ironed white handkerchief—the kind of handkerchief Western gentlemen used to wear in a coat pocket.

She looked at it, then at Ye-ye. She said nothing but wrapped it around her hurt finger and soaked it with her blood.

I pulled the cart in the direction she had pointed out, into a narrow dark alley paved in ancient cobblestones. Whole dead animals hung skinned and ready to buy from hooks along the top of these stalls. Fresh fish were sliced open lengthwise to show the still inflated air sacs, and the rich reds and blues of all the internal organs. I looked away from a cage of wild, dirty cats. These animals were meant for the stew pot --not for pets, and I clearly would not have wanted to brush the fur of these wild creatures. I looked back when a man asked to buy a small but hissing kitten. The merchant opened the cage and two other cats jumped out, spitting and clawing and scratching. They ran off into the market and disappeared into a sewer grate. Finally he caught the kitten by the scruff of the neck and stuffed it into the customer's cloth bag. Money was exchanged and the customer climbed back on his bicycle.

The smell in this part of the market made my stomach lurch. It was a powerful smell of blood and death and fear. I was glad when we reached the vats of stew snakes and soup turtles. We turned into another alley. This was no wider than the one we had just left, but there were no vendors here. Sunlight seemed brighter. The street was immaculately clean. There was neither litter nor dirt anywhere as if someone had scrubbed and polished the very paving stones.

Doorways here were rounded and made of stone. The doors, themselves were green, the color of wealth and the paving stones were red, the color of health. Elaborate wrought iron balconies dripped with trailing orchids and bougainvilleas. On every balcony, clusters of colorful songbirds sang from tiny perches within delicate bamboo birdcages. With every step, the cart lurched and bounced, so I walked slowly. An elderly gentleman wearing a neatly pressed, traditional, Mandarin style, gray suit sat on a doorstep smoking a long-stemmed pipe. He smiled as we walked by. Two grandmothers sat at a small stone table playing Ma-Jiang, an ancient tile game of luck and strategy. Their baby grandsons, fat in thick layers of quilted clothing, played with a toy truck on a blanket by their feet. I had an overwhelming feeling that I had stepped back in time. Of course, I knew we hadn't, but this so resembled Ye-ye's descriptions of what Chinese life used to look like in the days before the Cultural Revolution, that I felt tingly anyway. I walked slowly, breathing deeply of the scent of the flowers. It was a welcome contrast after the smells of pig's blood and cat urine we had left behind in the market.

It was a short alley and soon we were back in another section of the busy market.

"Ye-ye, that was a wonderful place!"

When he did not answer me, I looked back at him. He simply nodded and did not speak but I could see in his eyes that he was deep in memories.

"Ye-ye?"

"Oh, I am sorry granddaughter! Now it is my turn for daydreaming. This passageway so resembled my life of long ago that I . . ." his voice trailed off as I quickly found my place in the surge of moving bicycles and carts. This was a wider street, but had much busier traffic. Shop after shop of clothes surrounded us. One stall had all manner of athletic clothing, another all things for babies. One had only fine silk and still another all cotton quilted coats and trousers such as farmers wear in winter. I pulled the cart up next to a street lamp and lowered the arms.

"Ye-ye, if you could sit here a few minutes, I could move more quickly."

"Oh, good idea, granddaughter! It is time for a nap." He barely waited for me to leave before he curled over on his side and fell asleep.

I knew I should buy nothing in the first shop I walked into. I just wanted to see some beautiful things. I did not dare touch the silk dresses and jackets that hung there--each one wrapped in its own protective plastic sheet. I knew that I looked out of place, a dusty farm girl in such an elegant shop, but it was as if the colors beckoned to me. They were so rich; emerald green, ruby red and sapphire blue, each with gold threads forming pictures of chrysanthemums, peacocks or pagodas. I just wanted to feast my eyes on them if only for a few minutes, to take the images of them inside of myself so that I could carry their richness home with me.

"Step back from those dresses, girl! Farm girls' hands are so rough, just touching silk will ruin it. I am sure you do not have enough money to pay for what you could damage in here."

I did have enough money but I didn't tell this shopkeeper so. I had more important things to do with my money. I had to pay for my baby sister's or brother's permission to live. I was about to leave when I saw the basket on the counter. It was filled with tiny pink silk bows. Some had ribbon streamers with tiny pearls on them and some had bits of lace sewn into circles. Some were attached to hair clips and some to elastic hair wraps.

"Qing wen, Please, may I ask, how much are these?"

"Ah, each is eight yuan. They are very popular with the foreigners."

"Then I would like this one with the ribbon streamers and tiny pearls."

"Ah, a most excellent choice. But, what is a farm girl to do with such a delicate thing?"

"For now, I will only look at it. One day, soon, it will be a gift for someone special. Could you wrap it so my rough hands do not snag it, please?" I smiled at her as she carefully slid a pocket of clear cellophane over the bow.

After I had tucked this purchase into my trousers pocket, I walked to the clothing store next door. Rack after rack of sensible quilted clothing was jammed into a very small space. The racks extended to the ceiling. I tried on several things and finally settled on a dark blue print jacket and a pair of plain dark blue quilted trousers. I bought it two sizes larger than I am so that I would have room to grow before I needed another one.

As I was about to leave, I saw a turquoise jacket big enough to fit Mama until the baby came in one month. It was cotton, not silk, but still quite beautiful. The jacket she wore last winter no longer buttoned in the front over her belly. I bought this too from my fish money.

Three more stalls later, everything was fur: fur coats and collars for coats, fur hats and fur lined shoes and gloves. I chose a pair of red shoes with a warm fur lining for myself and another pair for Ye-ye in black. I bought a fur hat for Baba to protect him from the cold winds of winter. It had ear flaps that could fasten under the chin or up over the top of the hat.

I crossed over the street and was heading back to our cart when I passed a man with a cart full of baby things. I picked up a bamboo rattle with two bells inside a woven split bamboo ball. As I shook it, the two bells each made a distinct sound. I bought it and hurried back to the cart.

Ye-ye was still asleep and I did not try to wake him. I placed the packages in the back of the cart, then stood between the arms of the cart and pulled. My hands were sore. My shoulders ached from the strain. My arms and legs were tired but I knew there was no choice. Ye-ye was counting on me to get him home. I began walking toward the main road. Just before we left the market, I stopped and bought a box of noodles and vegetables cooked in sesame seed oil, some barbecued duck, some dried fruit, and refilled our hot drink bottle with jasmine tea.

When we reached the tree at the top of the hill where we had rested the night before, I woke Ye-ye and shared the meal with him. I suddenly felt very tired—even into my bones. Every part of my body pulsed with pain. I realized that blisters had formed on my feet and my hands. Every muscle ached. The heady excitement and business of the day had distracted me, but now the exertion of the day settled into a deep and painful weariness. The sun was still high in the sky, but I knew it would be tomorrow before I reached home— if I could keep walking that long.

伍

The Long Road Home

To know the road ahead,
Ask those coming back.

    I must have fallen asleep, for the next thing I knew, Ye-ye was shaking my shoulder and urging, "Mei Lin, you must get up." I was still sitting, leaning against the trunk of the tree. My back felt stiff and wooden as if my bones themselves *were* the tree! Ye-ye didn't wait for me to get up and was already settling into the back of the cart by the time I stood up. By the looks of things, he had already cleaned up the remains of our dinner hours ago. I could barely move my elbows, knees and shoulders when I first tried to stand. I stretched a little and yawned, stood between the arms of the cart, adjusted the rope over my shoulder and pulled.

    The sun was sinking in the western sky. Soon it would set and I would walk on in darkness. The sky was clear, however, so at least there would be moonlight to walk by. Things that had seemed so exciting as we approached the city now seemed dull and boring. The only thing I wanted to see was my home: Mama and Baba--and my own bed.

I walked on and on: one foot in front of another, one hill after another, one step after another. A wheel began to squeak: wee-ga, wee-ga, wee-ga.

"I must remember to grease that axel when we get home," said Ye-ye. I didn't answer. It seemed too much of an effort when no answer was required. "Mei Lin, are you alright? Do you need to stop for a while?"

"I'm fine. I want to get home as soon as possible." Actually, I was afraid that if I stopped now, I might never get started again. While I was moving, the pain was bearable. I was afraid that if I rested, I might stiffen up again worse than before. I might not be able to walk at all!

"Granddaughter, if I can help you, perhaps cheer you with a song . . ."

"Yes, you can help me. Help me stay awake by talking to me."

"Good! What shall we speak about?"

"I have been thinking of the Americans we met this morning. I am wondering why there are so many babies to adopt and why Americans and not Chinese adopt them."

"Ah, granddaughter, you ask difficult questions with painful answers! The answers are rooted in thousands of years of Chinese history. But, these are good questions for a long road as the answers are quite long. I will try to answer them although I am not sure I understand them entirely, myself. There are different kinds of knowledge, my gentle granddaughter. I must tell you that although I think I understand these answers with my head, my heart is much slower in this type of understanding."

The sun burned like a glowing pumpkin on the horizon. A solitary crane pierced the middle of it like an arrow shot across the sky. "Wee-ga, wee-ga," sang the wheel.

"As you know, Mei Lin, for many thousands of years, it has been the tradition among Chinese people that the eldest son is heir to all his father possesses. Yet, in return, it is his duty to care for his parents until they die. Actually, their care usually fell upon the wife of the eldest son, but what mattered most to married couples was producing a son to care for them in old age. Daughters cared for their husband's parents, not their own. To have no son meant to die of neglect and possibly starvation. A large family, with many sons, was insurance against illness and accident that at least one son would survive to care for a person in old age."

"But today we have much smaller families. Baba and Mama have only me. They will not die of starvation! I will not allow it. I would not marry a man who did not let me care for them."

"Before the New China was founded in 1949, you would not have had the freedom to even think this way. Girls had no choice as to whom they would marry or when. Your grandmother didn't even meet me until our wedding day."

"But Ye-ye, you loved Nai-nai very much!'

"I still do, but it took me many years to learn how to do that."

"Wee-ga! Wee-ga!" squeaked the wheel.

Twenty minutes passed before I dared to ask again, "Was our family *very* wealthy?"

Ye-ye paused and said nothing for a few minutes, then he sighed and said, "Yes, Mei Lin, we were. But I didn't know that then. Even though I was a learned scholar, I was truly ignorant. I had little understanding of the millions of people in our country who lived in desperate poverty. Worse, I didn't care. My ignorance has cost my whole family, especially your dear Nai-nai a great deal."

I felt my pulse quicken with sudden realization and blurted out, "Did *you* ever drive in an automobile?" I realized as soon as the words slipped past my lips that I had asked too eagerly. Ye-ye did not answer at first.

"Yes," he said. "I owned several very nice cars and I occasionally drove them for the fun of it, although I had a driver who usually did that for me." His voice sounded strained as if it was difficult to speak of these things.

"I'm sorry if I offended you, Ye-ye." I did not wish to see my grandfather uncomfortable because of my ignorance, so I quickly asked another question. "I know that when Chairman Mao started the Cultural Revolution, he questioned the traditional ways, and pointed out many injustices. How could all the good he did lead to too many babies without families?"

"Ah! It took many thousands of years for Chinese culture to evolve and grow. Chairman Mao tried to make sweeping changes in one lifetime. Much of what was good in the traditional ways was lost or damaged in this swift cultural movement. For example, many irreplaceable art objects were lost, damaged or destroyed simply because they stood for values contrary to the revolutionary effort. Ah, but in every war, there are casualties."

"Ye-ye, what does art have to do with babies?"

"Patience, child! It is a long road." His words were sharp, but the tone of his voice was warm and teasing. "I will get the story told long before you get us home. "

"I'm sorry, Ye-ye, I'm just impatient to know about the babies."

"Traditionally, there was no such thing in China as adoption. Aunts, uncles and cousins all lived together. If the parents of a child died, there would surely be an uncle or elder cousin to care for a child. There was no need for social welfare institutions. Families changed with the Cultural Revolution. Mothers began working in factories. Babies were left in the care of grandmothers or aunts during the workday much as your grandmother cared for you while your mother worked in a factory many li from our home. Your mother traveled home to see you every Sunday and missed you desperately, but it was the price she was called upon to pay for the sake of building a new China."

"Teacher Ma says this is good. Women were repressed before and now we are equal citizens. Still, I don't see how all this leads to babies adopted by foreigners?"

"In the 1980's our national leaders watched with mounting concern as the population of China continued to multiply. China was less than ten years from a crisis of crushing proportions. If the population continued to grow at the same rate, in a very short time, there would not be enough food to feed all the people."

"Did we grow more food?"

"There was not enough room. All the tillable land was already used. Great portions of China are desert and steep mountains made of rock. No, instead, our leaders took drastic measures. They instituted a national family planning policy to reduce the population of China. Young people were encouraged to wait many years before marrying. Your parents, for example were more than thirty years old before they married. By contrast, I was a mere twenty years old as were many of my generation. Your grandmother was only sixteen when we married.

"Under the new policy, each couple was encouraged to have only one child. Soon it was required that married couples must apply for a permit to try to have a child. Some provinces required young married couples to wait many years after the marriage to begin the birth permit application process. In some areas, this encouragement was enforced by neighborhood watch groups, who reported women who were known to be pregnant to local authorities. Then, the pregnancy would be medically terminated if she did not have a birth permit."

"They killed the babies before they were born? But I thought everyone loved babies!"

"Yes, I think most people do. This is why many women hide their pregnancies, tightly binding their bellies with cloth and layers of clothing so the growth will not show. Then they give birth in private without a doctor or midwife. But, once the child is born, there is no longer any way to conceal it. Even the best babies cry sometimes. Neighbors hear. If they want to win the approval of the local officials, they report what they hear. High fines are charged if couples were found to have had a child without a birth permit. So, many times, these babies whose mothers worked very hard at great personal risk to bring to life, are abandoned in a public place so that the officials will find them quickly. The baby will grow up in a social welfare institution. This way, the parents know that although it would be too risky to raise the child themselves, that the baby they love will at least live."

"But Ye-ye, wouldn't half of these babies be boys? I have seen only girl babies with the Da-bi-zi."

"You are observant, my granddaughter. Yes, half of *these* babies are boys. Some foreigners have adopted boys but most of the babies they adopt are girls. This is because of another reason. There is another group of babies."

It was dark now and a chill settled over me. A huge orange moon hovered over the eastern horizon.

"Sometimes a married couple has a permit to have a baby. When it is born, maybe half of the time, it is a girl. Because they can have only one child, many couples feel forced to give the girl away, leaving her in a public place where she will be found, although they will report her as stillborn. Then they try to have another child, hoping for a boy who will be able to care for them in old age. This is where most of the girls come from that the foreigners adopt. Usually the parents of these baby girls have a birth permit."

"Will my parents abandon our baby if it is a girl?"

"No, Mei Lin. Your parents are truly citizens of the new China. They feel a girl is as wonderful as a boy and will keep whatever baby comes to them. They want another child just for the joy a child brings. There was never a father more proud of a son than your father is of you."

I was glad it was dark. I could feel the color rising in my face and I could not take my hand off the cart to cover the smile of pleasure I felt curling the corners of my lips. I was proud of my parents, too. Clearly it was difficult to do what they had decided.

"Wee-ga! Wee-ga," sang the wheels as I thought.

"Ye-ye, Why do the Da-bi-zi want Chinese babies?"

"Unfortunately," Ye-ye continued, "there are many people who cannot have children for one reason or another. Until very recently, it has been" he paused a moment as if carefully choosing his words, "difficult for a Chinese couple to adopt a baby. They must first prove that they are unable to have children of their own. So the Social Welfare Institutions became overcrowded and the task of caring for the thousands of abandoned babies grew. Foreigners began to ask if they could adopt these babies and soon our leaders saw a mutually beneficial answer to a growing crisis. If foreigners would promise to love and care for the babies and treat them as their own children, then perhaps some could find homes.

"At the same time, there would be fewer babies in the institutions and the income the adoption fees would generate could provide better care for the babies left in the institutions. It seemed all around to be a workable solution—perhaps not the best solution— but a workable one. The adopted babies have parents who love them, give them an education and medical care they would not have in many social welfare institutions. The adopting parents have a family they had longed for. So, adoption builds a circle of love that spirals back to the children who must remain in the care of the provincial authorities."

Ye-ye stopped talking and I did not ask any more questions. My head felt heavy with too much knowledge. I wanted to think about these answers, sort them through, make sense of them.

"Wee-ga! Wee-ga! Wee-ga!"

It was not long before I heard another sound-- like that of a thousand locusts descending upon a grassy field. It was coming from the back of the cart and louder than the squeaking wheel. Ye-ye was lying on his back; his head thrust back and his mouth wide open. He was sound asleep and snoring quite loudly. I passed many hours alone with my thoughts, the bumps of the road, the silver light of a full moon and an endless song that went: "Wee-ga! Wee-ga! Wee-ga! Snooore!"

The air was chilly and the hairs on my arms stood up straight each time the wind blew.

The moon set.

The sky grew darker.

Just before dawn, as we approached the crossroads, I felt as if someone was watching me, following me as I pulled my cart down the road toward our village. I told myself that there was no such thing as ghosts; that demons which prowl the countryside in Chinese myths were things of childhood fear. Yet, there it was again; a rustling in the reeds that grew along the side of the road. "It is the wind!" I scolded myself: Certainly a girl old enough to be trusted with the kind of job I had just accomplished was no longer afraid of monsters in the dark!

Yet again, I heard a rustling in the reeds at the side of the road and something that sounded like a cat. "What is that?" I asked aloud as the words squeaked through the tight hole of fear in my throat. I don't know who I expected to reply for Ye-ye was too deep in sleep to hear me.

There was no answer.

I thought my mind was playing tricks on me and that I was so tired I was dreaming although I think I was awake.

I heard someone running away, the rhythmic pounding of feet dulled in the freshly hoed trenches between the mounds of a sweet-potato field. In the gathering gray light, I thought I saw the form of a thin, young man jumping over the plants and running across the field, away from us very fast. In my mind I could hear the fast beating of his heart and taste the adrenaline of fear in his throat. I could see no monsters chasing him, yet his fear was more real than mine. I stopped the cart and listened again. Yes, it sounded *like* a cat--but not exactly. I heard the sound of a motor and saw a single light moving up behind me on the road. A county police officer was headed toward our village of Longkou on motorcycle. He pulled over, removed his helmet, leaned on one foot and let the motor idle.

"Is there a problem, girl?"

"No, Xian-sheng."

"Just heading back from market?"

"Dui le," I said. ("That's correct.")

He cut the engine, stepped off his motorcycle and looked me over. "Aren't you a bit young for such a big job?"

"Bu shi, Xian sheng! (No, I am not, sir.) I came to help my Ye-ye, but he has hurt his leg. I stopped because I heard something moving in the reeds, but I think it was a cat." Just then it mewed again.

"Ah," he said, "I have heard this sound many times at this same place in the road. It is not a cat." He pushed aside the reeds and there, wrapped tightly in a brand new blanket was a tiny baby, not more than a day old. "You put this baby here!" he accused.

"No!" I gasped. My eyes were as big as the lid of a tea cup!

"Sir," Ye-ye roused from his sleep. "Look at her. She is only a child herself, hardly old enough . . . "

He looked at me for several moments. "No, I suppose not. Did you see anyone?"

"No, no-one." I half-lied. "I was scared at first when I heard the reeds move, I thought it was a monster." I left out the part about seeing the thin young man who was chased by his own fear through the sweet-potato field. I didn't understand how someone could abandon a baby but I knew that he had also taken considerable risk to make sure I would find her. Suddenly I wanted to protect him. So I left him out of the story and continued, "Then, I heard a sound that was like a mew and I thought it was a cat chasing a mouse in there. I was about to start back on my way when you came along."

"Humph!" he said as if considering the likeliness of my story. Then he looked back at Ye-ye. "Take your grandfather home. He does not look well. I will take care of this."

"What will you do? What will happen to the baby?"

"I will take her to the social welfare institute in Baoshan City. It is the closest one." He held the baby against his chest with one hand and started off on his motorcycle turning back toward the city we had left.

I leaned forward and strained against the rope as it cut into my shoulder. My hands felt raw as I squeezed my fingers around the grips. The cart seemed to have grown even heavier during those few moments while I rested. My every muscle strained against the weight of the wooden cart even as my heart strained against the weight of the certain knowledge I now possessed.

A New Day, a New Baby

Dragon father begets dragon son.

The sky began to lighten and the birds to sing, darting above the rice paddies, and snatching the insects that hovered in the mist above the water. I had long stopped thinking of anything when I finally saw the familiar outline of Longkou in the distance. My entire body was numb and my brain was numb too. My legs were locked into the rhythm of walking and my hands were cramped into the curve of the cart handles.

"Mei Lin!" I heard Baba's voice as if from far off. I thought I saw Baba racing like a ghost through the early-morning fog that drifted across the road. I dreamt I felt his arms embrace me. My knees gave way to exhaustion as I fell against his chest. He caught me and laughed, his voice sounding like an echo in a distant dream.

"Mei Lin. Let go of the cart handles. I will pull it the rest of the way."

But I could not let go.

I had held the handles so tightly and for so long that I couldn't release my hands from their grasp. Baba held me against his left shoulder and pried my fingers free on my left hand. Searing pain shot up my arm and then the arm dropped limp at my side. Baba shifted me to the other shoulder and pried my right arm free. I hung against him as limp as a cooked noodle. Baba was laughing yet there was tenderness and pride in his voice.

"Mei Lin. You are utterly exhausted. Truly a qian jin xiao jie, (a daughter of thousand pieces of gold)!"

I could not answer. He lifted me and placed me on the cart next to Ye-ye. I rolled against Ye-ye and absorbed the warmth of his body. I felt a tug as the cart wheel began to sing, "Wee-ga, wee ga!" I heard Baba's rich, melodious voice sing the first line of a lullaby, "Little bird, little bird, come sing your song for me. Little bird, little bird, can I fly away with you?" before I sank into a deep and dreamless sleep.

*   *   *

"Mei Lin, Mei Lin. You must try to get up." I heard Ye-ye and felt his hand rocking my shoulder. I opened my eyes and saw that I was in my own bed and that it was nearly sunset.

"Ai-ya!" I said. "Have I wasted an entire day?"

"No," said Ye-ye.

"No? It is nearly sunset!"

"Mei Lin, you have slept for two days. You must try to get up and eat something now." I felt like I was suspended, pulling myself up from under water. I have felt this way many times. I often had to dive into the river and release my fish traps from branches and debris that had caught them. Though I was on dry land, the sensation was the same. I willed myself to the surface of consciousness, yet every muscle ached. I raised my head a few inches from my pillow but my body refused to move any further and I dropped back down.

"Here," said Ye-ye. "I'll help you." He took my arms and pulled me up so that I was nearly sitting. He stuffed a rolled-up blanket behind me and let me lean against it "Drink this." He held a blue and white ceramic spoon against my lips. Slowly I slurped in what I thought would be the savory delight of Mama's chicken soup but choked when I tasted it. It tasted too strong: pig bone with ginger and dark vinegar soup! My throat was so dry it hurt to swallow, but it felt so good just the same. I took some more. "It is medicine soup to get back your strength."

"Two days?" I looked at Ye-ye. He was standing and walking effortlessly across the room. He placed the bowl of soup on the chest of drawers by the door and called to Mama.

"Well, a day-and-a-half," he continued. "You earned it. You are a girl but you did a grown man's work."

"Ah! She is awake at last!" The sound of Mama's voice nearly made me cry. I felt like I had grown so much older in the time I had been away from her, but I still longed to be a little girl and feel her hold me close.

"Mama, I have so much to tell you!" She sat on the edge of my bed and tenderly stroked my hair.

"I am sure you do, and you will in time. But I have much to tell you." It was then that I noticed that Mama looked a little thinner than the last time I saw her, still larger than usual, but thinner than I remember.

"Mama, the baby . . ."

"Came early. Your brother is very impatient to meet you." I heard a baby cry in the next room and the next thing I knew, Baba had walked into the room cradling a tiny baby in his arms. He bent down and laid him in my arms.

"A boy?" I asked, surprised.

"A boy. Are you disappointed? You look sad."

"No! I am still a little weary. No, a brother is just what I wanted." Though my thoughts had recently been of a sister, I knew in that instant that my words were the truth. I looked into his little face and his coal black eyes looked up at me. They were the same shape as mine, rounder than most Chinese, with long lashes. He was the most beautiful baby I had ever seen—but very tiny, almost like a toy. I bent down and breathed in the scent of him, all new and wonderfully full of life. I looked up at Mama and said, "Can I help you take care of him?"

"I will depend on you."

"What's will we call him?"

"We don't know yet. We will wait and have a naming ceremony in one year. Perhaps by then he will show us what he wants to be named." Until then, you can just call him 'Little Brother'."

"Di-di," I said as he wrapped his tiny fingers around my pinky. "He likes me! Di-di likes me!"

He cried again and stretched. Mama reached out and took him back. She rested him on her right hip and held him tightly with her strong arm. "It is almost time for our little dragon to eat again. Mei Lin, sit up a little more and finish your soup while I feed the baby. There are hard-boiled eggs in the soup for strength and ginger to make your blood begin to flow again after your long rest. Try to eat as much of them as you can.

Now I understood why it had not been mother's chicken soup! This was the traditional medicine soup for a woman who has just had a baby—to get her strength back. "Try to get up in a little while and walk. We will eat dumplings soon."

"Dumplings! It's not Chinese New Year!"

"No, but I want to celebrate the birth of my son and the return of my daughter, so I have made dumplings." Of course mama had made fish and chicken and noodles and several vegetables too in order to celebrate. But she knew it was only the dumplings I truly cared about.

I knew I had to get up. Mama's dumplings were the best in the world. And I was so hungry; I could almost taste them already.

Hot.

Steamy.

Stuffed with green onions and finely ground pork.

Drenched in rice vinegar and soy sauce.

Melting in my mouth.

I pushed myself up so that I was sitting up straight in bed. Ye-ye brought a cup of green tea. "Sip it slowly," he urged.

My head was swimming again. "Just go slowly. You have been lying down for a long time. Your body is not used to being up. Move slowly and give yourself time to adjust to the change."

When I had finished the tea, he urged me to slide my legs over the side of the bed. He pushed a small table over and placed the bowl of soup on it. He left the room and I finished my soup.

"Ah, Liu Lao. How nice to see you." I could hear Baba talking in the courtyard, "Have you eaten yet?"

"Yes, yes, I have only just finished! I came to see how Mei Lin is doing today. I heard the long trip was too much for her. Ah the terrible luck of this household! Yet, much of it stems from your own ignorance, Zhong Liang. First, you have a daughter rather than a son—and you decide to keep her. I offered you an opportunity to correct that situation. But, no, you stubbornly refused. Then your wife has a runaway crate of computer parts smack against her head and render her a helpless invalid. One day, a skilled welder. The next, useless! When will you learn Zhong Liang? When will you learn to follow my advice? I only give it for your own benefit! You should not expect a useless girl to perform a task that demands the strength and skill of a boy."

"Mei Lin is just fine. She is worth more than many sons." (I knew just which worthless son Baba had in mind.)

I smiled as I stood up and walked to the door. My legs were a little shaky and my head started to swim. My stomach lurched. I grabbed the doorpost and hung on until the swirling blackness passed and the sensation of needles stabbing my legs had stopped. Then I walked through our big room where Mama and Baba slept, where we ate and cooked and sewed at night. I walked past the family shrine. There was a small jade Buddha on a table with a black wooden plaque listing the names of our ancestors behind it. It was fragrant now with a fresh thank-offering of oranges and sweet jasmine. The scent of incense still hung in the air. I stepped out the front door and steadily, confidently walked out to the courtyard. I stopped a few feet from Baba and locked my knees. I was suddenly very weak but could not risk falling over!

"Oh, excuse me, Baba, I came to tell you that it is time to eat. I didn't know we had company. Good Evening, Liu Shu-shu."

"As you see, Liu Lao, Mei Lin is doing just fine. She is a remarkable girl."

"Um. I see." I thought he looked more than a little disappointed. "Well, I should be getting home. I only wanted to inquire about her. It seems the rumors I had heard were quite false."

"Thank you for your concern, Liu Shu-shu." I said. "I am heartened to know we have such a conscientious and caring village Communist Party chairman."

Liu Shu-shu walked out our courtyard moon gate, retrieved his bicycle, which he had left leaning against our wall and pedaled away.

When Liu Shu-shu was well down the road, Baba turned and smiled at me and, for the second time in three days, I fell into his arms, unable to walk another step. "You are a brave girl," laughed Baba as he scooped me up in his arms and carried me into the house.

"I do not like that man!" I sad, gritting my teeth.

"Mei Lin! He is our village Communist Party chairman! You will do well not to speak ill of him!" And then he whispered into my ear so that only I could hear, "Personally, I despise that snake. He is corrupt and conniving. He speaks the party line to officials in Beijing, but here, among us, he lives his old, poisoned ways. He has two faces, serving the party when it suits him, and serving himself most of the time. He is often wrong but he is hard to oppose, for he has many influential friends in high places that know him only as the loyal party servant he has shown them. Be cautious of him always. He is an evil man, but you didn't hear it from these lips! *These* lips," he said quite loud, smacking his lips together, "are lips that can *almost* taste dumplings—almost!" He plopped me into a chair.

Mama was putting dishes on the table. Ye-ye already sat at the table sipping at a small glass of *Double Happiness* beer. He poured one for Baba. The baby was strapped to Mama with a traditional cloth baby sling. It was not as fancy as the little blue baby seat the Americans used, but my brother didn't seem to mind. He seemed perfectly content; his ear nestled against the rhythmic beating of Mama's heart.

Baba began to serve the dumplings, first to Ye-ye, then smiling at Mama, he spooned out a large portion and placed it before her. He heaped dumplings into my plate as well. Finally, he sat down and began to pile them into his plate. "Ah! We have so much to celebrate." Ye-ye raised his glass toward the baby and said, "To the newest son in the house of Zhong! Gan bei!" He and Baba followed the traditional toast and drank down their glasses of beer. I ate a dumpling. Oh, it was like tasting perfection. I knew in that moment that there could never be a better moment in life. Ye-ye poured two more tiny glasses of beer.

"To my granddaughter, who did a man's job!" said Ye-ye, "Gan bei!"

They drank quickly and then slammed their glasses down on the table and quickly filled them up again, spilling beer on the table between the glasses. Baba wiped his lips on the back of his hand. This time Baba stood and raised his glass, "To the most beautiful, brave woman in all of China, the one who has given me two incredible children, the one I am honored to call my wife."

Baba did not say, "Gan bei!"

He did not drink down his beer.

He stood there, his eyes locked on Mama's. And, if only for a moment, Mama met his gaze! Slowly her cheeks and her neck turned red as she cast her eyes down and smiled. I sucked down another dumpling and acted like I didn't notice, but something powerful had just happened and I knew enough not to ask what it was all about. Baba continued to lock his gaze on Mama as he slowly sat and even more slowly drank his beer all the while locking his gaze on Mama.

"Enough beer!" said Ye-ye. "We must keep our wits about us and not become drunk. It could be dangerous if Liu Long Tang should come back."

"Agreed," said Baba. "Mei Lin, your Ye-ye has told us about his adventures, but we would like to hear it all again from your point of view."

So, I recounted the whole adventure for them. They gasped when I described Ye-ye's fall and laughed when I described the ugly, giant, ghost-faced "big-noses." When I told of selling the baby shoes, Baba slapped the table and laughed. "That's *my* capitalist daughter!"

"Ah! I nearly forgot!" Ye-ye walked over to a drawer in the corner chest of drawers and pulled out a wad of money. He handed it to Mama. "This is what Mei Lin made of your baby shoes."

Mama gasped. Tears rolled down her face as she counted out the money. "It is nearly enough for the birth penalty! We are very close if we add this to what we have already saved!" She turned to the baby on her breast and whispered, "You will not have to hide for long, you little illegal baby!"

"Will this make up the difference?" I asked and handed Mama my fish money. Mama counted it out and tears rolled down her face again. "What is this money from? Your Ye-ye has already given us the money from the sale of the melon and told us all about his visit with Qin Shu-shu."

"This is my fish money."

"So much! Didn't you buy clothes?"

"Yes! I got something for everyone. I saw the bag lying on the floor beside the door. I walked over and picked it up and handed out my gifts. Mama admired her jacket even though it would be a little big now. She said she could take it in. Baba tried on his hat and would not take it off for the remainder of the meal. He wore it with the earflaps sticking up and the chinstrap bouncing in the air with every movement of his head. The baby opened his big black eyes and watched as I shook the rattle in front of him.

While I was passing out the gifts, Mama put all the money together in one pile and counted it through again. She looked across the table at Baba but did not speak. One tear ran down her cheek as a smile spread slowly across her face.

"It is enough?" he asked and she nodded in silent reply.

Moon Festival

The palest ink
Is better than
The best memory.

   I had missed the first day of the new school term because of my weakness, but I was eager to get back to my friends and my schoolwork. I didn't want to get too far behind, so I begged Baba to allow me to go to school the next day. He argued that I was still too weak but agreed that, if Ye-ye would carry me on his bicycle to the crossroads each morning and greet me there each evening, I could go.

   He shouldn't have worried. I dutifully sat on the handlebar of Ye-ye's bike to the crossroads in the morning, but by evening, I was feeling too excited to sit still. My baby brother filled me with such wonder and happiness that I found new energy. I was so eager to get home to see him that I ran all the way to our house on the outskirts of Longkou. Ye-ye, maneuvering the bicycle on the deeply rutted dirt road, could not keep up with me. He shouted for me to slow down. I danced and ran in circles around him as he bounced around. "Can't you pedal just a little faster, Ye-ye?"

After two days, he told Baba he was no longer going to slow me down by waiting at the crossroads for me.

Before dawn on the sixth day of my brother's life, Baba quietly tiptoed out of our house and walked to the village. I knew where he was going.

As I heard him close the gate of the courtyard, I slipped out of bed and passed the family shrine. There was already a handful of slender red incense sticks burning there. Ye-ye is the only one in our family who still practices the old ways. Still, I thought it couldn't hurt. I lit some more incense sticks, held them between my hands and pressed my folded hands against my forehead as I have seen Ye-ye do many times, and bowed deeply toward the altar. "Watch over Baba and keep him safe." I prayed, just in case some god was really there. I asked the spirits of our ancestors to go before him and cover the eyes and ears of all those who should not hear and see what Baba was doing until it was done.

The baby began to stir and then cry with a loud, angry wail. Mama groaned and rolled over but didn't wake up. I went to pick him up so Mama could sleep. Uncle Charlie had brought us a crate full of baby formula from a business trip to Nanjing. I measured the powder into a baby bottle and shook it with some boiled water that was now cool enough to drink. I checked the temperature to see if it was still too hot for a baby to drink by taking a quick sip of the formula. All the while, I cradled Di-di by my left hip, chattering to him, "Oh, you hungry boy. You think you should get everything you want just when you want it? Well, it doesn't work that way. I, for example, had to wait eleven whole years just to get a little brother!"

I sat in a chair and lay him across my lap resting his head in the crook of my arm as I had seen Baba do, and put the bottle nipple in his mouth. He sucked greedily on it, gulping and sighing between swallows, squishing rivulets of milk out the sides of his mouth. I laughed and tickled his cheek. "Slow down, little dragon! You are so greedy you are wasting milk." I wiped it from his chin with my finger and dripped the precious drops back into his mouth.

When he finally sighed in satisfaction, I held him over my shoulder and patted his back until he released the bubble of gas from his stomach with a loud belch.

"Ah!" Said Ye-ye walking in from morning chores, "The ancestors have spoken their approval!" We both laughed and the baby gave a smile of satisfaction.

Baba had made arrangements with his friend Tang Gao Rong to meet at his desk in the Department of Civil Affairs to attend to official business--at unofficial hours--meaning, before Liu Shu-shu reported to work. Normally, a person would have to pass Liu Shu-shu's office as chief of the local cadre of the Communist Party, to get to the Department of Civil Affairs. In China it is often said that if the front door is closed, one should find a back door or an open window to climb through. This is usually an expression that means if you can't do things by the approved methods, try an alternate, unofficial way. This is what Baba did. Before Liu Shu-shu could find out and levy any additional fines, or impose any jail sentences for breaking the one child policy, Baba went and paid the standard penalty for having a second child and for having a child without a birth permit. So that no one would see or hear them, the documents were all signed and sealed in the half-light of early morning without ever speaking a word or turning on a lamp. Baba's thumbprint in red ink pressed over the characters for his name in the village book of life. He carried a copy of the certificate home.

He returned at dawn and withdrew the document from inside his shirt where he had worn it close to his heart. "Look, Mei Lin," he said, untying the red string that was wrapped around it. "Already, your brother is permitted to live because of your hard work with your fish traps and your fast thinking in dealing with the foreigners. If not for you, it would have been many months before we would have had this document." He grinned proudly.

I bowed my head and nodded. "Xie-xie Baba" I said as I handed him a warm bowl of congee.

"Mei Lin," said Mama from the doorway where she stretched and ran her fingers through her hair. "Do you know what day it is tomorrow?"

"Wednesday?"

"According to the lunar calendar, it is the fifteenth day of the eighth month and that means . . ."

"Moon Festival already! I have been enjoying little brother so much I have forgotten everything else."

"Fortunately, I have not. I have ordered some moon cakes from the bakery of Yan A-yi. Please remember to pick them up on your way home from school today if you want sweets for the celebration tomorrow."

I love moon cakes! Just thinking about them, my mouth began to water. With a whole boiled egg yoke baked inside to symbolize the golden moon, the flaky pastry is filled with sweet pastes of lotus seed or black beans or nuts. Mama took some money from the lacquer ware chest of drawers by the door and pressed it into my palm. I pulled up the leg of my school uniform pants and slipped the money inside my sock.

"Yes, Mama," I said. "I won't forget. Will Di-di be able to stay up with us and watch for the Jade Rabbit to appear in the moon palace? It will be his first moon festival."

Mama smiled. "It would hardly be a celebration of family harmony without him. However, it has been my experience that babies sleep and wake whenever they like and only a fool can tell them when they ought to be one way or another. Little son will be with us, though whether or not he will be awake, I doubt even your grandfather's Buddha could foretell. I don't even know that I will be awake for the festivities. I hope I will be able to stay awake until the full moon appears this year. Little babies have a way of wearing out their Mamas."

"If you fall asleep too early, I will wake you when the moon is full."

Just then, there was a loud knocking on the door. "Open this door!" Liu Shu-shu's voice angrily commanded.

Baba whispered to Ye-ye, "Oh this should be fun!" He walked slowly to the door and opened it, "Why Liu Lao. What a surprise to see you so early in the morning! Did you eat?"

"Zhong Liang, this is official business, not a social call!" Two uniformed police officers stood on either side of Liu Shu-shu. One was short and chubby as a panda cub, the other tall and thin as bamboo. Neither was smiling.

"What could be so official before breakfast in the morning?" asked Baba.

"Zhong Liang, I have received a report that there is a baby in this household. You know that we have a one-child family planning policy in this country. It is a rule for the good of the entire country. It is not at the discretion of individual citizens to choose to follow this policy or not. Pan Ching, son of Pan Ling said he clearly heard the cry of a baby coming from this house as he passed by here shortly before dawn this morning. It has occurred to me that it has been some months since I have seen your wife and perhaps that is the reason."

"Indeed? Is it possible that Pan Ching also knows the whereabouts of my missing chicken—the large black one with the bushy feathers on the top of its head? (Baba gestured here as if he had black bushy feathers on his head.) —the one that disappeared from my hen house this morning between 4 am and 6 am?"

"Zhong Liang, we are not here to discuss chickens! Do not change the subject." His neck was growing red even as his tightly pursed lips were turning blue, and a huge blood vein bulged out on his forehead. I got the feeling that Liu Shu-shu really wanted to stamp his feet and it was taking all of his self-control to keep from doing just that.

"You would like to meet my son?" asked Baba. I thought Liu Shu-shu would pop at Baba's words.

"You do not deny it!"

"No, of course not. My wife is just finishing his diaper change. Would you gentlemen like to come into my home? Did you eat yet?" Baba asked the policemen and motioned to the door as he stepped aside. I could almost see the air rushing out of Liu Shu-shu like a balloon with a small hole in it.

"That will not be necessary since you have confessed. Zhong Liang, you will come with us to jail! I have signed *no* birth permit on record for this household. You already have used your one allowed birth for this—this girl," He motioned toward me, a look of disgust in his eyes. He continued, "and you have an unregistered child living under your roof. This is a serious crime." The police officers each took one of Baba's arms. "How will your family live without you while you count the rats in your prison cell?" asked Liu Shu-shu. "You should have thought through the consequences of your actions much more thoroughly."

"I have, Liu Lao. I am sorry Pan Ling has caused you so much distress. He is not fully apprised of our situation, you see. Although it is true, that *you* did not issue us a permit for a second birth as is allowed by law for farming families, and my wife did recently give birth to a child, my son's existence is quite legal. I have already registered his birth and paid the penalties. Mei Lin, would you please show Liu Shu-shu your brother's birth certificate and the receipt for the fines assessed by the Civil Affairs officer?"

I picked the certificate up from the table and showed it to Liu Shu-shu. Then I showed him the receipt, on tissue-thin paper, stamped with a red seal of the village Civil Affairs officer and dated that very morning.

"Either this is a forgery or you are a thief! Where did a simple farmer get this much money?"

"Ah, Liu Lao, I assure you that neither is the case. As you know, I work very hard as does my whole family. Under the new encouragement from The People's government, we have engaged in some simple capitalist ventures. My daughter has been tending her fish traps and I have been selling her fish in the Baoshan City Qingpin market for nearly a year. My wife has been making baby shoes to sell in the shops to the foreigners. So you see, we did consider the consequences and earned enough money to pay for them."

The police officers let go of Baba's arms and looked at the documents. "They look genuine," the tall one said.

"Quite authentic," said the chubby one.

Mama came into the room then, holding the baby. "Mei Lin, where are your manners? Offer our guests some tea!"

"No thank you, we have to get back to the police station," said the short police officer. "Did you wish to report a stolen chicken?"

"No," said Baba. "We are still celebrating the birth of our son. Let the Pan family celebrate with us! Our good fortune will be their good fortune as well."

The tall one leaned over to get a closer look at my brother. "Ah, ugly baby!" He glanced at the family shrine. "Nothing here for bad luck demons to bother with."

Mama smiled. She didn't really follow the old ways, but it was like a game. She appreciated the policeman telling her in this backward speech, how handsome her son really was.

My brother opened his eyes and seemed to take in the whole situation.

"He has big ears," said the short one and smiled at Baba. "He will be an important man."

"This is not the end of this Zhong Liang! You think you are smarter than The People's government, but I am not done. This is deliberate treachery. No one has ever succeeded in breaking the one child policy in my village!" Liu Shu-shu turned, slammed out the door, left the gate swinging back and forth on its hinges and disappeared down the road angrily riding his bicycle, bumping over the ruts through a cloud of yellow dust.

The police officers turned and followed him bidding Mama and Baba good day before leaving and asking forgiveness for having disturbed our morning. The skinny officer gently set the gate back in position and latched it.

Baba stood in the doorway smiling as they moved away. "Until now," he said softly. "No one has succeeded until now."

Suddenly I realized I was late for school. I gathered my books and I too, ran out the door, but I did not run after I got to the road. I did not wish to pass Liu Shu-shu on the way into the village and decided I would rather be a little late.

Cold Winter - Warm Hearts

*Married couples tell each other
A thousand things without speech.*

Four months had passed since Moon Festival. The air had grown chilly and my breath hung in front of my face like a small cloud. I couldn't remember it ever being this cold before. I had used a stout stick to break through the thin ice. Hand over hand I pulled in the rope of a fish trap. The icy cold stung my fingers. I pulled quickly so the rope didn't freeze to my hands. Still, my fingers cramped and ached by the time the trap was on land. I removed a fish and held it up by the gill flap.

I had strapped Di-di to my chest and covered us both with Mama's big turquoise jacket—his head popping out the neck hole below my chin. I had used the traditional quilted cloth that Mama often used to carry him on her back, but I had turned him to face the world as I had seen the Americans do in Baoshan City. Now, as he saw the wriggling fish struggling to be free of my grasp, he too wriggled and squealed in delight.

"You want to help, huh? Well, some day this can be your job. I will be a rich Hong Kong capitalist by then. I will come to visit you in my fine automobile. If you are a good boy, I will let you use one of my fine silk pillows when you take a nap. And for you, a fine gold one, suitable for an emperor!"

Di-di gurgled and kicked his arms and legs happily.

"Oh, you are thinking about it, huh? What part of the plan don't you like?"

I plopped the fish into the basket of water on the handcart.

He kicked his little legs again and drooled. I dabbed the slobber up with my finger so it wouldn't freeze to his face and wiped the spit on my quilted pants. "Ah, so you think the automobile should be yours? Hum? Well, you can have one too, but you will have to work very hard. Fish traps are not easy work as you can see, especially in winter."

Quickly, I emptied the bamboo trap and inspected it for damage. Then I rubbed my hands together and blew hot breath into them before I baited the trap again and threw it back into the river.

I grabbed the handles of the cart and walked to the place where I had anchored the next line. Hauling in fish traps is always hard work but the time passed swiftly when Di-di was with me. I was thankful that none of my traps became stuck on debris at the bottom of the river. Sometimes, especially when spring rains swelled the river and brought branches and refuse from upstream, I had to dive into the water and untangle a trap before I could haul it in. Today was so cold that I was sure I would just let a stuck trap stay stuck. Nothing could make me dive into water *that* cold!

When we returned to our house, Mama was in the bedroom, her back to the door. She was holding the picture of herself and Baba taken on their wedding day. She sighed.

"What's the matter, Mama?" I asked.

"Oh, Mei Lin," she jumped, "I didn't hear you come in. I was just thinking of our wedding day. When I was a young girl, I would often dream of my wedding day. How much I had wanted a traditional red wedding dress! But, we were very poor and such styles were not politically acceptable at that time, so this drab, gray, cotton jacket is what I wore."

I looked at the picture closely, "Mama, you look so happy!"

"I was." Then she said brightly, "It was a small matter, and it is past. The character of the man you marry is of much more importance than the clothing you wear to your wedding ceremony."

I loosened the strap on the baby carrier and handed Di-di to mama as we walked back into the main room of our house. My hands burned as if a thousand hot pins pricked my skin.

"I never saw someone hold a baby like that, Mei Lin! You should hold him on your back. If anyone from the village sees you they will think you are ignorant."

"Liu Lao already thinks we are ignorant! Does it matter? I saw the Da-bi-zi hold babies like this in Baoshan City. I think maybe it is good for Di-di to see the world and learn. He is happy this way. You should see how he laughed at the fish this afternoon."

"Ai-ya! Such a girl. You are your father's child! You are always looking for new ways to do things better." Mama shook her head, but I could see a slight smile turn up the right side of her mouth before she turned away from me. She wrapped a warm baby quilt around Di-di and bound a red cord around it so it would not unwrap.

"Ah, Mei Lin, help me. I still cannot tie a knot with one hand!" I took the cord and tried to tie the knot but my fingers wouldn't work. She helped me and together we formed a sort of knot. Mama gently laid Di-di in his baby bed where he drifted off to sleep.

"Your hands look frozen, Mei Lin. You must warm them, but gradually or you will shock your system and cause great pain to your fingers." She poured a bowl of cold water and said, "Soak them in here until the water feels cold to you." I slowly eased my hands into the water and was gripped by a pain like scalding water normally yields. After a few minutes of soaking, when I experienced the water as cold, Mama added warm water from the teakettle. This too, felt boiling hot. When it felt only warm and I could wiggly my fingers, she added still warmer water until my fingers warmed enough to sense temperature properly and move and grip things.

Di-di awoke from his nap and she handed him back to me.

As I fed Di-di his bottle, Mama prepared a dinner of lotus root and winter cabbage, rice and fish. The days were growing shorter and already the sky was pink in the west when she finally sat, cradling a cup of tea. I heard the courtyard gate creak followed by a loud snort. The door burst open. Ye-ye tripped over the doorsill and stumbled into the room laughing. He dropped a large sack on the floor in the corner near the door. "Ah, what a daughter-in-law! She has hot 'cha' waiting for my return!" Mama smiled her half-smile and handed him the cup of tea she had intended for herself.

"You are early! I did not expect you for several hours." Again we heard the snort and a sound like something stomping the ground hard. "Well," said Ye-ye, "a water buffalo pulls a cart much faster than a man—or even a girl!" he said as he smiled at me.

"A water buffalo!" I shouted and raced to the doorway. The water buffalo snorted again and Di-di squealed in delight.

"Ah, four months old and already he knows a good deal when he sees it!" said Baba. Baba stood in the courtyard, unhitching a young water buffalo from our cart.

"I did not think we would be able to buy it this year, but Mei Lin's fish and this last batch of baby things brought exceptional prices. The little dresses sold even better than the shoes! I could have sold many more. We will be able to begin the planting this spring--with help!"

"We can plant even more!" I said. "We can plant something else that foreigners like to eat and sell it to the Golden Tiger Hotel Restaurant!"

"Always the capitalist, Mei Lin!" laughed Baba.

"Ah, this family of ignorant peasants has such bad luck!" said Ye-ye wrapping his hands around the cup of tea and glancing toward the family shrine.

"Oh Ye-ye, there are no demons or curses to guard against" I said.

"I used to be sure, Mei Lin, but the older I get the less I am certain of such things. What harm does it do to tease the evil away?"

I didn't answer him as I handed the baby to Mama and stepped into the courtyard. "I'll help you, Baba." I took the rope attached to the ring in the nose of the water buffalo and led her to the place where tufts of thick grass still grew between the river and the side of the road. Baba pounded a stake into the ground and we tethered her there to graze. She would be able to reach the river to drink and would have her fill of winter grass.

"Does she have a name?"

"Well, the man who sold her to me called her, 'Hong Rong.' Perhaps he thought the patriotism displayed by calling her 'Red Glory' would fetch a greater price!" We both laughed. Fortunately, for me, she was having a very stubborn day and he was willing to sell her at a very reasonable price! I think she panicked in all the confusion of the marketplace. She is really a very gentle animal," said Baba. "She will serve us well. For now, we will let her rest and eat. Later, you can bring Hong Rong into the courtyard for the night so that she does not wander onto the Pan family table as the main course for Chinese New Year."

I smiled at his joke and stroked her flank and she leaned into my hand looking for warmth or touch. She did, indeed, seem to be a very gentle water buffalo.

"Ah, Mei Lin, I have brought you something! Come inside for a while." Baba seemed excited. He stepped into the door of our house, slipped off his shoes and stepped into his house slippers. I picked his shoes up and placed them next to each other so they would be ready for him to step into on his way out the door and did the same with my own shoes.

He brushed past Mama pretending to need only the warmth of the cooking fire on his hands. Still, she blushed and busily returned to her work, placing dishes of food on the table.

He picked up one of the sacks and dropped it down next to his chair as he plopped himself down with a sigh. "Mei Lin, because of your hard work, we were not only able to purchase a water buffalo many months sooner than we had planned, but the Zhong family will be celebrating the New Year in great style this year. " He pulled out an exquisite red dress with gold embroidered chrysanthemums on it and held it out to Mama. It was made in the traditional style with black frog closures and a slit up the side of the leg. Her eyes grew wide. "For the most beautiful bride in all of China —maybe all the world!" said Baba. Mama looked at the floor. She dared not look at him. I knew she would cry if she did, for I was choking back tears.

How did he know? I wondered.

"Oh, and something else." He held out an oblong, red velvet box. Mama opened it ever so slowly to find a strand of perfect pearls.

"Oh!" she gasped.

"That's it. That was the exact sound I was hoping for!" And then, more seriously, "I was not a wealthy man when I married you but I became one on that day."

I didn't have long to think about what Baba meant. Soon he was pulling something else out of the sack.

"For our little emperor!" Baba pulled out a small quilted silk vest of black with red dragons embroidered all over it. It too had black frog closures on it. He shook it over my brother's head and the baby gurgled in delight.

He pulled out a rather ordinary white shirt for himself and another for Ye-ye and then he closed the bag and stuffed it under the table. "Well, I am hungry. Shall we eat?"

I said nothing. I knew Baba was teasing. There was something else in the bag. Mama flashed me a knowing smile. Ye-ye kicked Baba under the table.

"What?" Baba pretended innocence.

"Son, I am an old man and too tired to tease my precious granddaughter. Give it to her or I will."

Baba smiled. "Oh, did I forget something? Let's see if there is anything else in here." He peeked into the bag. "No," he said it in perfect imitation of Liu Shu-shu's voice, "I see nothing in here for a worthless mouth to feed." Then he flashed a grin and said, "Only something for my qian jin xiao jie" --daughter of thousand pieces of gold. He held out a green velvet box. Inside was a jade bracelet carved in the shape of a perfect green snake. Each scale was delicately etched. The belly was carved into the area where the jade streaked a shade lighter. It almost looked real! I was born in the year of the snake, so this is my good luck sign. No snake could ever devour me now!

"Xie-xie-thank you, Baba." I could barely breathe the words.

"Oh, and this." He held out a green silk blouse with gold chrysanthemums embroidered on it. "Green, the color of wealth for my daughter who plans to become a wealthy Hong-Kong capitalist." Mama and I were both getting teary eyed. I couldn't even say "Xie-xie."

"So much!" said Mama. "Did you save enough for food to see us through until harvest?"

"Yes, yes! There is plenty of food. There is even a little money left over. I tell you, the luck of the Zhong family is changing! So, you can't expect to welcome in a new year with old clothes, can you?" asked Baba. "Especially not a year that promises to be such a good year!"

"You should wear new clothes for the New Year celebrations. You don't want the evil spirits to recognize you, do you?" said Ye-ye.

"Oh, Ye-ye, you know I don't believe in evil spirits!"

Baba continued speaking to Mama, "You and Mei Lin have worked very hard. I know you sit by the oil lamp long after I go to bed sewing these things. And still, Mei Lin remains at the top of her class in school. Teacher Ma wants to put her ahead a grade. Her work is that good. It is your work and hers that has earned us this good fortune. Shouldn't you share in it?"

"Xie-xie," said Mama softly and looked down at the floor.

"Now can we eat?" Baba looked at Ye-ye. They both started eating with much enthusiasm. Mama and I just sat there blinking at each other.

"Did I do something wrong?" asked Baba with a mouthful of food. He turned toward my little brother who was lying in his baby basket. "Why are the women in this house so quiet tonight?" Di-di cooed like a little bird and shook his rattle.

玖

Prosperity in the New Year

A good fortune may forebode a bad luck,
Which may in turn disguise a good fortune.

For months, Mama had been preparing for Chinese New Year. Every nook and cranny had to be swept clean. This tradition began in ancient times to get rid of any lingering bad luck that might be hiding in the corners of a house. For Mama and me it was just an annual house cleaning.

Piles of gifts must also be amassed. Some of these were purchased new each year. Most were actually saved from gifts we were given in previous years that we never opened: an embroidered silk lipstick holder (Mama never wore makeup!) a decorative tea pot (how many tea pots can a person use?), a silk neck tie (Baba never had any use for these) a flower vase, a lacquered serving tray. Practically everyone we knew must be given a gift. Mama shifted through a pile of lists and gifts from past years, making a new list for this year. She decided whom she would give the existing things to and what new things she had yet to purchase. She kept detailed lists of gifts--what had been given to us for each of the past ten years and by whom, and what we had given to them. It would be very bad to give the same thing to a person two years in a row. And, although it was not unusual to redistribute gifts, it would have been even worse to return to someone a gift they had given to us-ever! For this reason, meticulous gift lists must be kept.

Baba had purchased dozens of red envelopes in the market. These "hong bao" had gold letters on them saying things like "luck" and "good fortune" and "wealth." Into each he placed a small amount of money. These he would give to children and lion dancers we encountered over the fifteen days of New Year celebrations. I always looked forward to receiving these from Mama and Baba's friends. Even in hard times adults always seemed to manage to scrape together a coin or two for every child they knew. This year had been a prosperous year, so I knew it would be a bounteous Chinese New Year for me as well. These hong bao were our spending money for the year. Some kids, like Liu Wei, spent his entire New Year fortune on candy and ate it within a few days. Others, like me, tried to make it last all year, doling out a few yen at a time for treats.

I always felt a little lonely at this time of year when I saw large families gathering: aunts and uncles with cousins of all sizes. We had no family other than just those who lived in our house. We did however, have many friends who were like family and we would visit and eat with them, exchange gifts and hong bao with the children.

Mama's closest friend was Yao Ting. She had one daughter two years older than I. Yao A-yi had worked in the same work unit as Mama at the factory. When Mama had her accident, Yao A-yi and Wan Jen came by bicycle every morning and brought hot soup for Mama to eat throughout the day. They swept our floors. On sunny mornings, they helped me wash our clothes and hang them on the bamboo poles in the courtyard to dry. Each evening they returned with more soup, took in the washing and sat by my mother's bed, stroking her hair, spooning the broth into her mouth. It was Yao A-yi who made my mother sit up in bed and made her try to walk one week after the accident.

It was Yao A-yi whom my Baba fetched in the middle of the night, one year later, to help Mama when my brother came. She never breathed a word of Mama's pregnancy or of my brother's illegal entrance into the world, giving us the precious time we needed to register his birth. She was as loved and trusted as any Aunt of blood relation. Her husband, Cai Chao had recently returned to the factory after being away for nearly five years. He had studied electrical engineering, earning a doctorate at the University of Vermont in America. Now he preferred to be called by his American name, Charlie—Uncle Charlie by me. They, and their daughter Wan Jen, would spend New Years Eve with us. They, too, had no other family. I could hardly wait. Wan Jen was the next best thing to an elder sister.

After I had carefully scrubbed the table, Ye-ye spread a long piece of gold-flecked, red paper along its entire length. He was humming a Chinese opera love song to himself as he did so, his voice warbling on the high notes. He took out his ink stone and a block of ink, several calligraphy brushes and some paperweights from the drawer. He weighted the paper down at the corners so it wouldn't move when the brush hairs dragged across it. Then, he carefully ground the ink into the ink stone and added a few drops of water. Soon, rich black ink formed of just the right consistency. He dipped his biggest calligraphy brush into it and whirled it around, soaking each brush hair completely. On a small scrap of paper, he tested the consistency of the ink by making several practice strokes. Perfect!

Then, bending at the waist, he hovered above the paper and lightly, and as smooth as a junk gliding upon the river, he stroked the combination of dots and hooks, slashes and strokes needed to make the words, "bright happiness in the new year to all who enter here."

He stood back and lightly fanned air across the top of the page to hasten the drying. When he was satisfied that the ink was dry, he carefully attached a spindle to the top and the bottom of the paper. He threaded a string through small holes in either end of the top spindle and called me to help. Carefully, we lifted the new scroll together and hung it on the left side of the front door so that all who entered could see it. Then he repeated the process on a second sheet of gold-flecked red paper as he wrote, "Good fortune follow your every step." This he hung on the right side of the door. A third banner hung horizontally across the top of the door proclaiming, "Happy New Year!—Xin Nian Hao!"

When he was done, he brought out a very elaborate gold paper in the shape of a diamond with the single word, "Fu" written in the middle. This he held up to the front door, considering the proper height before he marked a spot to drive a nail on which to hang it. I walked up behind him. "Don't you think you should hang it upside down, Ye-ye?" I teased.

"Ah, for one who does not believe in the old ways, you are a smart granddaughter! Yes, we will trick bad luck once again. We will hang the 'fu' upside down to announce that good luck has already arrived and bad luck need not waste any time here!"

Ye-ye hung the 'fu' on the door--upside down--and returned inside to clean up his brushes and ink. I wiped the table again and brought out grandmother's best dishes--what was left of them. The Red Guard had destroyed many of her most beautiful things when Ye-ye had been forced to move to the countryside during the Cultural Revolution.

Baba had been coaxing some spring blossoms into bloom on a windowsill. They had budded, and if luck was with him, they would bloom tomorrow, on the first day of the New Year. He placed these on Mama's lacquerware chest of drawers in the corner of the main room and carefully arranged them with some bamboo leaves to resemble a painting Ye-ye had made many years ago. He even used the same vase that Ye-ye had painted on the watercolor scroll. Placed close together, they almost looked like mirror images.

Mama and I had been cooking all week: slow-roasted duck in plum sauce, broiled fish, pork stuffed dumplings, shrimp stuffed dumplings, sweet cakes and candied fruits. We had prepared six different kinds of vegetables, rice and spicy noodles and of course, Mama's very best chicken soup.

Around eight o'clock, we heard bicycle bells ringing on the road. I raced to the door and threw it open just as Wan Jen hopped off the handle bars of Uncle Charlie's bike, "Xin Nian Hao! Happy New Year!" She shouted. Although cloth covered what she held so I couldn't see what it was, I knew she was holding an eight sectioned tray of traditional treats: things such as candied melon for good health, candied coconut for togetherness, watermelon seeds to ensure that we would have plenty in the coming year. Yao A-yi and Uncle Charlie walked their bikes in through the courtyard gate. Yao A-yi untied a box from the rack on the back of her bike. The smell told me that she had brought pork buns ready to steam and spicy vegetables. My mouth began to water and my stomach growled so loudly that Yao A-yi laughed out loud.

Wan Jen and I ran inside, giggling. She placed the tray on the table and hugged Mama. Then we raced off to the bedroom. I could hardly wait to show her the jade bracelet Baba had brought me from the market.

"Ai Ya, Mei Lin! This is beautiful! Your Baba bought you this? This is as fine a jade bracelet as a man gives a girl he wants to marry! Your Baba must be very proud of you!" I let her try it on, but already, Mama was calling us to eat. Afraid to wear something so valuable, I wrapped the bracelet carefully in the red cloth and put it back in the box.

"Guo lai, come, the food is hot," said Mama. Di-di was slumped over sideways in his baby carrier, sleeping on her back. He remained asleep for most of the dinner, which lasted for hours. Baba and Uncle Charlie were laughing a lot, drinking beer, "Gan bei!" they would shout, drink a swallow of *Double Happiness* beer, racing each other to bang their tiny, now empty glasses down on the table again.

Wan Jen and I spoke quietly to each other at our end of the table, leaving the adults to themselves except for the time when Uncle Charlie was speaking about his life in America. "Ah, yes, I had a car then. Everybody has a car in America. You really need one, there. It is a part of the lifestyle. You need to get from one place to another much more quickly than you do here. Time is very important in America."

"You know how to drive?" I asked.

"Yes, of course."

"Was it hard? How did you learn?"

"One question at a time!" cautioned Ye-ye.

"It is not hard," laughed Uncle Charlie. "Some of the other students taught me."

"Oh, I hope I can go to school in America some day!"

"You must study hard. Only the very best students are selected for this honor," said Yao A-yi smiling broadly at Uncle Charlie.

Uncle Charlie asked Baba how the farmers were receiving the new quotas and I lost interest in the conversation. Wan Jen and I returned to talking about her new pet kitten. He had long white fur and she liked to comb it and tie ribbons to it. She was teaching him to do funny tricks with a feather and a piece of string.

At about eleven o'clock, Baba and Uncle Charlie slipped outside. A few minutes later, I heard firecrackers popping in the street and ran to see what was happening. Hong Rong was bellowing in fright and pulling on her rope. Uncle Charlie and Baba were nearly doubled over with laughter.

Di-di awoke and began crying, frightened by the noise. Yao A-yi helped Mama remove him from her back and she cradled him in her good arm, cooing, "It's all right, little dragon boy."

"Honestly," said Yao A-yi to Mama, "Some part of a boy remains in every man!"

"Come, come," said Baba when the firecrackers had stopped. "We'll have to hurry to the village if we are to welcome the year of the rabbit in time for the lion dance." He soothed the water buffalo, stroking her neck and led her to the cart.

"Oh, must we go?" Wan Jen and I chorused.

"Why? You always love the Chinese New Year celebrations!" asked Mama: "The lion dance, the fireworks?"

Wan Jen and I both sighed. "This year," I explained, "Liu Wei will dance the part of the lion's head. He has been bragging about it so much, I am sick of it already."

"Liu Wei?" Asked Baba. "Are you sure? Only the best dancers are chosen to dance the lion dance on New Year's Eve. He has only been dancing one year—and from what I hear, not well. How could he have earned that place?"

No one answered. We all just stared at him. The silence spoke for us.

"Oh," he said, "That is how. He is the son of Liu Lao. Oh well, at least it should be entertaining."

"There is no regard for the old ways," sighed Ye-ye. "No one fears that the mountain gods will be dishonored by his sloppy dancing and bring bad luck to our village if this spoiled child of a fool is permitted such an honor."

"The old ways are nearly gone," said Yao A-yi. "Now, these customs are just for fun. I don't know anyone who fears dishonoring a god."

"Yes," said Uncle Charlie, "Most people in Longkou are more concerned about keeping Liu Lao happy."

"Ah," said Baba, "That explains it. There never was a river god with a temper as wrathful as Liu Long Tang's." We all laughed as we piled into the cart for the ride into the village. We tied Yao A-yi's and Uncle Charlie's bikes on the back and set off to join the festivities.

The River Dragon Roars

Good luck seldom comes in pairs,
But bad times never walk alone.

Mama and I had been up before dawn, boiling water in the courtyard to wash the clothes. We had just finished washing and had hung everything on the bamboo poles to dry when I heard a distant rumble. I looked up and saw a black wall of storm clouds moving in swiftly from the west.

"Mama," I yelled, "The rains are coming!"

"Of course!" said Mama, "I have just finished hanging out the washing. We will have to move everything indoors. Quickly, Mei Lin!"

Mama grabbed one end of a bamboo pole and I grabbed another. We carried it into the house together and hung it from hooks that Ye-ye had fastened to the ceiling beams many years earlier. Nine more times we returned to the courtyard to bring in the poles laden with wet clothing, bed sheets and blankets. When we

101

returned for the tenth and final pole, the sky seemed to open above us as sheets of water dropped upon our heads at once. Mama and I hung the last pole and we both collapsed into squats. So relieved to have gathered up everything before the sky opened, we laughed so hard we could barely stay balanced. The clothes would present a maze to navigate as we moved from one part of the small house to another. Other than a maze of pathways through the hanging clothes, there was now hardly any room indoors to stand. Fortunately, like most Chinese, we spent a great deal of our time squatting close to the ground.

"Surely, this will let up in a few hours and your Ye-ye can help me move the clothes back outside." Mama wiped water from her face with the back of her hand and splattered it on the floor. "What a mess!" She looked at the puddles forming on the floor from the dripping clothes and bedding. "Oh well, the fields need the rain. We should be glad. Oh! Mei Lin, you will be late for school. It will be too muddy to ride the bicycle. You will have to run." I grabbed my raincoat and stuffed my schoolbooks into my backpack. My hair was already tightly braided in two long queues, but was now wet. Hopefully, everybody else would have the same, damp problem.

For three days and nights, the rain continued. It seemed to keep coming harder rather than letting up. The air was hot and humid, too. After such a long, cold winter, we were almost relieved to be uncomfortably warm again. I wished my hair would dry, but that too seemed to be getting worse rather than better. It was small comfort to know that I was not the only one so sorely afflicted. Smells of wet wool and hair filled the classroom.

The principal stopped to speak with our teacher at the door. Ma Laoshe gave us a page of Math problems to work on, but I eavesdropped on their conversation.

"North of here, the river was still frozen until last night. The earth, except for the top layer, is still frozen. A warm front moved in just before the rains and has brought this sudden thaw as well as heavy rain. The river is swelling, and if the rains don't let up soon, the flood will work its way south to us. Don't alarm the children but be prepared to dismiss them at a moment's notice if the river begins to rise."

All through Chinese language and calligraphy classes I watched the rain. Ma Laoshe appeared more agitated as the day wore on. He scolded us for small infractions of the rules and piled on punishment assignments for homework. When history class finally ended and we were dismissed at the regular time, the rain had not let up. I was glad I had not brought a bike. I would have had to carry it home. The road had become a yellow clay quagmire. I walked home slowly through the driving rain, slipping and sliding in the slick mud. From time to time, my feet were sucked down in the soft muck up to my ankles. Where once a packed earth road had been, now mud oozed into the red cloth shoes and squished between my toes, matting the fur lining. One time, it sucked my shoe completely off, but I stood on a small pile of rocks with the other foot, and pulled the shoe out, scraped the insides as best I could and put it back on. Mud squished between my toes and bubbled over the tops of my shoes. I tried to pick rockier places to step from then on to avoid the sucking mud.

When I arrived home, Mama was squatting at the charcoal cooking fire and Baba and Ye-ye were sitting at the table talking. Di-di was sitting on Baba's lap banging a spoon on the top of the table and laughing.

"It's too much rain," said Baba, "Too much too quickly."

"Ah, there is always a lot of rain in spring," said Ye-ye. "Monsoons are never merciful."

"It has been a very cold winter. I have heard that the ground is still frozen to the north. The rains cannot soak into the soil. They have nowhere to go but to run-off and follow the river south--to us."

"It is only three days of rain. I have seen it rain for an entire week . . . "

"This hard? This is a lot of water in a very short time!"

"Hush," scolded Mama. "You worry about too much. Dinner is ready."

Rain continued to pour down in sheets, pounding on the roof and leaking into the cracks around the windows. Mama stuffed rags around the doorframe and around the windows where the powerful wind seemed to force rain through the smallest of cracks. But the rags soon soaked through and puddles formed on the floor. Patches of the roof began to leak. Small rivulets of water ran down the beams and dripped into pots and bowls that Ye-ye scurried about placing wherever he found dripping.

I did my homework by the light of the oil lamp and then washed the mud off my shoes, stuffing them with rags and hung them by the fire to dry. Then I helped Mama sew some baby things to sell at market and prepared for bed. My hair was still damp when I lie down, and as uncomfortable as that was, the rhythm of the rain soon lulled me to sleep.

I am not sure what time it was when I woke to the sound of Hong Rong bellowing in fright. I looked around in the darkness but Mama and Baba were gone. Someone—probably Ye-ye--had lit incense sticks. They were still smoking in the burner in front of the family shrine. Ye-ye didn't waste incense or ask the ancestors for help unnecessarily. I knew something was wrong. I threw my raincoat on over my pajamas. I decided to try to keep my shoes dry for school in the morning, so stepped out into the courtyard, barefoot. The moon gate was open and I could see a shadowy figure across the road, holding a lantern on what was now the eastern bank of the Nandu River! As I drew nearer, I could make out Mama, with Di-di strapped to her back, gently cooing at Hong Rong, "There you go. You're okay now. We'll take care of it."

"Where is the stake?" shouted Ye-ye above the roar of the rain and river.

The river was swollen, rushing with the power of a freight train. The water buffalo was nearly up to her belly in swiftly churning water. Mama was wading out toward her while Ye-ye stood on the edge of the road where the river now raced, inching higher moment by moment.

"I can't find it!" said Mama. "I'll have to cut the rope. I don't have time to search for the stake. The water is too cold." As mama sawed through the thick rope with a large meat cleaver she had brought from the kitchen, the water buffalo bellowed and pulled backward, fear showing the whites of her red-rimmed eyes. "It's okay!" mama stopped sawing to sooth her, stroking the frightened animal's massive neck. When the animal had calmed a little, mama began sawing at the thick rope again. Finally the rope was cut through and Mama pulled, urging Hong Rong toward higher ground. The panicked animal only bellowed louder and pulled back. "I think she's mired!" Mama walked over and felt down the animal's flank and down her leg. "Yes, she is knee deep in mud!"

"Wait!" Shouted Ye-ye. "I will get something to give her better footing."

"Mei Lin!" He turned around and saw me. "Grab a stout board from the pile by the side of the hen house and hurry here with it."

I did as he instructed. He handed me the lantern when I returned, took the board from me, and waded into the swollen, churning river, struggling against the current for balance. He stuck one end toward the water buffalo and tried to wedge it under her foot. She became panicked and lurched backward, dragging Mama off her feet. Without so much as a shout of surprise, Mama toppled backward, dropped her hold on the rope and disappeared beneath the swirling black water. I held the lantern high shouting, "Mama! Where are you? Mama?" Only the roar of the river answered me.

Baba came running. "I have moved all the chickens from the henhouse to the courtyard." He stood there a moment taking in the situation and the stricken looks on our faces. "Where is your mother?"

"I don't know!" I stammered choking on fear. "She fell and disappeared below the water!"

"An-Li!" he called her name. "Song An-Li!" he pleaded again to the river to give her back to him.

"Go, follow the river downstream!" shouted Ye-ye above the storm. "Mei Lin and I can take care of this beast. An-Li will likely swim to shore in a few meters." I hoped he was right. Mama had been a strong swimmer before her accident. She had taught me how to swim. Now, however, she had the added weight of a baby strapped on her back and only one useful arm. I didn't have long to ponder the likelihood of her swimming to shore. The water buffalo represented our chance for a better life. The whole family depended on us saving her from the jaws of the river dragon. Surely Baba would find Mama and Di-di and pull them out in time.

The Nandu River was rising rapidly. Already the water buffalo was shoulder-deep in churning water. I pushed my way into the river, sliding on the slick river mud, feeling it ooze between my toes and sucking me down like the grasp of an evil mouth, slurping in a noodle. The water was so cold it stung and instantly my feet and legs were numb. Ye-ye had found the rope and was holding the water buffalo, soothing her, patting her neck as Mama had done. "There, there, you are among friends." As the water continued to rise I hoisted myself onto her back, grabbing the horns that curled over her broad neck like a handle. She bellowed and pulled back, but her feet were stuck. Ye-ye grabbed a tree branch floating by and broke off the small branches. He slid the stick down along the side of her leg and released the suction holding her down. With the other hand, he gently lifted her stuck foot. He stroked her neck and cooed, "Now, was that so bad?" He gathered up the rope that remained of her tether. I lay on her back and stroked her neck. "You're okay. We'll get you out."

Just then, something large floated down the river and banked into her backside. I felt the jolt but the thing floated away and I never saw it. Hong Rong let out another panicked bellow and reared back. I dug my heels into her sides and hung onto her horns as she lurched forward and scrambled up to the road where she stood stamping her feet and snorting.

I slid off her back, slid my hand up her neck across her face, grabbed the rope attached to the ring in her nose and laughed, "Well, we did it! Ye-ye?" I shouted at the darkness, but again, for the second time in twenty minutes, only the storm and the roar of the river dragon answered me.

Although I told myself he had probably run down the road to help Baba, I feared the angry river god had swallowed him up as well. I could only hope the great dragon-river would spit him back, unharmed onto dry land.

By the soft glow of the kitchen lamp which spilled out the door, I hurried to tether Hong Rong inside the courtyard. Chickens were everywhere, fighting over limited places to roost. I brushed some aside and made a corner for Hong Rong to stand in. I lay some grain in the feed trough for her, hurried out the door and hung a large bag of rice straw for her to eat. I planned to race downstream to help Baba search the riverbanks for Mama and Di-di —and now Ye-ye as well.

My heart pounded as I ran to the riverbank where I had left the lantern. As I grabbed it and swung around, my heart froze in my throat. A flash of lightning revealed Liu Shu-shu coming down the road with two policemen and a cart. It was the same two policemen he had dragged to our house once before: the short, round, panda-faced one and the bamboo-pole, skinny one. I could see feet hanging off the edge of the cart. Although it was only for a second, the time it takes for one bolt of lightning to flash across the sky, I thought I recognized Mama's embroidered shoes on one of the pairs of feet hanging off the edge of Liu Shu-shu's cart.

"Mama!" I shouted as I felt something that was surely a hot dagger going through my heart and blocking the sound in my throat.

"Where is your decrepit grandfather, useless girl?" shouted Liu Shu-shu above the roaring of the river and the rumble of thunder.

"I don't know!" I shouted back. "He was here just a moment ago and suddenly he is gone. Perhaps he went to help Baba look for Mama and Di-di."

"Well," Liu Shu-shu spoke as if I was not there, and addressed the policemen, "Just put the bodies in here. We'll have to bring the coroner in the morning, but we can't be carting corpses around all night. At the rate the Nandu River grows, there will likely be more stupid peasants to pull from this dragon's mouth before long."

He turned back to me. "Tell your grandfather I have found them. I will come in the morning with the coroner. Have the burial fees ready."

The policemen pulled the cart through the moon gate and into the courtyard panicking the chickens. Several of them flew out the gate in a flurry. I rushed to chase them back in, waving my open raincoat and the lantern at them.

I numbly followed the cart into the courtyard and watched as one man lifted Mama's feet and pulled her to the end of the cart where the second policeman lifted her under the shoulders. Her head fell back. They carried her into the house and asked me, "Where do you want her?"

I couldn't answer him. A scream was lodged in my throat and would let no other sound come out.

"Just put them on the floor," said Liu Shu-shu impatiently. It was then that I realized that Di-di was still strapped to her back. I slipped between the policemen and quickly pulled the string loose to remove Di-di from the baby carrier before they could lower Mama on top of him. The cloth tie straps were wet and so they did not pull easily. Tears welled in my eyes. My fingers were numb and I could not grasp the knot well. My leg began to shake. "Take your time," said the skinny policeman. "We'll wait for you."

The knot yielded and Di-di slipped into my arms. His little eyes were closed and his face looked like he was still sleeping. Perhaps he never woke up from his sleep on Mama's back before he had drowned. I gently lay him next to Mama and wrapped her arm around him. The fat policeman smoothed Mama's face. I think he closed her mouth and eyes but I am not sure. That part is a blur, for as I was still watching, Liu Shu-shu shouted, "Hurry up! We don't have all night! Come get this other one."

It was only then that I noticed Baba--as they dragged him out of the cart.

"Pan Ling said he watched him try to rescue the woman and child even though it appeared they were already dead, floating face down in the river. The weight of the woman and child, the slick river bottom and the swift current were too much, even for such a proud one. Such a fool!"

I wanted to kick Liu Shu-shu. I wanted to run down the road and find Pan Ling and shake him. Why hadn't he tried to help rather than just let my Baba and my Mama and Di-di all die? Instead, I held in my tears and waited for Liu Shu-shu to leave. I would not give him the satisfaction of seeing me in a weak, girlish moment. I would be as strong as a boy.

When they had laid Mama and Baba side by side with Di-di tucked between them, the skinny policeman turned to me and whispered, "I am so sorry. In the morning, I will send my wife to look in on you if I cannot come myself. Will you be alright until then?

I nodded my head.

"I hope your grandfather comes in from the storm soon."

"Hurry!" shouted Liu Shu-shu. "The river continues to rise! Even now it washes over the road! We must get out of here before we have no avenue of escape!" They closed the courtyard moon gate and left. The fat one popped his head back through the gate and asked again, "Will you be alright here by yourself until your grandfather returns?"

I stared silently at him resolutely fighting back the tears that welled in my eyes as he closed the gate again.

I went into the house and raised the wick on the oil lamp. Then I hung the lantern on the post outside the courtyard gate to light the way for Ye-ye. I lit another lantern and washed the mud off the water buffalo, rubbing her cold legs with my hands to warm them and to move the blood through them. I stuffed rags into the crack below the courtyard gate where water had begun to pour in. The panicked chickens all scrambled for places to perch. I went inside and dumped all the wet clothes off three of the bamboo rods and piled the still damp clothes on the table. I hung the rods in the courtyard for the chickens to have a high place on which to perch.

Then, I went into the house, closed the door, and sat on the floor next to Baba. I wrapped my arms around my knees and began to rock as a sound like a bellowing water buffalo rose from deep within me. I waited with Mama and Baba and Di-di for Ye-ye to come home.

Alone

If you bow at all,
Bow low.

I heard someone banging on the moon gate and realized that I had fallen asleep. The sun was long past rising but I was sitting up and still dressed in wet pajamas. I opened my eyes and saw the bodies of Mama and Baba and Di-di all lying together on the floor and wished that I could crawl in between them to snuggle. I longed to hear Baba's teasing voice, and feel Mama's hand smoothing my hair. I wanted to see Di-di throw back his baby face and laugh out loud, but I knew I wouldn't. I knew they were gone. Their bodies already appeared somewhat gray in the harsh light of morning. I hardly recognized them.

Then I saw the lantern still lit and remembered that I was waiting up for Ye-ye. Perhaps it was he at the gate.

I opened the door and stepped into the courtyard. I was knee deep in thick, yellow water. Things were floating and crashing around in the courtyard: the laundry tub and the washbasin. Hong

111

Rong's wooden feeding trough had become a small boat. Chickens were perched on the laundry rods. They cackled angrily. They wanted to be fed and it was clear to them that there not only was no feed, there was also no ground upon which to peck the grain. Hong Rong was the only thing that looked normal, standing knee deep in water as water buffalo often do, slowly chewing on a mouthful of dried winter grass that I had hung in a corner for her.

I waded out to the moon gate and slowly pushed it open. The entire road was flooded. I realized that the river was flowing through our courtyard and was only centimeters from flowing through our house.

"Ah, there you are! Did we wake you up so late in the day?" asked Liu Shu-shu sarcastically. He was standing in a flat-bottomed river boat that was moved along by the two policemen who took turns pushing it with long poles. Beside Liu Shu-shu stood Jiang Shu-shu, the coroner. Then, without waiting for a response from me, he commented to Jiang Shu-shu, "What have I told you? Without her parents to constantly prod her, this lazy girl would sleep all day. What is the use of a girl?"

Jiang Shu-shu did not answer him directly. Instead he looked at me and nodded. "Zhong Mei Lin, I am so sorry to hear of the drowning of your parents and grandfather . . . "

"My grandfather!"

"Haven't you told her yet?" He flashed an angry scowl at Liu Shu-shu.

"Ah, I suppose it slipped my mind," he responded absently, as my world exploded before me and I stifled a sob.

"Slipped your mind?" He turned to me and softened his face. "Mei Lin, is there anyone in the house with you?"

"Just Mama and Baba and Di-di."

Jiang Shu-shu turned toward Liu Shu-shu. Blood vessels were popping out of his neck. "Have you allowed this child to spend all night sitting alone in a flooding house with the bodies of her dead parents, not even knowing where her grandfather is?"

"It is of little consequence." Liu Shu-shu made a nervous giggle. "They are all dead. She is alive. There was nothing she could have done about it."

"She is a child!" He turned toward me and softened his gaze. "Mei Lin, I am sorry to tell you like this, your grandfather, a truly noble man, died last night as well. He insisted on trying to pull your father out of the river. Your father was most likely already dead, but your grandfather, in his grief, clearly lost his judgment. He slipped in the mud. The river caught him up and spit him out several li from here. Longkou will be a poorer place without his wisdom to guide us."

"Bah!" snorted Liu Shu-shu. "He was a pompous old fool who never did properly re-educate."

"He was a learned and wise man," said Jiang Shu-shu very slowly and defiantly—bravely, I thought. "Zhong Mei Lin, do you have any other family members with whom you could live?"

"Yao A-yi and Uncle Charlie are the closest thing I have to family."

"They are not family!" snorted Liu Shu-shu. They also already have one daughter. It is against the one-child policy for them to adopt another."

"What will become of her, then?" asked Jiang Shu-shu. The girl cannot live here by herself!"

"Why, she will become a ward of the state, like any other orphan!"

"She'll be sent off to Baoshan City to the orphanage! Surely something else may be done. I could take her into my house until she is of an age that she can support herself."

"You have already raised five children, Jiang. Under the one child policy you are already an embarrassment."

"I raised five children before there was a one child policy!"

"The government will never approve it."

"Liu Lao, *you are* the government in this village. If you approve it, I am sure no one would question it."

"Are you suggesting that I should ignore the law?"

"No, of course not! It's only that . . ."

"She must be sent to a state licensed foster care home or a social welfare institute. There is no other way."

"A social welfare institute! There are all manner of deformed monsters there and idiots and senile, old people. Mei Lin is a bright girl. What opportunity would be afforded her there?"

"It is the law. There is no other way."

I felt the blood draining out of my face. Whether it was from the extreme cold of the water I was standing in as they argued my fate (as if I were not listening), or the sheer terror of the future that suddenly lay before me, I didn't know.

After a brief pause, Jiang Shu-shu asked brightly, "How does one go about becoming licensed as a state approved foster care home?"

"One would apply to me. If I deem them satisfactory, I send my recommendations on to the Bureau of Civil Affairs. A social worker will come out, inspect the home, interview the husband and wife and then the social worker will make recommendations. I know what you are thinking, Jiang. It would never work. You are a widower. They would never allow you to be a foster care provider for a cunning young girl. It would look very questionable."

"Liu Lao, I assure you, I was not suggesting anything that would even look like I was taking advantage of her much less the insinuation you make of taking a concubine! I would assure whatever authorities watch over such situations that she would complete her education. When she comes of age, I would give her my own contacts in business, as any father would. I would do this out of respect for her father and grandfather."

"Well, perhaps such an arrangement wouldn't *look* suspicious to you, Jiang, but you know how people talk. No, I am afraid that the only thing we can do is to send her to the social welfare institute in Baoshan City. Unless . . . "

I got a sinking feeling in my stomach as I realized that Liu Shu-shu was about to suggest the one thing that would be worse than living in a social welfare institute.

"Unless my wife would consent to our being a foster care family . . ." his voice lowered as he thought about the idea. "Then we could take the girl in. There could be advantages to it." His voice trailed off. Jiang Shu-shu's face fell.

"I am so sorry, Mei Lin. In future, if you need any fatherly advice, please come see me. I have raised five children. All are grown now and four are married or at jobs in the city. The youngest is in university. I know how to advise young people on many topics."

I could tell that Jiang Shu-shu was a very caring person. I wanted to throw myself at his feet and beg him to take me home with him, but I knew it was useless and I didn't want to give Liu Shu-shu the pleasure of seeing me in a weak moment. I wanted to honor my parents by remaining strong.

"So, back to the business at hand," said Liu Shu-shu. "We have come for the corpses."

"Bodies, Liu Lao. We prefer to say bodies," whispered Jiang Shu-shu. "These are deceased family members. It is more respectful and less shocking to say bodies—especially in front of a child. Please try to be just the slightest bit more sensitive."

"Jiang, I haven't time for this tender-hearted, molly-coddling. We have already wasted far too much time here. We have other corpses to collect. Let's get on with it!"

"Mei Lin, do you have any money?"

"Very little."

"There are four family members who must be cremated. Your baby brother may be cremated with your mother so we could only charge you for three. How will you pay for these services?"

I looked over at Hong Rong. I knew that I could no longer care for her, especially if I was to be sent to live at a social welfare institute--or worse.

"Would a young water buffalo in trade be enough to pay for three cremations?"

"Don't be ridiculous, child," snapped Liu Shu-shu. "What would Jiang Lao have to do with a water buffalo?"

"It would be more than enough," said Jiang Shu-shu, ignoring Liu Shu-shu as if he had not spoken. "I will sell her at fair market price and return the excess to you when all the cremation expenses are paid."

"All right then." Liu Shu-shu ordered the policemen. "Go in there and fetch the corpses." The two policemen jumped out of the boat and waded through the moon gate and into the house.

"Mei Lin, perhaps you and I should go into your house together and gather the things you will need to take with you," offered Jiang Shu-shu.

"Oh, don't bother about that! I will bring her back one day next week. My wife has plenty of clothes she can borrow until then."

Perhaps it was the fact that my legs were by now completely numb with cold, or the idea of wearing Xu A-yi's clothes, which were clearly the clothes of a matron and not those of a young girl, or maybe the facts that I hadn't eaten since dinner last night or slept more than an hour all night, all caught up with me at once. In the next moment, completely against my will, I felt myself slipping into blackness. Jiang Shu-shu leaped out of the boat and caught me in his arms just before I crashed into unconsciousness. Had he not, I feel quite certain that I would have splashed beneath the surface of the yellow water to join the rest of my family.

"The child's stone cold! Why she has been standing in these wet clothes all this time. We didn't even think. I must get her into the house. You!" He motioned to the fat policeman, "Stoke up the fire. We must get her warmed quickly or we will have five bodies to cremate."

He carried me into our house and lay me on the floor next to the charcoal cooking fire. Soon there was a roaring blaze. Jiang Shu-shu went into the bedroom and returned a few minutes later. He wrapped me in Mama's bed quilt and as he did so, he handed me a small bag, under the quilt so that Liu Shu-shu never saw the transfer. I knew I should not mention it as Jiang Shu-shu made a cup of tea. "Here, get some warmth into the inside of you."

While Jiang Shu-shu warmed me and the two policemen carried the bodies of Mama, Baba and Di-di to a second small boat they had been trailing behind them, Liu Shu-shu walked around our house picking up things and looking at them with a critical eye. He turned over Baba's vase, dumping the flowers on the floor and checked the stamp on the bottom. He whistled through his teeth. "Ming Dynasty! How did this piece of imperialist trash survive the Cultural Revolution?" I was afraid he was going to smash it, but he gently placed it back on the cabinet in front of grandfather's water color painting of it. He grabbed a bottle of Baba's *Double Happiness* beer, bit the cap off with his teeth and began drinking straight from the bottle. "At least this delay is not a total waste of time," he smiled and flashed a gold tooth and downed another gulp of Baba's beer. Then he wiped his mouth with the back of his hand and belched.

When the bodies were on the boat, Liu Shu-shu insisted it was time to go, even though I had begun to shake violently from the cold and my fingers were turning blue. The policemen tethered Hong Rong to the back of the boat and she waded along, bellowing in protest, behind the boat that carried what remained of my family, which trailed behind the boat that carried us.

We stopped first at the coroner's building where the boat of bodies, Hong Rong, and Jiang Shu-shu left us. I felt like a condemned prisoner as I watched him walk away. The policemen poled us a short distance farther. We got out of the boat and walked uphill to Liu Shu-shu's house. I was walking, still wrapped in mama's quilt, clutching the small bag Jiang Shu-shu had thrust into my hand while Liu Shu-shu was not looking. I hadn't dared yet to see what was in it. Liu Shu-shu's house was, of course, well above the water level and safe from any possibility of flooding.

He thrust open the door and called out sharply to his wife. It was dark inside and smelled like a chamber pot that had not been emptied in several days. A small woman with bent shoulders shuffled quickly forward. "I have brought you a gift! This young girl owes us her life. She is orphaned and totally indigent. We will feed her and clothe her until she is of such age, if that ever comes, that she can support herself. She will express her gratitude for our charity by sweeping, cooking, cleaning, and washing laundry and any other chores such a worthless girl can attempt. Xu A-yi made no response but stared blankly at me. Her silence and her hollow eyes spoke of sorrow and despair.

All this while, I had stood with my Mama's quilt still wrapped around me. It still smelled of Mama and in that moment, I felt her arms wrapped around me. I breathed in her smell and for just a few seconds, it blocked out the foul odor in the air. "You are a strong girl," I heard Mama whisper in my heart. "You will survive."

"You are a qian jin xiao jie, a daughter of a thousand pieces of gold," I heard the echo of Baba's voice in my memory.

My eyes had begun to adjust to the darkness and I glanced up to see Liu Wei sitting in the corner grinning at me. He was tilted back on two legs of a wooden chair, one foot resting on the lid of a blue and white porcelain chamber pot. He smiled a rather mean smile at me as if he could hardly believe his good fortune. Then, very deliberately, he held up his bowl of noodles and let it fall to the ground. "Oops!" he said and stared at me. When I did not respond, he yelled angrily, "Girl slave, clean that up!" Then he kicked over the chamber pot, spilling its rank contents on top of the noodles.

"Somehow," I thought to myself as I felt darkness swirling around me and swallowing me up again, "somehow very soon, I have to get myself out of here!"

In the House of Liu

If I keep a green bough in my heart,
The singing bird will come.

My days in the house of Liu passed slowly. Liu Long Tang roused me each morning before dawn by banging on the kitchen door and shouting, "Get up, worthless girl. It is almost daylight." I was to prepare his breakfast and polish his boots. I was then to empty his chamber pot of night soil into the neighborhood public toilet trench and clean the pot. Although I suspect he had never done this himself, he had definite ideas of how long it should take. He did not take into consideration the long queues of people waiting to use the toilets in the mornings. Most of them had to get to work so considered that their business was more pressing than mine. As an orphan girl, with no father to speak for me, I was no longer enrolled in school, so had no urgent need. Each morning Liu Long Tang scolded me. If I was later than he thought I should be—which was most mornings, he would forbid me to eat breakfast. "This is for your own good, lazy girl. Perhaps you will be faster tomorrow and then you will eat."

Liu Long Tang's uniforms were to be perfectly ironed with creases just so. I had never noticed him dressing so meticulously before I began caring for his clothes.

His wife, Xu A-yi was at least kind. From time to time, she slipped me a scrap of meat she had saved from her own food, or a piece of fresh fruit. She seemed, however, powerless to oppose Liu Long Tang but did her very best to pacify his frequent fits of temper. She moved in silence within the shadows of her own house.

Liu Wei . . . I still want to spit every time I think of him. He seemed determined to make trouble for me. One day he freed his father's precious pet canary from its bamboo cage, saying that I had done it. When I protested, Liu Long Tang said that I was insolent and punished me by cutting my food rations to one portion of watered-down congee per day until the bird could be recaptured. It was only a thin rice gruel he allowed me to eat with none of the extra bits of fruit or fish that Mama always added. At this he pronounced himself generous, and Liu Wei sat in the corner giggling like a simple-minded fool.

It was only three days later that a canary graced the cage again. Xu A-yi ran in from the alley saying she had simply left the cage open over night and the bird had flown in on his own. He seemed a different bird to me: thinner, younger and more filled with song than he had been before. When I mentioned it to Xu A-yi she shushed me and argued that he was thinner because he had lived in the wild for three days on his own, and had not been overindulged by her generous husband's sweet treats. He sang more because he was so happy and grateful to be home. She smiled sweetly toward me as she patted her husband's hand. So, without ever speaking of it directly, we shared the secret of how she had bought a new bird from her meager savings to replace the one that her son had freed. Xu A-yi and I became friends that day.

I do not remember any day, living in the house of Liu, that my stomach was ever full. Each night I slept, wrapped in Mama's quilt, on the floor, in a corner of the kitchen. The kitchen was not in the main part of the house but a separate shack attached to the back of the house. Liu Long Tang would lock me in each night, securing a padlock on the outside of the kitchen door with a key he wore on a chain around his neck.

The floor was made of ancient, crumbling bricks simply laid upon the earth. There was nothing to offer resistance to insects pushing up from below. At night, cockroaches as long as my fingers crawled over the pots and cooking surfaces. Rats and mice crawled in under the rotted door to look for crumbs. I kept a meat cleaver beside me as I slept lest some sewer rat think me a tasty morsel. (I vowed it would be his last thought.) They never bothered me, though. Perhaps there was enough to busy them in the specks of grease that clung to the pots and the crumbs that fell between the cracks of brick. Then, too, I seldom slept soundly. The slightest noise roused me. I would grab the meat cleaver and slap it against the chopping block. The rats and mice would scatter and I would gather a few more precious winks of sleep until they returned.

I asked Liu Long Tang for a rattrap but he denied the existence of vermin within his walls. "So you think the house of Liu is a dirty one? Then you can clean it." He handed me a well-worn brush and a bucket and told me to boil water and scrub every brick in the floor until it was clean enough to use as a dinner plate.

After that I never mentioned the rats again.

I kept the small bag Jiang Shu-shu had given me and secreted it away within a fold of the quilt. I had opened it one night after I had heard Liu Long Tang fasten the padlock on the kitchen door and I was sure I was alone. By the light of a full moon I had found my jade bracelet, Mama's pearl necklace, grandfather's pocket watch, and some money that Baba had stored in an old sock in a drawer in the bedroom. Jiang Shu-shu had probably found these things when he went into the room to get the quilt. Knowing him as we all did, Jiang Shu-shu guessed that Liu Long Tang would not bring me back to get my things—ever. Surely Liu would come back to take those things he knew he could profit by, but none of my family's belongings would ever be seen by me again. Jiang Shu-shu had quickly pulled out some things of value and given them to me.

On a warm spring day, with cherry blossoms blooming in the lane—really only a few weeks, but it felt like an eternity after the flood--I again heard the warm voice of Jiang Shu-shu as he stopped at the door of the Liu house one morning. Liu Long Tang was sitting in the courtyard smoking a cigarette and talking to his new canary. I was ironing Liu Wei's school uniforms. I was very carefully, deliberately creasing them crooked. (I knew that Liu Wei would never notice--but everyone at school would.) I could hear everything the two men said through the open window.

"Ah, Liu Lao! What a lovely morning to air your bird."

"Ah yes,it is, Jiang Lao. Have you eaten?"

"Yes, yes. And your wife, she is well?

"She is quite well. What brings you to my door Jiang Lao? You look as if there is something you mean to say."

"Ah, I was on my way into the village on some business. Qiang Lao died last night." I stifled a gasp. Qiang Lao was the sweetest old man, after Ye-ye, of course. He had been much older than Ye-ye, and had taught me the ancient art of weaving bamboo fish traps. He taught me to bait the traps and how to place them against the current to catch the most fish.

"Oh, it's about time. He hasn't been useful to the farming collective in too many years! At least he finally had the common sense to die." I could hear Liu Long Tang grinding the butt of his cigarette under the sole of his shoe.

"Um, ah, of course, of course you are as sad to see him gone as the rest of us," stammered Jiang Shu-shu, "but I thought, as long as I was passing along this way, I would stop to see about the girl. Is she getting along well?"

"Hum. I am not sad, Jiang. To say so is simply a cultural holdover of former times. As for the girl, she is a lot of trouble, but perhaps she will learn. As you well know, her family always had an attitude problem: thinking themselves superior. Her father was always butting his head into government business. Her grandfather was a pompous old dolt who never had anything reasonable to say: always quoting the ignorance of ancient poets and religious fools as if these words held some relevance today! But, she is young and appears to be of at least trainable intelligence. If anyone can work it out of her, I can. Perhaps the Zhong family stubborn streak may yet be broken."

"Hum," said Jiang Shu-shu. I could feel him choosing his words, not saying what he really wanted to say, much as Baba had often deliberately chosen his words when dealing with Liu Long Tang. "Well, I am sure you will succeed. Would it be possible to speak with her? I have business regarding her family account to settle."

"No, she is quite busy right now. I have sent her on an errand. I can take care of anything you need to see her about. If there is excess from the sale of that scrawny water buffalo, you can give it to me. I will see that she gets what is coming to her."

"Bu, xie-xie --No thank you. In fact, the animal did not bring as good a price as I had predicted. I was hoping to see if she had anything else to sell in order to pay the difference or perhaps she would like to work off the difference in my service."

"Hum. I told you it was hasty to accept that beast in exchange for your good work. The girl has nothing. I went to that pitiable pigsty they lived in and cleaned it out, myself. Most of the stuff was garbage. What little I could find of value, I sold to pay her keep but I am afraid it is already spent. As for working, she is so lazy I am afraid she will be a disappointment to you and an embarrassment to me. Perhaps I should send my son to pay off her debt, and then she could be indebted to him."

"Ah, that would not be necessary! I do not wish to trouble your son. I am sure Liu Wei has far more important things to work on. It is only a small debt I can wait for the girl to pay me back. If you would, tell her that I have inquired about her."

"Hao-de—I will."

"Hao—Good. Then I will be on my way."

Somehow, I thought, I must find a way to see Jiang Shu-shu. There is something he had not told Liu Long Tang—I could just feel it. I knew that there were other things of value in the house: some silver pieces of grandmother's, the blue Ming dynasty vase, some very old jewelry—some of it pure gold, grandmother's red bridal silk, all our silk clothing . . . where had all those things gone? Was Liu Long Tang holding back on Jiang Shu-shu or were those things gone before he got to our house to clean it out? What did Jiang Shu-shu know that he wanted to tell me? I unbuttoned the top button of my blouse and drew out Grandmother's jade Buddha. I held it between my fingers sliding its smooth side against my thumb as I thought. I must find a way to speak with Jiang Shu-shu without any of the Liu's finding out. I brought the Buddha up and absently slid the jade across my lower lip. I also wanted to see our house. Was our house truly emptied of everything? Didn't they forget or overlook at least one thing that would be of value to me? Hot tears ran down my cheeks. In all my treasures, I had nothing to remind me of Di-di. Had they left me anything of him?

Finding Strength

Virtue is not solitary;
It is bound to have neighbors.

As the morning of Qing Ming dawned, it was Xu A-yi who awakened me. She was quietly preparing food, packing a picnic feast for the traditional tomb sweeping day.

"Oh," she whispered, "Did I wake you? I am so sorry. My husband is not awake yet. I had thought I would let you sleep a little later this morning and get everything ready myself. He is always eager for us to tend his family graves early in the day so that he may have the greater part of the day for smoking cigarettes and playing cards with his old soldier friends."

As she spoke, I became aware of the sound of her voice drifting off in the background of my mind. This was the traditional day for Chinese families to sweep the graves of their ancestors, to bring offerings of food and drink to place at the burial sites, to share memories and family stories of those who have gone before us. I had no flowers or food offering to bring in order to honor my ancestors. I had no family to share my stories.

126

In years past, it had been a pleasant yet bittersweet day. Baba would pack up the handcart and Mama would make a picnic. Grandfather would bring brooms and potted flowers or tiny trees he had shaped just so. We would walk out to the mountainside burial grounds and clean grandmother's memorial stone. We would plant the flowers and arrange an offering of food to honor her. Grandfather would light firecrackers and Baba would burn incense and pretend paper money so that she would have plenty on her spirit world journey. When the area was clear and bright, we would eat our picnic and share our memories of grandmother. It was as if she was with us. Sometimes, grandfather would tell stories he remembered of other ancestors, although their tombs were near Beijing—far to the north--where our family had lived before the Cultural Revolution.

Grandmother's ashes were held in a chamber carved below the memorial stone. I knew this for I had helped Grandfather place them there and seal the small cavity for all time. Where were the ashes of Mama, Baba, Grandfather and Di-di? It suddenly occurred to me that I didn't know! In the gray light that precedes dawn, while Xu A-yi chattered on, hot tears escaped my tightly squeezed eyes. I suddenly felt so deeply alone I could hardly bear it. Against my will a sob escaped my lips.

"What? Mei Lin, are you crying? What is wrong?" Xu A-yi rushed over and wrapped her arms around me and held my head against her shoulder. It had been so long since I had touched another human being, that at her touch, something inside of me broke and a flood of tears escaped. I willed them to stop but they would not obey me. I cried in great gasping sobs, heaving for breaths of air. I ached for her to be my Mama and not Xu A-yi.

"You can cry. You can cry, but do not let my husband hear you," she whispered. "He thinks it is weakness. He will make it worse for you. Oh, sweet girl. You miss your Mama!" She stroked my hair and, wrapping her arms tightly around me rocked back and forth. "How well I remember the pain of losing my own Mama. I was

DAUGHTER OF A THOUSAND PIECES OF GOLD

so much older than you and still it hurts. It will never stop hurting, but some day you will be able to go on. You must. Do not give up. You are a strong girl. She raised you well. Honor her and leave this place."

I was so shocked at her words; I could hardly believe my ears. Here was the wife of my tormentor urging me to run away. "How?" I asked. "I have nothing. And, Liu Shu-shu never leaves me without guarding my way or timing my return."

"Make a plan. Make provisions. Someday soon, there will be a moment of opportunity and you must be ready to take it."

"Why do *you* stay?" I asked her.

"He is my husband." She paused for a moment. "He is a very powerful man. He has very powerful friends. Because of this, everyone in the village fears him. Your grandfather and your parents did not fear him and he hates them still for this offense. This is why he is so cruel to you—because they dared to stand up to him and they helped others to do so as well. Your grandfather was the real leader of this village. He is the one everyone respected. Your father followed well in his footsteps." She stopped and looked at me a moment to see if I was taking in all that she said. Then she continued, "My husband has no legal right to hold you here. He has not even filed the official papers to become a foster-care family. Officially, you do not exist in this house. So, no policeman would help him search for you if you were to leave this village." She waited for the words to sink in.

"I could live with Ting A-yi and Uncle Charlie?" I felt a surge of hope.

"No. I am afraid he has thought of that. They were both given government transfers and moved to Shanghai months ago. I have tried to find where they are, but without asking him directly, I am afraid that is not possible. Is there no one else?"

"No. No one."

"Surely your father has friends elsewhere." In that moment, I thought of Qin Shu-shu, at the restaurant for foreigners. Perhaps, he could help me. Although it seemed I could trust her, I did not want to reveal this last hope to Xu A-yi, lest Liu Long Tang drag it out of her after I had gone.

"Now," she said, "It is nearly daylight. I have already cleaned his chamber pot. It is beside the door outside. Take it, but do not go to the toilets. Go instead to the house of Jiang. He has important information for you. Do not delay there. Get back at the usual time."

I wanted to trust her, but I was afraid. What if she was setting a trap for me? But then again, why would she? The chamber pot was, indeed, clean. I desperately wanted to see Jiang Shu-shu, so I ran down the alley and out the road and instead of turning north toward the toilets, I turned south toward the river and ran till I came to the house of Jiang.

He was facing the rising sun and practicing Tai Ji. When he heard me approach, he stopped but did not seem surprised. It was as if he was expecting me. "Ah, Mei Lin. I know your time is short. I will get right to the point. I saw you behind the window on the day I stopped by after Qiang Lao's funeral. I want you to know your account is not as I told Liu Long Tang. If fact, the water buffalo was such a fine animal, she commanded a very good price. In addition, the day of the flood, I returned immediately to your family house and removed several things I thought might be of value to you either for purposes of sentiment or money. I have packed these things for you in a bamboo backpack. It is hanging in the left corner of my workshop. These are your things. You may feel free to come by any time and claim them. Until then, I will keep them hidden for you. The money from the sale of the water buffalo is also in the basket inside the blue Ming dynasty vase."

"Did you save anything of Di-di's?" I blurted out.

"I did. I didn't know if it would matter, or not, but there was a baby rattle with a bell inside it . . . "

"Oh thank you!" I said. "How can I ever repay you?"

"No. No, child. I am only just now repaying your father. I have owed him many times over. This is a small thing. These things will wait for you as long as I live. If they disappear one night, I will know that you are safely on your way." He pressed a key into my hand. "This is a copy of the door key to my work room, in case you should ever need it." I tucked it into my pocket and bowed again. "Now you must be away, Mei Lin, before Liu notices you are gone too long."

"Wait. One more thing! I must know, where lie the remains of my father, my mother, my grandfather and my little brother?"

"Ah! I am so sorry! I thought you would know. Their ashes lie safely with your grandmother, sealed within your family stone. Liu Shu-shu would not let you come to place them there. But I made sure they were honored."

"Xie-xie!" I choked on the words as I blinked back tears from my eyes as I bowed to the honorable Jiang Shu-shu.

I ran. No, I flew back to the house of Liu, touching the edges of happiness for the first time since the Nandu River had flooded.

I arrived back in the kitchen just as Xu A-yi finished packing the picnic. I realized that I had to pee—badly. I told her this and she laughed. "Take the chamber pot again," she said, "He is only just now getting up. I can hear him. He will suspect nothing. I will tell him that you have helped me prepare the food and are just now leaving for the toilets."

Indeed, when I returned, Liu Long Tang rewarded me with breakfast saying that at long last I was learning how to be responsible in my chores.

Outside, Liu Wei was grumbling and complaining. His father had told him to pack up a pedicart with the picnic and the brooms, some flowers and rakes—all the things a family would need to tend to the graves of their ancestors. "My back hurts. My hands hurt. My legs are too tired to be doing such menial labor. I am a scholar, not a common laborer."

When Liu Long Tang walked outside and found Liu Wei resting in the shade while the pedicart was still not ready, he scolded.

Liu Wei said, "You have no respect for my superior abilities. You treat me like a slave!"

"I treat you far too well, you lazy, worthless pig! Perhaps I should treat you like a slave."

We walked, Xu A-yi and I. Liu Wei pedaled ahead of us and his father rode on the cart with the lunch and supplies. The road was busy. Everyone was heading to the burial grounds. Liu Wei angrily rang his bell again and again, urging everyone to get out of his way.

It was not long before I began to notice a strange thing. A silence and something more—people were *not* looking at me but were silently stepping aside as we came near. When we arrived at the gate of the burial grounds, Xu A-yi took some incense from a Buddhist nun who was standing at a table at the entrance. She placed several coins in the tin cup at her feet and handed me several sticks of the incense. "Do you know where your family grave is?"

"I think I remember the way."

"Good. Go then. Meet me here at noon and I will take you to our family grave so you can share in our meal."

"I have no offering, no brooms . . ."

"You will not need them."

I ran up the hill and around the other side. Yes, I remembered the place. I remembered it well. It looked very different though. Someone had been here before me--more than one someone! It appeared that the whole village had been here before me. A thick carpet of fresh yellow flowers surrounded the family stone. Offerings of oranges and rice and even beer stood in front of the stone. I lit my incense from some hot coals at the Ping family grave and I stood on the flowers, holding the incense to my forehead and bowed to my family grave. Their names were all freshly carved in the stone.

Usually, the atmosphere at Qing Ming is busy though reverent and somewhat solemn. This day, it was absolutely quiet. I looked up and realized that I was surrounded by people. Yan A-yi, the baker from whom we always bought our cakes for moon festival stepped forward. "Zhong Mei Lin, we are all so very sorry to hear of the death of your parents, your young brother and your grandfather. The whole village grieves with you."

Ma Laoshe stepped forward. "You are a most excellent student, Mei Lin. I hope your grief will not keep you from school much longer."

In this moment, I realized that they all knew I was a prisoner in the house of Liu. How many of them would help me escape, I wondered.

They silently moved away, leaving me to myself. I stayed and remembered my parents and my grandparents and my baby brother. I thought of their smiles and the things that made them laugh. Although I missed them desperately, I felt at peace knowing at last that they were safely here and that so many people remembered them. I knew that although the whole village feared Liu Long Tang, they also respected my parents and grandfather, and I clearly knew the difference between fear and respect.

I also knew that I would leave there soon. That too became clear amid the scents of flowers and incense. It seemed that provision had been made and waited for me in the workroom of the village coroner. Opportunity was what I lacked. If I kept my eyes open and myself ready, I would be able to seize it the moment opportunity was presented to me.

I knelt in front of the family monument and scraped at the dirt with my bare hands. When I had made a small pile, I gathered it up and folded it into a piece of newspaper I had found blowing across the ground. Wherever I went, I would take some piece of my family's resting place with me.

At noon, I returned to the gate as promised but I was a different person than I had been that morning. I was more peaceful. I had a much clearer idea of what I must do. I was strong. I was, no longer a prisoner in the house of Liu but was again, a daughter of a thousand pieces of gold.

By the time Xu A-yi led me to the Liu family grave, Liu Long Tang was already drunk. It was a warm day and he had liberally quenched his thirst. He was eager to get back to the village to play cards with his old soldier friends so we ate hastily. He and Liu Wei punctuated their gulps wiping the grease from the grilled chicken on the backs of their sleeves. As soon as he was done eating, Liu Lao began to pack up, berating the rest of us for our laziness even in eating too slowly. The charcoal brazier was still smoldering when he put it on the wooden floor in the back of the pedicab.

"It will burn a hole in the wood floor," I whispered to Xu A-yi.

"I know, she said, "and tomorrow, when he is sober enough to notice it, he will blame me for the hole."

"No, he won't," I said as I loosened the cap on the large thermos of tea. I placed it on the back of the cart and shouted, "Ah!" as if surprised by an accident. I carefully allowed the water to spill out under the brazier with a satisfying hiss as it soaked the floorboards beneath.

"Worthless, clumsy, girl!" spat out Liu Long Tang as he brushed a few drops of tepid water from his trouser leg.

He climbed into his position on the back of the pedicab and commanded angrily for his son to hurry home. Xu A-yi and I walked back to the Liu house together at a much more leisurely pace; stopping often to admire the way blossoms fell across a stone wall or light danced upon a fish pond.

"Sleep now," whispered Xu A-yi when we reached the kitchen door, "while you have the chance." She placed the basket of leftover food on the table in the kitchen.

Liu Long Tang took his caged canary and a bottle of wine from the house. The men gathered in a public park not far away and hung their birdcages from the branches of the trees. They laughed and drank and played cards until well after dark. I could hear the sounds of their voices and the songs of their birds carrying through the alleyway.

As for me, I took Xu A-yi's advice. I wrapped myself in Mama's quilt and slept deeply. I awoke well after dark when I heard Liu Long Tang stumbling down the alley. At one point, I think he tripped into the sewer pit that ran along the side of the alley behind the house, but he pulled himself out and gathered up his birdcage. He was talking loudly to the bird as he walked.

"I am soooo sorry, beautiful bird!" His words slurred together. "Did I rustle your pretty feathers? Ha ha ha!" He passed the kitchen door but he did not stop to lock it before stumbling through the front door of his house.

In only a few moments, I heard the sounds of loud snoring echoing even through the brick walls of the house. I knew my moment of freedom had come.

I wrapped my few things in mama's quilt and gathered some leftover food from the lunch basket. I took ten wooden matches from the shelf over the cooking fire slid them into my pocket and, ever so carefully, slipped silently into the night. Though eager to run as fast as I could, I walked slowly so as not to make my steps heard until I was all the way to the river. Then, I hurried to Jiang Shu-shu's workroom. I opened the door with the key and in the darkness, felt my way along the wall until I found the bamboo backpack he had said would be there. I tucked Mama's quilt in along the open top edge and lifted the big basket onto my back and slid my arms through the straps. I carefully locked the door behind me and set off for Baoshan City. I remembered the way even in the dark. The same moon lit my way that night as had lit the way home so many months before. In my memories, I walked again with Ye-ye. Tomorrow morning, I would see Qin Shu-shu. Perhaps he would be able to help me in some way—even if I had no fish or melons to sell him.

Free!

Not the cry, but the flight of the wild duck
Leads the flock to fly and follow.

It was a beautiful, clear night. The air was crisp but promised of freedom and warmer days to come. Wearing a well-worn and patched, cotton, quilted jacket of Xu A-yi's, I walked along the familiar road from the village toward our farm. There is only one road from the village of Longkou to Baoshan City and it winds past the little farm house where my family had lived—when I had a family. From the distance, I could see the moon gate left open and swinging in a slight breeze. "Wee-ga!" a hinge creaked and I felt a sudden tightness in my throat. Ye-ye would not have tolerated that. If he were here, the squeaky hinge would have been oiled. As it was, the squeak seemed to announce the emptiness of the house. No one lived here anymore. The lantern I had left for Ye-ye so many months before still hung on the gatepost. The wind must have blown the flame out long ago, for when I shook it, oil still sloshed inside.

I used one of the matches and lit the lantern. I held it up to inspect the courtyard. Piles of river silt filled the corners and spilled over the threshold of the front door. Ye-ye's spring couplets still hung on either side of the door. Weathered now and faded from the sun, the ink had splattered in the rain and dripped down the red paper. The gold flecks curled up and were sticking out of the paper like scales on a long-dead fish. The words seemed to mock me as I held the lantern up trying to make out the ghost of their former beauty: "Bright happiness in the new year to all who enter here," and "May good fortune follow your every step." Defiantly, I stepped past them and held the lantern up high.

I suppose I expected to find the house as I had left it, so I was shocked to find that it was nearly empty. My footsteps on the wood floor echoed on the walls. Mama's lacquerware chest was gone. All the furniture Ye-ye had made was also gone. The dishes and cooking tools and most of the clothes were gone too. Here and there scraps of paper and a forgotten shoe littered the floor. Even the Buddha from my family shrine was missing, though the names of my ancestors, carved by Ye-ye into a black wood plaque, remained hanging on the wall where the family shrine had been. This I picked up and pressed against my heart. I would have to add the other names --though I lacked the carving skill of Ye-ye.

I peeked in the bedroom, but nothing remained there either except a few odd things on the floor. Liu Shu-shu, I supposed, had been pretty thorough in eliminating nearly every trace of my family.

All that remained of my family and my former life was held in the backpack basket—and in my memories. I slid the basket down my arms and sat it on the floor. I lifted Mama's quilt from the top, lay it on the floor and sat on it. Then, I carefully, removed each item. On the very top was a still warm jar of wolf-berry tea and some steamed pork buns! I ate the first bun in one gulp and saved the rest for later. I opened the jar and drank eagerly. Had Jiang Shu-shu known that I would leave tonight, or had he made the tea and buns each night waiting for me to take my chance? Either way, he had made provision for me!

What had Jiang Shu-Shu saved of my life? Each thing I lifted out brought a new wave of tears. Wrapped in the turquoise cotton jacket that I had bought for her, was Mama's earthenware teapot with the dragon-head spout and the tail curled into a handle. Di-di's birth certificate and mine rested along the side, bound in a leather folder and tied with a red ribbon. Mama and Baba's wedding license was with them as well as a small framed photograph of them on their wedding day. This photograph I held to my lips and kissed as tears streamed my face. I did not sob out loud, however. I was afraid Pan Ling would hear me and report me to Liu Long Tang. Grandmother's red silk bridal veil was next—the veil that had covered her face when she was brought in an old-style sedan chair to meet Ye-ye on her wedding day. Ye-ye's painting of the Ming vase with cherry blossoms was rolled up as a scroll, and the Ming vase itself, was near the bottom, wrapped in my green Chinese New Year silk outfit and the red dress Baba had bought for Mama. These, in turn were wrapped carefully in tissue paper. I wiped my tears on the sleeve of Xu A-yi's jacket. Di-di's quilted and embroidered baby carrier had been washed and carefully folded to pad the bottom. I felt a sudden wave of relief seeing it and something almost like joy swept over me when I came upon his bamboo baby rattle that I had bought. It rested near the bottom with a piece of cotton stuffed into the cage to keep the bell from jingling. Packed inside and around other things were six pair of cloisonné chopsticks that grandmother had brought with her from her home village. Ye-ye's calligraphy brushes and ink stone were wrapped together and rolled in a piece of cotton cloth. The jade Buddha from the family shrine rested inside the fur hat I had bought for Baba. The incense burner and the statue of the kitchen god were carefully wrapped in my school uniform. Lying on the very bottom were three of my schoolbooks and some letters from friends at school. The top one read:

> *"Dear Mei Lin, we are so sorry to hear of the tragic*
> *losses in your family last night. Teacher Ma asked*
> *me to drop off your math, history and literature books*
> *so you can keep up with the assignments. I hope you*
> *get this. You are not here and I do not know where*
> *you have gone. I will leave it all in your doorway. We*

*are now working on chapter 16 in Math and the
poetry unit in literature. We have done nothing new in
history today, but you may want to keep reading so
you will not be too far behind when you come back.
We hope you are able to return to school soon. Your
friend, Xiao-Xiao"*

Jiang Shu-shu had chosen well. He had preserved the best
of my life and returned it to me.

I packed all the things carefully back into the bamboo
backpack, adding the small bag Jiang Shu-shu had already given
me with my jade bracelet, mama's pearls and Ye-ye's pocket watch.
To this small bag of precious things I added another small bag that
Jiang Shu-shu had saved of gold and jade jewelry that Nai-nai
hadn't worn since the Cultural Revolution but that had been worn by
several generations of women in her family. I took off Xu A-yi's
jacket and hung it on a peg behind the door. Though she had been
nice to me, I wanted to leave behind every memory of the Liu
household. I stood up, picked up the backpack and started to walk
out the bedroom door, but I stopped when the lantern light caught
something shiny and pink on the floor in the corner behind the door.
I bent to pick it up. Still wrapped in cellophane, it was the silk and
lace hair bow I had bought in the Baoshan City Qingpin Market just
last August—less than a year and yet, a lifetime ago. It was the bow
I had bought to welcome a baby sister. I had never used it because
Mama's baby, my Di-di, turned out to be a boy. Still, it was like
finding a reminder of him. Tears welled in my eyes as I squeezed
the small treasure and slipped it into the pocket of my trousers.

Now, I was ready to leave. I shifted the weight of the basket
on my back and marched out the door. I turned and angrily yanked
down the spring couplets. "How dare you fade and mock me?" I
shouted at the ghost of the drippy letters. I tossed them into a pile in
the corner of the courtyard and with both hands over my head,
hurled the lit lantern on top of them. Immediately they ignited. I did
not stay to watch them burn. I walked out the moon gate and

carefully latched it behind me. I continued on the road to Baoshan City and did not look back.

All night I walked, stopping only to sip from the jar of wolfberry tea. By dawn, I had reached the "waiting tree" but it was too late to sleep. The farmers who had spent the night there were already gone. I hurried on into the city. My heart was light and my footsteps were quick. I had business to conduct. I had a future to arrange.

Soon, I was pushed and pressed on all sides. Bicycles swerved around me. Trucks loaded with livestock, careened in front and behind me. Handcarts and pedicabs zigged and zagged around me. Finally, I made my way to the service door of the Golden Tiger Restaurant. I pushed the buzzer and smoothed down my hair. Qin Shu-shu would help me. He loved my parents and he admired my hard work. He would give me a job. My troubles were surely over.

When the door opened, I saw the same teen-aged kitchen boy I had met there the year before. "Qing wen," I said, "May I see Qin Shu-shu?"

"Ah, I remember you! You are the girl with the fish and the melons. We do not need any today."

"No, I do not have any to sell today. I just need to speak to Qin Shu-shu."

"Qin Xian-sheng does not work here anymore."

"Where is he?" I felt a surge of desperation rising in my throat.

"Ah. No one knows. Perhaps he has been arrested. Maybe he moved to Hong Kong. He just didn't come into work one day about six months ago. No one has heard from him."

The boy started to close the door.

"Wait! Gan Yi-sheng! Is he still here?"

"Gan Yi-sheng? Oh, you mean the hotel doctor for the American tourists. You have to ask the doorman. I don't know anything about the hotel. I only know the kitchen."

He closed the door and I stood for a minute planning how to handle this new situation. I took off my backpack basket. If my cotton clothes didn't, this bulky, old-fashioned country backpack would surely mark me as a needy peasant girl. I hid it behind some potted trees by the corner of the American consulate courtyard. I walked up to the doorman and said, "My Ye-ye has sent me with a message for Gan Yi-sheng. Can you tell me where to find him?"

He laughed. "*You* have business with a hotel doctor? I don't think so! Our doctors are very good doctors. The hotel pays them lots of money to cure sick Americans. They do not go traipsing through the countryside treating sick peasants."

"No, you don't understand. No one is sick. My Ye-ye was once a good friend of Gan Yi-sheng. I have a message from him."

"Well, your Ye-ye's message is too late. Gan Yi-sheng retired last week. They had a big party for him. He has moved back to his family home in Shanghai. I hear he will be doing some teaching at the university there if you want to write him a letter."

"Xie-xie," I said and turned away from the door. Hot tears stung the corners of my eyes. I didn't know if Gan Yi-sheng was in that building or had moved to Shanghai. I only knew that there was no way that doorman was going to let me in. Angrily, I willed the tears to stop as I retrieved my basket backpack. I would come back at night when another doorman was working and try again.

If Gan Yi-sheng had indeed moved away, how would I live? How could I get a job? I was only 11 years old and I had no father to speak for me. I could not get a government job. I could not be a shop girl. The market! Perhaps I could find some work in the market. I could pluck chickens or scale fish! I walked past the American Hotel and the tourist shops. I walked over the highway on the pedestrian bridge and down into the Qingpin market. I walked past the man selling illegal tiger paws and rhino horns, past the man selling fake antiques and counterfeit American coins, and past the pearl merchant. At the vat of scorpions, I turned left and asked the first poultry man if he had any jobs. He had cages of pheasants and chickens, ducks and quails stacked one on top of another. All of them were clucking and chirping and quacking. It was so loud; I had to shout to be heard above the din.

"No, he laughed. I have seven sons and sixteen granddaughters. They all know how to pluck a pheasant."

"Xie-xie," I said. I continued down the row asking each of the merchants and farmers for work. They all dismissed me. Some waved me on as if I was a gnat. Others laughed at me. Some asked, "Where is your father to sign for you, girl?" I never answered this question but walked away.

Some small boys came running through the market clutching mangoes to their chests. All three were dirty. One, dressed in a ragged western style suit and rubber thong sandals bumped into me and pushed me off my feet. I fell in a mud puddle that smelled of pig blood and goat urine. "Stop!" shouted an angry merchant. But he was afraid to leave his market stall to chase the boys. An accomplice might be hiding--waiting for his chance to steal even more. The boys disappeared into a surge of the crowd.

A woman came to help me up. "Are you alright?" she asked.

"Yes, yes, I am fine. Did anything fall out of my basket?"

"No, I don't think so." She said. "It is a pity; your trousers look quite bad. Perhaps if you could wash them right away they might not be totally ruined. There are some faucets over here." She pointed the direction.

When I looked back to thank her, the crowds had swallowed her up just as they had swallowed the boys. I reached into my pocket, feeling sick with fear. The silk bow—was it ruined?

No! It was still wrapped in cellophane and it was perfectly dry! I pressed it to my lips and kissed it.

I walked toward the faucets, removed the basket from my back and put in down in a dry patch of ground. Standing in a corner behind a stack of animal cages, I wrapped Mama's quilt around me and took off the dirty pants and underwear. I put on my school uniform pants. When I was done, I folded the quilt again and placed it back in the basket and slid the pink hair bow into my uniform pants pocket.

At the faucet, I tried to wash my pants but it was hopeless. I ended up hanging them over a faucet and leaving them there. The underwear looked and smelled fairly clean when I was done. That, I lay across the back of some straw bales behind the animal cages. Then, I climbed up on the straw bales and while I waited for my underwear to dry, I leaned against my basket, ate another pork bun and sipped the last of my now cold tea. With the jar in my hand, and still sitting up, I fell asleep.

拾伍

The Police

You can only go halfway into the darkest forest,
Then you are coming out the other side.

"Girl!" I felt something slapping against the soles of my shoes. "Is she dead?"

"Girl! Wake up!" Someone else poked me on the shoulder with a stick.

Squinting through eyes unwilling to open, I realized that it was dark. Bare light bulbs glowed from the awnings of the market stalls. Moths and other insects fluttered in their glow. A crowd had begun to gather.

"I don't know how long she has been there," said an old, man with a face as wrinkled and brown as an apple left sitting in the sun for many days. "My wife went to lie down and found this girl here behind our stall, sleeping on our straw bales." He leaned on an elaborately carved wooden cane as if to punctuate his remarks. "We have been very busy all day and did not notice her coming. She looks like she came from the countryside. Does anyone recognize that school uniform?"

"Yes, I think it is from a village to the north of here. The village of Dragon's Mouth—I was there once on business," said a woman with a basket of snakes tied to the back of her bicycle. Forked pink tongues flicked in and out of the holes between the woven strips of bamboo.

"Are you lost, girl?" she asked.

"Where is your father?" asked another.

"What is your name?" a third questioned.

"What village are you from?" The first woman asked. "Are you from the village of Dragon's Mouth?"

"Wo shi," I answered groggily, rubbing my eyes. "I am from Longkou."

Finally, with both eyes, I could see that a crowd was growing dense. My chief interrogator was the wrinkled and toothless old man who nodded and smiled between each question, pointing and gesturing with his cane. Though groggy, I recognized one face in the crowd. I was, at first relieved to see him, though I shouldn't have been.

"I have met this girl before!" he shouted excitedly. "She sold some fish and watermelons to Qin Xian-sheng at the Golden Tiger Restaurant last year just before Moon Festival. It was highly unusual because he took her into the kitchen and counted out money directly from the safe to her—to a girl! He also allowed her to drink an American Ke Kou Ke Le™, which he never allows even the kitchen staff to drink."

"That's not so unusual!" said a young man on a motor scooter. "American products are expensive. I would fire anyone on my staff who ate my stock of American goods!"

"Then," the boy continued as if he had not heard this comment, "Then, Qin Xian-sheng spent nearly a half of the morning talking with the old man who was with her. He made us stop everything to prepare them a small feast as if they were some visiting emperors but he would not let us near them."

"What was he hiding, do you suppose?" asked a man wearing a Western Style business suit.

"I have wondered about this many times. They whispered together secretly, sitting away from the building, in a corner of the service yard and he insisted on serving them himself. Qin Xian-sheng serves no-one! Finally, when he came inside, I overheard him talking on the telephone. He said he wanted the hotel doctor to come outside immediately and treat the old man's swollen knee because it was too difficult for the old man to walk into the hotel. It was very important to Qin Xian-sheng that the old man be treated with the best medicine and the highest dignity even though he looked like a common peasant to me. I wondered then if he were a spy disguised as a simple farmer. Qin Xian-sheng stressed that the old man was a very important man and that he would personally pay any expenses involved. It all seemed highly suspicious to me at the time. This is why I have remembered it all in such detail."

The crowd nodded and murmured in thoughtful appraisal.

The kitchen boy realized that he had the full attention of the crowd so he took a deep breath, raised himself a little taller and continued with his story slightly louder and with more accusation in his voice.

"Then, when Qin Xian-sheng disappeared a few months later, I began to piece together these events with some others that also appeared suspicious to me."

"So, there was even more!" a woman exclaimed. She looked at me sideways as she scowled and clicked her tongue in a disapproving way.

"This morning, this same girl showed up at the hotel again asking to see Qin Xian-sheng. She acted as if she did not know he was gone! When I told her he had disappeared, she registered *no* surprise but instead asked immediately to see Gan Yi-sheng, the hotel doctor—the very same doctor who secretly treated the old man whom Qin Xian-sheng thought was so important."

"What is happening?" asked a thin, young man carrying a yoke with two baskets filled with bricks.

"I think they are all part of an international spy ring!" continued the kitchen boy.

"A spy ring?" asked a university student wearing black trousers and a white shirt with sleeves rolled up to his elbows. He was carrying an armload of books—some of which I recognized as American authors Ye-ye had spoken of with admiration: Fitzgerald, Steinbeck, Dickinson and Emerson. "That's crazy! What proof do you have?"

"I can tell you, there have been secret goings-on in that hotel. The hotel is, after all, located right next to the American consulate building. I believe there are tunnels leading to the American compound. It is mostly Americans who stay there. Ordinary Chinese who have dealings with the management level personnel of the hotel are suspicious if you ask me! Now that Qin Xian-sheng has so conveniently disappeared and this girl arrives without the old man, I think I am right. So, girl, is that your secret?" he looked at me directly, accusing me to my face, "Are you a part of a spy ring?"

If I were not so scared, I would have thought his delusions of international intrigue amusing. I did not look up at him, but kept my eyes respectfully downcast. Still, I could not help it. Perhaps because I was nervous or because the story was so ludicrous, I began to giggle. I tried to stop but it only became worse. Whenever I tried to speak, the only sound that came out was high-pitched laughter.

"I am calling the police!" cried a businessman. He removed one of those tiny light machines from his pocket, unfolded it and pressed it against his face. "I have heard enough. The police should take this girl into custody and find out the truth."

"Don't be ridiculous!" said the woman with the snakes. "She is a girl. She is nervous. Let me talk to her. Child, what is your name?

"Zhong Mei Lin." Faced with a rational person and a reasonable question, I was suddenly able to compose myself and answer sensibly.

"And you are from . . . "

"Longkou: the village of Dragon's Mouth."

"And are you the melon and fish girl."

"Shi."

A murmur went up in the crowd. "She admits it!"

"Hush!" The woman scolded. "Give her a chance!"

"Give her chance to the police! I have already called them. They will be here any minute. They will get to the bottom of this!" said the man as he clicked his little light machine closed and pocketed it again.

"Get to the bottom of what? So far we have a sleeping child from a small village a day's journey north of here. She has been to this city before to sell melons and fish to a tourist restaurant. Is there a crime?"

"What about the old man? What about the spy who fled to Hong Kong?"

"Zhong Mei Lin, who is the old man this boy refers to?"

"He was my grandfather."

"Was?"

"Yes, he died in the big flood that came with the spring rains this year."

"Ah. I am so sorry for your loss."

"Xie-xie."

"And why did Qin Xian-sheng think he was so important?"

"Before the Cultural Revolution, my grandfather was a famous professor. He knew all the writers whose names are on that boy's books." I pointed to the books the college student was carrying. "During the Cultural Revolution, he was sent to the countryside and reeducated through labor. He became a farmer. When my grandmother died several years ago, he did not want to leave her grave unattended so he chose not to move back to Beijing even though the possibility was offered to him—though without a university position as he was well past retirement age. He said he no longer had a life in Beijing and that his life lay buried in the hills of our village.

"Many years ago before our great Chairman Mao led the people in transforming our country, he had taught Qin Shu-shu at the university in Beijing. Qin Shu-shu was also a close friend of my father. He is several years older than my father but they shared many interests. Qin Shu-shu has always been like an uncle to me and like an older brother to my father."

"Ah," accused the kitchen boy, "It is worse than I suspected! You have been in close cooperation with the spy, Qin." In the distance, I could hear the "Bee-**ba**, bee-**ba**" of police sirens.

"I do not *think* that he is a spy. What I do *know* is that he has been a good friend of my family for many years."

"Make way, make way for the police!" shouted the man who had called them. He stepped out into the alley and motioned for them to come our way. People crushed to the sides of the narrow alley, crowding into the market stalls as the police car bounced down the, rutted, pot-holed road. Mud flew up on both sides of the car, splattering those who were closest to it. The police officer stepped out of the car and said in a booming voice, "I am Officer Wang. Someone reported that a spy had been captured."

"I think perhaps, that determination has been made prematurely," said the woman with the basket of snakes on her bike. She glared at the man who had called the police. Still straddling her bike and balancing the shifting weight of the writhing snakes, she said, "As far as I have been able to determine thus far, we have found a girl who is far from her home and who fell asleep in the straw bales behind this farmer's market stall." The old man, pleased to be the center of attention again, nodded like a doll with a head on a spring, and smacked his toothless mouth in excitement.

"This kitchen-boy," she nodded toward the boy, "Claims to know her and tells a fanciful story full of conjecture about her supposed entanglements with international intrigue. Personally, I think the boy has seen one too many spy films." She quickly filled the officer in on what had transpired before his arrival.

"So," he said, picking up the line of questioning. "Why have you come to Baoshan City to see this Qin Xian-sheng today?"

"He is a friend of my father's and I thought he could help me with a problem."

"Why didn't your father come?"

I took a deep breath and paused a moment. "He too, died in the great flood this spring."

"You poor child!" sighed the snake-woman.

"Is your mother not able to care for you?" the policeman asked.

"Mama" I choked and could not speak for a moment. "Mama, too died in the flood."

"Ai-ya!" The woman gasped. "Have you no one child?"

I hung my head and could barely speak. "I thought I had Qin Shu-shu. Gan Yi-sheng also greatly respected my grandfather and knew his writings well. I thought he could offer me some guidance. But the hotel doorman told me that he too, is gone. So, dui le--you are correct. I have no-one."

"One more question." Officer Wang spoke slowly with a tinge of puzzlement in his voice. "The flood was quite a while ago, before planting time. It is now nearly harvest. How have you been living these many months since then?"

"I don't know how to say this."

"Speak plainly, girl. Begin at the beginning. That will be easiest."

So, I did. I figured that if the kitchen boy had his way, I was already heading to jail for being a spy. The truth could produce no worse verdict. I began at the beginning and I told them how Liu Long Tang had taken me into his house. I told how he had made me work from before dawn until well after dark. All the while I spoke, the policeman furiously scribbled notes in this little book. I told how Liu Long Tang fed me nearly nothing and watched my every move. He even timed my trips to the toilet and locked me inside the kitchen every night with no bed to sleep on and rats to fight off. I told him everything. Then I told how I had learned from his wife, Xu A-yi, that he was keeping me in his house illegally and how the whole village, although afraid of the reprisals of Liu Long Tang, had quietly risen up in support of me--had made a way for me to escape. I told how Jiang Shu-shu had made provision for me and had gone ahead to my home and saved my family treasures for me.

When I had finished my story I realized that the crowd was very quiet. Finally the snake-woman spoke again. "This Liu Long Tang is no servant of the people. He is a snake and deserves to slither in a basket for the rest of his life!" The man behind her spit on the ground, emphatically in agreement.

"Yes," said the police officer. "He is well known to the provincial police. In fact we have been waiting for many years for him to do something that is clearly illegal--and for someone who is not afraid to file charges against him." He looked at me with a hopeful smile. "What he has done to you is clearly illegal. He had no right to detain you in his house in forced labor. By law, he should have turned you over to the provincial authorities immediately. We could have searched for next-of-kin and all this while you could have had plenty to eat and continued your education while living in the children's social welfare institute."

"Is that what will happen to me now? Do I have to go there?" I bowed my head in hopeless fear.

"You don't want to eat three times a day, sleep in a bed and wear clean clothes?"

"I have been told it is a frightful place, that monsters and imbeciles live there."

"Well, there are certainly some children with physical and mental handicaps there--but I would hardly call them monsters." He smiled warmly. "There are mostly children just like you who, due to one unfortunate circumstance or another, have been forced to live without their parents. The People's Government becomes their parent. It is not as good as living with a family, but it is much better than sleeping on a hay bale behind a stack of poultry crates or on a stone floor waiting for the rats." He smiled warmly as if to punctuate his comment before continuing. "I know the director, Ling A-yi personally. She is a very nice woman. You will like her." He held out his hand to me and helped me stand up. I picked up my basket and carried it to the police car. He opened the door for me and I put the basket on the back seat.

"Zhong Mei Lin!" The snake woman was calling out to me over the heads of the people pushing in around me. I stepped up on the floor of the car, holding the roof with one hand and the open door with another and faced her, looking out over a bobbing sea of black-haired heads. "I will come visit you at the social welfare institute," she shouted. "Do not be afraid. You will be safe and well cared for."

I wanted to believe her but two tears escaped from my eyes before I could stop them. What kind of monsters waited for me at the social welfare institute? I would find out in a few minutes whether I wanted to or not! I brushed the tears away as I climbed into the back seat of the police car and sat next to the basket backpack that held the remnants of my life.

拾陸

Qiu Qiang A-yi

Our greatest glory is not in never falling,
But in rising every time we fall.

The ride to the orphanage was all too short. There was less traffic in the middle of the night--not quite the press of crowds one finds in daylight. Though, in a city the size of Baoshan City, I think there must always be someone moving on the streets I was not sure what time it was, but, I guessed that it was certainly well past midnight.

I was disappointed that there were no tufted silk pillows on the shelf below the rear window of the police car, even though I don't think I would have lain my head on one if there had been. It took all of about one minute to sink in: I was in an automobile! Not a fine black car of a Hong Kong merchant to be sure, but a car just the same! I had never sat on such a soft seat before in my life. The ruts in the road seemed hardly noticeable. We bounced up and down but my bottom rested on a soft cushioned seat. The back of the seat wrapped around my shoulders in comfort, cradling me like a baby in a mother's arms. I rubbed my hands along the soft blue fabric of the upholstered seat. People on bicycles parted and made a way for us. Who would have thought less than a year ago that I would get to ride in such a fine machine—and so soon! I gulped back a wave of guilt for feeling so excited! "Oh Ye-ye," I whispered, "I would trade this moment in an instant to be able to pull you along in our hand cart again!"

The lights of the city swirled by. We passed a restaurant where an enormous, round, red paper lantern hung over each table. Below each lantern was a large lazy-Susan loaded with dishes of food. Women dressed in traditional Chinese silk dresses turned it. A lady dressed in a western style business suit reached out with chopsticks to choose some morsel of food to place on the plate in front of her. Gentlemen with closely trimmed hair, fine silk suits and colorful ties leaned back in their chairs and laughed, gesturing at each other that some tale they had just heard was too outrageous to be believed. From time to time, one or another of them brought a cigarette to his lips and then exhaled a puff of smoke that swirled around the lanterns before drifting slowly upwards into the draft of the ceiling fans.

They raised their glasses and toasted each other. "Gan bei!" I had a flash of memory of Ye-ye and Baba slamming their glasses to the table with these same words, toasting my brother's birth, but there was so much to see I soon lost the image though the deep sadness the memory had raised lingered like the smoke that hung around the diners' faces. I wanted to drink in the sounds, savor every flash of neon light. This is what it felt like to be a wealthy Hong Kong merchant. I decided I liked the feeling and sank back into the giddy comfort of the upholstered seat, still missing my family but determined to go on and make them proud.

We drove to a large building of smoothly polished, square, white stone. An enormous statue in the front courtyard depicted two children climbing up toward the sky. To one side of the building there was a play structure with slides and swings and climbing tubes. I had seen something similar only once at the children's park, but I had never played on one. It cost money to get in and money is something we seldom had until quite recently.

The policeman knocked on the door of the social welfare institute. Inside I could hear babies crying. The police man knocked again, only louder. After a long wait, a young woman came to the door. She was wearing a white coat that buttoned down the front and covered her clothing down to her knees. Her long hair was braided in two queues, just like mine. In the crook of her left arm she held a red-faced, squalling baby who was not more than a few days old. In her right hand, she held a baby bottle.

"I've got a new house guest for you," the policeman said.

"Well, bring her in." I could feel her eyes searching me up and down as we stepped into the dimly lit foyer. "She's a little old to have gotten lost, Officer Wang." She smiled wearily at the policeman. Then, she turned to me. "Do you have a name?" she shouted above the screaming baby.

"Zhong Mei Lin."

"Hum. That's unusual." She said with a tinge of bitterness in her voice. "Most of the older ones forget their names the moment they hit our doorsill. They remain loyal, protecting the name of parents who have abandoned them." She shifted the baby closer to her body and slipped the bottle into an eager mouth.

"She's an orphan," the policeman said dryly.

"They all are," she nodded over her shoulder toward the nursery within. "All these little nameless nobodies are orphans. None of them has parents willing to give them an identity. None of them has a father willing to use his connections to help them find a good job. They only have us a-yis."

"Her family was killed in a flood last spring. She has been through a lot since then."

"There are no other relatives?"

"All deceased."

"Lucky girl!" she sighed and shifted her gaze toward me.

"Lucky?" the policeman asked angrily. "How is having your whole family perish in your sight on the same night luck?"

"At least she has the memory of belonging to a family who loved her. Most of these children don't even have that much!"

"Ah," he said, considering her words.

"Ling A-yi is not working tonight, but once she arrives in the morning and hears of her, I am sure she will take personal care of her." The baby sucked eagerly at the bottle nipple. "Of course, she loves all of them, but she is especially fond of the girls who come to us older. She herself was orphaned when she was nine, you know."

"Yes, I, I did know that." It may have been the poor lighting in the orphanage entryway, but I thought I saw a slight rise of color in the policeman's cheeks as he said this.

"Well, there is work to be done. We can't stand here all night." The baby gasped for air, sighed and went back to eagerly sucking on the bottle. "I am sure you have criminals to catch or something." She smiled and continued. "Zhong Mei Lin and I have a bed to make."

The policeman turned, stepped out of the door and was swallowed up in the darkness.

"My name is Tai Qiu Qiang but the kids usually call me Qiu Qiang A-yi—Auntie--Qiu Qiang. A-yi at least pretends a little respect, but I let the kids call me Qiu Qiang. Tai A-yi seemed too formal for me. Besides, Tai is the home town name of our previous director. He named all of us after his village for several years. It's not a real family name and I'd much rather just forget him, anyway!"

Up until then I had been respectfully looking at the floor. But when she said her name, it struck me as so unusual that it startled me and I looked up. I wanted to ask, "Why do you have a boy's name?" but I thought better of it. It was not respectful to ask such questions of adults. I had enjoyed great freedom to ask questions and discuss things with my parents and my grandparents—far more than most Chinese children. I knew this, so, I said nothing and looked back at the gray speckled linoleum floor.

"Go ahead, say it!" she said. "The question will burn a hole through you until you ask it."

"I am sorry. I was rude to think it."

"It is okay, we are all sisters here."

"You are an orphan?"

"Dui—correct. I lived here for sixteen years. Now I work here." She cocked her head sideways at me for added emphasis, "Employment opportunities for orphaned girls are limited." I paused a moment to consider the implications of this information.

"Your name . . ." I began.

"Is a boy's name?" she finished my question.

"Dui."

"And you wonder how it is that an a-yi came to have a boy's name?" She was really good at this, though I supposed that with a name like that she must have answered such questions more than once before.

"Dui."

"Well, I will tell you. I was born in the season of Qiu while dead leaves lie on the ground. My parents abandoned me at seven days of age at the base of the city TV tower. They wrapped me in a blanket and lay me in a small nest of leaves in the corner of the pedestrian walkway. Dry leaves blew around me and covered me. It began to rain and few people were out walking in such cold, damp weather. I have been told I would not have been discovered had I not cried quite loudly and insistently—as loudly and as insistently as a boy would! I was nearly frozen by the time I was found, soaking wet and nearly hoarse from crying so long—yet, I had persisted in shouting so loudly that anyone passing by could not fail to notice me.

Finally someone did pass by on that cold autumn night and they did pick me up and bring me to this place where I was not expected to live. For several days they were sure I would die. The a-yis were surprised each time they came to feed me to find that I was still among the living. I was stronger than they thought. I was as qiang as any boy! So, when they realized that I would live, they named me. They called me Qiu Qiang--Autumn Strong. It's a boy's name but I earned it."

It occurred to me as she spoke that the orphanage staff had named her. Surely her parents had given her a name? Who had she been for seven days before she was Qiu Qiang? Were orphans expected to sever all ties with the past? I could barely choke out my next question.

"Will I be given a new name?" I asked in sudden panic. My family had not abandoned me. I didn't want to abandon them. In that instant, I resolved in my own mind that I would run away if they gave me a new name!

"No, you know your name. You have no reason to hide it. We only give names to children who have no names."

"Ah," I said, "Xie-xie."

"You will like it here. Most of the girls are pretty nice and Ling A-yi is wonderful. She works very hard to make this a model orphanage. She expects a lot of her girls, but in return, she gives a lot." I stumbled along behind her, only half hearing as she chattered on and on. The building was so large. It seemed to go on forever and ever, hallways turning this way and that; stairways and doors leading who knows where? And all of it was dark.

"A-yi?" I interrupted her.

"Umm?"

"Where do you keep the monsters?"

"Monsters?"

"Jiang Shu-shu did not want me to go to a social welfare Institute. He said there were monsters here."

"Monsters . . ." she muttered in disgust. "Is that what they say?" She paused a moment to control her anger. "There are no monsters here, only monstrous things that have been done to children!"

She felt down the wall for the next light switch and pushed the button. Dingy yellow light stretched down the next length of hallway.

"We had one little girl here who was set on fire by her father so that foreigners would pity her severe burns and her begging could earn him a tidy sum of money. The people's government intervened and took her away from him and brought her here to live in peace. The scar tissue on her face and neck kept tightening until she couldn't eat or breathe any more. She lived for several months but is dead now. Tell me, who is the monster: that hideously deformed little girl or her father?"

I had no answer. I think the blood had drained from my head. I felt dizzy and sick to my stomach. How could a father cause harm to his own child? I was certain beyond doubt that my own Baba would have died to save me just as he had died trying to save my Mama and Di-di and just as his father had died trying to save him. Until this moment, I had thought this was the way all fathers behaved toward their children.

She led the way down a hallway, up two flights of stairs and down another long hallway. At each turn she felt along the wall for a pair of small black buttons. When she pushed the upper one, light flooded the next stretch of hall or stairway.

"I think there is one empty bed in here." She motioned to a closed door. I opened it and stepped inside. Light from the hall spilled in. I could see two rows of ten beds. As my eyes adjusted to the dim light, I could tell that the left bed by the door was indeed empty. A thin, striped mattress was rolled up at the head of the metal box spring. Qiu Qiang A-yi led me to a closet behind the door. In a loud whisper she said, "On the top shelf you will find a pillow. Sheets and blankets are in there as well. You will have to feel around for what you need. Make up a bed as best you can without waking the other girls." As I felt around for the sheets and pillow, she kept talking. "In the morning we will figure out what else you may need." I made the bed with sheets I had found and a blanket that she pulled out of the closet. "We will also take that and keep any valuables for you." She motioned toward the basket on my back. "It is sad to say, but sometimes, special things can disappear--even among sisters. But we can go through all that in the morning as well. The toilet is down the hall, just a little further, on the left side. The bathroom is across the hall from the toilet room if you want to wash up a bit before you go to bed."

"Inside? Not only the bath, but the toilet is inside as well?" I had never seen such a thing.

"Yes, inside. You are in the city now!" she smiled. "There is a closet in the bathroom that has some pajamas in it. Find some that fit and change into them. In the morning, Ling A-yi will show you how to take a bath and let you know when your regular bath times will be. She will also explain the chore chart and the reward system. You will not go to school tomorrow because you will have so much to do to get settled in here. However, beginning on the next day, you will be enrolled in the public school and expected to keep up with regular school work as well as household chores. You are lucky to be in this social welfare institute. Ling A-yi insists that all of us must go to school and she has donors who guarantee our school fees. It wasn't like this when the former Director Tai was here. Only a few very exceptional students went to school then. I was not one of them."

She shifted the now sleeping baby to her shoulder and began patting her back. "You look so tired. You are not going to remember a word I have said by morning, are you?" She smiled at me.

"I will try to remember."

"Don't worry, if you don't, I'll repeat it--and the other girls will help you, too."

"Xie-xie."

"Now, get yourself to bed. As you can hear, I have more crying babies to attend to." She turned and started to walk away down the hall. Suddenly, she stopped and whirled around, her two long braids whipping around behind her. "Mei Lin?"

"Shi."

"Welcome home," she smiled brightly. I smiled back.

I couldn't wait to see the indoor toilet and the bath! I dared not put my basket down for fear I would never see it again. So, still wearing it on my back, I hurried down the hall. I opened the door and felt along the wall inside the door for the light switch as Qiu Qiang A-yi had done. Instantly the room was as bright as midday! The toilet was like nothing I had ever seen before. Instead of the concrete trench I had always used in the village or the outhouse we had at our farm, there was a gleaming white bowl submerged in a green ceramic tile platform that ran the length of the room. The whole room was made of green ceramic tile: the floor, the walls, everything! It was so shiny and clean! It was like a palace! There were even partitions between the toilets made of green ceramic tile! On the left side of each partition hung a small roll of white paper. Toilet paper! I had only heard about this once before from Uncle Charlie, but I had thought it was one of his silly stories. "Rich people (and all Americans)" he had told me, "use soft paper made just for the purpose of cleaning one's bottom, not old newspapers!"

On either side of the bowl were white ceramic pads in the shape of a footprint. I carefully took the basket off my back and set it down on the floor inside the door. I pulled down my uniform trousers and put my feet on the pads, straddling the bowl. Then I squatted in the usual fashion and relieved my very full bladder and the contents of my bowels as well. I used a few squares of the white paper to clean myself and threw the paper in the wastebasket. It was only then that I wondered where the water bucket to rinse the toilet would be. I couldn't find a water bucket and began to wonder if I was in the wrong room. Perhaps I had made a terrible mistake. Maybe this was not a toilet room. Maybe these bowls were used for something else--like cooking baby food and I had ruined one of them, dirtied it so shamefully!

It was then that I noticed the little silver lever on the wall behind each white bowl. I pulled up my trousers, walked over to the wall and then pulled down the lever. With a loud whoosh, water rushed into the bowl and swirled around. I jumped back in fright. A hole opened in the bottom of the bowl and the waste disappeared into it.

"Ai-ya!" I gasped and jumped backward even further. I was afraid I had done something wrong. Someone would find out and I would be in trouble. Quickly, I picked up my basket, clutching it to my chest rather than take the time to put in on my back, and hurried across the hall to the bathroom.

Three very large gleaming white porcelain tubs lined the far wall. They were at least twice as big as any tub I had ever seen. A child could actually lie down in one of these! The round metal tub I was used to, one could sit in, with knees scrunched to chin, while Mama scrubbed one's back and shampooed hair. Perhaps these tubs were so big because several children were bathed at once, I reasoned.

The walls and the floor here were also made of green tile just like the toilet room had been. To the right was a shelf stacked high with towels, as well as several bars of soap and bottles of shampoo. In the far left corner, six silver spigots stuck out from the wall above my head. Although they were large and cone shaped, I knew they were spigots because water dripped from one of them, and an angry yellow stain marked the spot in the tile grout where the drip landed. On the wall below each spigot was a pair of water faucets.

I put my basket down and walked toward the wall. I turned first one spigot, then the other. At first nothing happened, then with a rattle and a bang that rose from three floors below me, twenty streams of water shot out of the silver cone spigot above my head! In an instant, I was soaking wet—but warm. "Ah!" I gasped again in wonder. The water coming from the cones was warm! I stepped forward again, into the stream of water. "What a wonderful place!" I thought as I allowed the water to pour over my face and soak into my clothes. I loosened my braids and shook the loose hair against my back. I used some shampoo from the shelf and lathered up my hair. I stripped off the wet clothes and let the warm water run over my shoulders and down my back. I felt the dirt of the road and the grime of the market soaking out of my skin. I am not sure how long I stood there with water streaming over my body. I had never felt anything so wonderful. I wanted to stand there all night, until all remembrance of Liu Long Tang had been washed away and disappeared in the drain, but I suddenly realized that I was probably not supposed to be here—at least not at this hour. I grabbed a towel from the shelf and dried myself off.

I opened the cupboard door and found the pajamas. They were all different, a hodgepodge of colors and sizes. Nothing seemed to match. I found a top of neon green and hot pink with a basket of flowers embroidered on the left side. Then I found a pair of orange pajama pants and slipped them on. I wished I had some underwear.

I used a bar of soap, washed out my school uniform in the bathtub and wrung it out. I wasn't sure where I was supposed to hang it to dry so I took it with me and hung it over the foot of my bed.

Then, just before climbing into bed, I took Mama's quilt out of the basket and put it on my bed. I felt around the inside of my basket and found Mama and Baba's framed wedding picture and Nai-nai's red wedding veil. In pale blue moon light, I lay in the bed, snuggled under Mama's quilt and stared at the picture, thinking. I am a lucky girl. I had had a Mama and a Baba, a Ye-ye and a Nai-nai and a Di-di who all loved me. I still loved each of them. "You are still my Mama and my Baba," I whispered to the picture as tears escaped my eyes. I am not a nobody with a made-up name, but a daughter: a daughter of a thousand pieces of gold. I wrapped the picture in Nai-nai's bridal silk and tucked it under my pillow. Cupping my hand around the photo, I quickly fell asleep, dreaming not of monsters but of laughter and my family. I was home again.

Sisters and Brothers

The gem cannot be polished without friction,
Nor the person perfected without trials.

"Look! There's somebody in the empty bed!" I heard a tiny voice exclaim as I felt myself drifting in a deep fog of sleep. A cool breeze blew through the room as someone opened the door beside my bed.

"Well, if there is somebody in it, it's not empty anymore, is it, Mi-mi?" said a tall girl as she stepped into the hall. "You two are going to be late for breakfast, *again*," she warned and closed the door.

"Don't call me that baby name, Hua!" shouted the little one as she threw something, a shoe perhaps, at the now closed door.

"It's not a baby name, Tong Mi," said another girl sitting in the bed closest to me. "It is just a nick-name."

"It's a baby name when *she* calls me it! It's a nick-name when *you* use it."

"Hua just likes to tease you. Ignore her." I could hear her getting out of the bed and walking toward the little one.

"When did the new girl come?" Her little voice was coming from a higher place now and I guessed that the bigger girl had picked the little one up.

"She's been there half the night, Mi-mi. Didn't you hear her come in with Qiu Qiang A-yi?"

"No, I didn't! Why do I always miss everything fun?" Why didn't you wake me? You know how I hate to miss anything!"

"You think I should get out of bed, walk to the other end of the room, explode a firecracker over your head—because we all know you could sleep through a Chinese New Year parade . . .

"Don't tease me, I was tired that night."

"My point exactly! Anyone who could sleep through firecrackers and the drums of a lion dance could sleep through *anything*! What was I supposed to do?" There was a sound like something dropping and bouncing on a bed across the room and the little girl was giggling. "Don't! You're squishing me and I can't breathe if you sit on me."

"You can breathe, you faker! What did you want? Did you want me to jump on you like this--and shake you like this--shouting, 'Kuai Qi Chuang! (Quickly get up)'" the bed springs were squeaking as if someone was bouncing up and down on the mattress, "all with A-yi standing right there, not one meter from my bed?"

"You could have tried, Wu Dan. It was dark. You might have succeeded."

"And I might not!" The older girl jumped off the bed and landed on the floor with a thump. "No thank you. I didn't want to be peeling vegetables for a week just so you could be in on the excitement."

"Okay, okay! So who is she? Where did she come from?"

"Tong Mi, you are a very curious little girl! Here's a clean pair of pants that look about your size. Take off your pajama pants and put these on."

"What's curious?"

"It's what you are: always wanting to know everything! Here is a shirt."

"Is that bad?"

"Not really, but it sure wears on my patience! Now put on your sweater."

"I don't want a sweater, Wu Dan. I'm not cold. Who is that girl? I think she looks as big as you. Do you think you will be friends with her?"

"Ai-ya! You do not give up, do you?"

"I want to know."

"Put your shoes on. A-yi called her Mei Lin. I think it must be her real name. I don't think they made up a good name like that in the middle of the night. I do not know if she has a family name."

"Why don't I have a family name?"

"First, to have a family name, you have to have a family, Mi-Mi. *You* do not have a family. *I* do not have a family. I am *Wu*, because I was found in the *fifth* month and *Dan* because I was *all alone*. It is not a beautiful name like Mei Lin. A girl with a beautiful name had somebody who loves her."

"You love me."

"I love you but we're not family. A girl with a family name has a family."

"I thought you were my family! You are my Jie-jie!"

168

"Not really, Mei-mei. We live *like* sisters but we have different mothers and fathers. I call you Mei-mei but you are not really my little sister. You call me Jie-jie, but you don't really have a big sister —not really.

"We have Auntie's. They are like Mama's, aren't they?"

"I don't think so. A Mama doesn't go away at the end of her shift. I think they might be different in other ways, too. I don't know. I never had a Mama. You ask too many questions."

I stretched and opened my eyes. Dark blue curtains had been pulled back from the windows at the far end of the room and light streamed in. The windows were open, but white ironwork bars were locked over the openings. The walls were white and the floor was made of large white stone tiles. It was very bright. The beds were all made of iron. Some were gray and some were brown like mine.

"Look! She's awake!" The little one was not more than four years old. In an instant she stood beside my bed, peering at my face. "Who are you? Did you really come in the middle of the night? That's a pretty blanket. I wish I had a pretty blanket."

"Mei-mei, hush. Give her a chance." Her short bobbed hair bounced as she talked. "She just woke up." Then the older girl turned to me. "She is just excited to have a new girl in our room. I am Wu Dan. She is Tong Mi. The others have already gone down for breakfast. We are late *again* because she is so pokey!"

"Ni-hao." I smiled and rubbed my eyes, "I am Zhong Mei Lin."

"You were right, Jie-jie! She does have a proper family name!"

"Pay no attention to her." Wu Dan rolled her eyes in pretend disgust at the little girl. "If you hurry and get dressed. You can go to breakfast with us." Wu Dan folded her sheet and blanket and placed them in the net hanging above her bed. Then she rolled up her mattress and placed her pillow on top of the roll. She quickly placed a small cloth bag into the rolled up mattress. I knew it was something she thought she was hiding, so I didn't ask although I made a mental note to find out what it was sometime soon.

My powder blue school uniform pants were still wet, hanging on the end of my bedpost. "I have no dry clothes," I said.

"The clean clothes are in a basket over there." Wu Dan pointed to the basket in the middle of the floor as she hurried to help Tong Mi roll up her mattress. "There isn't much choice. Everybody has already taken the good things, but maybe you will find something that will fit."

I looked through the things. Most of the clothes were for children much younger than I. The only things I could find to fit were a pair of boys underpants, boys brown sweat pants and a matching sweatshirt with an appliqué of a mean-looking bull-dog on the front. This was actually a little big for me but it was a better choice than wearing nothing.

"Oh no! You're in trouble! Da ge-ge gets mad if anybody else wears those clothes," giggled Tong Mi.

"Da ge-ge?"

"His name is really Hui Na-Te but we all call him "eldest brother" because he is the eldest of the boys still living here. He Li-Ke was older, but he left last month and joined the army. So, now, Hui Na-Te is Da ge-ge. Don't worry about it," said Wu Dan. "He probably won't bother you on the first day." She snapped the quilt from my bed and quickly folded it.

"No!" I shouted. "I'll do it myself!" But it was too late. She turned over my pillow and found the framed picture wrapped in red silk.

"What's this?" She unwrapped the picture and looked at it.

170

"It's mine!" I shouted a little too loudly as I snatched it from her. In this new place, I felt fiercely protective of the pieces of my former life and my own identity. I didn't want to become just one of many like so many indistinguishable iron beds lining the walls. "Sometimes people have *personal* things!" I shot her a glance that said I knew about her personal stash.

"What is it? What is it?" chimed in Tong Mi.

"You don't have to grab!" scolded Wu Dan. "I only wanted to help. I didn't hurt it. I was just looking at it."

"I'm sorry," I said, cautiously handing it back to her. "It is a picture of my Mama and Baba on their wedding day."

"Your mama is very beautiful," said Wu-Dan. "You look a lot like her."

"Xie-xie," I said choking on the words.

"Let me see! Let me see!" begged Tong Mi "You have a Mama? I wish I had a Mama. What's a Mama like, Mei Lin?"

"A Mama," I felt the word sticking in my throat. I missed my Mama but I also felt sad that this *little sister* would never really know what a Mama is. Wu Dan took a broom from the closet and began sweeping the floor around her bed while I talked. "A Mama is a most special person. She gives you life and then she takes care of you. She sings lullabies when you are sleepy and holds your hand in scary places like the market, where a little girl could get lost."

"I'm a BIG girl!" She crossed her arms across her chest and stamped her foot.

I smiled and continued talking as I braided my hair into two long queues, "A Mama cooks your food and feeds you. She holds you in her arms and rocks you when you are sick. She combs your hair and tells you how happy her big girl makes her. Sometimes she scolds you but that is okay because a Mama always loves you even when you are naughty."

171

"I wish I had a Mama."

"I do too," I could barely whisper the words.

"Well, it will never happen, Mei-mei," said Wu Dan with authority. She handed the broom to Tong Mi. "Only babies get Mamas. You are four now. Mama's don't want girls who are four."

"Maybe," Tong Mi replied defiantly "Maybe somewhere there is a Mama who is waiting for a girl who is four!" She stuck her lower lip out in a pout and then began angrily sweeping the area under and around her bed.

We finished folding my bedding as Tong Mi swept around my bed. I put all my things back in my basket backpack—except my wet uniform pants. I was afraid to leave my basket. I didn't want to leave my things out of sight, so I hoisted it all on my back and headed down the stairs to breakfast.

Tong Mi chattered on, "Mei Lin. What is a Baba like? Did you have a Baba too? Is a Baba like a Mama only different? Where is your Mama and your Baba now?" Wu Dan and I rolled our eyes at each other and giggled. I knew we would become good friends.

At the foot of the stairs, we saw a policeman at the door talking to a woman with streaks of gray in her short, bobbed hair. "That's Ling A-yi," whispered Tong Mi. "She's my Mama."

"Not a Mama!" hissed Wu Dan. "She is very nice. She takes good care of us, but she is *not* a Mama. I think it is different."

I smiled at Wu Dan. "You are right." I couldn't explain it either, but there was something special about a Mama that amounted to more that all the tasks I had listed a few minutes earlier —a difference I couldn't describe but my heart knew anyway. We stopped to listen.

"How can I take in another baby?" the woman pleaded. "This is the third new child in two days. We already have two babies to every crib!"

"Well, now you will have three." The policeman said in fake cheerfulness. "Surely you don't expect us to keep her at the police station?"

"No, I know you can't. I just don't know how we will manage with so many. We had only six adoptions last month and twelve new babies joined us. Of course, there are fourteen scheduled to leave today. But that will only free us up to a little over twice our official capacity." She took the baby from the policeman and held her against her shoulder.

I gasped when I looked at her little face. She was the same size as Di-di when he had died. She was a fat, happy baby, laughing at us and gurgling. She had the same little rosebud kind of mouth he had. She was dressed in a hand knitted sweater and leggings with a matching cap. It was obvious that someone had loved this baby.

"She has a Mama!" whispered Tong Mi. "Did her Mama get lost in the market?"

"This one comes with a note," continued the policeman speaking to Ling A-yi, "so you won't have to work too hard making up a birth-date and a name."

"Jin Ying--little treasure" she read aloud. "Thanks, but naming them is not the hardest part of taking a new one. Feeding them, keeping them healthy, these are much harder."

"I am sure, but a name is a place to start."

"Come on," said Wu Dan impatiently. "Breakfast will be completely gone by the time we get there!" She grabbed both of our hands and nearly dragged Tong Mi and me down the hall.

Life by the Rules

Better to light a candle
Than to curse the darkness.

Ling A-yi called me into her office after breakfast, introduced herself and asked about my family. She sighed and patted my hand. "I know how you feel, dear. My own parents died when I was a little younger than you. Believe it or not, life will get better."

"It already is," I said brightly, but kept my eyes respectfully downcast.

"Yes, I had an interesting phone-call early this morning from the office of the provincial courts. I have heard all about the troubles you have had. That Liu Long Tang makes me sick. To think that he has gotten away with so much for so long! But that is not what I am talking about. I am talking about missing your Mama and Baba and the hole you feel in your heart right now . . ."

How did she know about that hole? I pondered the white tile floor but said nothing.

"What I want you to know," she continued as she placed a hand on my shoulder, "is that you will be happy again one day. I am."

She paused a moment and continued. "Tomorrow, you will go to school. "Hua and Wu Dan are close to your age and in your dormitory unit. They will show you the way. We will write a letter to your former teacher and request your school records so you will not lose your place."

"Ma Laoshe is the one to contact." Ling A-yi wrote his name down.

"Kang Yi-sheng will look you over this afternoon to be sure you are healthy."

"I am not hurt! I don't need a doctor." The only doctor I had ever seen was the one who had helped Grandfather when he could not walk. I didn't know what use a healthy person could have for a doctor.

"Don't worry. We hope you're not sick, but it's impossible to tell unless a doctor checks you over. It's just precautionary. Just do what she says She may give you some inoculations to keep you free from certain diseases. It may hurt a little bit, but you will be brave, I am sure."

"Wo Shi!"

"For today, you can just look around, find out where everything is. I will have one of the girls show you around after school to introduce you to Tang A-yi, our cook and Feng A-yi, our laundress and the rest of the Aunties."

"Xie-xie."

"You will be expected to roll up your bedding each morning and sweep the floor by your bed. Let's see," she consulted a chart on her desk. Your bath time will be every Wednesday and Saturday night at 6:20 p.m. You will only have ten minutes, so be prompt. If you miss your time, you miss your bath. When the weather is warm enough, you will be expected to take at least one bath or shower each week including washing your hair. If you do not, you will get points deducted from your reward chart. The Aunties will let you know when it is too cold to take a bath. At the end of each month, children who have done their chores and not lost any points will get a treat. Sometimes it is a piece of candy or fresh fruit. Sometimes it is a walk to the city park or other outing. You are expected to help the younger ones in your dormitory unit whenever possible."

My head was spinning. There seemed to be so much to remember. But, she kept going on! "Dirty clothes go in the basket by the door each night. As you already know, clean clothes will be in a basket in the middle of each dormitory room by morning." She paused a moment, scrutinizing my outfit, and then asked, "Have you met Hui Na-Te yet?"

"No, I haven't met him."

"You will." She smiled and arched her eyebrows, staring at the angry bulldog on my chest. "Let me know if he gives you any trouble. He thinks he has a personal laundry service because he has intimidated the others into not wearing the clothes he thinks of as his own. It is perfectly acceptable to claim a few items as one's own, but one is expected to care for these, oneself. Anything Feng A-yi washes is community property for any child to wear. If you have personal clothing items you wish to keep for yourself you may wash them out each Sunday. Feng A-yi will show you where to hang them to dry."

"My school uniform was dirty. I rinsed it out last night and it is hanging on my bedpost."

"Take it to her. She will show you how we do things here." She paused a moment and then interjected, "Students from this social welfare institute do not wear school uniforms. Our clothing is all donated. We are lucky to have clean clothes for each child. Sometimes, just finding something that fits for each one is a challenge. We cannot afford to also buy the local school uniform for each student."

"I understand. Where do I keep personal dirty clothes until Sunday?"

"There is a basket under each bed for personal items. Unless it is something wet, which will grow mold on it, you can keep dirty laundry in a bag inside that basket. If there is not a basket and laundry bag under your bed let Feng A-yi know. She will give you one. Wet things should be laundered immediately after you return from school each day."

"I will speak to Feng A-yi."

"Hao. In addition, we consider that everyone is a contributing member of this small society. You will be expected to find a way to make your contribution to the common good each afternoon after school and for half a day on Saturday. At four o'clock each Sunday afternoon, I post a new chore chart. Each child chooses to help with laundry, cooking, baby care or floor scrubbing. The more desirable chores go first, so be sure to be on time to sign up if you have a preference. Sunday is also a study day and sometimes we have visitors. Any questions?"

I had about a hundred, but I answered, "No questions."

"Hao. Shall we do this now?" She took my basket and placed it between her feet. She examined each item with me. "These valuable things will be safer if I keep them for you. This way they will not get lost or broken." She made a list, describing each of the items and then signed the bottom of the page. She asked me to check the list and then sign as well.

"What does this mean? Do you keep these things to pay for my food?"

"No," she laughed. "These things will be returned to you when you are old enough to leave the Baoshan City Social Welfare Institute. Until then, I will keep them somewhere safe."

"Where?"

"I suppose I could make room right here," she stood and opened the closet behind her desk with a key she wore on a chain around her neck. "Your basket will fit if I lower this top shelf. This closet is always locked. I personally keep the only key."

"What if something happens to you?" I continued to look respectfully at the ground.

"My, you think of everything!"

I peeked up at her and saw that she was smiling at me. Embarrassed to have been caught, I quickly looked down again. She said, "I see that you are a girl who knows her own mind."

"Xie-xie." I said though I wasn't sure if she meant it as a correction or a compliment. Either way, Thanks were the appropriate response. Thanks for a compliment would require a show of embarrassment. Thanks for the opportunity to receive correction and redirection was more normal and required no emotional response, only a determination to do better.

"To answer your question, this is why we have this paper, listing all the things that belong to you. Let us make a second copy so that you can keep one as well."

"May I keep some things with me?"

"Yes, but you do understand that you run a risk of losing or breaking these things."

"I want to keep my mama's quilt on my bed and the picture of my Mama and Baba."

"Is that all?"

"No, I also want my school books, the top of my school uniform and the letters from my friends. And this, belonged to my grandmother." I pulled the red string and removed the jade Buddha from beneath the sweatshirt. "I have never taken it off since the day she died."

"You may keep it if you are not afraid to lose it *and* if you keep it under your shirt. I don't want the others to become jealous. None of them has anything like that."

"I understand. Sometimes I may need to get something out of there." I pointed to the basket.

"You can look at your things anytime I am here. If you take something or put something back, bring your list and we will write notations so we know which of us is responsible for which things. Is that good?"

"Hen hao, very good."

"Now, I believe you have a visitor."

"A visitor?" I turned around as Ling A-yi opened the door. A beautiful woman in a western style business suit walked in. She had pearl buttons down the front of a beige silk blouse, wore black high-heeled shoes and carried a black leather briefcase. When she turned to set the briefcase down beside a chair, I saw that her hair was elegantly twisted up the back of her head and held in place by a carved wooden comb decorated with cranes flying over a waterfall and cherry blossoms. She held her hand out to me but I kept my hand at my side. "Zhong Mei Lin, you look well this morning. Did you eat yet?" She asked as she sat down.

"Yes, yes, I ate." My mind was racing. I was trying to figure out who this woman was. How did she know my name? I could not place her but she did look familiar. I must have looked puzzled for she laughed.

"You don't know who I am, do you? Perhaps if I wore my hair down in long queues I would look more recognizable? I am sure you would know who I am if I was riding a bicycle with a basket of snakes on the back!"

"Ai-ya!" That's who she was: the snake woman! She did not at all resemble the peasant woman I had seen on the bicycle last night.

"I have other things to attend to," said Ling A-yi. "I will leave you two to get acquainted. If you need something, you can push that button and a bell will ring. I will come." She went out and closed the door.

"Here, I thought you might need these." The woman handed me a bag with my underwear and discarded trousers in it. They had been cleaned and dried. The underwear was bright white and smelled like flowers. The trousers were blue and also smelled quite nice. The stains were gone. "I have a small clothes washing machine and electric dryer in my apartment. I threw them in with my own washing last night."

I thought, "They have machines that can do this? —and so quickly!" But, aloud, I only said, "Xie-xie!" and nodded my thanks to her.

"Oh, and I believe this belonged to your grandfather. He loaned it to me once. I'm sorry I couldn't return it to him in person while he was alive." She handed me a freshly laundered and stiffly ironed, man's, white handkerchief. I looked at her in disbelief. I had met this woman more than once before! She was the same woman who had given us directions when Ye-ye and I had been lost in the market.

"Sit, Sit!" she urged me. "We have not been properly introduced. I am Han Yue Mei. Yesterday I took a day off from work. I had been cleaning all day and was in the market last night picking up some snakes my father had ordered for a banquet he is having tonight to celebrate my younger brother's graduation from university: dragon soup, you know."

"I had no idea," I said as I slid slowly into the chair next to her.

"I am, actually, a provincial court official and am quite interested in your experience. Last night, after you left, I delivered the snakes to my father's house and then went straight away to the local police precinct."

"You did?"

"When the police officer returned, I spoke with him at length about this Liu Long Tang. It seems that provincial officials and the police have been watching him for quite a few years but have not been able to find anyone willing to come forward and make a formal complaint against him. The only one was a Zhong Chou about three years ago."

"That is my grandfather!"

"He accused Liu of corrupt government, embezzling funds intended for the people's collective and imposing higher quotas on the farmers than is allowed by law. Unfortunately, Liu must have been tipped off about the investigation, because there was no evidence to convict him. Papers and ledgers had mysteriously disappeared. Witnesses would not speak against him. No one was willing to come forward and substantiate your grandfather's claims. Liu Long Tang discredited him as a senile old man and no one but your father came forward to refute this claim. Your father was dismissed because his only testimony was one of support of your grandfather. He is on record as having said, 'If my father says it is so, then it is.' This is a very loyal statement, but hardly what we would admit as evidence in legal proceedings of this gravity. So, with no solid evidence and nothing to go on but the hearsay of this one, courageous old man, the case was put aside—until now."

"Why now?"

"Mei Lin, You can help us finish what your grandfather started three years ago. Your testimony last night was very condemning. But, we need solid evidence. We don't want to arouse his suspicions by conducting a formal investigation. We're afraid he'll destroy evidence or intimidate witnesses again. You have lived in his house. You know his habits. If I know whom to see, I can slip into the village and collect the evidence we need, posing as a simple farm girl. I need to collect the evidence and call in the police in one swift movement. What I need to know from you is who else will support your testimony? Who would have evidence we need."

"The whole village! The last time he raised the quotas, he made *everyone* angry. It is more than they can bear. Ye-ye said he has become like the worst of old-time landlords, growing rich while the people get poorer. There are rumors that he has a fat bank account in Hong Kong. Everyone wants to get rid of him but they are afraid to oppose him! He has many powerful friends in Beijing."

"He is not nearly as powerful as he thinks--or the people fear. Many of his old friends have died or been sent to jail for crimes similar to those we suspect him guilty of. If you could give me some key names, we could quietly investigate without raising too much suspicion in the village. Do you know who could help us? And, just as important, do you know whom I should avoid?"

I gave her several names beginning with Jiang Shu-shu as well as directions to their homes and places of business. I told her what I knew about what he had done to each of them. I told her about Xu A-yi's baby girl that he had drowned with his own hands. I told her about the trouble Teacher Ma had teaching only subjects Liu Long Tang approved of. I told her what Baba had said: that Liu Long Tang spoke one way to the officials he reported to in Beijing pretending to be a loyal party member and a caring leader, but that he acted a completely other way in our village, holding to ancient traditions and repressive ideologies. I told her Liu Long Tang's habits and when he was likely to be away from his house and how to avoid him until she had her evidence.

When I was done, she smiled. "With your help, we will finally cook this snake!"

"Xie-xie," I said and smiled at her.

She returned my smile. I looked respectfully at the ground, but I sensed she was waiting for me to do something. I looked up and she was still smiling at me and holding out her right hand so I extended my right arm toward her and shook her hand in the Western fashion.

"I'll let you know how we progress." She said. "Here is my business card. If you need *anything*, please call me. You have been a great help."

I walked with her to the front door of the building. She opened the door to leave just as a bus pulled through the courtyard gates. A brisk young woman in a gray business suit hopped off the bus. She was carrying a briefcase and a clipboard. An older man followed her talking into one of those fold-up light machines. "Yes, we are here now. I don't think the notaries have arrived yet. I don't see their car. I will talk to you after we have the babies."

One after another white-faced foreigners filed off the bus. They were very tall with noses that stuck out from their faces. They were noisy and laughing. They carried bags of diapers, baby bottles and baby clothes but no babies. One couple had two other children, girls about six and eight years old. Both girls looked Chinese! Another couple had one child. This boy had yellow hair. I had never seen a child with yellow hair and I couldn't stop staring at him. I was so distracted that I didn't notice in which direction Han Yue Mei had left. When I thought of her again, she was already gone.

Some of the foreigners took pictures of the fountain in the front of the building. One took a picture of me standing in the doorway. The businesswoman made some announcements and they quieted down. Then, they gathered their things and filed one by one into the building. I stepped aside and let them pass. I was struck by the fact that they smelled peculiar: more like flowers than like people. Together, their scent, their whiteness, their sheer size, and their ugly, protruding noses, presented an overwhelming presence of strangeness.

Ling A-yi came out of her office and greeted the woman in charge. She bowed her head toward the foreigners and motioned for them to follow her to a large room across the hall. Some of them sat around a big wooden table. Others milled around the room looking out windows or at the pictures of babies that covered the walls. Tang A-yi brought in a large service tray with lidded cups of brewed green tea, which she set on the table. Ling A-yi motioned for the foreigners to take some. A few did. Most didn't.

Finally, two young women came running up the steps to the social welfare institute. They nearly flew into the conference room.

"Sorry, we are late," they said to Ling A-yi and the businesswoman and man and then shook hands in the western fashion with all of the foreigners. "There was a terrible accident on the road near the airport. We had to go the long way around but traffic was blocked in every direction."

"Well, we are all here now," said the man with the phone. The young women set up piles of papers and official document folders from the provincial government. They placed a ceramic bowl of red ink on the center of the table.

Two by two the foreigners sat at the table with the notaries. The notaries asked each of the foreign couples the same questions. "Why do you want to adopt a Chinese baby? Will you care for this baby as if it were your own? The foreigners signed papers and sealed everything with their thumbprints dipped in red ink.

When all the people had signed papers, the Aunties lined up outside the door and came in one by one carrying babies. They would call out a name, "Lu Fu Mei" and the businesswoman would look at her clipboard and call out the corresponding names of an American couple. "Kathy and Bill Ke. . ." This is about as far as she would get before the adopting mother would start crying and take the baby from the Auntie. Sometimes the fathers cried, too. Mostly, the men followed every movement of the baby from behind the lenses of a camera. After a while they would take a turn holding the baby. They seemed not to notice anything else in the room but that one baby.

All in all, I saw twelve babies, each under one year of age turned over to the Americans and two little girls, one about two and the other three-years-old. Some of the babies cried. The toddlers hid behind their auntie's white coats screaming in fear. All of the white-faced women cried black tears, which streaked their cheeks. The adoptive mothers of the toddlers squatted down holding out brightly colored toys and smiling at the little girls. Eventually, curiosity got the better of them and they each grabbed for the toy with a squeal of delight and allowed the foreigners to take them away from their Auntie. At this, the Auntie would leave the room and stand in the hall fighting back tears. Qiu Qiang A-yi was the last Auntie in line.

"Are these babies going to live in America, A-yi?"

"Yes, lucky babies!"

"Can I go to live in America?"

"You think you can just decide to go? You have to be chosen. And, Americans don't want girls as big as you. They want little babies!"

"I am a good worker."

"That doesn't matter. You are not cute and little. Americans want cute, little babies. Cute and little is lucky. Old and hard working is—just old and hard working." She smiled and hugged me. But, that means you and I will have a lot of time together and I won't have to worry about you leaving me until you are all grown up!"

Kids ran in the door from school just then for lunch break.

"Hey, girl!" a teenaged boy's voice bellowed the length of the hallway. He was at least three years older and half a meter taller than me. "Who said you could wear my clothes?" He was wearing a pair of green and yellow plaid leggings that were twenty centimeters too short for him. His hairy shins stuck out below the tight hems that threatened to stop the circulation in his legs. Above it he wore a pink sweatshirt with a heart and a misspelled English word, "Sweatheart" emblazoned through the middle of it.

"Very attractive." I said and giggled as I walked past him. "Was that the only thing you could find in the laundry basket this morning?" I could see color rising in his neck. "Someone should teach you . . . "

And something rose within me in that moment, too; something like my Baba and the way he liked to tease. And that something danced in the corners of my eyes and sprang like a cat at Hui Na Te.

"Manners?" I said teasing, "Of course, you are so right. We haven't been introduced, have we? Wo Jiao—I am called—Zhong Mei Lin. You must be Hui Na-Te."

"Dui."

"Look," I whispered and bent closer to him. "I don't want any trouble. I don't like this mean bulldog any more than you like that 'sweat heart.' This was the only thing in the laundry basket when I got up this morning and I would have been wearing pajamas all day if I hadn't put it on. What I really don't like are boy's underpants!" I yanked at the uncomfortably thick waistband.

"You got my underwear, too!"

"Well, it was better than nothing!" I winked at him, letting him know, that I knew, he probably had no underwear on—or too tight girl's underwear.

"Can we cut a deal?" he whispered, almost pleading.

"I'll think about it." I turned around quickly, my braids swinging behind me and thumping against my back.

I started walking back to my dormitory room to get my uniform pants so I could take them to Feng A-yi.

"How long?" he shouted after me.

"What?"

"How long do you think it will take for you to think about it?"

"Oh," I smiled. "I think I'll make a decision in time for you to go to school this afternoon. After lunch you will *probably* be able to at least *look* like a boy--if not," I snapped the underwear waistband again, "*feel* like a boy again."

I closed the dormitory door behind me, threw my things on my bedsprings and quickly changed into my own underwear and freshly laundered blue cotton pants. Oh, they smelled nice! I took off the mean bulldog and put on my powder blue uniform top with the black and white stripes down the sleeves and zipped it up to my chin. I folded the brown sweat suit and tucked the baggy boy's underpants inside one of the legs.

I didn't know anyone else was there until I heard a scratching sound coming from the floor on the other side of Wu Dan's bed. She was lying on the floor, writing on a scrap of paper.

"What are you doing? Aren't you going to eat lunch?"

"I will in a minute, but first I have to save a moment."

"What?"

"Promise you won't tell?"

"I promise."

"Someday," she got a far-away look in her eyes, "I will be a great writer. I am saving pieces of my life by writing them down. Clean paper is hard to find, though. I take it from the waste paper basket in Ling A-yi's office when I can find some." A look of shame crossed her face. "Sometimes she only uses one side of a page before she makes a mistake, crumples it up and throws the paper out. I smooth out the papers and use the blank side. Mostly I write between the lines of things she has written. Someday, these pieces of my life will become a book." She pulled out the cloth bag I had noticed earlier from under her mattress. It was stuffed with small scraps of wrinkled paper all crammed with tiny, tightly spaced words. Each sheet had a different topic heading on it. "Tong-Mi and me" was one. "Our new orphanage director" said another. She handed me the one she had been writing on. I read, "Mei Lin. A new girl arrived late last night. She has been assigned to the bed next to mine. Her name is Zhong Mei Lin and she seems very nice for a girl with a real name. I think, at long last, that I will soon have a close friend my own age."

"I think so, too," I smiled at her. "Let's go to lunch." She stuffed her papers back in the bag and then stuffed the bag into the rolled up mattress. I grabbed the brown sweat suit, clutched it to my chest and we linked elbows giggling as we ran down the hall. Na-Te was standing in line in the dining hall. He looked at me when I walked in. I held up a sleeve of the sweat suit and waved it at him. He stepped out of line and said, "Give that to me!" A fat Auntie looked across the room at him.

"Not so fast, *Da ge-ge*!" I whispered and leaned toward him.

"What do you want?" he hissed.

"First, I want you to be polite."

"Qing—Please?" he said with exaggerated politeness, "Ba yi fu gei wo--May I have my clothes?"

"Second, I want you to promise to do your own laundry from now on."

"Laundry is woman's work!"

"Well, you are partly right. Laundry is work."

"Those are *my* clothes."

"Not if you don't care for them."

"I ought to . . ."

"Do your own laundry from now on?" I held the arm of the sweat suit up and threw it over my shoulder. Then I rubbed my cheek against it is if it were a pet cat.

He sighed heavily, frustration and resignation rising in his breath. "I ought to," He hesitated as if the words caused him pain to speak before he blurted out, "I ought to do my own laundry from now on."

I handed him the sweat suit, turned toward Wu Dan and said, "Gosh, I'm hungry!" Then I turned back toward Na-Te and said, "Did you eat yet? Perhaps you would like to join us for a noodle or two?" I didn't wait for him to answer. I linked elbows with Wu Dan again and strolled casually toward the stack of bowls.

拾玖

Baby Love

If you enjoy what you do,
You'll never work another day in your life.

Every day, for that first week, I was assigned a different afternoon chore so that I could try them all. I quickly learned that I clearly despised peeling vegetables with Tang A-yi. Not only was it boring, but I also cut almost every one of my fingers on the sharp knives. Worst of all, Tang A-yi chattered endlessly. I needed all my powers of concentration to keep my thoughts on the closeness of my fingers to the blades of the knives. Because her constant chatter cut into my thoughts, it was very hard to think around her and therefore, tedious just to be with her. There was also no way to escape her as she sat on a stool not three meters away from me.

Laundry was somewhat better in that regard. Feng A-yi hardly ever said more than whatever words were barely necessary. The work however was much harder. Two hundred babies produce a LOT of dirty diapers! More than a thousand dirty diapers a day can produce a powerful stink the like of which I hope I never again experience. Second of all, in order to become clean, diapers must be boiled and stirred in a big pot. Then they are fished out with a pole, wrung out and laid one next to the other over hundreds of clothes lines zigzagging all over the courtyard! Then, the children's clothes were washed each day in similar fashion but in a different pot of washing water. Wet clothes are heavy!

Scrubbing floors was not too bad. Cao A-yi, the housekeeper was not too chatty and not too picky about how things were done. But, squatting on stone tile floors, scrubbing for two hours a day seemed to last an eternity! As soon as I had scrubbed one part of floor, someone would track dirt across my beautiful floor. The worst part is that this chore stayed with me long after I had completed it. My legs were so stiff I could barely walk to dinner and my back hurt for days afterward.

By far, the best job was taking care of babies. We dressed babies and changed their diapers. We fed them bottles of warm baby formula, burped than and tickled them. We carried them when they cried and put them in baby chairs so they could sit and play with their fingers. We played games with toddlers and wiped up baby spit. We changed wet sheets and sang silly baby songs. We lined up bigger babies on potty-chairs and whistled a signal to pee. Then we clapped when the babies produced the pee our whistles had called for.

The best part of taking care of babies was Qiu Qiang A-yi. She laughed a lot and I found myself laughing when I was with her. Guo Jing A-yi, the fat Auntie who also worked in the nursery, lived with her mother-in-law. Each Saturday, she brought in small treats, which she shared with all the Aunties—and the girls who were helping to care for babies. "Yes, yes, eat! That is what I bring them for. My mother-in-law loves to cook. She is retired now and has nothing to fill her time, so she cooks for us."

My time in the nursery passed so quickly! On that first Sunday, I was first in line to sign up for a whole week of baby loving!

"Wu Dan, come with me! We can sign up together and it will be fun!"

"No, I don't like babies. They stink and they spit on you."

"You would rather scrub floors?"

"I would rather do anything but care for babies!"

"Come-on Wu Dan, we can do it together!"

I don't know what changed her mind but on Monday afternoon, she was already in the nursery when I arrived after school.

"You always arrive late for work?" she challenged me.

"I'm not late! You're early. I didn't think you wanted to do this."

"Well, I thought it might be different if we did it together."

"Okay, girls, the babies are just getting up from their naps. Let's get their diapers changed and get them out of their cribs. Little ones can sit in the padded baby seats and look at each other. Some of the older ones can sit in the walker-chairs. If we get this whole room-full of babies up and changed, you can spend the last part of your time playing with them."

They all woke up at once! When one cried, they all cried. Ri-Yong, Ji Qiao, Yang Lan, Wu Dan and I hurried to pick the loudest ones up, change their wet diapers and put them down in the play area. Pretty soon, only a couple of the babies were crying and Wu Dan and I carried these with us as we played with the babies. We hid our faces in our hands and cried, "Surprise! I am here!" The babies laughed and we did it again. They laughed harder. One of the ones who cried the loudest and the longest was little Jin Ying, the baby who arrived the day after me.

"She is spoiled," said Guo Jing A-yi.

"She misses her mama," said Qiu Qiang A-yi. "She is used to being picked up the moment she cries. She is used to being fussed over."

"She'll get over it."

"Um," said Qiu Qiang A-yi. "She is a sweet baby. She would make any Mama happy. I will see if Ling A-yi will submit the paperwork for her to be adopted as soon as possible."

I didn't want to care about this baby. Every time I looked at her, that tiny rosebud mouth reminded me of my own sweet Di-di. And yet, I felt my heart pulling toward her each time she smiled at me."

"Wu Dan," I whispered one night long after lights out.

"What?"

"Maybe we should each pick a special baby to care for, like a little sister."

"No babies."

"That's it? Just, 'No babies!' Why not?"

I heard a slow sigh and a groan. "For a girl who is so smart in school, you are *so stupid*!"

"You take that back! Why are you being so mean?"

"I am not mean. I am your friend. Friends tell you the truth. Sometimes babies get adopted. You care about them and then you never see them again. It can break your heart."

"Isn't it better for the babies, though, to have someone care about them especially?"

"Yes, but it is safer for your own heart, to find a sister who is too old to be adopted. Trust me, I have made this mistake before. Don't care about babies. Pick someone older if you want a special little sister. This is why I have Mi-mi. I think I would be different if I had had a big sister like me when I was as little as she is. I wanted someone to protect me so badly! But, things were very different back then. This was a different place—a much worse place. Ling A-yi was not our director then and Na-Te was not Da ge-ge. Back then, the big kids got away with it when they picked on the little kids and stole our food. There was a lot of fighting. I cried every night."

"I don't care what you say. I think I will take special care of Jin Ying. She has already stolen my heart."

"Not Jin Ying! She is the worst one. She will surely get adopted. If you must care about one baby in a special way, choose one that will likely not be adopted. Guan Fang Mei cannot walk. The Americans want beautiful babies who are healthy. No one will ever take her away from you. Her legs don't work right. She is too sick. She needs someone to care for her and treat her special because no Mama ever will."

"Well, it sounds like we have our special babies then."

"What?

"It sounds like Guan Fang Mei has stolen your heart just as Jin Ying has stolen mine. Our babies have chosen us!"

"Mei Lin, I think this is a mistake."

Mistake or not, Wu Dan and I were always first in line on Sunday afternoons to sign up for chores. As much as possible, we rushed home from school to care for our babies--though, rushing is not what I would call it. The older students in each dormitory unit had to stop every day, to pick up the preschool children from their dormitory unit at the preschool and bring them home. Wu Dan, Hua and I were responsible to pick up Tong Mi, Xiao Yue, Ai Lin and Fu Yuan and walk them home. This was not as easy as it might sound. Four four-year-olds run in four different directions at the same time. Even harder, was getting them to walk past the bakery and candy stores without stopping. They pressed their noses against the window.

"When I get some money, I will buy some of those red fish candies," said Xiao Yue

"I will buy sweet sesame seed rolls," said Ai Lin

"I will buy a tang hulu" said Fu Yuan, "A long stick with six fruits—no ten fruits--on it and lots of extra thick red candy coating the outside so that it looks like red glass. And I won't bite it either. I will let it sit on my tongue until the sugar is melted and *then* I will bite the fruits one by one."

"Come, come," urged Wu Dan. "You don't have any money and you won't ever have any money, so why even think about it?"

"Someday I'll have money," insisted Tong Mi. "When I have money, I'll buy you a treat, Jie-jie. What do you want?"

"I don't want anything!" said Wu Dan as she grabbed the little one's hand. "I don't want to think about it. I just want you little kids to hurry up and get back to the dormitory."

Hua, of course, didn't help much. She was not particularly eager to get back and would dawdle as much as the preschoolers. She walked on the same sidewalk but pretended not to be with us. She looked at all the boys on the street, and for some reason, they all seemed to look at her. Would they still follow her down the street with their eyes if they knew how mean she was? After we checked the little ones in with Ling A-yi, Wu Dan and I hurried to our babies.

We often went back to the nursery after dinner to tuck them into bed for the night. Of course, we helped care for all the babies but Jin Ying and Guan Fang Mei received special care.

Two times in that first month, I returned to Ling A-yi's office.

"Ling A-yi, I have brought my list. I need to remove one thing from my basket."

"Ah! Yes, Mei Lin." She looked up from the papers she was writing on, opened the top desk drawer and withdrew her copy of the list. I carefully crossed off the item from both my list and the office copy and we both pressed red inked thumbprints beside the crossed-off item.

First, I removed Di-di's colorful cloth baby carrier so I could carry Jin Ying on my back even while I was washing baby bottles or changing another baby's diaper. Two weeks later I returned again to remove Di-di's bamboo baby rattle. I decided that it was better to remember him in the laughter of another baby than in a bamboo rattle that sat in a closet.

I sat Jin Ying on a blanket I had laid on the floor. I shook the rattle and the little bells bounced around inside the split bamboo ball. She reached out, grabbed the handle and shook it. She was pleased with herself and laughed so hard she toppled over. I caught her and eased her backward. She lay on her back, shaking the rattle and making happy baby sounds.

Guan Fang Mei was lying on the blanket next to her. Her crooked legs each wiggled in a different direction. For a while she was content just watching Jin Ying play with the toy. Then she began to reach for it herself and cry because she couldn't take it from Jin Ying.

"Okay, it is time to share," I said

"I don't think that's a good idea," said Wu Dan.

"Of course it is. There is only one toy. They have to learn to share."

"But Jin Ying is a much stronger baby with a much stronger temper. Guan Fang-Mei will fuss a while but she will give up soon."

"No. We must teach her not to give up. She should share the toy." I took the rattle from Jin Ying and gave it to Guan Fang Mei. Her face lit up as a broad smile slowly spread from one corner of her mouth to the other--just as a storm cloud filled the face of Jin Ying. A piercing scream of pure anger split the room! Her whole body stiffened. She kicked the floor with her feet and pounded the air with her tiny fists. Her whole face became as red as the Chinese flag.

"You need to share!" I said firmly, and walked away, letting her cry. Each time she looked over at Fang-Mei, she got angry again, screaming with renewed vigor. Sweat began to run down her face. "I can't give it back to you if you act like this," I said. I walked away again. She screamed even louder. I ignored her until her screams became pitiful little sobs of sadness.

When I had finished changing a diaper on Dou-duo, I went back and picked up Jin Ying. She wrapped her arms around my neck and clung to me, shuddering and gasping for breath.

I paced the floor, holding her close to me and began to sing a lullaby I remembered Baba singing: "Little bird, little bird, come sing your song for me. Little bird, little bird, can I fly away with you?" She buried her face into my neck and soon fell asleep.

Spring passed into summer.

At breakfast one hot morning, Ben-Ming who was only three started crying and throwing things, screaming and growling like a bear. He had only just recently graduated from the nursery to the dormitories. Guo Jing A-yi picked him up. Everyone knew Ben-Ming couldn't talk right. "What's this about?" she demanded of the kids sitting on that side of the hall.

"Every morning that big boy takes his congee." Xiao Bo pointed toward Da Wei.

"And every day at lunch that boy," he pointed toward Gang Fung "Takes his noodles!"

"Is this true?" A-yi asked, looking at Da Wei as he slurped down the last of the congee.

"I don't think so. This is mine."

"Yeah, it's yours if that's *your* second bowl!" said Mingsha.

Guo Jing A-yi grabbed each of the offenders by an ear and set them up scrubbing pots in the kitchen. She brought another, extra-big bowl of congee to Ben-Ming.

Ling A-yi came into the dining hall and announced, "Boys and girls, we have a famous person in our social welfare institute." She snapped open a newspaper and held up the headline for all to see. *Orphan Girl is Key Witness in Provincial Government Case!* She read aloud, "'In a true turn of events, an orphaned girl, Zhong Mei Lin currently residing in the Baoshan City Social Welfare Institute, has become the key to finally provide evidence needed to free the village of Longkou from the repressive tyranny of a double-dealing official. The young Zhong was orphaned in last spring's flood and held illegally as a slave in the house of the corrupt Liu Long Tang. Helped by other villagers, Zhong escaped her captor. She provided crucial evidence that has long eluded investigating officials.' Well, as you can see, it goes on and on, describing the case in great detail. I will paste it to the door and you may each read the entire article if you choose."

Everyone, abandoned their congee and crowded around the door—even the cook!

"Well, who could have guessed that our Mei Lin was the key to the biggest government corruption case our province has seen in decades!" Tang A-yi patted my back then turned away. "Children! Children! Your bowls must be cleared and rinsed before you go. Don't forget!"

"My hero!" teased Na-Te as he slid up behind me.

"She is a hero!" defended Wu Dan.

"And she's my Jie-jie, too!" Tong-Mi threw her arms around my knees and hugged tightly.

The next day, I heard the sound of a little boy's crying coming from the boys' toilet. Another little boy was shouting, "You leave him alone!"

A gruff voice responded, "Stop kicking me you little bug! I'll squash you."

Another small voice scolded, "You big bullies! It's not his fault. You took so much of his food he was starving." I heard the sound of fists punching what I could only imagine was the little boys. I was about to barge in there myself when Da Ge-ge pushed past me and burst into the boys' toilet room. I heard several hard punches. Then Da ge-ge shouted, "When will you learn?"

He emerged from the boy's toilet carrying Ben-Ming. A bump that looked like a purple egg was growing on the little one's head. He was crying and clinging to Da-Ge-ge's neck.

"Take him to the infirmary." He handed the little boy to me. "I'll be right back."

He disappeared into the boys' toilet and emerged moments later carrying Xiao Bo whose left eye was black, red and purple and was nearly swollen shut.

"Wait a minute," he said. He went back into the toilet room and shouted. "If either of you touch Mingsha, I'll *kill* you. Do you understand?" The only answer was silence.

We raced down the stairs and to the infirmary where Hu-Shi A-yi placed cool cloths on their bruises and washed the blood off the scrapes in Na-Te's knuckles.

"I thought you were a poet and a thinker, not a fighter," she said.

"I am, but unfortunately, some people only listen when you talk with your fists," he said.

Sweetness and Sorrow

Have a mouth as sharp as a dagger
But a heart as soft as tofu.

The steamy days of summer gave way to autumn. It was still hot, but at least I could sleep at night without sticking to my sheets. Na-Te sometimes sat with Wu Dan and me at meals, but mostly he seemed to deliberately go out of his way to ignore me. He spent most of his time with the older boys like Feng Cong, who was playful and always getting into trouble—but he was not mean.

One Sunday afternoon, right after lunch, Cong found a long string of firecrackers, which he lit and threw in the window of the girl's toilets. Ni-Na picked it up and threw it back out the window where it landed on the ground behind Cong. Guo Jing A-yi came running out from the nursery and grabbed him by the ear. "You make so much noise during baby nap time! Listen! You woke them all up! Babies are screaming. They are tired, but it is not possible to get so many babies back to sleep when they are also scared—thanks to you! You come now. You will help in the nursery for the rest of the day!" She led him away, still holding onto his ear as Ni

Na, Pan Xiao Mu and Mingsha peeked out the girls' toilet room window and giggled.

Another time, Cong and Hei Lin "borrowed" one of Tang A-yi's large service trays and rode it all the way down three flights of stone steps. Not only were they both still alive when they reached the bottom, but Cong was excited to do it again! The tray, however, was seriously bent and Tang A-yi was seriously angry. Again, Cong was led away by his ear, this time to wash dishes and peel vegetables. Hei Lin, was let off with a warning. Tang A-yi had surmised that he was much too young to have thought up such a deed by himself. Na-Te was never directly involved in the mischief, but he was always in the crowd of boys who gathered to watch and cheer them on.

Na-Te was a different boy, however, when these other boys were not around. He was very quiet and made mention of things other people never noticed. "Do you hear that sound?" he asked one day as we were walking home from school. There were a hundred city sounds flying through the air; taxi horns, motor noises, construction noises, but I knew which one he meant. "It is a yellow wagtail warbler! They are quite typical on the plateau steppe region, far to our north. I wonder how it found its way so far into the city? He must have gotten blown off course."

"How do you know so much about birds?"

"My parents were naturalists. They were both killed five years ago in a rock slide while studying the Temminck's Tragopan, an incredibly beautiful but endangered bird that lives in the mountainous forests of the southwest. I continued to live with my grandparents, but when they both died one after another in the year of the Ox, I was sent here.

Another time, Na-Te left a drawing of a perfect white lotus blossom on the bench in the dining hall where I usually sat. The most striking thing was that he signed his name, not in the simple letters of modern Mandarin, but in the elegant old style calligraphy that Ye-ye had taught me.

"Where did you learn this style of writing?" I asked.

"My grandfather was a highly skilled calligrapher. He taught me everything I know."

"My grandfather taught me grass writing as well!"

I was beginning to see that he was really not as big and scary as the bulldog on his sweatshirt would make one think. He liked to draw and make things. This side of him—the side the other boys would never know, became a secret between the two of us.

Tong Mi became sick in September, just as the new school year began. Measles. She was burning with fever and had spots all over her. She had to be sent to the infirmary for three weeks while she recovered so that the fever would not spread to other children. After the infectious danger had passed, Wu Dan and I went to visit her one afternoon after school and found her sitting in her bed playing with a little sock doll. The sock had once been a boy's white sock. What had once been a red band around the top of the sock, was now red shoes and mittens on the doll. Another sock, a black one, had been unraveled and the yarn used to make a wild, curly mane of hair. A few of the threads had been sewn to form eyes and nose and mouth. The doll wore a little dress made of scraps of rags: sleeves of blue, shirt of red and skirt of purple. It was probably stuffed with other rags.

Wu Dan picked up the doll and examined it. "Where did you get this?"

"Da ge-ge give it me."

"Da ge-ge?"

When I saw him that night in the dining hall, I noticed his bare ankles sticking out between the bottom of his sweat pants and the tops of his shoes. I walked up beside him and said, "Thanks for the little doll you gave Tong-Mi."

"Ah, I could have made something really nice if I had more to work with."

"You are an artist and a good brother."

"She's a good little kid."

Wu Dan and I spent every afternoon caring for babies. Often Tong Mi went with us. After dinner we helped her get ready for bed and did our homework. Then we returned to the nursery, cuddled our babies, fed them one last bottle and tucked them in to sleep for the night.

One October Monday, we arrived in the nursery to find Na-Te already working.

"I thought you only did *men's work*," I challenged him.

"Well," he said, "You are half right, I do work."

"I didn't know you were fond of babies."

"Not really. I didn't sign up early enough so this was all that was left."

"Oh."

"Mei Lin, may I speak to you in the bottle room a moment?" said Wu Dan, grabbing my arm and shoving me toward the room where we prepared the bottles of baby formula. "It's really important."

"Mei Lin," she hissed in exaggerated impatience as she shoved me into the room and closed the door behind us, "For a girl who is so smart in school, you are REALLY stupid!"

"Again? Now what did I do?"

"Mei Lin. Boys don't sign up for baby care because there was nothing else! This is the first job to get filled! He signed up to work here because he likes *you* and I mean LIKES you."

"Me? Maybe he likes you."

"Not me! I've seen that look before. He's got it bad, and it's aimed in your direction."

"It?"

"It and I mean IT! He looks at you exactly the way Officer Wang looks at Qiu Qiang A-yi. Have you ever seen the way she wraps her arms around him? It's not so she doesn't fall off the back of his motorcycle! Those two are going to get married, I just know it!"

"Getting married! I'm not getting married! Na-Te is a very nice boy. I like him when he is not with other boys. But I am not going to marry him. He is like a brother."

"You be careful, Mei Lin! He is not thinking of you as a sister!"

There may have been something to her observations because it seemed that from then on, poor Na-Te got stuck with nursery duty surprisingly often.

One cold November night Ling A-yi told Tong Mi to take a bath even though it was not her regular bath night. Ling A-yi, herself helped her wash her hair and trimmed the scraggly ends. She said that tomorrow would be an important day, but she did not say why. In the morning, Wu Dan helped her get dressed and we went to breakfast together as usual. As we were heading out the door, Ling A-yi stopped us. "Tong Mi will stay with me today. Do not take her to preschool."

"Why?" asked Wu Dan.

"I think it is best if we not talk about it until after school today."

But, Wu Dan and I did talk about it all the way to school.

"Something is not right. Why isn't she going to preschool today?"

"Perhaps she has to see the doctor."

"She's not sick anymore."

"Maybe she has to get some inoculations so she doesn't get sick again, and they don't want to frighten her before it happens."

"Maybe," said Wu Dan, but I could tell she was still distracted.

At lunchtime, she led the way as we raced home from school. I was nearly breathless by the time we reached the front door but Wu Dan tore through the building calling for Tong-Mi. She looked in the dining hall but she was not there. She looked in Ling A-yi's office but that too was empty.

"Where is Ling A-yi? She demanded of Dong A-yi as she passed the office door.

"Ah, I think she said she had some papers to file with the courts and she would be back around three o'clock."

"No!" gasped Wu Dan. She ran up to the dormitory room and looked in the basket under Tong Mi's bed. Her doll was missing, too. She ran to the nursery and looked around, counting babies. Seven were missing.

"She's gone, too, isn't she?" she shouted across the rows of baby cribs.

Qiu Qiang A-yi walked toward to her, "Wu Dan, we thought it would be better for *her* this way. She has hope for a wonderful new life. If we told you beforehand, your grief would have made it very difficult for her to feel free to go. As it was, you dressed her just like any other morning and gave her the confidence and freedom to join her new family. She experienced no anxiety. Ling A-yi had a good talk with her this morning before they came, and she was very happy to go with her new parents. She could hardly believe that she finally had a Mama *and* a Baba. She kept asking them questions but they of course didn't understand a word she said. She held both their hands and skipped out the door with them. They brought the cutest little musical panda bear for her and dressed her in the sweetest little blue sweater and hat set . . ."

It was then that I heard a sound I recognized, a sound like a bellowing water buffalo rise from deep within Wu Dan. She fell into Qiu Qiang A-yi's arms and sobbed like a small child. I had heard this same sound escape my own lips once and I ached with her. I sat beside her as silent tears streaked my own cheeks. But Wu Dan was like a wild animal and would not let me touch her. She pushed me away and ran to our dormitory room where she unrolled her mattress and lay on it. I unrolled my mattress and sat silently beside her as she cried. I could find no words to soothe her pain. I think this is because there were none.

We did not go back to school that afternoon, but stayed in the nursery. Wu Dan hugged Guan Fang Mei and held her close. She sat on the floor rocking her back and forth, whispering in her ear, "You won't leave too, will you?" Tears streaked her cheeks again and again.

That night, as we lay in bed, I called out, "Wu Dan, are you still awake?"

"Shi."

"I know she is your special little sister, but I want you to know I miss Mi-mi too. If it means anything to you, I am here. I am not going anywhere. You are not alone."

"Xie-xie." Her voice grew strained. "People come and go around here so quickly. I want to hold on but just when I think it is safe to care again, they go and switch my life around. I feel like a big piece of my heart has been torn out and moved to America and

I'll never see it again. I thought she was too old to be adopted. I thought it was safe to care about her."

"I know, but think of all the good you have done for her. She is ready to love a Mama because of all you taught her about Mama's *and* about loving someone."

"What do I know? I'm just an orphan girl too stupid to know I shouldn't hold onto memories and I have no right to dreams! Memories and dreams both hurt you. Only *right now,* the present moment is safe—even if it hurts."

"Don't you talk like that! We have to have dreams. Our dreams are our hope and our future dancing before our eyes. They show us the way. And our memories," I pulled out the jade Buddha and rubbed it against my cheek. "Our memories tell us who we are and how we got here. Most important, they tell us *how* to get where we are going. Both memories and dreams help us get through *right now*—especially when *right now* feels this rotten."

"Do you have dreams, Mei Lin?

"Me? I want to be a rich business woman and drive a black automobile with curtains on the windows and two tufted silk pillows on the back shelf. No! I will have my chauffeur drive me."

"Oh, Mei Lin, you are so funny! Let's be sisters forever."

"When we are old enough to leave the orphanage, we could get jobs as sales clerks in a big Hong Kong department store and live together. We could wear green shop uniforms with green velvet shoes and sell fancy dresses. We could save our money and go to university. You will become a famous writer and I will become a wealthy business woman."

"What if one of us became rich and famous and the other didn't?" she asked.

"Then we would share our good fortune until the other found her dream as well. What would happen if one of us got married?" I asked.

"Married? Well, Hui Na-Te will have to agree to let me live with you as well."

"Na-Te! I will not marry Na-Te! He is like a brother to me." I picked up my pillow and bopped it over her head.

"He is *not* your brother! Open your eyes!"

"Very touching!," a voice from across the room growled. "Now, will you two go to sleep?"

"Oh Hua!" we both shouted together and threw our pillows across the room at her.

戴拾壹

Longing for Love and Belonging

Make happy those who are near
And those who are far will come.

In late December a deep cold spell fell upon Baoshan City. The social welfare institute, like most buildings south of the Yangtze River, had no central heating system. Stone walls and tile floors held the cold and made it even colder indoors than it was outdoors! A thick layer of ice formed on the inside of the exterior walls and the windows.

At night, I lay awake in my bed shivering and knew that I was lucky. I had a gray wool blanket just like everyone else, but I also had Mama's quilt. Though the quilt was warm, what I really longed for was Mama! I remembered that, on cold nights, she would heat a large round, river rock in the cooking fire, wrap it in a towel and place it at the foot of my bed where it would keep my feet warm until morning. When it was so cold that I could not sleep, she would carry me to her bed. I would sleep then, safe and warm, snuggled into her side, with her arms wrapped around me.

I couldn't help it, although it had been nearly ten months since they all had drowned, my eyes flooded again. It was so cold, the tears burned, freezing a track of ice as thin as rice paper, sliding toward my ears. All around me, I could hear girls crying and moaning their misery at the cold, while others chattered their teeth.

Even though it was long past lights-out and no one was supposed to be talking, I said aloud, "I remember my mama."

"Well aren't you the lucky one, *Miss Hero*!" said Hua bitterly.

"What I remember is that on very cold nights, she would call me into her bed and wrap her quilt around the two of us--together."

"Spare me the sentimental mush!"

"This isn't sentiment, it's science!" I said impatiently. When there was no smart answer from her, I continued. "It was warmer with two in a bed than just one. Perhaps, if we double up, we can both share two blankets. If we lie close to each other, we can keep each other warm."

"Oh, it's worth a try!" said Wu Dan as she threw her blanket over me and crawled into my bed. She was already wearing a sweatshirt and two sweaters and a pair of quilted pants instead of pajamas. We all were.

"I'm not sharing!" said Hua, "especially not with a little kid who's going to wet the bed."

"Suit yourself," I said. Everybody else paired up, sharing one bed and two blankets. Only little Fu Yuan was left alone because Hua wouldn't share. "Come here, I said, you can share with Wu-Dan and me." She threw her blanket on top of us and crawled into the bottom of our bed, so that she was wedged between us and her feet were near our stomachs. Pretty soon the room quieted down and everyone fell asleep.

At breakfast, everyone, except those in our dormitory room looked tired. Dark circles hung under nearly every eye. They were all short-tempered and complaining about the cold. Ji Qiao snapped at Xiao Ping, "Watch what you are doing! You nearly stepped on my foot!"

"But I didn't. Don't be so bossy, Ji Qiao!"

Ni-Na and Gao Zhu, two second graders, both fell asleep in school.

After school, Wu Dan and I hurried to the nursery. The babies were all tightly swaddled so their arms and legs couldn't move and knock the blankets off. They were buried under thick quilts, lying quietly in soft, dark caves. Three of them snuggled together in each crib.

"Work quickly, today, girls," said Qiu Qiang A-yi. Her breath hung in a cloud around her mouth. "Don't let the babies out to play. It is too cold for them. Just change their wet things as fast as you can, and tuck them back into their beds."

Changing the babies was a huge job. Each baby had at least six layers of clothes and blankets on. These must be removed quickly, the diaper changed, bare bottoms wiped with warm soapy water, dried and then a new diaper and dry clothes put back on. When we got to the sixteenth crib, there were only two babies tucked beneath the covers. These were the newest babies--only a few days old. Yesterday there had been three. "A-yi, where is the third baby?" I asked.

"If you don't want to know an answer, you shouldn't ask a question."

"A-yi?"

She did not answer and acted as if she had heard no question.

"A-yi, where is the third baby?" My voice rose in what would surely be considered a disrespectful tone by most adults.

She looked right at me. Then, after what seemed a very long pause, she answered very slowly, "Sometimes, when it is very cold, babies die."

"Die?"

"The end one in that crib kicked her blankets off. She was frozen when I came to wake them this morning."

"Frozen?"

"Blue."

"To death?" I thought of Di-di and my throat closed in.

"It happens. It is regrettable, but it happens. More often the older ones who move around a lot are victims. It is better if you don't think too much about it. There are one hundred and ninety two other babies to care for here. It is best not to invest too much of your heart in any one."

My pulse raced at her words. There was one baby here that I had invested my heart in. *She* was older *and* strong *and* smart enough to figure out how to loosen her swaddling wrap.

I rushed over to the crib my Jin Ying shared with Duo Duo and Yang Lan. In my mind she was as gray and stiff as Di-di was the last time I saw him. I pulled back the quilts and her fat pink cheeks dimpled up in a broad, sweet smile. She was very definitely alive and laughed when she saw me. Clearly angry to be swaddled so tightly, she wriggled her whole body.

She had been learning to walk before it grew so cold. She was learning to talk and said at least twenty words. She pleaded with me to pick her up, "Bao!" I changed her diaper and then wrapped her back up and tucked her into her bed. She screamed and struggled against me when I wrapped her in the swaddling blanket. "Play! Play!" she howled.

Wu Dan pretended not to hurry, but she checked on Guan Fang Mei. I thought I caught a hint of relief on her face, though I doubt she would have admitted she was worried if I had asked.

"The weather report says that it will be even colder tonight," said Qiu Qiang A-yi. "I am glad I won't be working the night shift tonight. Burr!" She rubbed her arms and shivered.

"Do you think other babies will die tonight?" I threw the cold question right out there in the middle of the room where it hung in the air like the cloud of our frosted breath.

She didn't answer me.

"A-yi?"

"One should not ask questions to which one does not want the answer," she repeated.

"If we come back after supper and swaddle them all tightly, and then tie a cord around the swaddling blanket so they can't wiggle it loose, and then snuggle them all together under the quilts, they should be warm enough, right?"

She didn't answer me.

Jin Ying was screaming angrily. My chest tightened in response to her emotions. I was beginning to cry just listening to her. I ran to Ling A-yi's office. She was just locking up for the night. "Qing wen, I don't have my list, but I need something from my basket?"

"What is it?"

"I need my mama's turquoise coat."

"It is so big! How will it keep you warm?"

"It is big enough to put over Jin Ying and myself together. I can carry her under my coat like I once carried my Di-di."

"Mei Lin, you are getting far too attached to this baby. You know I have submitted her paperwork for adoption. She needs a Mama."

"I," —the word caught in my throat. I had asked no question, but still I got an answer I didn't want to hear. "I can keep her alive and healthy until her Mama comes for her." I said it far more bravely than I felt.

"Alright then, we'll just make a little notation on this sheet that your copy of the list will not agree. Get the coat."

I hurried out the door intending to return to the nursery, but stopped when I nearly ran into Na-Te. His nose was red and his eyes were red. He had only the bulldog sweat suit on and a thin sweater that didn't close in the front.

"You look terrible!"

"Xie-xie," he said sarcastically. "You, on the other hand, look great."

"Are you sick?"

"Sick? I think I passed sick three days ago. Am I still alive?"

"What are you doing out of bed?"

"Trying to stay warm. I thought if I could keep moving, I would stay warmer." I can't explain it, but in that moment, I felt something very warm move in my heart and it was flowing in his direction.

"Wait! Wait right here." I ran back in the office. "Ling A-yi, I need one more thing." I rummaged through to the bottom of the basket and felt the soft fur of Baba's hat. I removed the jade Buddha that was wrapped inside it and placed that back in the basket. Instead of making a notation that the item had been removed, I just crossed it off the list as if it no longer existed. Then, I hurried back to the hall.

214

"Baba always said that the head was the most important part of the body to keep warm when it is cold outside," I told Na-Te

"Or inside?" He smiled.

"Put this on. Then go back to the infirmary and wrap up in a blanket. You will keep warm. You must get better."

"Xie-xie." He pulled the earflaps down and attached the chinstrap. "I feel better just knowing you care whether I live or die." He stroked his head and made a purring sound like a contented cat. "I will never give you back this hat."

"Please don't wear it in July!"

He walked slowly away, coughing and sneezing as he went. Half-way down the hall, he turned and shouted, "Mei Lin, you have made me very happy. Now, I **know** I must get well."

As I watched him walk away, I noticed that the sleeves of his sweatshirt were about ten centimeters too short. The legs were also too short by several centimeters. He wore no socks and his toes protruded from the front of his shoes. It suddenly occurred to me that Da ge-ge wore the same lousy bulldog sweatshirt day in and day out, winter or summer, not because he really liked it, but because it was the only outfit in the orphanage clothing inventory that fit him.

Whenever we received donations of new clothes, there were usually dresses, coats, shoes, sweaters and pants outfits for little girls and lots of stuff for babies. The bigger the size, the fewer choices there were in the clothing collection. I don't know why it had taken me so long, but I suddenly realized that the bulldog expressed nothing about his personality other than the fact that he was desperate enough to wear almost anything--even a ridiculous pink heart with a misspelled English word on it. I had never heard him complain—except to demand that he be allowed to wear the one outfit that fit him. Right then, I decided that I would do something about that--and soon.

When I arrived back in the nursery, I picked up Jin Ying, unwrapped her swaddling blanket and strapped her to my chest in the baby carrier, facing outward like Di-di always preferred. Then I put Mama's big jacket on over both of us. With a small knitted cap on her head, and her face buried under the coat up to her cheeks, only her little black eyes peeked out. Though I knew she would much rather be on the floor, she giggled at her new freedom.

"Mei Lin!" scolded A-yi when she saw me. "You should not take her out! Now she will scream all night. She needs to learn that she is not a special case. She needs to learn to stay in the bed."

"A-yi, she already knows that she is a special case. Her Mama taught her that. I think, if you will let me, I could keep her with me and she will be warm all night."

"This is not practical. She will keep you up half the night!"

"It will be better for me than lying awake *the whole* night wondering if she is too cold."

"I should not let you do this."

"Please, A-yi?"

"I should ask Ling A-yi before I give you permission. No one has ever asked to do this before."

"She has already gone home for the night. She was just leaving when I got to her office to get my coat."

"Please A-yi?" chimed in Wu Dan, holding a shivering Fang Mei. "Her legs don't even stay in the right direction long enough to wrap her up tightly."

Qiu Qiang A-yi looked up at the little holes in the ceiling tiles for a few moments and then answered. "Okay, I will switch with Dong A-yi for tonight. I will check in on you at midnight. If anything happens or if you think better of the idea halfway through the night, and you need to bring the babies back, I will be sleeping here in the staff bed or tending to the babies."

In the dormitory, Wu Dan and I pushed our beds together. We lay across the two beds. Wu Dan, Fu Yuan, the two babies and myself, all snuggled together: cozy and warm under three blankets and Mama's quilt. True to A-yi's warning, the babies each woke during the night and fussed, but we rubbed their backs as I softly sang:

Ay, Ay, Ay.

Little one goes to sleep on Jie-jie's back.

In your sweet dream whom will you meet?

You will dream of little birds safe at their mother's side.

When the little birds grow up, their mama leads them flying.

Ay Ay little one goes to sleep on Jie-jie's back.

Little treasure grows up fast.

This wide world is for you to fly.

When I finished the song, Fang Mei sighed and drifted off to sleep. Jin Ying was already fast asleep.

For the remainder of that week while the cold front hung over the entire province, Wu Dan and I snuggled our two babies and little Fu Yuan through the night.

Fu Yuan slept at my right side across the foot of both beds. I lay on my left side with my back to Fu Yuan and my body curled around Jin Ying. Fang Mei was next to her and Wu Dan lay across the head of the bed, with Fang Mei wrapped in her arms.

Two more babies died of cold that winter and six more in the sickness that swept through the orphanage. But *our* babies, stayed fat and warm and healthy.

As preparations for Chinese New Year began, I asked to take some money out of my basket.

"Mei Lin, I can't imagine what you need that much money for. I am not sure I feel comfortable giving this much money to a child, but it is after-all, your money." She counted it out and handed me a stack of colorful, red and blue and green Yuan. "Don't be spending this on foolishness."

"I won't, A-yi. May I use the phone?"

"Yes, yes." She motioned to the one on her desk.

Though I would have preferred her to be gone, it was clear she had no intention of leaving. I took the business card out of my pocket and dialed the number.

"This is Zhong Mei Lin. Could you come visit this Sunday afternoon? There is something I would like to ask you. Xie-xie." I hung up the phone.

"Mei Lin, what was that all about?"

"A surprise." I left before she could ask any more questions.

On Sunday, Ling A-yi was gone for the day. I showed Han Yue Mei into Ling A-yi's office. "I was glad you called." She said. "I am so sorry I have not been back to visit. I intended to, but I have been very busy. You did see the newspaper I sent, didn't you?"

"I did. Thank you for sending it, but that is not what I want to speak to you about. I am sorry to bother you but I don't know who else can help me."

"What is the problem?"

"Not a problem, really, just something I need help with. First of all, I want to make sure there is a surprise for every child in the orphanage for Chinese New Year."

"That is a lot of children Mei Lin!"

"Perhaps the older ones who are no longer in the nursery could each have one piece of candy and one small hong bao."

"I don't think I . . . "

"I have some money from the sale of my water buffalo, but I have no way to get to the stores and get this many things by myself —at least not without being found out. The babies in the nursery don't need candy, but they do need some toys. If I could give you the money, would you buy some baby toys and some candy and some hong bao's for the older kids? Could you also go to a bank and get me two hundred five-Yuan notes to put in the hong bao's? This way the little ones can each buy their own treat at the candy store."

"This is what you want?

"Yes, but I want it to be a surprise. I don't want anyone to know where these things came from."

"I can help you."

"I need one more thing."

"What is it?"

"There is a boy, perhaps you will see him when you leave this room. He is nearly fifteen and he always wears a brown sweat suit with and angry bulldog on the front of it. There are no other clothes here that fit him. He needs some nice clothes suitable for a boy who is really an artist and a poet and too old and too nice to be wearing an angry bulldog on his chest."

"What did you have in mind?" she asked, raising her eyebrows as she smiled.

"I know exactly what he must have. He should have nicely tailored black trousers and black socks befitting a scholar. He should have black shoes that are comfortable but that also look nice —something stylish but also practical. He needs a white shirt that buttons down the front and an undershirt. He needs a nice sweater, something conservative but tasteful and," I paused a moment, almost embarrassed to say the word in front of such a properly dressed adult. "I need some underpants for a boy his size."

She smiled. "You like this boy a lot, huh."

"He is like a brother to me, that's all. He is very nice and he will soon outgrow the clothes he has been wearing. No one ever donates clothes for boys to the orphanage—especially not for teenage boys."

"And that is the only reason?"

"Dui."

"I will help you." She smiled sweetly. "I will have these things delivered in time for the first night of Chinese New Year."

"Hao, though perhaps you could have the clothes for the boy delivered as soon as possible. He has nearly outgrown the sweatshirt and pants he wears every day."

"I will see what I can do." She stood to leave but then turned and said, "You are an amazing girl, Mei Lin. You worry about this boy and the other children when you are an orphan, yourself. Most people would be angry about what they have lost. You look for what you can give! Your parents must have loved you a great deal, for you have learned a great deal about love."

"They did love me. Of all the things in the universe of which I am sure, this is the thing about which I am most sure."

On the following afternoon, a delivery man arrived. Ling A Yi nearly turned him away insisting that she had not ordered anything from an expensive department store. He checked his clipboard and commented, "It's paid for and I am responsible to deliver it to this address. Is there a Hui Na-Te residing at this address?"

"Yes. Yes, there is, but he . . ."

"Has a paid-for package."

In the end, she saw the wisdom in accepting the delivery and called Na-Te into her office to open it. I didn't want it to seem obvious that I knew what was happening, so I waited outside her door pretending to scrub the floor--although it was not my job. A few minutes later he burst out the door and raced up the stairs to the boys' dormitory room. I waited for him to come down. --And waited and waited. That section of floor had never been scrubbed so thoroughly.

He finally walked down the stairs, adjusting his shirtsleeves under the sweater. He carried himself with a new dignity. His hair was combed and pulled to one side. He seemed older and more mature and incredibly handsome. The sight of my elder brother took my breath away and caused my heart to stop if just for a moment.

"Na-Te?" I asked as he walked toward me. "Is that you in those clothes?"

"Shi."

"Ni zhen hao kan! You look good!"

"Xie-xie!" He grinned a huge grin and then continued, "I also . . . " He snapped the waistband of his underwear. " . . . *feel* good!"

I giggled and hid my face behind my hands.

"You had something to do with this, didn't you?"

"No!" I lied unconvincingly.

戴拾戴

Happy, Sad Adoption Day

You think you lost your horse?
Who knows, he may bring a whole herd
back to you someday.

Chinese New Year was very different in bustling Baoshan City from what it was in my small village of Longkou. For one thing, the lion dancers appeared to have been chosen for the honor because they were extremely skilled, not because their father had intimidated everyone on the planning committee. The fireworks were also of a far greater number and quality. Some of them seemed to begin with a rumbling in my stomach, their glow lasting long into the night.

Some festivities happened right outside our front door. Everyone in the city was walking in the streets. Young boys ran around setting off long strings of red firecrackers, rendering the air clouded with the smell of gunpowder. Drummers announced the presence of the lion dance. Crowds followed the red and green and gold lion, watching his antics as he visited shops looking for hong bao, the red envelopes of lucky money that merchants hid for him to find.

The little ones who could keep their eyes open that late, sat by the dormitory windows, looking down from above. Some of us older orphans went outside to welcome the year of the dragon from the wide front steps. In Longkou and in the social welfare institute, as in most of China, we did not celebrate individual birthdays. Chinese New Year is everybody's birthday. At midnight, on the first night of Chinese New Year, we advanced in age one year. Wu Dan would be twelve and I thirteen! In the smell of gunpowder from firecrackers, the drum beat and the excitement of the crowds, I almost felt happy, though the hole in my heart still ached for Mama and Baba, Ye-ye, Di-di and even Nai-nai who had been gone the longest.

I was standing with Wu Dan and some of the older girls, watching the parade when Na-Te walked up behind me and put his hand on my back. I felt his touch like warm energy tingling through my skin and into my bones. He bent and whispered into my ear, "Come with me." The brush of his breath upon my ear made my knees feel weak.

"We're not supposed to leave the step," I pointed out.

"Just for a moment? We'll be right back, I promise." His words blew across my cheek causing my throat to grow tight and dry.

"I . . ." his hair touched my face ever so slightly and my lungs forgot how to breathe.

"Please, Leave Wu Dan here. Watch where I go and follow me."

I don't know exactly why I did it. It had something to do with the way he looked in those clothes, and something to do with the way he pouted and nearly pleaded. And, I am sure it had something to do with the way my heart was pounding. It beat so loudly; I thought someone might hear it even above the firecrackers and the drummers in the street.

"I have to go," I said to Wu Dan. I knew she would think I meant that I had to go to the toilet, but I didn't exactly *lie* to her. I slipped behind her and slid against the wall, down the steps and followed where Na-Te had gone, around the corner of the social welfare institute, across the street, past the candy store and into the next alley.

No sooner had I turned that dark corner, away from the noise of the parade, than someone grabbed me around my back and clamped a hand across my mouth.

"Qing, bu yao jiao—Please don't scream?" he whispered and released his hand from my mouth. He pressed me tightly against his body. I giggled, confused but not afraid. I breathed in the familiar scent of Na-Te and was surprised to find it dizzying at this proximity.

He said, "I think you are very beautiful, and kind, and generous, and smarter than any girl I know. It would make me very happy if you would let me –what I mean to say is-- I want to kiss you —Qing, ke yi ma?"

"Kiss me?"

"Hao ma—May I? I want this like I have never wanted anything in my life."

My mind raced. I should say, 'No!' and run away. An honorable girl would say 'No,' --wouldn't she?" What would Baba say? I didn't know. We had never talked about these things. Yet, as much as I wanted to resist, I felt myself longing to kiss him.

"I don't know how the sun will ever shine again," continued Na-Te, "if you say, 'No'."

I closed my eyes and turned my face toward him. He pressed his lips against mine and I pressed back.

It was not as soft as I had thought it would be. Neither was it as sweet. His breath smelled of black bean and garlic paste. Somehow, I had always imagined that a kiss would taste more like duck-sauce.

He slid his hands down my arms and laced his fingers between mine. We stood there a moment, just breathing. I was listening to my own heart pounding in my throat, matching time with the frenzy of distant drums. I held Na-Te's hands, keeping my balance though I felt like my head was spinning. My thoughts spun, too! It wasn't an entirely undesirable experience, yet I wondered if I had done something terribly wrong. It felt forbidden, but I wasn't sure. I had never seen Baba kiss Mama—had never even seen him hold her hand as Na-Te now held mine. In that moment, I missed Mama even more deeply than before. Some part of my growing up was not complete and she was not here to see to it properly.

"We should get back," I said, "Before anyone misses us."

"Dui," he said. "You go first."

I ran back to the white stone stairs in front of the Baoshan City Social Welfare Institute. I slipped back into my place beside Wu Dan, just as the dancing lion shook apart a head of lettuce, which a shopkeeper had left out for him. The children cheered from the windows above, "Faster, faster!" In a wild, racing rhythm, that matched the wild beating of my heart, the dancer inside the head of the lion searched for the hong bao hidden inside the lettuce. The lion's bearded mouth opened and closed as if chewing, all the while spewing out leaves of lettuce. The lion's head tilted, his green eyes rolled, the great pink eyelids closed and then fluttered open again as if the lion was pondering something delightful. Everyone laughed.

"Where have you been?" asked Wu Dan. "You are missing all the fun!" But she didn't wait for an answer and I didn't offer one.

Later that night, long after everyone else had gone to sleep, I lay in my bed, and pressed my lips against my fingers, remembering the feel of Na-Te's lips against mine and pondering what Mama would advise. I kept the photo of Mama and Baba under my pillow that night. Although I wished I could have had a talk with them about these things before they had happened, now that they were done, I didn't want them to see me kissing my hand and know my thoughts about Na-Te.

It was after dinner, on the fourth day of Chinese New Year, that Ling A-yi sent Xiao Hui to fetch me. When I arrived at her office door, she looked up, removed the lid from her teacup, sucked in a long slurpy sip of tea and abruptly said, "Sit down."

I sat and she continued to look at me over the top of a pair of skinny reading glasses. She had piles of folders on her desk. "Mei Lin, you have known this day would likely come, although I doubt such knowledge could make it easier for you. I am not sure that telling you is the best thing, although it is clear to me now that not telling Wu Dan before Mi-Mi left cost her great pain. Sometimes it is hard to know which way to proceed."

I felt a sinking feeling in my stomach. I knew just which day she was talking about.

"Today?"

"Tomorrow morning." She removed the eyeglasses and lay them down on her desk.

"Can I stay home from school? I want to get her ready. I want to see her go to them."

She rubbed her eyes. "Don't you think it would be easier just to know it will happen and let us take care of the details?" Concern creased her face. I knew she wanted to spare me pain.

"No, I don't think so. I think it will hurt more if I don't do this." I fought back the tears, "I want to say good-bye to Jin Ying. I want to send her off to her new life."

"You can go tuck her into bed and say goodnight right now."

226

"I want to take her to her mama and baba. I want to see that she is safe with them."

She looked down, tapped the end of a pen against the desk, closed a folder that lay open in front of her and looked up at me. "Normally, I would say, 'No,' to a request like this . . . " Her voice trailed off and she paused a moment. "But I think you are quite mature. I must impress upon you that it is *very* important that you show her how happy you are with her new situation. She must not see you cry or hear you say anything negative about her new life. You must convey that you are happy for her. This will help her know how to feel. If you let her know that you are sad, you will confuse her and delay her happiness with her new family."

"Dui."

"If you feel you cannot control yourself, you will leave the room—for her sake."

"I will not cry."

"Then, you may stay home from school tomorrow morning."

"Xie-xie."

I ran to the nursery. I did not cry. I picked up Jin Ying and fed her a bedtime bottle.

"You know, you spoil her. She is nearly sixteen months old. You should make her drink from a cup." Said Qiu Qiang A-yi.

"I know, A-yi, this will be the last bedtime bottle I will give her."

"You know?"

"I know."

I held Jin Ying in my arms and hummed a lullaby until she fell asleep. A-yi turned down the lights for the night. I continued to hold her, studying the features of her sweet face. I wanted to remember every detail. When A-yi said it was time to go, I kissed her forehead and carefully lay her between her two crib-mates. I pulled up the blanket and whispered, "Goodnight little sister. Tomorrow will be a special day for you."

I awoke next morning long before anyone else. I dressed and combed my hair in the darkness. Then, I went down to the nursery. The babies were just waking. I stood and watched Jin Ying sleep until she opened her eyes. When she saw me looking at her she laughed and raised her arms for me to lift her out of the crib.

"Jie-jie—elder sister!" she called out to me.

I smiled back at her and picked her up. "It's a special day! I said with far more excitement than I felt. I took her to the dressing table and took off all her clothes. I wrapped her in a blanket and held her while I poured some warm water into a bowl. I dipped a washcloth in the warm water and washed her face with it. She giggled and wriggled away from the cloth.

"Oh, you like that, huh? Well it will be quick today because this room is still cold, but I am sure you will have a lot more baths next summer if you tell your Mama that you like them." I washed her quickly, unwrapping one part of the blanket at a time as I washed and then quickly dried first one arm, then the other, her shoulders, one leg and then the other, her front and her back. She smelled so fresh and clean when I was done. I chose the prettiest clothes in the basket. Over them all, I put a soft pink jacket with a *Hello Kitty* patch on the pocket and a pair of knitted green wool pants. Set against her pink cheeks and her rosebud mouth, the soft pink jacket made her more beautiful than any baby in the room. "Oh, your new mama will surely cry for joy at the sight of you, *Little Treasure!*" I choked on the words.

"Mama," she said.

"That's right, lucky girl," I said brightly, "You will meet your new Mama today. She will probably not resemble your first Mama at all, but don't hold that against her. She has come a great distance to find you." I put on her shoes and noticed that already they were tight. "Tell your Baba you need a new pair of shoes." I said.

"Baba," she repeated. She toddled around the floor, hanging onto my pants leg while I picked up her pajamas and threw them in the dirty clothes basket.

"Oh, you are getting really good at that," I cheered her on. "Pretty soon, you will be doing it all by yourself!" She lost her balance and sat down hard. She cried. I scooped her up, hugged her and said, "You're fine," as I patted her back. "No crying is allowed today. This is a happy day. You will get a mama and a baba today."

"Mama."

"Mama *and* a baba. A baba is really special, too. I had a Baba once."

"Baba."

"He was funny and he made me feel like an empress! He died and I miss him terribly. *You, Little Treasure,* will go to America in a few days and I bet you will ride in a fine automobile. My Uncle Charlie said that everybody in America drives a car."

She clapped her hands although I am sure she had no idea what I was talking about.

"Will you think of me when you rest your head on one of the silk pillows at the rear window of your car?"

She giggled.

All around me, the Aunties were scurrying to get the babies up and dressed. Today there was added work because the nine babies who were to be adopted must be cleaned up, fed and dressed before the foreigners arrived—even if they weren't the first babies awake.

I did not go downstairs to eat breakfast. I could not bear to leave Jin Ying for one minute longer that I had to. I stayed in the nursery and fed her some congee, spooning it into her mouth.

All too soon, Ling A-yi was at the door. "They should be here any minute," she said.

In that moment, I remembered something. "A-yi, may I get something from my basket?"

"Now? Can't it wait until later?"

"Later will be too late. I need it now. It is very important."

"Alright, bring the baby. The Americans will be here very soon. We can stop at my office on the way to the conference room. I will leave you in my office for a few minutes while you look in your basket, but will come back for you when the foreigners are ready for the babies."

I dug around the inside of the basket while Jin Ying stood, holding onto the corner of Ling A-yi's desk, bouncing up and down. "Ma-ma, Ma-ma," she babbled excitedly. She knew something was different about this day.

"Dui! That's right, your mama's coming!" I said with exaggerated cheerfulness.

Finally, I found it. I rubbed my hands across her head, smoothing down little spikes of downy baby hair that were sticking up all over her head. I unwrapped the pink silk bow from the cellophane and clipped it to her hair. Four thin ribbons streamed down at varying lengths. At the end of each ribbon was a small pearl. Set against the blackness of her hair, it was, perhaps, the most beautiful thing I had ever seen. I whispered in her ear, "Don't ever forget your Jie-jie."

"Mei-Lin, it is time." Ling A-yi peeked in the office door. She looked at the baby and smiled. "She is the most special baby ever adopted from this social welfare institute."

I picked up the baby and carried her into the hall. I could hear some of the parents crying and exclaiming over their new babies in the conference room. Three aunties remained in the hall, holding babies. I stood at the end of the line. Finally, my time was gone. I looked at Jin Ying and said, "Are you ready? Your mama and baba are right in there!"

I kissed her little head, stepped through the door, and announced, "Jin Ying!"

The woman with the clipboard called out "Michael and Elizabeth Talbot."

Elizabeth Talbot stared, "Oh Michael, she is even more beautiful than her picture!"

"She takes my breath away," he said.

I put Jin Ying on the ground and held her hand. I squatted down and pointed to Elizabeth Talbot and said, "Mama."

"Ma-ma, Ma-ma!" she babbled.

Elizabeth squatted down and held out her arms. "Here's Mama!" she said, black tears of mascara streaking her face.

Jin Ying broke free of me, raced six steps by herself and fell into Elizabeth Talbot's arms.

A pretty woman with brown hair that fell around her face in soft waves, she had a gentle smile. She was wearing American Levis and a red sweatshirt with the Chinese word love, "Ai" written in black on the front of it. Elizabeth Talbot picked up Jin Ying and held her close against her shoulder. She kissed her and said, "Here's Mama," again and again. She wiped the black tears from her face with the back of one hand. Then she motioned to the woman with the clipboard to come close to us and turned to me. "Xie-xie," she said in Chinese while bowing to me. Then, in English, she said to the other woman, "Ask if this girl is her A-yi."

Through the translator we spoke, "No, only Jie-jie," I said, "but I care for her every day."

"She is so beautiful and happy, I can tell someone has loved her."

"I have loved her very much. She is a very special baby."

"What is your name?"

"Zhong Mei Lin."

"How old are you?

"Thirteen."

"She is a very special girl," said Ling A-yi, placing her hand upon my shoulder. She has taken exceptional care of this baby. When it was very cold earlier this winter, some other babies died. She took Jin Ying into her own bed to keep her warm each night." I looked up at A-yi. I didn't know she had known this.

"You kept my baby alive?" asked Elizabeth Talbot.

"Dui."

"Thank you for caring of her until I could come get her. I will be forever grateful."

"Bu ke qi--It was nothing. I did it because I love her." I had been respectfully looking down at the floor but I peeked up at her and said, "I am afraid you will not thank me when you realize how I have spoiled her." I looked back down as my guilt hung on my shoulders. "She still drinks from a bottle and will not even try a cup." Then, I said hoping to wash away some of my guilt, "She still wears a diaper at night, although in the daytime she does very well in split pants."

Elizabeth felt with her right hand under her left arm for the baby's bottom and looked shocked to realize that the baby's bare bottom was sticking out of the fold in her knitted green trousers. "Oh my!"

"She talks a lot and will tell you when she has to use the toilet."

"That's good! What word does she use?"

"'Xiao bian' means she has to pee and 'da bian' means poop. If she says 'da bian,' you had better run."

Elizabeth laughed. "Maybe we'll just keep her in diapers a little longer." She handed Jin Ying to her husband. Michael Talbot looked a little afraid to hold her, like she might break if he held her too tightly, or pee on him if he squeezed her. The baby started to cry. "You'd better take her back, Hon," he said and gingerly handed her back to Elizabeth.

"Okay, sweetheart, Mama's here."

"Mama," said Jin Ying laughing again. She was clearly content in her new Mama's arms and delighted to be the center of so much attention.

Michael Talbot zoomed in on them through the lens of his video camera and the three formed a cozy little circle. All around them other parents with babies were forming their own cozy circles. There was a lot of noise in the room. Babies cried, mothers cried, translators talked while the woman with the clipboard shouted instructions.

The parents began to undress the babies and put clothes on them that they had brought from America. Jin Ying wore red and white, striped leggings with no split in the back, a white shirt and a soft red sweater. On her feet, they put white socks with tiny lace cuffs and the cutest pair of little red shoes I had ever seen. They were shiny and had three tiny red roses on each toe. I was glad to see they were not too tight. But Jin Ying had other ideas. She wanted her old shoes.

"Bu yao!" she shouted and kicked the new ones off.

"Well," said Michael Talbot. "I think I just learned my first bit of Chinese. I would take that to mean, "I don't want those!"

"If memory of college Chinese serves, that *is* what it means," laughed Elizabeth. "She sounds like a normal toddler to me!" She patiently put the shoes back on. "Wo yao," she said.

Over this they put a pink coat with a white fake-fur trimmed hood and matching pants that were attached to the coat. Elizabeth took all the baby's orphanage clothes and folded them in a pile with the clothes of all the other adopted babies. She began to take the silk bow out of her hair, but I stepped forward and placed my hand on hers. The translator was no longer in this part of the room. Although it had been nearly a year since I had spoken English with Ye-ye, I searched deep into my memory to find some of the words I wanted. I knew there were holes in what I wanted to say and my speech was not good. "This hers. I give it her. Her remember me."

"You speak English?

"Not well."

"Much better than my Chinese!" laughed Michael Talbot.

"We learn school, two hours only week."

"Xie-xie," said Elizabeth refastening the bow in the baby's hair. "She will keep it always." She had tears in her eyes again. "We will have her first portrait taken with this bow in her hair." She motioned to the photos of babies covering the walls of the conference room.

"And we'll send you back a photo of her to keep for yourself, Mei Lin," said Michael Talbot. I could see Ling A-yi looking at me across the room. It was time to leave.

I bowed to the Talbots and said, "Thank you adopt her. She have good life."

"Thank you for taking such good care of her." They returned my bow.

I left the room and stood in the hall, listening, unwilling to move away. But, I did not cry even when I heard Jin Ying cry and call out for me, "Jie-jie, Jie-jie!"

I could hear Elizabeth soothing her, "Mama's here. You're okay." But she didn't stop crying. I ran to our dormitory room, opened the window and looked down at the street below. Jin Ying was kicking Elizabeth, trying to wriggle out of her arms while reaching behind her Mama calling, "Jie-jie." I watched the Talbots stand on the front steps of the Baoshan City Social Welfare Institute as the woman with the clipboard snapped a photo of them together. I watched them step into the bus, and I watched the bus drive away. Jin Ying did not stop crying, "Jie-jie!"

I closed the window, unrolled my mattress and lay on my back. Tears rolled back from my eyes, filled my ears and cascaded onto my pillow.

戴拾叁

The Red Jacket

Better do a good deed near at home
Than go far away to burn incense.

"Come on, Mei Lin, sign up to work in the nursery again? It's not as much fun without you."

"I can't, Wu Dan. I'm just not ready." I picked at some noodles with my chopsticks.

"Jin Ying left twelve days ago!"

When I didn't respond, she said softly, "I wish I was Jin Ying!"

"Me too," I sighed and smiled at her.

"She'll have a good life!"

"I know."

"And we still have each other," her face brightened and she smiled an exaggerated, silly smile at me.

"We'll always have each other," I laughed. "You're not going to get adopted, are you?"

"Not a chance! We are sisters for life!" I held up my hand toward her.

"We'll always be together no matter what!" She laced her fingers through mine and gripped tight.

"No matter what?" She looked left and right, and then said, "You had better warn Na-Te."

"Na-Te? What are you talking about?"

"I see how he looks at you. I see how you pretend not to look at him."

"Oh, you're crazy!"

She continued jokingly, "I would understand if you were avoiding me in the nursery to spend more time in the kitchen with Na-Te, but I thought you hated scrubbing floors."

"I do. I mean, I do hate scrubbing floors, not that I avoid you in order to spend more time with Na-Te!" I could feel my face getting hot. "It has nothing to do with him, okay?" This was not coming out well. My tongue was twisting all over itself.

"So, it is good for you to pout and sulk but it was not good for me?"

"What?"

"You were the one who practically dragged me into working in the nursery in the first place. You insisted that we choose a special little sister to care for. You never considered why I was so against the idea, did you?"

"No, I . . . You never said . . ."

"There was another baby, Mei Lin. Her name was Yang Lan —the same name as one of the babies who shares a crib with Jin

Ying. We called her Lu-Lu. She was every bit as sweet as your Jin Ying. Every bit! And she was *my* special sister. How do you think I feel every time I see than new baby with my special baby sister's name? You thought I was just a cold, cruel, baby-hater, didn't you? I'm not, Mei Lin. I am just tired of hurting. That's why I chose Tong Mi after Lu-Lu was adopted. I thought she was too old to be adopted. I never saw anybody over three get adopted, and she was already four! I thought it was safe to care about her. But, it wasn't."

"Oh, Wu Dan! I didn't know!"

"I don't want to care about anybody, but I can't help myself. I do care. I have decided that from now on, I will just care about people who won't leave me. That's why I care for Guan Fang Mei. No one will ever adopt her. The foreigners only want perfect babies."

I stood there speechless.

"And, I care about you!" she continued. "You just said we'd be sisters forever, but I can't be a sister if you lock me out of your heart. If you hurt, I want to share it with you. Sisters are for bad times as well as good times."

"We are sisters."

"Should I sign up to scrub floors with you?"

"Fang Mei needs you," I said with a conviction I hardly felt.

"I know--and I need you. Won't you please sign up to work in the nursery?"

Her words struck me deeply. It had never occurred to me before that everybody here had an aching heart. What right, then, did I have to expect special treatment for mine? I returned to the nursery that week, though it felt like I was just going through the motions. I was not impatient to get to the nursery after school as I had been before. I did not care to go back after dinner to bed down babies and to sing lullabies. There were plenty of babies but none of them stole my affections as Jin Ying had. None of them had a smile as bright. None of them laughed as sweetly.

As I dressed for bed that night, I commented, "I don't know what's wrong with me. I know there are plenty of babies here, but none of them makes me want to call her little sister like Jin Ying did."

"You're not letting them," said Wu Dan. "That's why they don't. Just pick any one," she urged. "They all need somebody to care for them—especially the sick ones."

"What if I love a sick one and she dies?"

Wu Dan looked up at me and then fixed her gaze at the floor. Her chin quivered. This girl, whose very name is a daily reminder that she was all alone when she was brought to the orphanage in the fifth lunar month, was quiet a full minute, staring at the floor before she asked, "What if she dies and nobody ever loved her?"

Wu Dan's comments rang in my ears. In the days after that, we played with all the babies in turn. I played with the pretty ones as well as the ugly ones who had holes in their faces where their upper lips should have been. I said I was being fair. In truth, I knew I wasn't allowing myself to spend enough time with any one baby that I would begin to see her unique personality or to care about her. Even thought she was a half a world away, my heart still clung to my sweet Jin Ying.

Several large boxes of toys had been delivered during the fifteen days of Chinese New Year celebrations. I could scarcely believe how much Han Yue Mei had been able to purchase with the money I had given her! There were lots of toys to play with now: colorful plastic rings that stacked on a rocking tower, blocks that squeaked with pictures of farm animals on them, balls and tops, and some cups that nested one inside another. The babies turned these over and looked inside, they chewed on them and the older ones stacked them to make a tower.

"Mei Lin," offered Qiu Qiang A-yi one afternoon as I was squatting near the floor playing with Duo-duo and Shan-shan who sat laughing in the new bouncy chairs. "I have noticed that you don't seem to be quite yourself lately. I stood when she spoke to me and she put her arm across my shoulder. "It has been my personal observation that sometimes, just talking about what bothers me helps, even if I cannot change the circumstances."

"Xie-xie, I said. "But, I don't know how I would make words to describe this empty hole in my heart."

"Well, you think about it. My offer is always open."

Two days later, I noticed Qiu Qiang A-yi about to leave. As she opened the door, I could see Officer Wang parked at the curb, waiting for her on his motorcycle.

"A-yi?" I asked without thinking. The word just leapt from my mouth.

"What is it Mei Lin?"

"No, I'm sorry, I shouldn't have said anything. It is a terribly personal question."

"Well, ask it. I'm only a few years older than you, more like an elder sister than an Auntie. If I don't like it, I won't answer it."

I looked down at the ground, thinking of how to phrase it but there was no tactful way. "Do you ever kiss Officer Wang? I mean, is it okay to kiss a boy? Do you have to be married first?"

"Whoa! I thought you said one question! So far we're working on three and I am on my way out the door!" She put her hand on my shoulder and looked right in my eyes. "The answers are yes, maybe and no. We'll talk more tomorrow, especially about maybe."

True to her word, Qiu Qiang A-yi and I had a talk. I can't remember everything we talked about, but I do remember feeling a lot better afterward. No, I had not dishonored my family name—yet. Perhaps in the old China such a gesture would have marked me for life, but in the present day, disgrace was still a few steps away.

Wu Dan and I were on our way downstairs for dinner when Chen Song met us on the steps. She said that Ling A-yi had a package for me in her office.

"A package for me?"

"From America. It has your name on it. I saw it."

Wu Dan and I went to retrieve it. We carried it with us to dinner and set it in the corner of the dining hall while we ate. Both of us pretended not to care, but we hurried through our watery rice and vegetables. In the relative privacy of our dormitory room, (with only seventeen other girls watching) I opened the box.

"Who is it from?" asked Mingsha.

"Why did Mei Lin get a box?" asked Su Xi.

"Where is *my* box?" said little Zao-Zao.

"You didn't get a box. Only Mei Lin got a box," explained Xiao Ping with all the authority a first grader can muster.

Finally the tape gave way and I opened the box flaps. On the top, were several large sheets of clean but crumpled up white paper. I smiled a broad smile and handed them to Wu Dan, "I guess whoever sent this was thinking of you. As small as you write, that should give you room enough to write a whole book!"

She happily began smoothing out the papers. Just below this was a small cardboard folder. When I opened it up, there was a picture of Jin Ying smiling sweetly and holding a stuffed toy panda. She was wearing a beautiful pink dress of some kind of sheer material over another layer of deeper pink satin. It had a delicate lace collar and a dark pink sash around the waist. On her feet were white lacy socks and sparkly white buckle dress shoes. She had

had a haircut and her bangs were even. In her hair was my pink silk bow with the pearl and ribbon streamers. "Oh!" I gasped, "She is so beautiful!"

"And happy," said Mingsha.

"I wish I had a pretty dress like that," said Zao-Zao in a dreamy voice.

"Well, I don't!" sneered Hua. "It is not practical. It would be ruined by one day of kitchen work or washing diapers."

"I think," said Su Xi, "If you own a dress like that, you are a princess and you don't have to do laundry or scrub floors."

"Is Jin Ying a princess now?" asked Mingsha her eyes growing wide.

"I think," I said remembering my Chinese New Year clothes, "that when you live in a family, sometimes you have clothes for special days that you don't wear when you do house chores. One year, I had special clothes just for Chinese New Year. Jin Ying lives in a family now, so maybe she has this extra dress just for a special celebration."

I opened a second folder that had been just below the first. I recognized Michael and Elizabeth Talbot and Jin Ying, nestled in her Baba's arms smiling so big, both her dimples showed. But there was also a golden haired boy, about the same age as Na-Te and a brown haired boy who looked to be about seven. It hadn't occurred to me that Jin Ying would have siblings. Very few children in China had brothers and sisters since the one child policy had begun. I had nearly forgotten that families in other places often had more than one child.

Under the pictures was a red jacket made of soft fluffy material. It looked very comfortable and warm. There were two kittens playing with a ball of yarn appliquéd on one pocket and fuzzy black pom-poms at the end of the drawstring ties for the hood.

Pinned to it was a note written in both Chinese and English. *I hope this keeps you as warm as you kept our sweet Jin Ying through the cold winter nights.* I slipped the jacket on and continued looking in the box.

There was a huge bag of candy with a note that said, "Please share with your sisters." The girls cheered and clapped. I took one piece and then passed the bag to Mingsha. Another bag was filled with all sorts of hair ribbons, pom-poms, barrettes, ponytail elastics and other hair ornaments. I clipped two red barrettes in my hair and took out a pair of sparkly red pom-pom pony-tail elastics, secured them to the end of my braids, and passed the bag.

"Let me see!" shouted Su Xi.

"Everyone can share," I said. There's plenty here for everyone to have a new one every day if we take turns!"

At the bottom of the box was a cardboard camera; the kind you use once and then have the film developed. With it was a pre-paid mailer to a film company in the part of Baoshan City where the Golden Tiger Restaurant and Tourist Hotel is located. I remembered having passed it on previous trips in that area to see Qin Shu-shu.

"Wu Dan, take my picture!" I handed her the camera and then posed. "Here, now you put on the jacket and I will take your picture."

She put on the jacket. "Oh, Mei Lin, it is so soft! Can I wear it sometimes?"

"Of course, we are sisters."

"Let me try!" said Su Xi. So, Wu Dan took off the jacket and put in on Su Xi. It hung, nearly touching the ground. We all laughed. I snapped her picture. Each of the girls tried on the red jacket and I took their pictures--all except Hua who sat on her bed working a page of Math problems.

"Do you want to try it Hua?"

"No I want to do my Math. It is very hard with all this noise in here."

"Oh, Hua, grow up. Stop acting so jealous!" said Wu Dan.

"I am *not* jealous," said Hua. "I am just . . . trying to do Math."

"She is *so* jealous," confided Wu Dan in a whisper to me.

I turned the camera on her and took Hua's picture anyway without the red jacket on.

That night, as I lay in bed, I pictured Jin Ying smiling, two dimples in her cheeks. She was wearing the pink dress and nestled securely in her new Baba's arms. The only man I had seen with any regularity, since my arrival at the social welfare institute was officer Wang, and he only from a distance as he waited for Qiu Qiang A-yi to come out to him. I missed Jin Ying but in missing her, I also missed my Baba and envied her spot nestled in her Baba's arms. Sometimes the longing not just for Jin Ying, but for my old life, was so great as I drifted off to sleep that I could not stop the tears. I learned to cry silently, though, so no one would tease me for being a baby or for thinking my longing was any deeper than theirs. At least, I consoled myself; I had once had a family. But, sometimes I thought that because of that, maybe I knew even more deeply what I was missing than the girls who had never had a Mama to brush their hair at night or a Baba to swing them up in the air or tell them that they are a daughter of a thousand pieces of gold.

Releasing Promises & Seizing Opportunity

To attract good fortune,
Spend a new penny on an old friend,
Share an old pleasure with a new friend
And lift up the heart of a true friend
By writing her name
On the wings of a dragon.

After breakfast the next morning, Ling A-yi called me into her office as Wu Dan and I were lining up the preschoolers at the front door for our walk to school.

"Mei Lin, you will stay home from school this morning to see the doctor.

"I am not sick."

"No, of course not. It is for some routine paperwork that I am required to file."

"What paperwork?" I asked suspiciously. "Does Wu Dan have such paperwork? Does Hua?"

She seemed impatient as she drew her lips into a tight, thin line.

"No they do not."

Fearful of being different and afraid of what that difference might mean, I said, "Then I won't have such paperwork either!"

"The choice is not up to you. It's not even up to me at this point. We have been directed to do this paperwork by the Department of Civil Affairs."

"Have I done something wrong?"

"No, nothing like that. In fact, it may turn out to be very good news."

"What good news?" I demanded far more urgently than was appropriate for a well-raised daughter of China.

Ling A-yi paused a moment and sighed. "I wasn't going to tell you until I knew if it was going to go through. I didn't want you to get your hopes up and then have them dashed."

"Hopes of what?"

"The American couple who adopted Jin Ying has requested to be allowed to adopt you. It seems that not only were they very impressed with you when they met you, but the baby was inconsolable, crying day and night, mourning for the loss of you. Although she is now adjusting well, they think it is cruel to separate you from her and they want to keep you together." They have already petitioned the adoption officials in Beijing and requested that official papers be filed for your adoption."

"Adoption?"

"Adoption."

"I am thirteen years old. I am too old! Nobody over three years old is ever adopted."

"No, although it is very unusual for someone to request a child of your age, the law states you must be less than fourteen."

"I would live in America with Jin Ying?"

"If it all works out. As I said, it is all highly unusual. It is premature to get your hopes up now. So much could go wrong."

My mind was spinning. I tried to sort out each piece of the puzzle.

I would live in America.

I would see Jin Ying again!

I would have a mama and a baba . . . not the same mama and baba, of course, but a family.

I would leave Na-Te and Wu Dan in China: Wu Dan, my forever sister, the truest friend I had ever known.

Jin Ying's parents cared enough for me to ask--just for me— not somebody else! They wanted me!

My heart was tearing in two. I would have to choose between my dream: a life with a chance of a future and my promise to be a sister forever to Wu Dan.

"No," I said. "I do not wish to go."

"Well, at your age, your consent is required for final adoption. At this step in the process, however, I am afraid I must prevail. You will see the doctor today as scheduled and I will submit the paperwork. I think it is in your best interest; a great opportunity and I hope you will take some time to think this over carefully before you are faced with the final decision. Do not decide impulsively. Your future is at stake."

I had never experienced Ling A-yi as so forceful.

Wu Dan was still waiting in the hall with the preschoolers when I left the office.

"I will not be going to school this morning," I announced.

She looked at the floor and did not acknowledge me. "Come on little ones. Time to go to school." She said a little too cheerfully as she led them out the door, down the wide stone steps and across the street to the preschool building.

I ran up to the nursery and threw myself at Qiu Qiang A-yi. She enfolded me in her arms and I sobbed like I hadn't sobbed since the morning of Qing Ming.

"A-yi, Americans want to adopt me. They want to take me to America."

"I know."

"How can I go? How can I leave Wu Dan?"

"Life often places difficult decisions upon us."

"A-yi, I can't decide this!"

"Then trust Ling A-yi to decide for you. It is a wonderful opportunity."

"Wu Dan and I are going to be department store sales clerks together. If we get good enough grades, maybe we will be chosen to attend university. . ."

"You think you will *both* have these opportunities--and at the same time? You have no understanding of the limited options available to a girl who grows up in a social welfare institute! Don't you think I had dreams of university? The two career choices offered me were working in a social welfare institute or joining The People's Republic Army. It was really no choice. Could you see me with a rifle?" She leveled a baby bottle on her right forearm and pointed the nipple at my heart. "If I had your choice I would *fly* out of here! You are being offered a golden star! Grab hold of its tail before it passes you by!"

"How can I break my promise to always be a sister to Wu Dan?"

"In your heart, you will *always* be a sister to Wu Dan. Aren't you still a sister to Jin Ying even though she is in America now?"

"Yes, but . . . "

"A sister would love you enough to let you go. A true friend would not hold you to this promise. Besides, you don't know what opportunity may be presented to Wu Dan in the future."

"Mei Lin, I thought I might find you here," said Ling A-yi. "The doctor is downstairs in the medical examining room. Please go there at once."

During lunch break, I sat with Wu Dan, rearranging the noodles in my bowl, but unable to swallow any of them. Na-Te came and sat with us and I felt like I would throw up. *How could I leave them?* He and Wu Dan chatted away about nothing. I grew sicker by the moment.

"Excuse me, I feel sick," I said and got up from the table. I went upstairs and lay on my bed until it was time to return to school. Qiu Qiang A-yi's words echoed in my mind, "You think you will *both* have these opportunities--and at the same time? You have no understanding of the limited options available to a girl who grows up in a social welfare institute! If I had your choice I would *fly* out of here!" A girl from a social welfare institute has no father to speak for her; to enroll her in university or arrange a job with an employer. A girl can't do these things on her own—at least not without great difficulty. I knew that I would have to go with the Americans. It was the choice my Baba would have made for me.

When the building was quiet enough that I was sure Wu Dan and Na-Te had returned with the others to school, I got up and walked there myself. I went through the whole day in a fog. The teacher asked me a question in Chinese Language class but I wasn't even aware that she had spoken my name. The whole class laughed.

As we walked home from school, Wu Dan was chattering on about a hundred different things. "Did you see what Fei Yau did in Math class? Honestly, I don't know how she gets away with so much. If you or I tried that we would be punished."

I couldn't hear her. I felt like I was under water, drowning.

"Mei Lin, what is the matter with you?" she jumped in front of me, yelled at me, waving her hands in my face, with nine of the elementary school kids standing around us, and a sea of bicycles careening around us because of our sudden stop.

"Nothing, I just don't feel well." *How could I tell her I had chosen to leave her, to break my promise to her?*

"Hey, you are talking to *me*! I *know* you! Remember me, Wu Dan?" She danced in front of my face crossing her eyes. All nine elementary school kids' eyes were riveted on me.

"Can you just let it go? Can we talk about it later?"

"Ah! So there is something!"

"I don't want to talk about it right now. Not here."

We stopped at the preschool and picked up the little ones.

Just as we ushered them in the front door of the social welfare institute, Wu Dan closed the door behind them so that she and I were alone on the front steps. "They told you, didn't they?"

"Told me what?"

"That's why Ling A-yi called you into her office and why you stayed home from school this morning, isn't it?

"What are you talking about?"

"Your adoption."

"You knew?"

"And I knew I wasn't supposed to know."

"How did you find out?"

"Well, you know how I look through Ling A-yi's office trash can for scraps of paper to write on?"

"Dui."

"Two days ago, I found a paper in there that looked pretty empty. There was lots of room between the lines and it was written on only one side. I didn't even look at what it said at first. I was just writing along between the lines when I noticed your name. It was just a note from the Central Adoption Committee in Beijing, notifying Ling A-yi that an American couple had requested to adopt you. They wanted to know if she thought you would be agreeable to the idea and if she thought it was a good idea for you. If so, she was to fill out the appropriate forms and return them to Beijing as soon as possible."

"You knew and you didn't tell me?"

"How could I tell you? I wasn't supposed to know and maybe Ling A-yi would decide it was not a good idea."

"You knew and you didn't tell me."

"I would have told you but I . . . "

"But you let me feel sick all day wondering how *I* would tell *you*. You let me tell Ling A-yi that I didn't want to be adopted . . . "

"You *told* her you didn't want to be adopted?"

"I did."

"Why?"

"I promised to be your sister forever. We are going to work in a big department store and sell fancy dresses together, aren't we?"

"You're crazy! It's a dream, Mei Lin! We'll never have the kind of opportunities we dream about!"

"We'll have each other."

"No we won't Mei Lin! We won't have any choice. When it is time to leave the social welfare institute, we will go where they tell us. We will work the jobs they assign us to. It is fun to dream, but happy dreams are not reality—not for orphans!"

"I didn't think it was a dream, I thought it was a plan—a plan we both shared."

"Mei Lin, it was a dream, a foolish dream of a couple of kids. You are faced now with a real opportunity. You are crazy if you refuse! Believe me, I wouldn't refuse if this was my choice!"

"You would leave me?"

"You bet I would! And, I certainly wouldn't waste an ounce of guilt on breaking my promise to you!"

Late that night, I lay in bed, holding my picture of Mama and Baba and thinking. How could I leave the land where they were buried? But, I knew I already had. Some part of me already knew I would leave when I scraped the handful of dirt from their graves and wrapped it up in newspaper. I had planned to leave their resting place forever by taking a small part of it with me!

I couldn't sleep. I thought I heard a muffled sob coming from the direction of Wu Dan's bed.

"Wu Dan," I called out. "Wu Dan, are you awake?"

There was no answer.

Goodbye, Hello

Wherever you go,
Go with all your heart.

I tried to put the idea of adoption out of my mind. I tried to forget that I might be leaving China.

But I couldn't.

Some days raced by. At these times, I gathered moments into my memory much as Wu Dan did. Unlike her, I did not write them on scraps of paper. I only tried to hold images in my mind: memorizing the patterns the morning sunbeams cast upon the floor of my dormitory room, the way Wu Dan's hair bounced when she talked, the musical sound of Qiu Qiang A-yi's laugh.

At other times, the days dragged, threatening to swallow me in dread. I wondered what America would be like. Would it be different from what I knew in China, or were people the same all over the world? I thought about seeing Jin Ying again. Would she run to me or would she have forgotten me already? What were American schools like? Would I be able to make friends, or would they laugh at me because my hair is not yellow and my eyes are not completely round and my English is not good?

I talked with Qiu Qiang A-yi quite a few times about my anxieties for the future. She was excited about my decision to go with the Talbots and promised to write back to me as often as I wrote letters to her.

She shared a bit of her hopes and dreams, too. I learned that she and Officer Wang were, indeed, hoping to marry as Wu Dan had suspected. At present, she lived with seven other women who had all been orphans. Officer Wang lived with his family. They were saving money and waiting to be assigned an apartment, she explained.

Finding an apartment in China is not a simple matter. All housing is controlled by the government. Young married couples often wait many years to be assigned a place of their own. They live with the husband's family until they are assigned an apartment. But, this was not an option for her because officer Wang's two older brothers and their wives were already living in his parents' small apartment--and both of the wives were expecting babies. The family had made it clear that it would be very good if Officer Wang could move out before the babies came.

Even if they could find some small room to live in, she said, they did not have much money and would not have a very elaborate wedding ceremony. They would probably just appear before the Officer of Civil Affairs and have some papers signed.

I thought about the picture of Mama and Baba on their wedding day. They both looked so happy wearing the simple gray padded jackets. I thought of the day I had come home to find Mama looking at the picture and remembered how much she wished she had had a proper dress for such a special day.

On my last visit to her, I gave Qiu Qiang A-yi the red silk dress that Baba had bought Mama for Chinese New Year only one year ago!

"This was my Mama's dress," I said. "You have cared for me much like she cared for me. If you like it, you can have it for your wedding.

"Oh, Mei Lin! It is exquisite! I have never owned anything so beautiful. Are you sure you want me to have this? You should keep if for yourself."

"I think Mama would have wanted you to have it—to thank you."

After refusing the gift two more times and listening to me insist three more times that she keep it, she clutched the dress to her chest, bowed and closing her eyes, said, "Xie-xie, Mama de Zhong Mei Lin."

I spent every spare minute with Wu Dan. She did not want to talk about the future and my inevitable departure. She only wanted to live in the present. "The future is frightening. The past is painful. Only the present is pleasant," she said.

On the Saturday before I was scheduled to leave, she persuaded me to cut my hair into a short bob like hers. "It is more practical and more modern," she argued. "America is a very modern place. You will fit in better with a more stylish haircut, she said, finally admitting what would soon happen." She borrowed some shears from Feng A-yi's sewing box. I stood in the girls' bathroom holding my hands over my eyes. My thick hair, hanging unbraided, reached past my bottom. She held the shears level with my shoulders and cut. Long strands of black hair soon littered the white tile floor. I shivered. I thought of each five centimeters of hair like a year of my life, much as a ring of a tree represents a year of its growth. It felt so final, as if she was cutting away my life in China, making room for new growth in America.

Unfortunately, I had neglected to ask Wu Dan if she had ever cut hair before. Her enthusiasm belied the fact that she had no idea what she was doing. When she had cut all the way around my head, I was left with one side six centimeters shorter than the other. "Don't worry," she said as I looked critically in the mirror, "Now I will even it out."

She cut again beginning on the longer side. This time, the other side was longer, but by only about four centimeters. It was an improvement, but with continued improvements like this, I would soon be bald!

"Wait!" I held up my hands as she licked her lips, poised to trim yet again. I raced down to Ling A-yi's office. She was reading some forms and looked up when I stood in the open doorway.

"Mei Lin! What have you done to your hair?"

"I was trying to cut it so it would be more stylish when I meet my new parents, but it is more difficult than I had thought. Please, may I get some of my money and go to a hair salon to have it done properly? Wu Dan could go with me. We could be back before dinner."

"It seems like the only reasonable solution, doesn't it? It would have to be from your money. The orphanage certainly has no money for salon haircuts!"

I took down my basket and counted my money. I counted again. There was exactly as much money here as when I had entered the orphanage. "A-yi, I am confused. I took out money to buy things for Chinese New Year, but all of my money is still here."

"Your friend from the provincial courts didn't want you to know. She, with the help of several wealthy businesswomen has set up a small charity to contribute to the care of the children here. The gifts for the children and the clothes for Na-Te, as well as several other baskets of clothes, and diapers, and the steamed eggs you all ate for breakfast on the first day of Chinese New Year were all donated by this charity. She returned your money."

So I withdrew two hundred Yuan. Wu Dan and I walked to the Lotus Blossom Hair Salon on the corner of Nanjing Street and Guangdong Boulevard.

As I stepped in the door, a bell rang and everyone looked up. Two hair stylists were sitting in their chairs, eating bowls of noodles, paging through magazines which they had draped over their knees while they commented on the spring fashions.

"I need a haircut," Insaid.

"Yes, you do," said one with a blond streak in the front of her hair.

"What butcher shop did you escape from?" asked the other who was wearing a very short black leather skirt.

Wu Dan's face glowed as brightly as a red paper lantern!

"Well, you've come to the right place," said a third woman who was massaging the back of a patron. "Can you pay?" she scrutinized my well-worn clothes.

"I have money."

"Come up here," the one with the blond streak motioned to a beige vinyl, padded bench I was to kneel upon. It had rests for my elbows that could bear my weight as I leaned forward and held my head over a bowl. She poured water on my head until my hair was wet. She squeezed out most of the water, and asked me to lean back so that I was upright. She stood over me and lathered the shampoo, massaging my scalp until thick foamy bubbles formed like peaks of whipped egg whites. These she scrapped off my head and splattered into the bowl. Then she sprayed more warm water on my hair and lathered it again. She rinsed my hair again and again until it squeaked when she rubbed it. Then she wrapped a towel around my head and asked me to sit in the salon chair she had previously been sitting in.

"Now, what did you want me to do with it?"

"I want something like that!" I pointed to a soft-focused photo on the wall of a girl with a sharply angled haircut, chin length in the front but short and layered in the back.

"Oh, very fashionable!"

"And, I want you to do the same thing to her," I pointed to Wu Dan.

"Are you sure, Mei Lin?" said Wu Dan with wide eyes.

"We're sisters, aren't we? We're in this together."

Wu Dan didn't protest in the customary way, but quickly knelt at the water basin.

After our hair was cut, the stylist dried it by blowing hot air on it while shaping it with a hairbrush that had plastic spikes in place of boar's bristles. We looked at each other and giggled. We paid for the haircuts and I also bought a spike-style hairbrush for each of us. Wu Dan and I walked back to the social welfare institute arm in arm with a giddy confidence, allowing our hair to blow in the breeze and laughing almost the whole way. It was as if, all by themselves, the haircuts had made our plain blue cotton trousers into filmy pink dresses and we had stepped out of the pages of one of the fashion magazines the stylists had been reading. We stopped at the candy store and bought a bag of nougat morsels rolled in sesame seeds and honey.

That night, I gave Wu Dan my red jacket. "When you wear it, remember me."

"You know, Mei Lin, there is an ancient myth that an invisible red thread connects two lovers from the day they are born," she said stroking the soft sleeve of the jacket. "The fabric of their lives unravels until they find each other. Perhaps there is a similar thread that connects good friends and keeps them connected long after they part."

"Sisters," I corrected. "Sisters are forever."

Finally the day arrived. I stood in the hall at the end of a long queue of Aunties. Each one was holding a baby. Everyone else was supposed to be in school, but when I looked up, Na-Te was standing at the door of the dining hall. He walked toward me.

"Zhong Mei Lin, I will never forget you." He bowed toward me in a very formal fashion. The morning sun glinted off his hair in red and purple bursts of light as he moved. I wanted to reach out and throw my arms around him and kiss him again as I had on the first night of Chinese New Year, but of course that was impossible in a hall full of Aunties. He thrust toward me a soft package wrapped in newspaper, and tied with twine. "I wish you much prosperity in America. Please do not ever forget me." Then he turned and walked briskly toward the back door of the orphanage and out into the alley where we hung the laundry on sunny days.

I followed him down the hallway and stopped at the doorway. "Hui Na-Te!" I shouted after him. He stopped and looked at me. "I could never forget you." He stopped and nodded once toward me but shook his head, and said nothing in reply before he started walking down the alley kicking stones.

"Hui Na-Te!" I shouted again, unwilling to let him go. He looked up but I could find no words to express the ripping I felt in my heart. I looked down again, sighed, turned around and started back inside.

"Zhong Mei Lin!" he called out.

I stopped, turned to face him. He held his hand over his heart and said slowly. "A part of me goes with you. A part of you stays here with me forever."

I nodded sadly and turned back to the conference room. There was nothing else to say. He had, as usual, said just what I was feeling and he had said it just right.

I put the package he had given me in the top of my backpack basket smoothed down the front of my old school uniform which, by now, was much too short, and ran my fingers through my springy new haircut.

Then, I took a deep breath and hoisted the basket onto my shoulders. "I am a daughter of a thousand pieces of gold," I said to myself. Carrying all that remained of my life in China, I stepped through the door of the conference room and into my new American life as I announced my own name: "Zhong Mei Lin."

I recognized the Talbots right away and didn't wait for the adoption facilitator, the woman with the clipboard, to announce their name. I stood before them and bowed.

"Hello Father," I said in English and bowed toward Michael Talbot.

"Hello Mother," I said and bowed toward Elizabeth Talbot.

Elizabeth Talbot was smiling warmly.

"What have you done to your hair?" said Michael Talbot.

His words plunged me into despair. *Already I was a failure as a daughter to them! Of course, I should have asked their permission before cutting my hair. What had I been thinking?*

"I am so sorry, Father! I will grow it back." I bowed to him again.

"Don't pay any attention to him, Mei Lin," said Elizabeth Talbot. "What do men know about hairstyles? It looks very cute on you. You look much more mature and stylish. You look like a Chinese-American girl." She put her hand on my shoulder and I dared to peek up at her. She was smiling at me and then she put her arms around me and hugged me. I felt my body go stiff. Wasn't I too old for this kind of baby stuff? Didn't they know I was thirteen?

Unlike the babies, I was not required to undress in the conference room, return all my clothes and put on clothes the Talbots had brought. Though the clothes I wore were the same ones

I had brought with me, not owned by the social welfare institute, Ling A-yi accepted several new outfits from the Talbots in exchange for my clothes. I was glad to see that Wu Dan and Hua would have new things to squabble over.

When they were ready to leave, Michael Talbot offered to take my backpack basket and I allowed him to. "What do you have in here, kid? Rocks?" This thing weighs a ton!"

"I will carry it," I quickly offered.

"No. I'm kidding. I'll carry it."

The three of us stood on the broad white steps of the Baoshan City Social Welfare Institute. Another father from the group of adoptive parents snapped a photo of us. Michael and Elizabeth Talbot stood on either side of me, each with an arm around me. I stared straight ahead and smiled so wide it hurt.

"That's the close-up of the happy family," said the other dad. "Let me get one from across the street so you can see the whole building." He ran across the street, snapped a couple of pictures and ran back. "I took an extra one, with the telephoto-zoom. That window was open a minute ago." He pointed to my dormitory window. "There was a sad-faced kid up there wearing a red jacket, leaning against the window frame. The light was hitting it just right. It was a striking image--too good of a shot to pass up."

I looked up, but no one was there.

My Name Is Zhong Mei Lin

*The superior person can find herself
in no situation
in which she is not herself.*

I could barely believe it when we walked through the front door of the Golden Tiger Hotel. The doorman, who would not have let me pass through this very door, less than a year ago, held the door wide and said, "Good morning, Miss." I wondered if it was the fashionable hairstyle or the Americans who walked on either side of me that made the difference.

The hotel was like nothing I had ever seen. The smooth stone floor was so highly polished that my face reflected back at me. From ceilings that looked like they were made of pure gold hung an enormous electric lamp of carved glass prisms. Tiny rainbows reflected off of it and danced around the room. In the lobby was a sailing ship that was bigger than I. The entire thing was intricately carved of jade.

The rooms were spacious—almost as big as our farmhouse.

The mattresses were so thick you couldn't roll them.

Each hotel room had what the Talbots called *a bathroom*. The Talbots each went in there, one at a time. Then they asked if I needed to use the bathroom. I didn't need a bath as much as I needed a toilet, and I told them so. Elizabeth Talbot smiled and opened the door, "We call it a bathroom, but there is also a toilet in there."

"How odd," I thought, "to put a thing as filthy as a toilet in the same room with a tub used to get one's self clean! It seemed a great contradiction to me. Yet, if this was the American way, I reasoned that I must get over my revulsion and do as they do. I went in and closed the door.

There was, indeed a bathtub on the left side and a sink on the right. In the middle was a thing that must be a toilet, but I couldn't figure out how it worked. It was sticking up from the ground and there were no footpads or platform to stand on. I tried putting my feet on the rim, squatting over the bowl, but it was so slippery, I bruised my foot when it slipped off and splash-landed in the bowl.

"Mei Lin, are you okay?" asked Elizabeth Talbot from the other side of the door.

"I will not be much longer!" I said. At least I hoped I wouldn't. I had to pee badly.

I tried again. This time I approached the thing head on. *Americans must have superior strength* I reasoned, *if they can stay balanced, while squatting on a toilet with such a narrow opening!* This time, I *faced* the American-style toilet instead of backing up to it. I took off my shoes and socks, so my feet would be less likely to slip, completely removed my trousers so I could climb up on that high rim (which was impossible to do with my pants pulled down), hung onto the water tank on the back and peed. American toilets were a lot of work!

Elizabeth Talbot had three outfits laid out on one of the beds when I came back into the hotel room. "Why don't you take a shower and choose one of these outfits to change into?"

They were all new clothes. I had never had three new outfits all at once. Perhaps they intended for me to choose one and then they would send the other two outfits back to Wu Dan and Hua. I would choose the ugliest outfit. It was a difficult decision. They were all beautiful but all strange looking. In the end I chose the one that was less durable and not at all practical. This way, Hua and Wu Dan would have useful clothes that lasted longer. It was a dress.

The skirt was much too short. My knees were visible. It was embarrassing to have so much of my body uncovered. I knew that city girls often wore dresses—with skirts even shorter than this, but I was a country girl and had never worn any dress before. My legs had never seen daylight. I feared I had made a terrible mistake, but when I came out of the bathroom again, the Talbots were both smiling.

"You look lovely," said Michael Talbot.

I did not argue with them. I respectfully kept my eyes down, bowed and said, "Xie-xie." *At least no one will see me* I thought.

"Well then, shall we go out to show off our beautiful daughter to the good people of Baoshan City, and maybe see if we can find some lunch along the way?"

A wave of panic rolled through me. He expected me to leave this room half naked!

They headed to the door and I followed. What was I afraid of? I was an American girl now. I was expected to dress like an American girl. As soon as lunch was over and we left the Hotel, I remembered what I was afraid of.

It seemed to me that people grouped together staring at me and my white parents and my naked legs. I imagined that they whispered their shock to each other. *Americans will ruin that girl*!

Only one stately-looking old man sitting on a street corner with a green bird in a cage, looked on approvingly and spoke out loud. "Very lucky girl!" he said nodding to me, and then bowed to Michael Talbot, giving him a thumbs-up. "Thank you adopt China girl." He smiled broadly revealing three teeth missing from the front of his mouth.

We walked through a small park where grandmothers sat playing Mahjongg. Tongues started clicking as they whistled their stern corrections at me. "You will catch cold, girl!"

The Talbots walked on oblivious to my embarrassment. Elizabeth Talbot took my hand and said, "Now, we are going to buy some things for you. We want you to pick out some things for when you are older. Every girl needs pearls. Do you like natural seawater pearls or cultured pearls?"

I had Mama's pearls. I didn't want any others, so I said, "I no pearls."

"Well, if that's the way you feel about it, of course, you don't need to buy any." I could see she looked disappointed, maybe even offended. We walked on in silence, browsing through a few small shops and into the open Qingpin market.

Finally Michael Talbot broke the silence. "Perhaps there is something else you'd like? If I remember correctly, we are just one turn away from the jade market."

We turned into the street of the jade market. My arms ached, remembering the last time I was here with Ye-ye. I felt the jolt of the cart again as it hit the rut in the road and heard him say, "Well your grandmother is certainly worthy of remembrance. However, do you think you could reminisce on a smoother section of road?"

"Oh, look! Isn't this beautiful?" Elizabeth picked up a delicately carved pendant of a hummingbird and held it against my chest. It was truly lovely but if I wore that, I would have to take off the jade Buddha that had belonged to Nai-nai. "I no want!" I said.

265

"You are a very difficult girl to please," said Elizabeth Talbot growing impatient with me.

"Honey, honey, I am sure she has her reasons. It *is* just gorgeous, though there is no accounting for taste. Let's just buy it and we'll give it to Jenna for her twelfth birthday."

"Jenna? Who is Jenna?" I asked.

"Your sister! The baby we adopted when we met you. What was her Chinese name, Jing Yin or something?" Elizabeth Talbot looked like she was searching her brain for the right words.

"Jin Ying!" I said.

"Yes, that was it! Her name is Jenna now. She is doing very well. I can't wait until you can see her again. You'll hardly recognize her. She has gained five pounds and is running everywhere.

"Jenna?" I asked.

"That's right. And, while we are on the topic, I was thinking of naming you either Molly or Maya. Do you have a preference?"

"No!" Each was equally horrible. Neither one was my name.

"Okay then, I think it will be Molly," said Elizabeth Talbot.

"My name Zhong Mei Lin," I said quietly, while my insides were exploding. I wanted to run back to the social welfare institute but I did not wish to dishonor Ling A-yi. I wanted to run to Qiu Qiang A-yi. What I really wanted was Mama—*my* Mama, not Elizabeth Talbot!

"Well, if you insist, we can keep part of that," she continued thinking out loud. "Zhong is too hard for most Americans to pronounce. How about if we call you Molly Lin? That sounds cute."

Not only was I standing in a public market nearly naked, now I felt myself being stripped of my identity. "My name Zhong Mei Lin."

Your name *was* Zhong Mei Lin. Your new name is Molly Lin

Talbot."

"Wo jiao Zhong Mei Lin!" I whispered to myself as I stared at the ground. I would not abandon the memory of my parents, no matter how these people disgraced me. I would always remember who I was!

The walk back to the Golden Tiger Hotel was long and entirely silent.

That night, Elizabeth Talbot said, "Molly, I bought you a suitcase to put your things in. You'll have to leave that old basket here. It just won't fit on the plane. She went in to take a shower. Michael Talbot had gone on an errand with another American father, so I was alone for a few minutes. I carefully removed Na-Te's package from the top, untied the cord and opened the newspaper. There, rolled up tightly, was the bulldog sweatshirt. I held it up to my face and breathed in. It still smelled of Na-Te. I held it against my face, remembering the sound of firecrackers and the smell of gunpowder and the excitement of his lips pressed against mine as I let the bulldog absorb my tears, which now ran freely. I carefully removed all my things and packed them into the new suitcase, laying the bulldog sweatshirt on top, carefully smoothing it flat so it wouldn't wrinkle.

The next day, I got dressed and put on the same clothes the Talbots had given me the day before. I thought that I would honor their choice rather than wear my own comfortable clothes. These clothes were not dirty, but still Elizabeth Talbot seemed angry with me.

"You must wear clean clothes each day," she said.

"These clean. No spot!" I had no idea what she was concerned about. All my life, I had been careful not to get dirt or spills on my clothes. Putting something in the laundry that was not dirty was a waste of water as well as disrespectful to Mama or to Feng A-yi who washed the clothes. I was often able to wear the same clothes for a week before they needed to be washed.

Elizabeth Talbot finally laid the other outfits on the bed and pointed to each. I chose one and changed. This one was more comfortable. Purple corduroy jeans and a pink and purple top with a thin silver stripe. There were no sleeves, however. Still, I suppose I was more comfortable with naked arms than naked legs.

After breakfast, we went for a walk and passed a schoolyard where children were playing.

"Why don't you play with them?" said Elizabeth Talbot.

"Can I play with you?" I obediently asked a group of girls playing Chinese jump rope.

"Why are you with foreigners?" The smallest one asked.

"I was orphaned and am being adopted by these Americans," I explained. "In a few days, I will go with them to America."

"Are those American clothes?"

"Dui--that's right."

"Okay, you can play," said the eldest girl.

I lined up with the jumpers while two girls held the elastic cord around their legs. On my third turn, while I was jumping, crisscrossing the elastic strings and snapping myself out of the middle, Nai-nai's Buddha popped out of my shirt and bopped me in the nose.

"What is that?" asked Elizabeth Talbot who had been watching from the schoolyard gate.

I grabbed it and tucked it back under my shirt.

"No! I want to see what it is." She marched toward me, gesturing toward my neck.

"Nai-nai," I said. I couldn't remember the English word for father's mother.

"Let me see that!" she demanded.

I obediently pulled it out and held it out to her.

"This is a Buddha!" she said and turned to Michael Talbot. "Our daughter is wearing a jade Buddha! Where did you get it?" she accused. She turned back toward her husband and said, "You don't suppose she stole it from the market do you?"

Michael Talbot scrutinized it. "No, I think she's had this a while. The thread looks rather faded."

"But, Mike, it's a Buddha! Why didn't we think of this? I thought the orphanages raised them without religion! I was prepared to deal with a child who had no religion. How are we going to deal with a child who is Buddhist? I don't know how to raise a Buddhist? Lord, I don't know if I can live in the same house with a Buddhist. What if she insists on practicing some weird religious rituals and chanting, burning smelly incense and all?"

"Well, I guess we'll have to learn. We can't just go yanking it off her neck. She has been living in this culture her whole life. Hopefully, she'll grow into ours and maybe we'll have to grow into hers a bit."

"*But Mike!*"

"Beth, we can't tell her what to feel. She's too old for that. We'll have to take this one step at a time."

"I *can* demand she respect our religion in *our* house!"

"Of course, but we'll have to respect her, too. Think of it as just a piece of stone—like the hummingbird. For all we know it means nothing more than that to her. Let's not make too big a deal out of it right away. She has enough changes in her life to get used to. Let's wait until we can communicate better to find out what significance this small piece of jade holds for her."

"I don't know how you can take these things so lightly, Mike."

Elizabeth Talbot stomped briskly off in the direction of the hotel. Michael Talbot called out to me, "Zhong Mei Lin, let's go!"

In that moment, I began to love him. I wasn't sure what I had done wrong, but I knew I had caused a terrible argument between my new parents and it had something to do with Nai-nai's Buddha. I also knew that Michael Talbot had called me by *my* name.

America, the Confusing

She who learns but does not think is lost!
She who thinks but does not learn is in great danger.

We traveled for almost an entire day and night and arrived in America an hour before we had left China. It wasn't magic. It was Geography. We had crossed the International Dateline. As confusing as this concept was, it was nothing compared to what I would soon encounter.

The most noticeable difference for me was the sky. The sky is very blue in America. In big industrial cities like Baoshan City, it was brownish gray. Even in my little village of Longkou, it was never quite as blue as in America.

There are cars everywhere in America, big cars. And trucks? One American truck could carry a fleet of Chinese trucks! There were no water buffalo in the streets, no handcarts or pushcarts laden with goods wending their way down the street. There were far fewer bicycles. The most amazing thing about bicycles was this: I never saw one that was black! In China, almost all the bicycles are black. In America, they are pink and white and turquoise and neon green but almost never black! They look different, too. There are many different styles and sizes of bicycles in America. Although there are some differences in size and occasionally in color, in China, most people ride the same style of black bicycle.

We stopped in five airports before we arrived at the one that was closest to my new home. Waiting there for us were about as many people as live in Longkou. I wondered who among them might be the American version of Mr. Liu and who was Jiang Shu-shu. They had balloons and signs that said, "Welcome to America!" Some of them were waving American and Chinese flags. I felt like I was walking in a dream. To these people it was two o'clock in the afternoon. To my brain, it was two o'clock on a morning after I hadn't slept for a day and a half. My body craved sleep. My memory of this day is swirls of images but a few things remain quite clear.

Most of the women were crying and hugging Elizabeth Talbot. The men were shaking Michael Talbot's hand. Some people came very close to me, putting their face right next to mine and shouted as if I were hard of hearing, speaking very slowly. "I—am—Cindy--Fernwelter! I—am—a—*friend*—of—your--mother."

I recognized one little boy about seven years old. He had soft brown hair and eyes like Elizabeth Talbot. He smiled at me. "Hi, I'm Jake." He held out his hand and I shook it.

"I am Zhong Mei Lin."

"Are you going to be my sister?"

"I already am your sister."

"How do you say big sister in Chinese?"

"Jie-jie."

"Hey! That's what Jenna always says when she's sad!"

"Jie-jie, jie-jie!" I heard an excited voice I would have recognized anywhere. I searched the crowd and finally saw her struggling to get down from the arms of a blond-haired boy who looked slightly older than Na-Te. She had indeed grown.

"Mei-mei—little sister! I shouted through the crowd, "Jin Ying, guo lai—come here!"

The older boy put her down and the crowd parted between us. She ran to me squealing with delight, both of her dimples punctuating her happiness. I picked her up and held her tight. I breathed in, searching for her familiar scent but I could not find it. She smelled like something entirely American—like flowers! It didn't matter. I had her back. She had not forgotten me.

She started talking—in English! "I know you. You from China. Me, me from China!" She walked around the room telling everyone who would listen, "This my Jie-jie."

Everyone was crying. Even people who had arrived on a plane at the next gate stopped and cried when they saw her dancing around showing me off to everyone.

It was at least a week before I could sleep at night and stay awake all day.

"This is what we call, 'knock you off at the knees—jet-lag!" said Michael Talbot the second morning at breakfast. He was drinking something foul smelling and brown. "It's coffee--an American icon," he said when I wrinkled my nose at the nasty smell. "Get used to it."

I was eating a fried egg and something called toast and jam that wasn't too bad--although scratchy on my throat. I heard a click-click-click drawing nearer, growing faster. Before I knew it a large tan animal hurled itself into my lap and wriggled a cold black nose into my face. I screamed and shot up to my feet, dumping the animal off my lap, sharp claws raking my thighs even through my jeans. I screamed like I had never screamed in my life. Terror had gripped my soul and I could not shake it loose. I crawled up on the chair and stepped on the table trying to escape the demon-creature.

273

I was screaming, crying and shaking my hands and could not stop.

Jin Ying was sitting in a high baby chair with an attached tray. She had been picking up small cereal circles and eating them. She drank milk from a cup with a plastic spout on it.

Seeing me scream and stand on the table, she began to laugh.

"Taffy, sit!" she yelled and the shaggy tan animal sat.

"What that?" I cried.

"It's a dog," said Jake, my new Di-di.

"A cocker spaniel" said the Da ge-ge, Evan.

They were all laughing. "She's really harmless," said Michael Talbot.

"Molly, why don't you come down, now," urged Elizabeth Talbot.

Tentatively, I took one step toward the seat of the chair. I had never seen such a frightful animal before. It moved quickly and had sharp, white teeth.

The dog jumped up and barked at me.

"Ai-ya!" I screamed and jumped back on the table.

"Molly, you can't stand on the table," said Elizabeth Talbot emphatically.

"Evan, take Taffy back down to the garage and hurry up or you'll miss your bus," said Michael Talbot. "I think we'll have to introduce these two a little more slowly. Jake, get going. Summer vacation doesn't start for another week! Don't forget your lunchbox."

Jin Ying was in pajamas, so, still trembling, I picked her up and carried her to our room.

"That's all right," said Elizabeth Talbot. I'll take care of

Jenna," and she took Jin Ying from my arms.

I wanted to be useful. Perhaps if I was useful, Elizabeth Talbot would forgive me whatever it was that still had her so angry with me. I cleared the plates and glasses from the table and stacked them in the sink. At first, I could not turn on the water although I knew it was a spigot. Finally, after playing with it a while, I figured out that I should pull up on the lever above the spigot to make water flow, turn it left to make it hot and right to make it cold. I soon washed up the whole sink full of dishes, rinsed them and stacked them in the other sink.

"Oh, no dear, you don't need to do that!" I heard the echo of Wu Dan's voice in Elizabeth Talbot, *"For a girl who is so smart in school, you certainly are stupid, Mei Lin!"*

"What had I done wrong now?" I wondered.

"We have a dishwasher," said Elizabeth Talbot opening a white panel to the left side of the sink and sliding out a blue rack. "We don't wash dishes, we just stack them in here."

"No wash dishes?"

"Well, the machine washes them. I'll show you later. Right now, the boys are leaving for school and your baba is leaving for work. I have a doctor's appointment for the baby. I couldn't get two appointments at the same time, so yours will be tomorrow. Do you think you'll be alright if I leave you here alone for a while?"

"I be alright."

I decided that I would make good use of my time and do all my laundry. I poured hot water into the bathtub and threw in my clothes. I took a bar of soap from the ledge and rubbed it on the dirty spots. I scrubbed the cloth, beating it against the side of the tub, rinsed it and rung it out. I drained the tub and filled it with clean water and rinsed the clothes again. I found a large pot in the kitchen and carried some of the clothes in it. I went out the back door to find the bamboo poles to hang them on. I could not find them. When I looked at the house for some clue as to where they might be, I saw no racks by the windows upon which to hang bamboo poles. "Americans must not hang laundry on bamboo poles," I thought.

I remembered that we had used rope at the social welfare institute when there was not enough bamboo, so I looked for rope. But, there was none--anywhere! I went back into the bathroom and hung my blue quilted pants and a shirt on the rod that supported a plastic curtain, which hung by the bathtub. I needed more space, so I took the towels in the bathroom down and folded them. I hung underwear and socks from the towel bars. I still had nowhere to hang the dress and the purple jeans and shirt that I had worn in China, or my old school uniform. I hung my uniform pants over one chair in the kitchen and the purple jeans over another. I hung the pink and purple and silver striped shirt from the handle on the black glass door under the cooking fires.

There was a large rounded window in the dining room with curtains that only went half way up. I removed the curtains, folded them and placed them on the dining-room table. Then I hung the dress and the rest of the clothes on these brass rods.

I had just finished when Elizabeth Talbot came charging in the door.

"What have you done to my house, Molly? Everybody walking by on the street can see this mess you've made. What *have* you done?"

"I wash clothes." I barely spoke and stared at the ground.

"You have turned my house into a Chinese laundry!"

"I Chinese. This laundry." I kept my eyes respectfully fixed at the ground, trying to figure out what wrong I had done.

"Don't be funny, Molly! We have a washing machine and a dryer! What do you think we have them for? Oh, dear God, look at my floors! Get this mess off my curtain rods and wipe that water up before it ruins my wallpaper or warps my hardwood floors!

She began furiously pulling clothes off the curtain rods and the chairs and throwing them on the floor of the kitchen. She was crying and saying, "I can't do this! What was I thinking adopting a teenager?" She was blotting water off the dining-room wall. "This is nuts! This is nuts! I think I'm gonna' go crazy!" She was wiping up puddles on the floor with a kitchen towel.

I couldn't believe she was throwing my clean things on the floor. I had just scrubbed all these things clean and now I would have to clean them again. I knew it would be disrespectful if I raised my voice to my mother but my mother had never raised her voice to me. Elizabeth Talbot was not my mother and she was acting very rude toward me, so it mattered less to me. I couldn't remember the words to speak in English so I began yelling in Chinese.

"Why did you bring me here? I want to go back to China! I hate it here. I hate you! You don't even like me, why did you adopt me if you don't even like me?" Yelling it all felt good. Knowing that she probably didn't understand more than a word or two of it felt even better.

"Don't just stand there!" she shouted at me. "Help me clean this mess up!"

I picked up my clothes and carried them back to the bathroom and threw them in the tub so I could wash them again. I began running water and she came into the bathroom.

"In here, too? You've got this stuff all over the place in here, too? God, give me patience!" she threw her hands in the air and stared at the ceiling. "I think I'm going to explode! You'd better send some grace now, God, because I'll do something regrettable or I'll go crazy." Elizabeth Talbot was talking to someone who wasn't there--and crying.

"You don't respect me!" I yelled back in Chinese. "I work

hard. I only try to please you but I can't seem to do anything right! Everything about me is just wrong for you!" I was crying.

"Mama, mama!" Jin Ying ran into the room. "Too much Noisy! Oh boy, messy here!"

"Yes, your big sister made a big mess." Elizabeth Talbot said. She reached out an arm to me, "I'm sorry, Molly. I think I lost my temper because I am so jet-lagged. We'll work this out, somehow. Gather this up and we'll take it downstairs," She said. "I'll show you how to do laundry."

The first thing I learned in America is this: Nobody does any work here. Machines do everything.

I wrote a letter to Wu Dan every day and told her all of these things I had learned about America. I enclosed an envelope and some blank sheets of paper she could write back. Elizabeth Talbot took me to the post office and told me to also send an international postage coupon so that Wu Dan wouldn't have to pay to mail the letter.

When he came home from school, Jake piled up a stack of books on the coffee table in the living room. "I am going to teach you to read American." He said. "I am very good at it." He spread open the book across his lap and snuggled next to me on the couch. He pointed to the words, "I am Sam. I am Sam," He read. "Now you do it," he said, pointing to the words.

"Sam I am," I read.

"Good, Mei Lin. Pretty soon you will be as good a reader as me!" We read for nearly an hour, "*Hop on Pop, The Cat in the Hat*, and a dozen others before he declared, "I'm pooped! We'll do more work tomorrow."

Evan walked in from his school, slammed his books on the counter of the kitchen, removed a carton of milk from the refrigerator and began pouring it into his mouth. I must have been staring. He swallowed, put the carton down and wiped his mouth with his sleeve. "It's not as bad as it might seem," he said. "I have perfected the art of never letting my lips touch the carton. It just saves the unnecessary and intermediary step of dirtying a glass." He repeated the procedure, closed the carton, slipped it back in the refrigerator, removed six cookies from a jar on the counter and walked down the hall to his room.

"Dad's birthday is this weekend," said Jake drawing my attention back. "What are you going to give him?"

"We no have this tradition in China. What is customary?"

"You don't have birthdays?"

"No. Well, some rich, city people might, but I never did."

"Don't Chinese people get borned?"

I laughed. "Yes, we born, but not celebrate this day special way."

"How do you know how old you are?"

"Everybody celebrates birthday all together on same day every year."

"Do you get presents?"

"No. Do you get presents?"

"Yeah! In fact, I'd say that's what makes a birthday, a birthday."

"What is your custom?"

"Well, you have to eat birthday cake and ice cream and everybody has to sing, *Happy Birthday* to you **and** you get presents."

"What kind presents?"

"Whatever you like. Sometimes we make presents and

sometimes, if we save our allowance, we buy presents. I usually make presents because I never save much allowance."

"What is allowance?"

"You know, if you do your chores, you get paid. Don't tell me you didn't have allowance in China, either."

"No, we didn't."

"No wonder you wanted to come to America! Stick with me, I'll show you the good stuff."

"What will you give your Baba?"

"Hey! Baba is what Jenna calls Dad! Anyway, it's his birthday on Saturday and I am going to give him a new baseball 'cause he likes to play catch with me."

"And it is customary for everyone to give him a gift for his birthday."

"Yes."

"Thank you very much, Jake. You have helped me very big deal."

I knew exactly what I would make Michael Talbot for his birthday, something he did not have, a symbol of importance. But first, I had to find the cloth.

While Elizabeth Talbot was cooking dinner, I asked her, "I want make something. I need buy cloth. I have money."

She never stopped stirring the ground beef she was browning in the pan. "I'll take you tomorrow after your doctor appointment."

"Xie-xie," I said, then left the room to get away from the sickening smell of searing beef.

I put all my money in my pocket before the doctor

appointment. I had no idea how much it would cost, but I knew what I wanted.

We went to *Textile Emporium.* I selected just what I had in mind and had the clerk cut it. When I took it to the cashier and handed her my money.

"What's this?"

"Money."

"Play money. I need real money."

"It real money. It Chinese money."

"You'll have to take this to a bank and have it exchanged. I can only take American money." She snapped a wad of chewing gum in her mouth.

Elizabeth Talbot had been browsing at a display of summer craft projects. When she heard the ruckus she came over and looked at my money on the counter. "Oh, I didn't even think," she said. "I'll pay for it and you can pay me back later when we exchange your money."

Afterward, we went to the bank. "I'm sorry, I can't exchange this," the teller said. "I can only convert dollars to Yuan. I cannot convert Yuan to dollars. It's illegal. This money is useless outside of China.

"I will earn American money. I will pay you back."

"Don't worry about it," said Elizabeth Talbot.

I closed myself in my bedroom, slipped on the bulldog sweatshirt that still smelled of Na-Te, and cut and sewed, carefully tucking and folding the fabric just so. By week's end I had produced two perfectly round, beautifully tufted pillows for the back shelf of Michael Talbot's car. I could hardly wait to give them to him.

I noticed right away that there was something customary in

birthday celebrations that Jake had forgotten to tell me. I had not wrapped my gift in colorful paper. It was also shocking that Michael Talbot opened these gifts in the presence of those who had gathered to wish him well. In China, we did not wrap gifts and we *never* examined them in front of the gift giver! Who could have guessed that American traditions could be so opposite? I stood nervously holding my gifts behind my back until it was my turn.

"Molly has something for you," said Elizabeth Talbot when he had finished opening all the packages on the table.

"You do?" He turned to me. "Well come on Mei Lin. Let's not keep it a secret."

"I make for you," I said and held out the pillows.

Evan snorted a mouthful of milk out his nose. Jake laughed himself so silly; he got off his chair and rolled around on the floor.

"Boys!" said Elizabeth Talbot. "That is enough! You don't need to be so rude."

"But mom," said Evan.

"They're pink!" shouted Jake and began holding his sides, laughing again.

"Enough!" said Michael Talbot. "They're beautiful."

"I do something wrong?" I asked but could not look up.

"They're pink!" shouted Jake again.

"Jake, go to your room!" said Michael Talbot.

"Pink not good?"

"Pink is for girls!" shouted Jake on his way down the hall.

"I so sorry I offend you," I offered. It seemed in that moment that I would never get anything right. Everything good I tried to do turned out all wrong in this place. I was no longer a daughter of a thousand pieces of gold. I was a daughter of mud, a mistake, a regret, and a burden! I should never have left China. "Excuse me, please?" I said and walked to my bedroom and closed the door. I sat on my bed, writing another letter to Wu Dan. "How could I have become such a great failure in such a short time?" I wrote.

There was a knock at the door. "Mei Lin, may I come in?"

I couldn't believe Michael Talbot was asking my permission to enter a room in his own house. "Mei Lin, it's Baba. May I come in?" I burst into tears. I could not bear to hear the name Baba applied to anyone but my Baba, Zhong Liang. As nice as he was, Michael Talbot was not he! I wiped the tears off my face, got up and opened the door.

"Mei Lin, it was very nice of you to make me such a thoughtful gift. I remember seeing such pillows when we were in China. They go on the shelf by the back car window, don't they?"

"Dui."

"Do they have a special significance?"

"Successful and important people have them. They are the only ones who have cars. You had a car but you did not have any pillows. When I was a girl in China I often dreamed of becoming rich enough to rest my head on such a pillow."

"You are a very sweet girl. You may rest your head on these pillows of mine any time you ride in my car. I am very proud to be your Baba."

I burst into tears again.

"Did I say something wrong?"

"I so sorry! I try, but I cannot call you Baba. It hurts my heart."

"Well, we can't have that! I only use 'Baba' because Jenna always did and I thought it would be a more comfortable word for you, at least at the beginning."

"I had a Baba once. I love him very much."

"I had no idea! I thought you had grown up in the orphanage."

"No, my whole family die in the flood one year before you adopt Jin Ying."

"You must miss your family a great deal."

Fresh tears spilled from my eyes. "I no want make you mad, but--you not Baba."

"I understand." He paused a moment and then asked, "What was he like, your Baba?"

"He a good man, help many people. He very funny--and love me. He call me 'daughter of a thousand pieces of gold.' This highest praise for Chinese girl. Here, I show you picture." I took out the photo of Mama and Baba from under my pillow and unwrapped it from the red silk bridal veil that had been Nai-nai's.

"Why did you keep it under there?"

"I was afraid you would be mad if I honor my other Baba in your house."

"Mei Lin, I could not be angry to share such a sweet sensitive daughter with this good man. I consider it an honor." He took the red veil from me, "May I?" He laid it on the center of the dresser. Then he placed the photo on top of it. "I want you to remember them always."

"I thought you would destroy this picture if you ever saw it."

"Why would I destroy the memory of someone who created something as wonderful and beautiful as you? They must have been very fine people to have raised such a special daughter. It is only right to keep their memory alive. I am sorry their time came so soon, but am so glad I get to share this bright and beautiful daughter with them."

He held his arms out and I stepped toward him. He hugged me. I did not hug back, but I let him hug me. "What would *you* like to call me?" he asked.

"Would it be okay if I call you Dad like the boys do?"

"Sure! But, do you think you could manage to say "Daddy" from time to time. I always wanted my girls to call me 'Daddy."

"Thank-you, Da-dee." I bowed deeply, showing my greatest respect.

All-America-Girl

Be not afraid of growing slowly
Be afraid only of standing still.

I had been living with the Talbots for nearly a month, when I decided it was time to settle in. I removed my suitcase from under my bed and finished unpacking it. I placed the jade Buddha on the dresser with Mama and Baba's photo. I put the incense burner in front of it, although I had no incense to burn. I carefully scratched the names of Ye-ye, Baba, Mama and Di-di into my family name plaque. This, I leaned against the wall behind the Buddha. I took a small glass jar from the recycling bin under the kitchen sink and carefully poured the dirt from our family burial place into it. I placed the jar on the dresser in front of the name plaque.

I spread Mama's quilt across my bed, covering the white eyelet cover Elizabeth Talbot had put there. That thing gave me shivers each time I saw it. In China we wore white only for a death in the family. Each time I saw all that white on my bed. I thought of the funerals I had not been allowed to attend. Though dirty and a

286

little faded, the bright colors of the quilt cheered me and I felt Mama with me every time I looked at it. When I was done, the room I shared with Jin Ying had begun to look like a home I could recognize and feel happy in.

I was especially comfortable whenever I was wearing Na-Te's bulldog sweatshirt.

This had become a problem. Every time Elizabeth Talbot saw me wearing it, she groaned and said, "Not that stinking sweatshirt again! Go back to your room and take it off! I am sick of looking at it! You have a closet full of clean clothes! What is wrong with them?"

"Nothing wrong. Very beautiful. Thank you very much."

"If you are cold, why don't you wear that nice red jacket we sent before we adopted you?"

"No have red jacket."

"Why don't you have it? Didn't you get the package?"

"Got package but no more have jacket now."

"What happened to it."

"I so sorry. I give to Wu Dan."

"Didn't you like it?"

"I like it very much. Xie-xie," I bowed to punctuate my thanks. "But, she not be adopt. She need more. Keep warm in cold winter."

Elizabeth Talbot wiped a corner of her eye and shooed me away. I was sure I had hurt her feelings by giving away the jacket she had given me. *Everything I do turns out wrong*! I thought.

To be honest, the bulldog sweatshirt did sort-of reek, especially after I wore it through a couple of hot June days, but I couldn't bear to wash it. Even though it now smelled of me, it also still smelled of Na-Te, our scents mingled together. If I pressed my face into the back neckband and took a deep breath I remembered how it felt to touch him. Not much scent remained on Mama's quilt but I could find her in it if I searched and breathed deeply. These were the only scents in this new place familiar to me.

In addition to Nai-nai's Buddha pendant, the Buddha on the dresser, became a problem immediately after I put it there. While I was watching Jessica Laughlin on the WKRE TV-*evening-news-with-a-heart,* Elizabeth Talbot went to get Jin Ying up from her nap. Jessica was talking about a young girl who had just had heart surgery. Jin Ying was crying, standing in her crib. Elizabeth Talbot was singing, "You are my sunshine, my only sunshine, you make me happy when skies are gray. . . ." And then she must have picked up the baby because the crying stopped. The next thing I knew, she was shouting, "Molly! Get in here this minute! I will not have this-- this obscene *thing*--this half-naked man displayed in *my* house! Remove it immediately. I don't ever want to see it again until you are a grown adult. At that time you may decide what to do with it in your own house. Do I make myself clear?"

"Very clear," I said, although I hadn't a clue as to *why* she was so incensed. There was, after all, a sad, half-naked man hanging on a cross on the wall in her bedroom, so I knew it couldn't really be the half-naked part, though that was the only clue she had given me as to the cause of her anger. What was it about the Buddha that angered her so much? The happy Buddha looked like more fun than the tortured Jesus, but I figured that if this Jesus was so important to the Talbots, He was important to my happiness as well. I would be the daughter they wanted.

The Talbots were Catholic. They hoped that I, too, would become Catholic. To do so, I attended extra religion classes every Wednesday evening.

Every Sunday, we went to St. Stanislaus Church. Instead of bowing while holding sticks of incense as Buddhists do and chanting and meditating, everyone stood while singing and knelt while saying the same words together. Instead of each family laying

288

offerings of oranges and rice on an altar, only one family each week brought offerings of wine and little pieces of bread. Then, they sat and listened to a man who was wearing a long dress talk. That part was the same except that the only Buddhist teacher I had ever heard sat while he spoke and the Catholic priest stood while he spoke. When all that talking was done, the people filed row by row to the front of the room and ate the little white pieces of bread.

"You can't eat the bread," said Jake, "Because it is really the Body of Christ. If you eat it and you are not Catholic you will go straight to the bad place that I am not allowed to say; you know, h-e-double-hockey sticks!"

"He must be mistaken!" I reasoned. Eating the body of a person was *inhuman*! I must have misunderstood. These people didn't act like cannibals. Still, he was taking classes to be allowed to eat the Communion bread, so he might have learned some secret I hadn't.

I didn't really believe anything concerning religion, Buddhist or Catholic, and didn't understand what all the fuss was about. To me, it didn't matter. I only liked the Buddha because he was a piece of home. Perhaps the Buddha reminded Elizabeth Talbot that I was too Chinese and not American enough. Maybe, if I could lighten my skin, round my eyes and make my nose bigger she would be happy with me. For two days I tried to keep my eyes wide open all the time in an effort to make them look bigger and rounder. But, Daddy stopped me and asked, "Mei Lin, do you have something in your eye?" so I gave it up as hopeless. I would never look like them.

I finally decided that belief was secondary to obedience—but obedience was secondary to my own safety. To be on the safe side, whenever I was in the church, I made sure to always sit on the end of the pew so I could make a quick escape if someone decided to eat *me*.

The smell of American cooking—especially searing beef, which we ate almost every night---made me sick to my stomach. We ate this meat, or chicken, usually with a potato; baked fried, shredded, boiled, mashed, or au gratin, along with some uncooked vegetables, that I found flavorless, and cow's milk that gave me cramps. Breakfast, too was usually cold cereal and milk. I had never eaten cold food in my life! Mama had insisted it was unhealthful. I think she was right. I had constant stomach cramps and diarrhea. I was grateful for food, and the supply was plentiful, but I longed for something tasty like hot and spicy vegetables or anything cooked in black bean sauce. I began having dreams about mountains of pork dumplings dripping in soy sauce and vinegar and deep fried egg rolls with shrimp and cabbage inside.

Of everything I missed, however, the lack of rice and noodles nearly drove me crazy! Every day of my life, I had eaten rice—often twice a day—and some type of noodle for lunch. After all, the Chinese word for lunch literally means, "eat noodle!" The Talbots occasionally had noodles, but they drowned them in some sort of milk sauce that gave me cramps and gas, or a thick tomato sauce that also reeked of the unpalatable beef and made me burp. I would gladly, forever, give up my fantasies of dumplings, steamed buns and hot breakfast foods, for just one bowl of rice or unadorned noodles each day!

It was a very hot day in August, and I suppose the heat contributed to my discomfort, but when Elizabeth Talbot placed before me a slab of meatloaf with mashed potatoes and lettuce and tomato salad, I felt my stomach lurch. I just could not force myself to eat this one more time. I pushed it away from myself and announced, "I am not hungry. May I excused?"

"Sure," said Dad. I walked down the hall to my room.

"Mike, I don't know what her problem is. She has been sullen and disruptive since the day she arrived! I know she has got to be hungry. She refused the grilled cheese sandwiches I made at lunch, too and I don't think she ate but a single piece of toast for breakfast."

"Do you want me to talk to her?"

"I wish you would. You seem to have a better way with her than I do."

He finished his dinner then knocked on my door.

"What's the matter, sweetheart?" he asked. "You've got to be hungry."

"I'm sorry," I said. "I want be good daughter, but I think America food make me sick." I explained the whole problem to him and he gently laughed.

"I'm the one who should be sorry," he said. "I guess we've been pretty insensitive. We just expected you to fit into our ways right away and didn't think about you missing your own ways. Each time we went to China for two weeks, I would have died for a decent hamburger and a cup of coffee. I don't know what we were thinking. Let's go shopping!"

We drove for nearly an hour to the United Asia grocery store a few towns away. "It probably won't be just what you remember, but maybe there will be some things that are close. You just show me what is good. You and I will cook a fabulous dinner tomorrow night!"

I pushed the shopping cart up and down the aisles, my mouth salivating! There were cans of pickled quails eggs and fresh lotus root, dried seaweed and rice noodles. In the freezer case were ten kinds of bao zi ready to steam and as many kinds of dumplings. There were cans of shark fin soup and fresh bean curd. There was mango juice and huge jars filled with bite-sized morsels of Lychee jellies. Best of all there was noodles and rice. Dad bought 20 pounds of rice and three cases of Ramen Noodles!

All around me, signs were written in Chinese. When we got to the checkout, the cashier announced each price in Chinese.

"You'd better handle this," whispered Dad. "I'm in over my head."

I chatted with the cashier who had recently emigrated from Taiwan but also spoke Mandarin. We laughed about the strong taste of beef and how we couldn't understand why Americans liked it so much.

That night when we got home, I cooked up four cups of rice which Dad and I sat and shared. I ate at least six times as much as he.

Elizabeth Talbot walked into the room, looked at the large bowl of rice in front of me and said, "I thought you weren't hungry?"

"Well, technically, she wasn't hungry for American food," said Dad. "But, she was starving for Chinese food." He pointed to the bags of groceries on the counter.

Elizabeth picked up the can of soup, reading the English side of the label and said, "Oh, ick! Shark-fin soup. I feel sick just thinking about it."

"And that's just the way she feels about hamburgers and milk and cheese."

"You're kidding!"

"Dead serious." He smirked. She said nothing, ran to her room and closed the door.

That night, I wrote a letter to Wu Dan. I told her about the Chinese grocery store. "I finally found some signs of civilization!" I said.

In September, I started school. As I had arrived in America during the last week of the school year, it had seemed pointless to begin school then. I attended St. Stanislaus Junior/Senior Catholic High School. I was in the eighth grade in the junior high school. Evan was a junior in the senior high school.

Instead of the entirely comfortable cotton warm-up style school uniform I had worn in China, I wore a scratchy green and blue plaid skirt, white blouse, plaid necktie, green sweater and itchy green knee socks with black and white saddle shoes that gave me new blisters with every step. I felt uncomfortable. I felt self-conscious. I felt ridiculous!

Boys wore the same kind of shirt and sweater, but got to wear black trousers and black shoes. It looked much more comfortable!

I rode the bus with Evan the first day and he walked me to my homeroom.

"Look," he said, "Everybody is nervous on the first day. You got your schedule in your trapper," he tapped on the cover of the large notebook I carried. "Don't be afraid if you get lost."

"Why I get lost?"

"When you change classes."

"Change class? Students move from room to room, not teachers move to the students?"

"Right. Students move but you only have three minutes to do it in, so don't think you have time to stop at your locker between classes. Take all your books for morning classes now."

"Oh, this very different! In China, teachers get lost. Students stay in one place all day."

"Really? Cool! Now listen, it tells you right on your schedule which room you go to. A, B and C tells you which wing to go to and G means the gym. The room numbers are next and the first number tells you which floor. 1 is first floor and 2 for second and 3 for third floor. Don't worry if you get lost. I did my first week—lots. Just stop and ask somebody for help. Okay?"

"Okay," I said.

I looked around the classroom and found a seat. I don't know what I was expecting, but I was shocked to be in a classroom with so many white people. In my mind, classrooms should be filled with black haired people with almond-shaped black eyes. There was one boy who was not white. His skin was as dark as the outside of a well-used wok. I had never seen a human being in that color before and I couldn't help staring at him.

"What chew lookin' at?"

"You. Your skin is black!"

"So, you notice that, huh?" Everybody laughed.

"I never saw a person with black skin before." I continued. "Does it hurt?"

"Does it hurt? What?" Then he laughed. "You think I'm burnt? Where you from, girl?"

"China."

"You a Commie?"

"No. I don't think so. What is Commie?"

"You know, a Communist? I thought everybody over there was a stinkin' Communist."

"I no stink. I American Chinese now, so I shower every day! I smell like flower."

"Oh, man you are good! What's your name?"

"I am Zhong Mei Lin, but sometimes people call me Molly Talbot."

"That's cool! My name be Be-Bo but the teachers call me Tyrone Percie Bennett."

"What classes you got?"

I showed him my schedule and he said, "We got History and Religion together. History is first period. You want to walk over together?"

294

"Yes, Thank-you."

Be-Bo became my first friend in America.

In English class I saw a girl with black hair and almond eyes. I was so excited to find a familiar looking face; I walked right up to her. "Excuse me," I said. "You are Chinese?"

"Nah, I'm American. My name's Ellen Dawson. I was born in Korea but was adopted when I was tiny, so American is all I know." She talked so fast I could hardly understand her.

"I adopted!" I said hoping she would see the connection between us.

"That's nice," she said and called out to a yellow-haired girl across the room, "Marissa, are you trying out for cheering this year?"

I didn't fit in at school any more than I did with the Talbots. I was a slow listener. By the time I understood what people had said and translated it in my head, they were already on the next topic. Holding a conversation was nearly impossible.

Every class depended on reading. Jake had been teaching me all summer, but he was only in second grade. I needed to read like an eighth grader. I was used to being the smartest kid in school. Now, I felt just plain stupid. The only class I excelled in was Math, which had never been my best class before! There I didn't have to speak, only work equations on the chalkboard.

"Molly, would you show the class how you solved problem 78?

That I could do! If I had had to *tell* how I had done it, I couldn't do it.

We had been at school about six weeks, when suddenly it seemed that everybody was talking about the Halloween dance party.

"What you going as, Molly," asked Be-bo.

"I don't know." I had no idea what Halloween was or what "going as" implied.

Ellen said she was going as either Marilyn Monroe or Madonna; definitely something that required a blond wig so no one would guess who she was.

"I was thinking of going as an African American," said Be-bo. "Maybe you could go as a Chinese girl. I bet nobody else will think of those costumes!"

"Maybe I go as African American and you go as Chinese girl so we confuse them," I said.

"Ha! That'd be cool," he said slamming his hand on the desktop. "You wanna' do it?" We both laughed.

Later that night, I asked Evan about it. He dragged a big box out of the attic. He and Jake rummaged through it, pulling things out.

"You could be a ghost," said Jake. "This mask glows in the dark. It's really cool."

"How about a fortune teller?" Mom wore this to a party one year. Evan held up a wild printed skirt and a wig with gold bangles hanging off it.

"Remember when Dad went to that party as superman? He got his cape caught in the car door and didn't realize it was flappin' outside until they got there!" laughed Jake.

Later that night, as I said "goodnight" to Mama and Baba's picture, it occurred to me that Moon Festival must have come and gone and I hadn't even known which day to celebrate it. I was losing China, but I didn't feel like I was gaining America. I was drifting in some uncharted nowhere-land between countries and I felt it must be as vast as the Pacific! The worst thing was that I still had not been able to please Elizabeth Talbot. She seemed to always be angry with me for no reason that I could determine. I would never be the all-America-girl she wanted!

戴拾玖

Finding My Way Home

Knowing is not as good as loving;
loving is not as good as enjoying.

Daddy and I had a standing date on the first Saturday of every month. We would drive to the Oriental grocery store. There, I always chatted with the same grocery clerk. It was the only time I read or spoke Chinese and I thirsted for these tidbits of language like a Mongolian horse thirsts for water after crossing the great Gobi desert. I had learned her name was Lin Pi-Jen. She was a musician and played the pipa, a Chinese string instrument. She had a daughter born in the year of the horse—the year after me and Wu Dan. (Although by the American way of calculating we were only a month different in age and born in the same year.) There were lots of Chinese people in the area. In fact, there was a Chinese language school on Saturday mornings not far from our home.

"How are you doing?" she asked on our November visit. "Are you all-American-girl yet?"

"No. I'll never be that! I have made friends with the dog, but people are more difficult. I can't seem to fit in. My adoptive mother is the biggest problem. She doesn't like me. I don't know why she adopted me."

"What do you do for her, to make her life better?"

"I mostly try to stay out of her way. Whenever I try to help with the baby, she comes and grabs her away from me. Whatever I do is wrong. I always make her angry."

"You must work harder to be a good daughter."

"How? I have done everything I can think of."

"You must find out what is important to her and give it to her."

All the way home, I pondered, "What is it that Elizabeth Talbot wants from me that I have not given her?" I couldn't think of what it might be.

On the day before Thanksgiving, all the Talbot cousins and aunts and uncles gathered at Grandma's house in upstate New York. It was a long drive, but it was worth it. I got to rest my head on a silk pillow as we drove. I dreamed of China and of watching dusty peasant girls with broad bamboo hats, pulling handcarts loaded with watermelons and baskets of fish, while I drove past them, dozing on silken comfort.

I knew the moment I met her that Grandma Talbot liked me. She hugged me when I walked in the door and said, "It's about time I get to meet my newest granddaughter! What took you so long to get here?"

"Oh mom, you know how busy we've been!" Dad rushed up behind me and kissed her.

"I know, dear, but a grandma needs to hug her grandchildren more often than twice a year!" She hugged and kissed Dad, then each of the boys and Mama. Then she took Jin Ying from Mama and said, "Oh how big you have grown, my little empress!" She sat in a chair taking off the baby's coat all the while talking. She kissed the little girl over and over until she giggled. "Now you tell grandma, *how much does Jenna love grandma*?" She sang the words.

"So big!" said Jin Ying and threw her arms up over her head.

"Oh, what a smart girl! You remembered our game." She put the baby down and said, "You go play with your cousins. *I* want to talk to Molly Mei Lin." She wrapped her arm around my shoulder much as Auntie Qiu Qiang had often done. She was shorter than most Americans, about as tall as Auntie Qiu Qiang but six times as round. She wore a red and white checked apron over blue jeans and a pink turtleneck. "Come into the kitchen, dear, I'm baking pies today and I need your help. The arthritis in my fingers is so bad with this cold snap in the air that my fingers can hardly hold the rolling pin to roll out the dough."

I knew how to roll out dough! I had done it often with Mama when she made dumplings. The American rolling pin was very big, though and much heavier than I was used to. I lay my hand in the middle of the rolling pin and began to roll. It was very hard to do.

"Like this dear," said Grandma Talbot. She held the little handles on the ends instead of pressing down on the middle. It was easier to roll the heavier rolling pin this way. I could see that there were differences between rolling small dumpling wrappers and big pie crusts.

We had a great talk. She asked me all about life in China and what I was finding different about America. We laughed a lot and she stopped every once in a while to hug me again. "I'm so pleased you decided to come join our family, dear."

"I too," I said, "but my heart hurt when I think Wu Dan and Guan Fang Mei will never be adopt." She asked who they were and I told her about each of them as we peeled apples and stirred them in sugar and cinnamon.

"Never say 'never,' dear. We can't tell the future. Maybe someday a family will come along for each of your friends."

I knew better, but I thought it smarter to keep such thoughts to myself.

On Thanksgiving Day, the uncles set up folding tables added to the end of the dining room table, extending it into the living room. All the other furniture had to be pushed aside to make room for the huge table. The boy cousins came in then and put the chairs around the table, counting three times to make sure there were enough. Aunt Susan spread out three tablecloths and Aunt Tina placed a plate in front of each chair. The girl cousins all came and lay the silverware in the proper places. Finally, there was room for everyone to find a place at the table. We stood behind our chairs and, as steam rose off an enormous brown bird with it's head and feet cut off, each person had to name one thing they were thankful for before we could eat.

"I am thankful for making the basketball team," said Evan.

"I am thankful for apple pies," said Jake.

"I thankful everything," I said, "Everything that is China and everything that is America." *One holds my past,* I thought *and the other my future.* I remembered that Wu Dan didn't like to talk of past or future. "Most of all, I am thankful for right now," I said and smiled at Grandma.

"I am thankful for this whole big beautiful, hungry, healthy family!" said Grandma.

When everyone had spoken, Uncle Larry asked a blessing and we all sat down. Grandma had made a huge bowl of rice. "Now, nobody touch this. This is Molly Mei Lin's rice," she said as she put it on the table right in front of my place.

"Whoa! How come she ranks?" teased Evan.

"Alright, she gets the rice, I get the bird!" said Uncle Bob.

"Okay, I'll give you the bird but every drop of chestnut stuffing is mine!" said Uncle Pete.

"Boys!" said grandma in a teasing way. "Honestly, some part of a boy remains in every man!" I stared at her, remembering the night Baba and Uncle Charlie had lit firecrackers scaring Hong Rong and making Di-di cry.

I tasted all the food. Turkey was good. But, that was all! Mostly, I ate rice. I liked being at grandma's house. I wished I could stay there. I seemed to fit-in better there. But Sunday, we drove back home to New Jersey.

On the Monday after Thanksgiving, a letter arrived from Wu Dan. Guan Fang Mei had been adopted. There was surgery to straighten her legs in America. She might even learn how to walk. Wu Dan was trying to be brave and think of what was best for Guan Fang Mei, but I felt her fear and aloneness grip me about the throat. How I wished I could be back in China with her!

About two weeks after Thanksgiving, I returned home from school to find a clean pile of laundry on the dresser in our room. Some was for Jin Ying and some for me. I began sorting it, putting it in the proper drawers. Suddenly, staring up at me, neatly folded and freshly laundered was the snarling face of Na-Te's bulldog. *I* hadn't put it in the laundry hamper! Whenever I was not wearing it, I usually hid it between my mattress and box spring. But that morning I had been in a hurry. Had I left it on my chair? Did Elizabeth Talbot pick it up while picking up Jenna's clothes? I grabbed it and held it against my face and breathed in deeply. Mountain fresh scent! I dropped to my knees and sobbed, pressing the bulldog into my face. She had stolen Na-Te from me! An even more awful thought seized my mind and gripped my heart. I looked at my bed. Mama's quilt was clean! The white patches were no longer gray, but sparkling white. I buried my face in it and searched for some hint of Mama. Sometimes, if I found just the right spot and breathed deeply, there was still a trace of her there. Again and again, I pressed the worn quilt to my face and breathed in, but all traces of Mama had been washed away and replaced with Downy freshness. Once again, I heard that sound of a wounded water buffalo rise from deep within my very soul.

She knocked on the door, "Oh, for God's sake, Molly. What is *wrong* with you?" I sobbed bitterly. I would not let her in. I locked the door of my room and would not come out.

"Molly Talbot, you open this door right now!"

I would not.

I wrapped myself in Mama's quilt and held Na-Te's bulldog sweatshirt to my chest and rocked back and forth. I could not stop. Every time I thought I had stopped, I would think of Mama and of Na-Te and I would cry again. I would think of Wu Dan alone without Guan Fang Mei and I would cry. I would think of what a mistake it had been to come to America and I would cry.

I *will run away*. I thought. *I will go back to China where I belong*.

When Dad came home from work, I heard them talking.

"You'd better talk to her, Mike. She won't even let me in the room."

"What happened?"

"I don't know. She's just so moody! I never know what to expect from her. You'd think she'd be thankful that I cleaned that thing so that she never had to miss it."

"What thing?"

"While she was at school today, I washed that reeking, awful sweatshirt and that thread-bare rag of a quilt she dragged home from China. By the way she reacted, you'd think I'd killed somebody!"

There was a knock on my door. "Mei Lin, it's Daddy. Would

you let me in sweetheart? I want to talk."

I took a deep breath, wiped my face and opened the door.

"I can see you are pretty upset." He stared at my tear streaked, red face and swollen eyes. "Your Mama's upset . . ."

"*That woman* NOT my Mama! She hate me!"

"Mei Lin, she *loves* you! Whose idea do you think it was to adopt you?"

I did not answer.

"She fell in love with you the first day she met you. When Jenna started crying for you it broke her heart. She wanted to take you home right then. She thought it was unfair to keep you two apart. She made inquiry about you before we even left China. She started the paperwork for your adoption the minute we got home from China."

I didn't react. I stared at the floor, but his words were sinking in.

"We couldn't afford two adoptions so close together, so, although she had planned to stay home with Jenna for a few years, she went back to work part time to make enough money to pay for your adoption. This *woman* has given her heart and soul for you. The thing she wants most in the world, the *only* thing she wants from you is to be your Mama."

"She can't be my Mama! I have a Mama."

"Okay, okay. This is the Baba/Daddy thing all over again, isn't it?"

I didn't answer. I just stared at the ground. *What had he just said? It was the key Lin Pi-Jen had told me to search for! The thing she wants most in the world is to be my Mama.*

"Can she be your Mom?"

"I no think she want me. Everything I do always wrong for her. She hate me."

"She *doesn't hate* you. It seems that everything *she* tries to do for *you* turns out wrong, too. She thought she was being nice, washing your things while you were at school so you wouldn't miss them. And you reacted by screaming at her and locking her out of your room."

"She washed away my Mama!" I held the quilt up and sniffed it and cried with renewed vigor, shaking and sobbing.

"Oh God!" said Elizabeth Talbot, standing in the doorway. "That was your Mama's quilt?"

"It still smelled like her." I took in a deep breath and then continued, "If I closed my eyes and wrapped it around me, I could still feel my Mama." Elizabeth Talbot walked into the room. Tears were running down her face. "When they carried my whole family away, dead, Jiang Shu-shu wrapped me in it and hid my family treasures under it and I knew I would survive."

"Your whole family at once?" asked Daddy "Not just your Baba?"

I stared at the ground. "When I slept on the floor of Xu Shen-shen's kitchen, I wrapped myself up in her quilt, and Mama kept me safe from the rats."

"Rats?" Elizabeth Talbot shivered.

"When I escape from him and walk to Baoshan City by myself in the night, I had Mama's quilt in my basket. It was like I carry her with me. She give me courage."

"Escaped?" She wiped the tears from her face with her hand.

"When I was sent to Baoshan City Social Welfare Institute, I snuggled under this quilt and my Mama wrapped her arms around me and kept me and Jin Ying and three other girls warm through a night cold enough to kill babies."

"Why have you taken so long to tell us all this?" asked Daddy. He was crying too.

"I didn't think you wanted to know China-me. You only want *Molly*, all-*America* girl!"

"No! I want you to be *you*!" said Elizabeth Talbot. "I only call you Molly because I thought an American name would help you feel more comfortable with American people. Molly is a special name. It was my Mama's. She died many years ago and I still miss her. You were such a wonderful girl, I thought you deserved a very special name."

"You like me?"

"I *love* you! I am sorry. I guess I have done everything wrong. Can you forgive me?" She sat on the floor and wrapped her arms around me. "I had no idea. I thought I was helping."

"I thought I was helping *you*!" I said. "I washed dishes. No! All wrong. I washed clothes. No! All wrong! I take care of Jin Ying. No! You only do that."

"No, it wasn't wrong. It's just that I didn't want you to do it the hard way when we have much easier ways. I don't want you to work too hard. I want you to enjoy being a kid for a while. You don't have to be responsible for the baby. That's my job. You can play with her whenever you want. I just didn't want you to feel that I had adopted you as a nursemaid for the baby. I wanted you to know I only want you to be a daughter. I adopted you because I love you."

She wrapped her arms around me and drew me toward her. I rested my head on her shoulder and she rocked me back and forth, rubbing my back. We were both crying.

Maybe Elizabeth Talbot was trying to be a mom as much as I was trying to be a good daughter. Maybe neither of us knew how to do that right?

I leaned back. "Would it be okay if I call you, 'Mom'?"

"It would be wonderful!"

Dad sat on the floor and wrapped his arms around both of us.

We sat on the floor together like that, until Jin Ying came running into the room. "Hey, What's going on in here? I wanna' play too!" She jumped between us and rocked back and forth. We all wrapped our arms around her and hugged.

Asian Angel

If you walk on snow.
You cannot hide your footprints.

Mom's birthday was on the nineteenth of December. I wanted to give her something very special but I didn't know what that might be. If I could only go to the mall to look around, I knew I would know what I was looking for once I saw it. I sat at my desk counting my allowance money.

Taffy sprawled on the floor of my room. She groaned and rolled over on her back looking hopefully at me. I reached out and rubbed her belly with my foot.

On the Saturday before Mom's birthday, Dad had taken the boys to a Giants football game and Mom had taken Jenna with her to do some Christmas shopping. I was supposed to stay home and nurse a sore throat. I knew that I was not permitted to walk to the shopping center alone. Mom said that it was too far for a girl to walk alone, but I was sure she meant an American girl because it was less than ten li from our house. I would only be walking, not pulling a handcart. I reasoned that I was certainly old enough to take care of myself. Besides, I would be back before anyone knew I had gone so there would be no harm done.

I put my money in my pocket and zipped up the front of my parka. I hadn't gone a single block before I wished I had also worn a hat and some gloves. I put up the hood of my parka and stuffed my hands into the pockets. Still, the icy wind stung my face and whipped through my pants. I crossed the busy highway using the stoplight and walked up the Sunset Lake Bridge. At the top of the bridge, I looked down and saw a small boy, about the size of Tong Mi. He was standing on the ice at the edge of the lake walking toward the middle. I realized with alarm, that the ice was not firm. In fact, there was open water in the middle of the lake. I had broken such ice many times trying to haul in fish traps. He could easily fall through.

"Boy!" I shouted, "No go there!"

"What?" he said.

"Go back. Ice no good."

"You don't make any sense," he said. "You talk jibber jabber!" The ice groaned. Water sloshed in the open area.

"Lie down!" I said. "Lie down and wiggle to land." He waved a dismissive hand at me and in that instant three things happened all at once. I realized that I had been so excited that I had been speaking Chinese, the ice cracked, and he disappeared below the surface. In a flash, I saw Di-di in the freezing river. I saw Mama and Baba and Ye-ye all lying gray in Jiang Shu-shu's boat.

I leaped in front of a car. The breaks screeched it to a sudden stop and a fat bald man leaped out of the car screaming, "What kind of crazy prank was dat? You tryna' get us bot kilt?"

I shouted back, "Call help. Boy in water!" and pointed at the hole in the ice.

"Sweet mother of God!" said the man. "Hang tight! The firehouse is just down the street."

I did not hang tight. I ran off the bridge, threw off my coat and kicked off my shoes while running. Then, I slowly, carefully lay across the ice and wiggled out to the place where chunks of ice floated in brown water. I reached into the water as icy needles of pain shot through my arm. I felt something soft bobbing in the muddy water just below the surface and I grabbed on and pulled. Unfortunately, his body and waterlogged coat added just enough to my weight to cause the ice beneath me to crack. I felt it crack, like a slow-motion tickle running along the length of my body from my armpit, down to my feet. I dared not even breathe. In the next instant, I was plunged into the icy water. I gasped for breath and willed myself to breathe against the cold, which was closing in around me, squeezing the life from my body. I put my feet down and was surprised to discover that I was able to touch the slimy, mucky bottom.

I heard sirens.

I was chest deep in frigid water and my feet were already numb. I had only been in the water a few seconds, but I knew I didn't have much more time. I clenched the hood of the snowsuit with one hand and hurtled my whole weight against the ice in front of me, jumping up and throwing myself backward against the surface of the ice until it broke.

The wail of the sirens grew louder. Soon, the hillside at the edge of the bridge was swarming with rescue workers. Some were in wetsuits. They pulled a cord and a yellow rubber boat appeared out of a bag! A news crew from WKRE TV-*evening-news-with-a-heart* arrived and started filming. Jessica Laughlin was standing on the shore in a red WKRE parka talking into a microphone.

A man in a black and neon yellow firefighting outfit lay across the ice, spreading his legs behind himself and holding a pole across the front of himself. He hurled a length of rope across the ice into the open water where I stood.

"Here girl, grab the rope!"

I swung my arm wildly but my hands would not move. I could not grab the rope. My fingers didn't work. I didn't know if I still held the boy's hood. I could no longer feel my arms or legs. I saw him grab my hand although I could not feel it.

"My name's Rich," he said. "What were you doing out there?"

I couldn't answer him. My teeth were clenched. He hauled me up on the ice. "You're a whole lot heavier than you look!"

"Boy!" I said.

The firefighter pulled me harder, I felt a ripping pain in my armpit, but my hand must have been frozen shut, clamped onto the boy. My arm wouldn't come out of the water. The firefighter pulled on the seat of my pants, dragged my legs out of the water and spun me around. Still, my arm stayed stuck in the water. The thing I was holding onto floated under the ice under me

"What the devil?" he said. "Oh dear God in heaven! Dave, we got us another swimmer!" The man in the wet suit crawled on the ice and came around the other side of the hole. Then he slid in and grabbed the child. I looked at the little boy, only long enough to see that his face was grayish-blue. I was too late. He was drowned like Di-di.

I should have made him get off the ice. I should have gone down there in the first place and not shouted to him from the bridge. I should have remembered how to speak English! I hadn't done anything right and now a child was dead.

They pried my hand off his parka and lay the boy on the ice. They quickly dragged us both to shore and wrapped us in blankets. One team of rescue workers attended to him and another to me.

"How long were you in the water?" asked the red haired woman.

"Me? Two or three minutes. The boy? At least five!"

She and the man named Rich lay me on a rolling bed and slid me into the back of an ambulance. They snapped about a dozen plastic packages that grew hot in a few seconds. They packed these around me and wrapped me in a blanket.

"I'm Tara and I'm here to tell you that you're gonna' be just fine," she said. "We're just going to take you to the Medical Center and have you checked out. Mostly, we've just got to get you warmed up but we want to do it gradually."

Suddenly I started shivering violently and my teeth chattered.

"That's okay. It's just your body's way of generating more heat," said Rich.

"She's stable," said Tara taking off the blood pressure cuff and hanging a stethoscope around her neck. "Pulse normal, BP normal, temp is still low but rising steadily. Let's roll." Rich turned to me. "You're gonna' be fine. We'll be right back. We're gonna' stow a couple pieces of equipment and then we'll be on our way."

I looked out the door of the rescue vehicle and could see the TV cameras focused on the boy in the other vehicle.

I couldn't go to the hospital! If I went to the hospital, Mom and Dad would have to come pick me up and then they would know that I had at least started to walk to the mall by myself. I had to get out of here!

I sat up, held a heat pack under each arm and slid out the side door. Every movement sent a sensation of a thousand needles jabbing my arms and legs. Everyone was so focused on trying to make the boy breathe again, that no one noticed me slip out the side door and walk to the place where I had dropped my coat. I put it on and slipped on my shoes although I could neither grip my coat zipper to close it nor tie the laces of my shoes. I tucked the heat packs into my armpits and clamped my arms down on them. Shivering, teeth chattering, I walked home.

Almost instantly, my jeans grew stiff and hard, freezing to my skin. Each step drove sharp crystals of ice into my legs, making tiny cuts in my skin, burning as they bled.

The physical exertion of walking caused blood to begin circulating throughout my body. It felt like a thousand pins were stabbing my arms and legs. I wanted to scream for the pain in my hands.

Upon entering our house I made my way to the bathroom. I remembered how Mama had prepared a bowl of cold water from my frozen hands and I knew exactly what I needed to do. I stripped off most of my clothes, moaning at the pain, and drew a cool bath. I couldn't get the jeans off, so I stepped slowly into the tub, screaming out loud against the searing pain in my foot. Gradually, I eased my whole body into the tub, submerging myself in the water as much as possible. When I could tolerate the temperature without pain, I drained a little water out of the tub and added warmer water.

Gradually, over the course of two hours, I stopped shivering and began to feel warm. I dried off, put on my bathrobe and slippers and made a cup of tea in the microwave and dumped my wet clothes into the empty washing machine.

I turned on the portable TV on the kitchen counter just as Jessica Laughlin said, "Tonight's 'story with a heart' is a mystery. An Asian angel risked her own life to rescue young Jonathan Powers from Sunset Lake earlier today." Scenes of Rich, sprawled across the ice, pulling me, and then the boy out of the water flashed across the screen.

"Witnesses say the girl saw the four-year-old boy fall through the ice, flagged down help, and then wasted no time, diving into the frigid waters to pull him out. Rescue workers had prepared to transport her to Jersey Shore Medical Center for treatment." The cameras cut to footage of rescue workers loading up a rescue vehicle. "When they returned moments later from stowing gear, the Asian Angel had vanished. Melinda and Todd Powers would like to thank this teenager who saved the life of their youngest son." There was a picture of a little boy with bandaged hands sitting in a hospital bed flanked by a man and woman. Jonathan is currently in stable condition." Then, my face flashed on the screen. It was not my best photo! My hair was crusted in icicles. My lips were blue. "If you know the identity of this Asian angel, please call WKRE TV today.

Just what I need, I thought. *Now Mom and Dad will find out for sure that I had planned to walk to the mall by myself!*

Meeting the Public

The object of the superior person is truth.

"Hey, Mei Lin!" shouted Be-Bo as he ran toward me down the hall. "I seen you on TV last night. That was some hairdo!"

"What are you talking about?" I slammed my locker shut and walked into homeroom.

"Hey ice maiden!" shouted Karl.

"Very cool, Molly," said Marissa and smiled in a way that told me she had just made a joke. "Can I be the president of your fan club?"

"Behold, an Asian Angel walking in our midst!" said Brian, kneeling on one knee pretending to have some sort of trance-induced vision.

"Class, please find your seats!" said Ms. Bordum. "Molly, obviously, some of us saw the evening news last night. Would you care to talk about it?"

"There is nothing to talk about. I saw the picture, too. I'll admit that girl might have looked similar to me, but I was home all afternoon taking care of a bad sore throat." I stuck out my tongue to reveal a throat lozenge I had been sucking on. I felt my face turning as red as my cherry stained tongue.

"Molly, that was YOU! I would swear to it," insisted Be-Bo.

"Tyrone, sit down," said Ms. Bordum. "If the lady says it was not she, then you must be mistaken."

"But, Ms. Bordum . . ."

"No buts but your butt in your chair."

The bell rang and we took attendance, listened to announcements and stood for morning prayers. The second bell rang and Be-Bo badgered me all the way to History class.

"Look Be-Bo, just put it down."

"You mean 'just drop it'?"

"Oh, yeah, that's what I mean. Leave me alone!" I spun into the History classroom, sat down and acted like I was busy getting ready for class.

He brushed past me, came back, leaned over and whispered in my ear. "Look, I don't know *why* you don't want to admit to doing something that good, 'cause personally, if it was me, man, I'd be eatin' up them news reporters!" He put his nose about an inch from mine and smiled a big goofy smile that made his cheeks really fat. "I *know* it was you I saw on that television last night." He looked straight in my eyes (Which was kind-of scary because I don't think I had ever done that with another person in my life!) and then continued, "I think I'll just be proud to know you whether you like it or not."

"Tyrone, find your seat!" said Mr. Ditweiler as if he was bored having to say this sentence yet again in his life.

The whole day went like that. Every class was the same. No one had any doubt, though none of them expressed it quite as emphatically as Be-Bo. They were all sure I was the mysterious Asian angel. I was exhausted by the end of the day and couldn't wait to get home to my room and close the door.

Evan had basketball practice, so I sat by myself on the bus and stared out the window all the way home. I almost didn't get off the bus.

There was a WKRE News van with a satellite dish on the roof parked in front of our house. Jessica Laughlin was standing in front of our house and a camera man was filming her. They all turned when the bus stopped. She ran from our front step to the sidewalk in front of the house, and stood just to the left of the school bus door. The door opened and I felt all eyes focused on me. I wanted to hide under the seat and pretend I didn't live there. Instead, I slung my backpack over my left shoulder and stepped out the door. Jessica Laughlin asked, "Are you Molly Talbot?" and thrust the mike in my face.

"You make big mistake," I said. "My name is Zhong Mei Lin."

"Are you the Asian angel who pulled little Jonathan Powers from Sunset Lake yesterday afternoon?" she looked clearly confused.

"I not pull anyone from lake," I said truthfully.

She dropped the mike to her side. "What do I do, Tim?" She hollered to her camera man.

"Find another lead," he said.

"Another lead? We must have had forty phone calls all positively identifying a girl named Molly who lives at this address.

"Are you sure your name is not Molly?" she asked again without speaking into the mike. I felt Ye-ye and Nai-nai, Mama and Baba and Di-di and a whole column of Zhong family ancestors all standing behind me. Baba had called me a Daughter of a Thousand Pieces of Gold. This is highest praise for a Chinese girl. These people wanted to make me a hero. *But, what right did I have to accept their praise or even hold Baba's words in my heart if I was too much of a coward to even accept the punishment for my disobedience?*

I knew Mom and Dad to be fair. Surely they would not reduce my food rations to nearly nothing as Liu Shu-shu had done. What punishment was I afraid of?

Dad's car pulled into the driveway. "Mei Lin, are you okay?" he called out.

Mom opened the front door of the house, "Oh there you are! I was beginning to think you had missed the bus. What? What's going on?" she asked and stepped out on the lawn in her slippers. She wrapped her arms around herself and rubbed her arms to keep warm.

Suddenly I knew what punishment I feared. What I feared more than anything was their disapproval. What I wanted more than anything was for them to be glad they had adopted me.

I ran to Dad and hugged him. "I'm sorry."

"What happened, Sweetheart?" He motioned to the camera man to put down his camera and then turned so our backs were toward him.

"Are you Mr. Talbot?" shouted Jessica Laughlin.

"Excuse me, I was speaking to my daughter," Dad answered.

"Is this Molly Talbot?" she persisted.

"Let's go in the house where we can talk," said Dad to me, wrapping an arm across my shoulders.

Mom came up on the other side and put an arm around my waist. "Molly, what happened? Why are all these people on our front

318

lawn?"

We stepped into the house and closed the door.

"I'm sorry," I repeated. "I thought I would just be gone a little while and that you would never know, but then the boy fell in the lake and there were TV crews and . . .

"Woah! Molly, where did you go?"

"I was going to go to the mall."

"By yourself?"

I nodded.

"You know that isn't safe. There are no sidewalks along the busiest roads!"

Detail by excruciating detail I explained the whole mess.

Well, said Dad, "It seems clear to me that you should be grounded for at least a week for breaking the rule about walking to the mall by yourself. It simply is not safe. There is no excuse. You deliberately disobeyed a rule we set up for your own protection. It has nothing to do with your ability to walk that far, and everything to do with our need to be sure you are safe. Do you understand?"

I shook my head, looking down.

He took my chin in his hand and gently tilted my face upward. Then he looked right into my eyes. I was not afraid. I saw only love in his eyes, not anger or disgrace as he continued speaking, "But, I am going to suspend your sentence because I am so proud of you! You are truly--what was it you told me your Baba called you, *a daughter of ten thousand pieces of gold*?"

"It is only one thousand," I smiled.

"No," he paused and looked right in my eyes again, "*You* are worth *at least* a hundred thousand pieces of gold," he smiled back at me.

"A hundred million pieces of gold," said Mom as she took my hand. "Let's go meet your public."

Sisters Are Forever

Great souls have wills
Feeble ones only have wishes.

I was sitting on the couch in the living room in front of a cozy fire, munching on my favorite Chinese-American snack food; a chunk of uncooked Ramen noodles. In the corner, little lights twinkled on the Christmas tree. Jake sat on one side of me crunching a handful of potato chips. Taffy curled up on the couch on the other side, keeping my feet warm. Jenna was on my lap drinking apple juice from a sippy-cup. Together we read one of Jake's picture books. Jake read one page and I read the next. Jenna patted the pictures and kept interrupting us to ask questions.

"Where's the bunny now?"

"The bunny's not on this page."

Then she turned the page back until she found the last picture we had seen of Peter Rabbit.

"Why he has no clothes on?"

"He lost them in Mr. McGregor's garden."

"He should not go there if his Mama say, 'No'," she scolded.

Sometimes, when I got frustrated with her interruptions, I would start "reading" in Chinese until she shouted, "No Chinese! Do it right."

Dad had come home from work early and was in the kitchen putting the finishing touches on a birthday cake for Mom. He was whistling the Happy Birthday song. He placed a glass vase holding five yellow roses on the dining room table.

"Who died?" I asked remembering the carpet of yellow flowers covering my family burial place on the day of Qing Ming.

"Died? Why would you think somebody had died?"

"Yellow flowers are traditional color for burial of special person."

"Ah! Not here," said Dad.

"Why *five* roses?" I asked. "I think most people buy them by the twelve!"

"You'll find out," said Dad mysteriously, "and twelve of something is called a dozen."

"But if not for burial, why yellow? I think red roses are American romantic color. Red is Chinese color for happiness and celebration. I think red is best color for Happy Birthday, too."

"Nope, it's definitely got to be yellow. Just wait. You'll find out why soon enough."

Evan came in from playing basketball in the driveway with his friends. His cheeks were bright red from the cold.

"How can you stand to play out there?" I asked and shivered.

"At least I don't go swimming in this kind of weather." He threw the basketball at me.

"Hit the shower!" shouted Dad, "and make it snappy. Your mother will be home from work at any minute."

Evan had finished his shower and was standing in the hallway wearing only a pair of gray sweatpants when Mom walked in from work.

"Boy, am I starved!" I had back-to back meetings all day with no time for lunch," she said.

"Well, I have prepared a gastronomical delight: a birthday celebration fit for a queen!"

Mom hung up her coat, slipped off her black dress shoes and sat in an easy chair in the living room staring at the fire. She sank back and put her feet up on the footstool.

"How's the birthday girl?" asked dad as he bent down to kiss her.

"I'm sorry. To be honest, I worked so hard all day that it doesn't feel much like a birthday."

"What would make it feel like a birthday?" asked Dad.

"I don't know . . . just being home I guess."

"I know," said Jenna pointing to the dining room table, "Flowers!"

"Oh, roses definitely help," said mom gazing into the next room and smiling broadly at Jenna. "I think I am beginning to feel much more festive already. Come here my littlest sunshine. Kiss your Mama."

Evan had returned from downstairs and now had on a clean tee shirt with his sweat pants and a fleecy sweatshirt. "Hey, Dad, you messed up. There's five roses. Shouldn't there be four!"

"Nope, no mistake."

"What?" shouted Mom jumping out of her chair, setting

Jenna on the floor. "You *know* something? The call came! Today? While I was in meetings all day, THE call came?"

Dad was grinning ear to ear. She threw her arms around him and shouted, "Today of all days?"

He shook his head, "Yes."

"Oh this is the best birthday, ever!" She put her head on his shoulder and began crying.

"Roses always make Mom cry," said Jake.

"Why?" I asked confused.

"It's not the roses, it's what they mean," explained Evan.

"Will somebody explain to me what is going on?"

"Well," said Evan, "You know how Mom always sings that corny "*You are my Sunshine* song?"

"Yeah."

"She always says we are her sunshine. Each of the yellow roses represents one of her *sunshines*—one of us kids."

"There are only four of us."

"Obviously not."

"What?"

"You see, for a long time I was an only child. Every year for mother's day and on my birthday and her birthday, Dad would buy Mom a single yellow rose. When Jake came along, he gave her two on mother's day, two on her birthday, one on my birthday and one on Jake's birthday."

Mom and Dad were crying and hugging each other, so Jake picked up the explanation. "When we got Jenna's referral picture, Mom bought three yellow roses and put them in a vase on the table and propped Jenna's picture up in front of it. Dad saw it and knew right away. They started carrying on like this." Jake and Evan rolled their eyes at each other in mock disgust.

"We're getting a new baby?" I asked.

"Maybe," said Evan. "If they ever stop bawling, maybe they'll let us in on the surprise."

"Is it a brother or a sister?" hollered Jake.

"A sister," said Mom. She looked right at me and started sobbing again.

"Darn," said Jake. "We need more boys my age around here. When are you going to get another boy?"

Mom started laughing and crying at the same time. "Mike, we're not done!"

"Well you always wanted a full house," he grinned. "I guess we'll build an addition.

"Don't worry," said Evan, "She always gets like this when we get a referral. She did this when we found out about you." Then he looked at Dad, "So, where's the picture?"

"I don't have a hard copy yet. The agency e-mailed a photo this morning. I downloaded it as wallpaper on the computer. Go into the study and look at the computer screen."

I picked up Jin Ying and all four of us ran down the hall to Dad's study. Evan and Jake got there first and blocked my view so I couldn't even see.

"What does she look like?" I asked.

"Looks like she's is about your age," said Evan, stepping back. "She's wearing a red jacket just like the one we sent you before we adopted you."

"Wu Dan!" I gasped, my knees suddenly weak. I dropped down into the office chair. "See," I said and hugged Jin Ying when I could finally talk, "I told her that sisters are forever!"

I reached up and touched the face on the computer screen. "You and I *are* going to be sales clerks together in a big department store and sell fine silk dresses. We *will* share an apartment and go to university together. You were wrong. You *will* be a famous writer **and** I *will* be a rich business woman. My chauffeur will drive us around in a big black car with pink tufted pillows on the back shelf. It *is* a plan, not a dream."

Mom and Dad were standing on the doorway watching me. They were hugging Jake and Evan between them. I stood, and carrying Jenna, walked toward them. They each wrapped an arm around my shoulder, drawing me into the circle of love that is our family.

CHINESE WORDS

A! Oh!

A-yi Auntie, a title of respect used by a younger person speaking to a somewhat older woman.

Ai-ya! An exclamation of surprise.

Baba Daddy

Baoshan Precious Mountain. Baoshan City is the closest city to Mei Lin's village.

Bei ke qi Don't mention it.

Bu Negates whatever follows it but never stands alone as a word.

Bu shi I am not

Bu, xie-xie No thank you

Da bi-zi Literally means "big noses" and is slang meaning white foreigners.

Da ge-ge Eldest brother

Di-di Younger brother

Dui Right or correct

Gan bei Cheers!

Guo lai Come here

Hao Good

Hao-de I will

Hao ma May I?

Hen hao Very good

Hong bao Red envelopes used to hold lucky money for Chinese New Year

Hong Rong Red Glory

Ke Kou-Ke Le *Coke-a-Cola™"*

Kuai Qi Chuang Quickly get up out of bed

Jie-jie Elder sister

Lao A title used between adults in the countryside, similar to Mr. but not quite as formal

Longkou Dragon's mouth

Laoshe Teacher

Lao-zi The ancient ones

Ma-Jiang A popular but ancient tile game of luck and strategy

Mei-Guo-ren-men Literally means "beautiful country people" and refers to Americans

Mei-mei Younger sister

Nai-nai Grandma-specifically, father's mother

Nandu Hard to cross

Ni hao Hello

Ni hao ma? How are you?

Qian jin xiao jie Daughter of thousand pieces of gold

Qing Indicates a question will follow that will make a request. Although it can never stand alone in Chinese, it roughly translates as "Please?"

Qing ba yi fu gei wo? May I please have my clothes?

Qing, bu yao jiao Please don't scream.

Qing, ke yi ma Please may I kiss you?

Qing pin Poor, or in dire straights. Qingpin market is like a very large farmer's market.

Qing wen Please, may I? or May I ask?

Shen-shen A title of respect used by children in the countryside referring to an adult woman, similar to the American tradition of speaking of a parent's friend as "aunt"

Shu-shu A title used by a child in the countryside in speaking to or referring to a male adult. Similar to the American custom of calling a parent's friend "uncle."

Tai-tai A title of respect used in formal situations and in business dealings meaning, "Mrs."

Wei-guo-ren-men Literally, "Foreign county people" or Foreigners

Wo bu yao "I don't want"

Wo jiao "I am called" or "my name is."

Xian-sheng A formal title of respect used in the cities and in business dealings. It is similar to the title, Mr.

Xie-xie Thank you

Xin Nian Hao Happy New Year!

Ye-ye Grandpa- specifically: father's father

Yi-sheng Doctor

Dear Readers,

Thank you for reading *Daughter of Thousand Pieces of Gold*. I hope you enjoyed the story as much as I enjoyed sharing it with you.

If you liked this book, please tell your friends by "liking:"
https://www.facebook.com/PegHelminskiAuthor

and
Please leave your comments on the
Daughter of a Thousand Pieces of Gold book page at **Amazon.com!**

If you are part of an adult book club or
China-Adoptive-Parents Group, Please visit:
www.mnhpublications.com
for a free discussion guide.

If you are a teacher and wish to use the book as part of classroom instruction on China or Family Life/Adoption, please visit:
www.mnhpublications.com
In the "For Teachers" section you may download
a free teacher's curriculum guide.

For group sales and FCC chapter fundraisers contact:
publisher@mnhpublications.com

Finally,
If you are a student who read this book,
and especially if you were adopted from China,
I'd love to hear from you!
peg@mnhpublications.com
or:
Peg Helminski
1251 NW Maynard Road, Suite 177
Cary, NC 27513

Xie-xie ni!
Peg Helminski

CPSIA information can be obtained at www.ICGtesting.com
Printed in the USA
BVOW03s1858210813

329225BV00010B/223/P